PRAISE FOR MARIAH STEWART

~The Wyndham Beach Series~

ALL THAT WE ARE

"Mariah Stewart writes beautiful bo

"A hopeful and emotional novel
friendships, and life's never-ending s

—@harlequinjunkie

"I have loved this entire series but this one is THE BEST ONE YET! I loved everything about this book—the characters, the story line, the pacing—all of it!"

—Owl Reviews on *Goodreads*

"The Wyndham Beach series is one of my favorite comfort reads . . . Everything that I love about this series is here in abundance—the gorgeous setting, the wonderful and now very familiar characters . . . the gorgeous female friendships, and a plot that is uplifting, comforting, and life-affirming."

—@Salboreads

"This is the final installment of the Wyndham Beach series and I am sad to see it end! I have loved this series because it isn't like your typical beach romantic story line . . . I appreciate that the series includes women not only in their 30s (the children) but the mothers play a prominent role. Stewart . . . looks at family dynamics in their entirety."

—@stumblingintobooks

"A wonderful story that will touch your heart. The book focuses on the friendship of three lifelong friends as they support each other through grief, new relationships, second chances, and hope."

—*Harlequin Junkie* (top pick, 5 stars)

"One of my comfort programs is *Virgin River*—it's a TV program I can unwind with. The Wyndham series by Mariah Stewart has become my bookish equivalent. I love that the ladies—Liddy, Maggie, and Emma—are in their fifties and navigating life and relationships as older women, as mothers, partners, and working women. This is a book filled with mostly nice people; with friendships, and family; with a glass of wine at sunset and a blooming, wonderful bookstore, and I really enjoyed my time at Wyndham Beach."

—@salboreads

"Mariah Stewart writes about women with real-world problems and does it well. A highly recommended series featuring mature heroines."

—*Bayside Book Reviews*

"An authentic portrayal of someone's messy life and there is a lot to relate to here. There's a couple of romances, lots of friendship, and some drama, too. Overall, a really enjoyable read, especially if you like character-driven stories in an idyllic setting."

—*Novelgossip*

"I love this series because it's a romance with generational characters. It is refreshing to read a romance that involves various ages and still covers real-life struggles and decisions, and is still topped with an HEA."

—@stumblingintobooks

"Mariah Stewart has been one of my favorite authors for such a long time. *Goodbye Again* has all the things I love so much. There are a lot of big themes in this book—there's substance along with the lighter love story. I love losing myself in the world Stewart builds, and if you haven't been there yet, I'd greatly recommend it."

—@shoshanahinla

AN INVINCIBLE SUMMER

"*Oh* my. This book was simply *gorgeous*! Each of the characters we're introduced to leaves a mark on your heart. The love that was both lost and found is enough to turn the biggest skeptic on to the idea of everything happening for a reason, and in its own time. All in all, it was a wonderful cast of characters with varied lives that are intriguing, heartbreaking, and uplifting in equal parts."

—*Satisfaction for Insatiable Readers*

"This is my first by this author, and it certainly won't be the last. Her writing is extremely engaging, and the author really brings to life the dynamics of longtime friendships and relationships and all the ups and downs that come with them. I couldn't help but fall in love with this book."

—*Where the Reader Grows*

"A multigenerational story line, an idyllic setting, and a new series from one of my tried-and-true authors? Yes, please! As much as I loved the setting and the premise of this one, the characterization is where it really shines. Maggie and her two lifelong friends were all such lovely, authentic women."

—*Novelgossip*

"This story hooked me from the beginning and kept me dangling all the way through: cheering, crying, and just absorbing the decisions as Maggie finds her path to true happiness. A wonderful story I just fell for!"

—*A Midlife Wife*

"What makes this book so readable are the relationships and how the past ties into the future. Isn't that the way it is for all of us? *An Invincible Summer* is a fast-paced, easy-to-read story delving into the relationships we have in life and how they both break and sustain us."

—*Books, Cooks, Looks*

"I really loved these characters and this story. The characters just felt real and flawed in the best of ways. I found myself caring about each of the characters, which has me really excited that this book is just the beginning to a series. I will definitely be continuing on, as I want to see what happens with some of these other characters. I just want more, if I'm being honest! Read this book if you are a fan of women's fiction, contemporary fiction, or are looking for a great summer read."

—*Booked on a Feeling*

"This book was raw and real. Stewart crafted beautifully imperfect characters that allow us to see ourselves in their struggles. I spent the majority of the novel on the edge of my chair, cheering for Maggie and her daughters. This book also gives off what I'd consider *Virgin River* vibes, so if you like that series, grab this one and give it a try."

—@stumblingintobooks

"What a down-to-earth, heart-filling, and sentimental read. Full of friendships, forgetting, and moving forward. The relationships and characters are realistic, charming, and the plot is a bit elusive to keep you on your toes. A very enjoyable read about love, loss, and second chances, and it is a page-turner."

—@momfluencer

"This novel by @mariah_stewart_books is what a women's fiction novel is all about. There's a bit of romance, friendship, and complicated relationships. I really enjoyed how this book highlighted the messiness that life can be, but [it was] done in a lighthearted way. And the overall theme of learning lessons from the past and the courage to move forward on to new phases of one's life was endearingly told."

—@tamsterdam_reads

"There is so much I loved about this read. The setting of Wyndham Beach is gorgeous. I could smell the sea air, feel the warmth of the sun as the women took their coffee and sat watching the horizon. I could feel Maggie's pull to return to her roots. I loved the female relationships in the book. Maggie is a strong but supportive mother who brings her children through crises but holds out for her own choices, and the independence of her own life. The gatherings with her friends are glorious—tattoos, rock concerts, and the warmth of conversations between women who really know and understand each other. This was such a celebration of life and especially of women of *all* ages."

—@salboreads

~The Hudson Sisters Series~

THE LAST CHANCE MATINEE

"Prepare to fall in love with this amazing, endearing family of women."
—Robyn Carr, *New York Times* bestselling author

"The combination of a quirky small-town setting, a family mystery, a gentle romance, and three estranged sisters is catnip for women's fiction fans."
—*Booklist*

"If you like the Lucky Harbor series by Jill Shalvis, you will enjoy this one. Stewart's writing reminds me of Susan Wiggs, Luanne Rice, Susan Mallery, and Robyn Carr."
—*My Novelesque Life*

THE SUGARHOUSE BLUES

"A solid writer with so much talent, Mariah Stewart crafts wonderful stories that take us away to small-town America and build strong families we wish we were a part of."
—*A Midlife Wife*

"Reading this book was like returning to a favorite small town and meeting up with friends you had been missing."
—*Pacific Northwest Bookworm*

"A heartwarming read full of surprising secrets, humor, and lessons about what it means to be a family."
—*That Book Lady Blog*

THE GOODBYE CAFÉ

"Stewart makes a charming return to tiny Hidden Falls, Pennsylvania, in this breezy contemporary, which is loaded with appealing down-home characters and tantalizing hints of mystery that will hook readers immediately. Stewart expertly combines the inevitable angst of a trio of sisters, a family secret, and a search for an heirloom necklace; it's an irresistible mix that will delight readers. Masterful characterizations and [a] well-timed plot are sure to pull in fans of romantic small-town stories."

—Publishers Weekly

"Stewart [has] the amazing ability to weave a women's fiction story loaded with heart, grit, and enough secrets [that] you highly anticipate the next book coming up. I have read several books from her different series, and every one of them has been a delightful, satisfying read. Beautiful and heartwarming."

—A Midlife Wife

"Highly recommend this series for WF fans and even romance fans. There's plenty of that sweet, small-town romance to make you swoon a little."

—Novelgossip

"These characters will charm your socks off! Thematic and highly entertaining."

—Booktalk with Eileen

~The Chesapeake Diaries Series~

THAT CHESAPEAKE SUMMER

"Deftly uses the tools of the genre to explore issues of identity, truth, and small-town kinship. Stewart offers a strong statement on the power of love and trust, a fitting theme for this bighearted small-town romance."

—Publishers Weekly

DUNE DRIVE

"Rich with local history, familiar characters (practical, fierce, and often clairvoyant centenarian Ruby is a standout), and the slow-paced, down-home flavor of the bay, Stewart's latest is certain to please fans and add new ones."

—Library Journal

ON SUNSET BEACH

"Mariah Stewart's rich characterization, charming setting, and a romance you'll never forget will have you packing your bags for St. Dennis."

—Robyn Carr, *New York Times* bestselling author

COMING HOME

"One of the best women's contemporary authors of our time, Mariah Stewart serves the reader a beautiful romance with a delicious side dish of the suspense that has made her so deservingly popular. *Coming Home* is beautifully crafted with interesting, intelligent characters and pitch-perfect pacing. Ms. Stewart is, as always, at the top of her game with this sensuous, exhilarating, page-turning tale."

—Betty Cox, *Reader to Reader Reviews*

AT THE RIVER'S EDGE

"Everything you love about small-town romance in one book . . . *At the River's Edge* is a beautiful, heartwarming story. Don't miss this one."

—Barbara Freethy

"If you love romance stories set in a small seaside village, much like Debbie Macomber's Cedar Creek series, you will definitely want to grab this book. I easily give this one a five out of five stars."

—*Reviews from the Heart*

The Mercy Street Series (Suspense)

Mercy Street
Cry Mercy
Acts of Mercy

The FBI Series (Romantic Suspense)

Brown-Eyed Girl
Voices Carry
Until Dark
Dead Wrong
Dead Certain
Dead Even
Dead End
Cold Truth
Hard Truth
Dark Truth
Final Truth
Last Look
Last Words
Last Breath
Forgotten

The Enright Series (Contemporary Romance)

Devlin's Light
Wonderful You
Moon Dance

Stand-Alone Titles (Women's Fiction / Contemporary Romance)

The President's Daughter

Priceless

Carolina Mist

A Different Light

Moments in Time

Novellas

"Finn's Legacy" (in *The Brandywine Brides*)

"If Only in My Dreams" (in *Upon a Midnight Clear*)

"Swept Away" (in *Under the Boardwalk*)

"'Til Death Do Us Part" (in *Wait Until Dark*)

Short Stories

"Justice Served" (in Thriller 2: Stories You Just Can't Put Down)

"Without Mercy" (in Thriller 3: Love Is Murder)

The Head That Wears the Crown

MARIAH STEWART

Montlake

Text copyright © 2023 by Marti Robb

Published by Montlake, Seattle

www.apub.com

Amazon, the Amazon logo, and Montlake are trademarks of Amazon.com, Inc., or its affiliates.

ISBN-13: 9781662512728 (paperback)
ISBN-13: 9781662512711 (digital)

Cover design by Caroline Teagle Johnson
Cover image: © Zastavkin / Getty; © MirageC / Getty;
© Eugene Partyzan / Shutterstock; © Jade ThaiCatwalk / Shutterstock

Printed in the United States of America

For Robyn Carr

Chapter One

One thing I want to make clear: before this whole thing started, I was pretty much like anyone else. Maybe even pretty much like you. I worked five days every week, and took a one-week vacation every summer at the Jersey Shore with my ex-sister-in-law and our kids. I'm not going to tell you things didn't get . . . well, *tense* sometimes, but the house was free—thanks to the ex-sister-in-law, who owns it—and the kids got to spend the week with their cousins on their father's side, which is all my ex-sister-in-law cared about since the kids rarely saw each other and she was very fond of them (not so much fond of me).

Now that I think about it, they rarely see their father, either. He's more interested in his new wife and the new family—the one they started before he was my ex—which is perfectly fine with me, since he's not the man I thought he was when we got married. Of course, I was twenty-two at the time, but even so, I should have known better than to marry a man who didn't think Big 5 basketball was all that (it's a Philly thing).

Anyway, my seventeen-year-old son, Ralphie—why, why, why had I let his father talk me into naming that boy after him?—and my fourteen-year-old daughter, Juliette—who tells everyone her name is *Jules* because Juliette is *so* not cool—and I live a block off Porter Street in South Philadelphia in a row house that looks a lot like every other row house in the neighborhood. We have take-out pizza on Friday nights from Giorgio's and take-out Italian two nights a week. And by take-out Italian I mean I stop at my sister Roe's on my way home from work and pick up enough for the three of us of whatever she made that day.

Roe—short for Rosalie—is the youngest of us three girls. She can also be one of the most annoying people on the face of the earth (one-time runner-up for Miss Negativity USA), but we love her anyway. She's a fantastic cook—she cooks four weekdays at Robotti's Italian Garden—and feeds us on two of those days. Hard to bitch too much about someone who keeps you and your family well fed, but that's a totally separate issue from the fact that she's still a PITA a lot of the time. But, like I said, we love her anyway.

I was telling you how this whole crazy thing happened.

So I was at the Italian Market on Ninth Street on a Saturday morning in early April, lugging around the usual. Meat and cheese from Di Bruno's, pasta from Talluto's, thinking about stopping on my way home to pick up bread and cannolis from Isgro's, when I got the feeling I was being watched. You know that feeling, right, when those little hairs on the back of your neck start to tickle? I'd just remembered I'd said I'd pick up mussels for Roe when I noticed a dark-haired man staring at me while he was pretending not to. He was tall, dark, and, yes, handsome—the latter being a bit of an understatement.

Which begged the question: Why was he watching this fortysomething mom of teenagers, who was rocking the beginning of a few varicose veins and maybe a little arm flap? Not to mention the grays that my hairdresser expertly covered the first week of every month (the same hairdresser who'd been dropping some not-so-subtle hints that I might want to put a little Botox on my Christmas list this year). At first I thought I was imagining that it was me he was looking at—I mean, I need a little more maintenance these days, but don't get me wrong, I haven't exactly let myself go (I've been told I can pass for thirty-five in the right light—thirty if you're on your fifth beer and/or your third shot of Jack Daniel's). I will say with all modesty, all things considered, I still look pretty good in a pair of yoga pants.

So I moved on to the fish market. When I came out, I could swear I saw him again near the butcher shop, but Ninth Street was crowded, and when I looked back he was gone. By the time I'd gotten to my car, I'd forgotten all about Mr. Tall, Dark, and Handsome (as Sin).

On Sunday morning, I took the kids to Mass at Saint Monica's. Which was no easy feat, people, getting teenagers up early on a Sunday morning to go to church. But the last promise I made to my mother before she passed—God rest her soul—was that I'd keep the kids in the church. You make a promise to your dying mother, you keep it, right? I couldn't afford the tuition to Catholic school these past two years, but I could insist they go to church and to CCD (that would be Confraternity of Christian Doctrine, for those of you who never sat through Catholic education classes). When they balked, I reminded them they were doing it to honor their grandmother, who'd be turning in her grave if they didn't go. Since both my kids loved my mother, they went. Oh, sure, sometimes they grumbled, but they went.

So anyway, on Sunday, we were coming out after Mass ended, and I was standing on the steps talking to Mrs. Hill, who was an old friend of my mother's, when I looked out across the street, and there was the dark-haired guy from the market. Only this time he was with two other men. They were both shorter than him, one being somewhat squat and shaped like a fireplug and the other tall—though not as—and very, very thin. Like, cadaver thin, and he wore a bowler-style hat. The three of them were wearing black suits and white shirts and dark glasses. And they were all watching me.

My first thought—after thinking they were grossly overdressed for a warm day in April—was that they were human traffickers watching my daughter, who, while only fourteen, looks more like sixteen. She's petite, only five feet two—I'm only two inches taller—and she has long chestnut-brown hair and green eyes, both like mine, and she's perfectly

3

proportioned, if you get what I mean. She's still growing into her looks, but already you can see she is going to be a stunner before she's of legal age. I looked around wildly for Juliette, who I found standing in the middle of a group of girls she's been friends with since kindergarten.

I excused myself to Mrs. Hill and tried to find my son in the crowd, but he was down on the sidewalk. At over six feet tall, he's not hard to pick out in a crowd. He has dark curly hair that he keeps just long enough to tumble over his forehead because some old girlfriend told him he looked adorable that way. His eyes are green like the rest of us, and he's built pretty well since he plays a lot of sports. I called his cell and told him to get his sister and take her home. Now. He started to argue—he was talking to some cute girl I vaguely recognized as an old classmate of his—but apparently something in the way I said "NOW!" convinced him to move. He grabbed his sister and hauled her off the steps and down the street. She was obviously annoyed at having her big brother interrupt her like that, so she was no happier than he was.

I watched the three men across the street, and, while I didn't want to prematurely overreact—there could be a perfectly logical explanation why they seemed to be everywhere I was—if they took so much as one step in the direction of my kids, I was hitting 911. But they hadn't moved and didn't seem to notice Juliette was gone. They were still watching me, which raised the question: Who traffics forty-four-year-old women?

I walked home with several friends who dropped off as we reached their streets, and I was watching over my shoulder every so often, but nobody was there. Soon it was just me on this sunny Sunday morning heading for home, alone. I convinced myself it was all in my imagination and laughed at myself for being so silly. Like a guy who looked like that would be looking for me, right?

I had a lot of explaining to do to my kids when I got home.

~

The next morning, I pulled into the parking lot at my office building in the far Philly suburbs where all phases of the business of insurance were conducted. It wasn't quite eight thirty in the morning, so I sat in the car for another few minutes listening to the local morning radio sports talk show on WIP. This morning they'd picked up on the ongoing argument from Friday's show: Which Philly team had the largest fan base, and was it deserved?

No-brainer. The Eagles. And yes. Yes, it was.

I listened to a few callers who tried to make a case for the Phillies or the Flyers, and a few 76ers fans called in before I turned off the car and opened the door, a cup of Wawa coffee in one hand and a tote bag in the other. I locked up and started through the parking lot.

I was one car row from the entrance when I saw them. All three of them, and I realized this was no coincidence.

My blood froze in my veins, and my legs turned to rubber. I dropped my coffee—and damn it, there was still half left—and ran for the door.

"What's your hurry, Annie?" Debbie Wilson, the receptionist for my department—that would be claims—had been halfway up the steps when she heard the splash.

I blew past her and rushed into the building, past the security guard, and hightailed it down the hall to my department as fast as my size seven-and-a-half ballet flats could take me. Once safely in my cubicle, I dropped my tote—pissed off more than I can tell you that I'd wasted a half cup of Wawa Colombian that had been fixed perfectly—and fell into my chair, gasping for breath.

I was so out of shape, and I regretted having dropped my gym membership back in the fall when I was going through a budget crisis. My heart was beating like crazy and my hands were shaking uncontrollably. I didn't know who those men were, but they were definitely following me.

Which made no sense at all. I mean, why?

I couldn't think of one good reason unless my ex's family put a hit out on me. Which wasn't inconceivable.

I sat for a moment to calm myself, trying to decide what to do. I walked back out to the lobby and stopped at the security guard's station, peering around the corner to make sure they hadn't followed me into the building, but the only people I saw were people who belonged. I tapped Glenn, the guard, on the shoulder.

"Glenn, there are three guys outside in the parking lot who don't work here."

Glenn shrugged, not bothering to raise his eyes from the newspaper spread out across his desk. "So maybe they're here for a meeting and they're early."

"I think they're following me."

He looked me over, head to toe, then back again. "Why would they be following you?"

"I have no idea, but maybe you could find out."

"Sorry. Can't leave my post."

So I went to the receptionist's desk, where Debbie was just getting set for the morning. Computer booted up, coffee on one side of the desk, and a cheese danish from the snack room on the other.

"Deb, did you see the—"

"Oh, hey. Too bad about your coffee. The stuff they're selling downstairs this morning sucks." She sat on her chair and swiveled around to look at me. "I think you got a splash there on your skirt."

I looked down. Yep, that was a splash of the coffee I should have been drinking. I grabbed a tissue from her desk and tried to blot away the evidence.

"Did you make it in time?" Debbie asked.

"In time for what?"

"The bathroom. Isn't that where you were rushing to?"

"Um, no. Listen, Deb—did you happen to notice three men in dark suits standing outside the building this morning?"

"Yeah, Rich, Lennie, and Joe. The undertakers. I mean, the under-writers." That Debbie. What a jokester.

"Not those three. Three different men. One really short guy, a medium-tall guy, and one really tall guy. The medium-tall guy looked like a cigar with a bowler, but the *tall* tall guy looked like your best fantasy." Surely Deb would have noticed him.

"Nope. Are you having a meeting this morning? Want to leave their names?" She opened the center drawer of her desk and took out a small notepad and a pen.

"I don't know their names. They were standing right out there next to the **Parking by Permit Only** sign." I tossed the damp tissue into the wastebasket next to her desk.

She shook her head. "There wasn't anyone there when I came in except Elena Crockett. She was having a problem parking that big new Benz of hers."

Elena was the president of Philadelphia Fire, Casualty, and Liability Insurance Company—PFCLIC—my employer.

I walked to the wall of glass that wraps around the reception area and looked out, but no one was there who shouldn't be.

I turned around, and Debbie was staring at me as if waiting for an explanation.

"These guys have been following me all weekend," I told her. "At least, I'm pretty sure they were."

At first she didn't say anything. Finally she said, "If you think you're being followed, you should call the police."

"You're right. Of course. Why didn't I think of that?" I nodded and went back to my cubicle, where I picked up the phone, then immedi-ately hung up. Did I call the city police or the police out here in Chester County? Would that be the state police? Did the township we were in have their own police department?

I tried the state police. After reporting that I'd seen the same three men in the same places I'd been in over the past two days, I was asked a barrage of questions: Did I recognize any of them? Know their names? Did the men make contact with me? Did they approach me? Speak to me? Attempt to touch me? Threaten me in any way? Then the trooper on the other end of the line sighed and asked, "So what exactly did they *do* besides be in the same places you were in?" and I had to admit they'd done nothing *personal* to me but I felt they were following me.

"But you saw them in all public places, right? Not near your home or hanging out around your car?" he asked.

"No," I said quietly. Maybe I had overreacted.

"Okay, I have the report, but there's nothing I can do for you. You don't know their names and they haven't committed a crime. Let me know if they contact you. Or maybe try the Philly police since two of the incidents happened there." The trooper hung up before I even got out a thank-you.

While I looked up a number online for the Philadelphia police, the phone rang, and before I knew it, I was embroiled in hot negotiations with an attorney trying to push me into settling an accident case for which our insured had absolutely no liability since it was caused one hundred percent by his client. The man didn't know what he was in for. I was a crack negotiator.

Mondays were always tough, because we had people calling in to report accidents and we had our regular workload to deal with, so my phone rang nonstop. I'd skipped breakfast and was famished by one o'clock, which was my first chance to get up from my desk. I had about ten minutes to eat lunch and check in with my BFF, Marianne McDevitt, who worked in underwriting and was the person who put me on to the job I have now. Before I knew it, it was four thirty and time to leave. I managed to get out by five forty-five and still had to drive back to the city. Before I left the building, I stood inside the front door and scanned the parking lot, but I didn't see my three amigos. When I got to my car, I sent a text to both kids to see what was going on at home.

Homework, from Jules. Nothing, from Ralphie.

All the way home I thought about whether or not to call the police and what I'd say if I did. The state trooper had raised some good points. I decided to calmly examine the facts of the situation as I parked my car. Then I wondered what the facts really were.

Parallel parking on any street in South Philadelphia was always a challenge, so I focused on that. I grabbed my tote bag from the passenger seat, got out, and locked my car.

And walked smack into Mr. Tall, Dark, and . . .

"Who the hell are you, and why have you been following me?"

I tried to back away, but I was between him and my car. Tweedledum and Tweedledee were on the sidewalk on the opposite side of the street watching and standing in exactly the same position, their arms folded over their chest.

"You are Annaliese Gilberti Cancelmi." A statement, not a question.

I didn't bother to respond, since he already knew who I was.

"We've been looking forward to meeting you." I detected an accent in his soft voice. "You've no idea how much."

"So you could send me to Dubai in a shipping container?" What else could it be? I didn't owe the IRS.

"Why would we do that?" He appeared to genuinely ponder the question.

May I say, up close, he looked even better.

"Because that's what human traffickers do." I met his gaze head-on. I couldn't help but notice how chocolaty brown his eyes were. I momentarily wished I were thirty again, because he was clearly close to fifteen years younger than me.

He frowned. "Mrs. Cancelmi, is there someplace quiet where we can talk privately?" I was still trying to place his accent. Not quite French. Not quite Italian.

I'd heard it before—a long time ago.

"Who are you?" I asked again, this time in a somewhat more civilized tone. "Why have you been following me?"

"Please. We mean you no harm. On the contrary. Please. A few minutes of your time. Any place you choose. I swear on my life no harm will come to you."

That accent again. It floated through me like a distant echo.

I stared at him for a very long time. Finally, I said, "There's a coffee shop right down there at the corner. I'll meet you there in one hour."

"Thank you. Very much, we thank you." He looked relieved as he backed away and nodded.

"Watch the traffic." He was crossing the street backward, as if not wanting to turn his back on me. Rush hour around here, no one stops for anything or anyone. "And don't call me Mrs. Cancelmi."

I muttered under my breath, "I'm not Mrs. Cancelmi." My mom didn't change her name when she got married. Her family name was Gilberti, and she went by that, and we girls were given her last name at birth. If my father cared one way or the other, he never showed it. I didn't care either way, but when I got married, my mother asked me to respect her family name by keeping it, as she had, so I did, which was just one more reason my ex's family was happy to see me go. The kids of course carried their father's name. I tried hyphenating—you know, like the Brits do, so they'd be Gilberti-Cancelmi, but that didn't fly with Ralph Senior's family, either. Besides, can you see a six-year-old having to learn to print that in first grade? Yeah, me neither.

Anyway, I went into the house and closed the door behind me, wondering why I'd just agreed to meet with these guys, if I should just go ahead and call the police like I'd planned, or if I should hear him out.

In the end, it was the accent that pulled me in, that accent that conjured up memories of things I hadn't thought about in a long time.

Well, the accent and the fact that he was hotter than any guy I'd ever seen in the flesh. Besides, at that point, curiosity was killing me.

Chapter Two

It was Juliette's night to start dinner, so everything was ready when I went into the kitchen. I'd picked up a baked pasta dish from Roe the night before, so all it needed was thirty-five minutes in the oven. My daughter had made a salad and had the dining room table set. She'd picked a few tulips from my poor excuse for a backyard garden and placed them in a pretty vase that had belonged to my mother. I hadn't seen it in a long time so I wasn't sure where she found it, but I appreciated her effort to make the table look cheery.

"Smells good." I dropped my bag on the counter. "Looks like spring in the dining room, Jules. Nice."

Juliette rolled her eyes, but she wasn't fooling me. She was as pleased by the compliment as she was with how nice the table looked. She followed me into the dining room with a pitcher of water and began to fill the glasses.

"Call your brother and let's eat before it gets cold." I plated the pasta, and before I could pass the dishes around, the kids were seated at the table. Ralphie was always ready to eat, so getting him into the dining room was never a problem.

"So what's doing at school this week?" I asked, listening and eating, discussing the usual: sports, tests, the new kid who transferred from some school in Jersey and got suspended when drugs were found in his locker, the ongoing conversation about which colleges Ralphie wanted to visit in anticipation of sending out applications in the fall, and where he was most likely to get a scholarship, all the while keeping an eye on the clock. I didn't want to alarm the kids, so I didn't want to appear as if I was rushing through my meal. By the time we finished, over fifty minutes had passed.

"Ralph, it's your night to clear, rinse, and load the dishwasher." I stood as if I wasn't in a hurry, as if my heart wasn't racing wildly, and picked up my bag. "I'm going down to Barb's for coffee. I won't be long." I'd done this before on occasion, so there was no red flag.

"Could you bring us something for dessert?" This from Juliette.

"Sure. I'll see what she has tonight."

It took me two minutes to walk to the corner. When I arrived at Barb's, the three were seated at the only table occupied, the one closest to the back wall. They all looked up at the same time I walked in, but I didn't acknowledge them.

"What'll it be tonight, Annie?" Barb's daughter, Lynnie, was behind the counter.

"I'll have a large decaf," I told her as I eyed the pastry counter. "And put three cream puffs in a box for me, please."

I took the mug she passed over the counter and moved to the station to fix my coffee, willing my hands not to shake. I was trying to act normal. Dropping a container of half-and-half on the floor would blow it.

"Annie, your cream puffs," Lynnie called to me.

"I'll get them on the way out." My focus was on the table where the three men waited patiently for me.

When I got within five feet of the table, all three stood and the handsome one held my chair out for me. I felt Lynnie's eyes on me. I could almost see her jaw drop and hear the gossip chain revving up. I sat and put my coffee on the table and studied each of their faces in turn as they sat as well. Mentally I thought of them as the Fireplug, Dead Man Walking, and George. The first two were self-explanatory.

I thought of the good-looking one as George because he reminded me of a young George Clooney—in his *ER* days—only maybe even a little better looking and taller. He could also be more jacked than Clooney, but that was just a guess.

I realized they were studying me at the same time.

"Okay, what's this all about?" I asked as I took my phone from my bag and put it on the table next to my mug.

"We appreciate your meeting with us," George said softly. *That accent again . . .*

Fireplug and Dead Man Walking sat silently. Of course they knew exactly what was going on and were obviously content to let one man speak for them.

"What's your name? Where are you from? Why are you stalking me? What do you want?" I whispered as I glanced at my phone. I had 911 ready to go. All I had to do was hit the call button. "I'll give you five minutes."

The three exchanged a long look before George began to speak.

"My name is Maximilien Belleme. We"—he indicated his companions—"are from a small country in Europe. Saint Gilbert. I believe you've heard of it?"

He'd pronounced it *San Zjil-bear*, and that distant bell began to ring again, louder this time. *Saint Gilbert . . .*

"But I'm afraid our conversation is likely to take more than five minutes," he added almost apologetically.

"Saint Gilbert." I pronounced it as he had, and in that moment, I heard the soft voice of my grandmother. Grandmere, we called her when we were speaking to her. Otherwise, we usually referred to her as Gran.

"Grandmere." I didn't realize I'd said it aloud until George—er, Maximilien—said, "Ah, you remember her."

"Of course I remember her. She died when I was nine, but I remember . . ." I struggled to recall exactly what it was I did remember.

"Her voice. Her accent. Yours is the same. She smelled like violets. She spoke slowly and softly and very properly." I closed my eyes and she came into focus. "She always wore the same jewelry. Earrings that looked like golden roses. A ring that had a big red stone. She let me try it on once." I frowned as I opened my eyes. I hadn't thought about that in . . . God, I couldn't remember how many years it had been. And why was I babbling?

"Gran always seemed old, and she was sort of . . ." I searched for the right word to describe her as she was in my memory. "Otherworldly, maybe? She was tall and very beautiful, and her smile was always sort of sad, like she had a sad secret." I closed my eyes again, trying to picture her face, but the only face I saw was my mother's. I realized I was still babbling and snapped back to the present. "Why are we talking about her?"

"What do you know of her childhood?" he asked.

"Not much. But my mom said once that Gran had grown up in a house much larger than the row house we lived in. And one time when Juliette asked for a pony for Christmas, Mom made some comment about Gran having had a whole stable of ponies when she was little. Whenever one of us asked about her, Mom would say something like, 'It's complicated.'" I shrugged. We'd been pretty young when Gran died. "That's it. That's all I know."

"What do you know about her family?"

I tried to remember everything I'd heard over the years.

"Gran had sisters named Jacqueline and Amelia. Jacqueline died. Her mother's first name was Elizabet. My mom was named for her. Everyone would spell it with an *h* at the end to make it Eliza*beth*, and Mom would get annoyed and correct them. Eliza*bet*."

"What else?"

"Her parents died during the Second World War and so did her brother. He was older than she was. That might be when Jacqueline died, too, but I'm not sure about that. Gran had to leave her home because . . . I don't know why, I think it had something to do with the war. Someone helped her get to England—her and Amelia—and she met my grandfather there. After the war ended, she came here." I shook my head. "My mom never said much more than that. She said her mother didn't like to talk about the past. Mom's aunt Amelia visited one time. She lived in London, I remember that. Gran's house was big, and it was like a museum. There were so many fancy things there." Fancy things that had fascinated us as small children, things we were never permitted to touch.

Except sometimes when I got to visit with her all by myself. Memories flew past my inner eye with the speed of children running frenetically down a long, dark hallway.

"Is that all?"

I nodded. I wasn't sure where this strange conversation was going. "Why are we talking about all this, about *her*? Can we just get to the point?"

His eyes met mine as he leveled his gaze. A long moment passed before he spoke. For that moment, I forgot I was looking at a man I'd thought was going to pack me away and put me on a boat to Dubai.

Then he spoke, and the spell was broken.

"Your grandmother was Her Royal Highness, Grand Duchess Annaliese Emelie Sophia Elizabet of the Grand Duchy of Saint Gilbert."

"Huh?"

That's all that would come out of my mouth. I stared at him, then at the other two men, who were nodding silently.

Finally, I found my voice.

"Obviously you have her mixed up with someone else. My grandmother was a war refugee. She came to this country with nothing but her new husband."

"And the jewelry she managed to smuggle from Saint Gilbert in the hems of her clothing," he said softly. "And a small Bible with a white leather cover."

That got my attention. Actually, it sent a chill up my spine. My mother often read from it, but after she passed away, I'd mostly forgotten about it. Then three years ago I found it in a box of random things I'd cleared out from my mother's desk. Mom had been gone for almost eight years, but it had taken that long before I could face going through her personal space. The last time I saw that white Bible was a week ago on the top shelf of the small bookcase in my bedroom.

"How would you know what she took with her when she left her home?" *How could he possibly?*

"My grandfather was the man who helped her escape when the Germans invaded Saint Gilbert in 1941," Maximilien said with quiet pride. "He led her, her sister Amelia, and my grandmother through Switzerland into Italy and on to the coast of France, then to England. She met your grandfather there. He was an American war correspondent. They fell in love, married, and when the war ended and his work there was done, they came to America and settled near Philadelphia."

He seemed to be watching my face, so I tried really hard not to show any emotion whatsoever. I never knew my grandfather. He died when my mother was twenty, before I was born, but I did know he was a journalist and that he'd met my grandmother in England during the war.

"When your grandparents arrived in this country, they moved into a home outside the city. Your grandfather taught journalism at a college. You've seen the house, of course?" He paused. I nodded, and he continued. "Have you not wondered how a college professor in the late 1940s could have afforded such a home?"

I shook my head. I had no idea where this was going, but I remember that house. My mother grew up there, and both my grandparents died under that roof. It looked like a mini-castle surrounded by a black iron fence. It was furnished with antiques, some quite fancy. When we visited as a family we had to dress up and we had to wear gloves and we were told not to speak unless we were spoken to. Cecilia, who's two years younger than me; Rosalie, two years younger than Ceil; and I would sit quietly on a stiff dark-green velvet love seat with our hands folded in our laps, and we'd watch our grandmother chat softly with our mother on the other side of the large room while we squirmed uncomfortably on that horsehair-stuffed torture device. We were served tea in paper-thin china cups with gold roses painted on the inside, and we'd sit in the very formal dining room and eat delicious tea cakes that our grandmother had baked in her old-fashioned kitchen. Everything about that house was old fashioned, as was Grandmere. We never wondered why. We were kids, and that's who she was, and that was that.

After my grandmother died and the house and most of its contents were sold, a few furnishings were divided between my mother and her brother, and each of the grandchildren were given something from the house. I thought of the delicate set of china with its painted roses packed in boxes in my attic.

It occurred to me then that this man knew far more about my mother's family than I did, and I thought I had figured out why.

"I get it. You think I have the jewelry? That maybe my grandmother gave it to my mother and my mother gave it to me? Whatever my grandmother supposedly smuggled in her clothes? Well, you're too late. I have no idea where Gran's things went after she died. So if you've come to rob me . . . so sorry. You're wasting your time." I put my hands on the table, about to stand.

"We haven't come to rob you, Annaliese." Maximilien removed a leather pouch from the inside pocket of his jacket and placed it in the center of the table.

I stared at the pouch, then looked into his eyes. I saw nothing but sincerity there. Yes, I still wasn't sure I shouldn't call the cops, but there was something . . .

Anyway.

"Open it. Please." Dead Man Walking spoke for the first time. He, too, had that soft accent.

I reached for the pouch and slid it to my side of the table and opened it, my eyes still locked with Maximilien's. I could feel several objects inside, so I tilted it and lowered my gaze, watching, incredulous, as the contents tumbled out.

My grandmother's gold earrings. Her ring with the big red stone. A necklace I'd never seen before that looked like gold spun into gossamer threads where more red stones—some the size of my thumbnail—rested between the crossed filaments.

I know my jaw dropped. I picked up the ring and brought it closer, and knew it was the same one that had graced my grandmother's hand. In that moment, I could have sworn I smelled violets, and I had to fight back sudden tears.

Suddenly weary, I looked up and met Maximilien's eyes again.

"Will someone please tell me what this is all about?"

Chapter Three

I was still on the living room sofa staring blankly into space the next morning when I heard the kids moving around getting ready for school. It was too late to run upstairs and pretend everything was normal, so I curled up and pulled an afghan over me. I'd been up all night scouring the internet for anything related to Saint Gilbert and my brain was muddled, so I brushed over the fact that I'd slept downstairs in the same clothes I'd worn to work.

The kids bought my story that I hadn't been feeling well as they went past me into the kitchen. Some minutes later they came back through the living room, Juliette with a Pop-Tart in one hand and the other outstretched, palm up, for lunch money. I took care of her, then waited for my son to come along. He did, I handed over the cash, and off they went to catch up with their friends, arguing over the fact that Jules had taken the last Pop-Tart.

They closed the door behind them, and after waiting a few minutes to make sure they weren't coming back for a forgotten book or permission slip, I sat up, pushed off the afghan, and called my boss and claimed a migraine. Then I made coffee and called my sisters and told them to get over to my house immediately.

"I'm getting ready to go to work," Roe protested. "I can't drop everything on a whim."

"This is not a whim," I told her. "This is important. Life-changing, even."

"Oh my God, Annie! You have a life-threatening illness!"

"No, Roe, I'm not sick. I—"

"You met someone. I'm calling Ceil right now. We'll bring wine to celebrate."

"No new guy. Roe—"

"One of the kids got arrested. Oh God, was it drugs? You need bail money?"

"Dear God in heaven, Rosalie, just plead a migraine and get your ass over here."

I hung up before her imagination went totally off the rails, and I called Cecilia. No such craziness from her. Ceil was the practical one, the one with the most level head. I told her I needed to talk to her about something very important, and she just said, "On my way."

I could almost hear her shrug through the phone. It took a lot to rattle this woman, and since she had her own business as an interior designer, she could take time off when she wanted.

She was there before Roe, even though Ceil lived in Center City and Roe lived three blocks away. Ceil was the tallest of us and very slender. She had honey-blonde hair that was cut short and streaked with highlights, and she always looked very chic. Today she was dressed casually in black leggings and a taupe top over which she'd tossed a navy cardigan. She never forgot her earrings and always had some funky ring on one of her middle fingers and wore big, round tortoiseshell sunglasses that made her look like a VIP.

Roe, on the other hand, was somewhere in the middle, heightwise. Not as tall as Ceil, not as short as me. She had long, very dark curly hair that had a tendency to frizz in the humidity of Philly's summers and very long, dark curly eyelashes. She arrived wearing the white pants she always wore to the restaurant and a white tee. She carried about fifteen extra pounds because she was always tasting what she cooked and never had time to work out. I tried to get her to run with me in the early evening, but she was either still at work or too tired. She always looked—how to say this in a kind way—disheveled. Like she'd just rolled out of bed and hopped onto the subway.

I poured coffee for them and declined to answer any questions until the three of us were seated around my dining room table. Then I started off by asking them what they remembered about our grandmother.

"She was tall and beautiful, but she always dressed sort of strangely, like, not modern. And when we visited her, we had to sit on that old Victorian love seat with our backs ruler-straight and our legs crossed at the ankles." Roe wrinkled her nose. "We had to wear white gloves and use our best manners. I remember that was the last thing Mama always said before she rang the doorbell at Gran's house. 'Best behavior, girls.'"

"Gran was beautiful and very aristocratic. Elegant," Ceil recalled. "Just the way she held herself, and the way she spoke. I wanted to be just like her. She always liked you best."

"No, she loved all of us the same," I protested, though I knew Ceil was right.

For some reason, Gran warmed to me in a way that was different from the way she was with anyone else. The year I turned eight, things changed. At least one day every month, Mom would take me to Gran's and literally drop me off at the driveway. Gran would be waiting for me at the front door, and she'd hug me and close the door behind us as if shutting out the rest of the world. Those were very fun days for me. Gran and I would bake together, sometimes the little cakes she was so fond of, sometimes something else. On sunny days we'd go outside and explore the glory of her garden, where she'd planted so many beautiful flowers. She'd always let me pick a few to take home to Mom.

On those days, I saw a completely different Gran. She seemed happy to be with me and interested in every part of my life. Who my friends were, what I was learning in school. I'd always thought it was because I was her oldest grandchild, but I figured as my sisters grew older, they'd be invited to Gran's house for one-on-one time so they could get to know her better, too. Now I wasn't so sure that was her motive in wanting to spend time with me. I think it was more she wanted *me* to spend time with *her*, if you get the difference. Unfortunately, we never had time to explore whatever her real agenda might have been because of her unexpected death.

As if she could read my mind, Ceil said, "Annie, you were the only one she ever invited to spend time alone with her."

"Did you resent that?" I asked.

"Are you kidding? We weren't the ones who had to spend the afternoon sitting on those stiff chairs with the scratchy fabric poking through our clothes," Roe said.

That's not exactly what happened on my solo visits.

Ceil brought the focus back to where it belonged. "Gran always made me think of the old European royals you'd see in those 1930s movies Mom used to watch on TV."

I sighed and silently thanked Ceil for the segue. "Because that's what she was."

Roe tilted her head to one side as if she hadn't heard what I'd said. "She was what?"

"She was European royalty. Her Royal Highness, Grand Duchess Annaliese Emelie Sophia Elizabet of the Grand Duchy of Saint Gilbert."

My words hung over the table. It appeared my sisters were having the same problem processing it as I'd had. They turned to look at me at the exact moment wearing the exact expression, obviously waiting for me to say something that made sense, so I told them about the three men I'd met the night before and the story Maximilien—Max, by the end of the meeting—had told me.

I paused. "Actually, Max's grandfather was the man who helped Gran escape."

Roe looked up from her coffee and made another of her faces. This time it was her *WTF* face. "What kind of crazy shit is this?"

"I swear I'm not making this up."

"It sounds like a scam. They must want something." Roe frowned. "But what?"

"That was my first thought, too. But then they gave me this." I got up and got my bag and took the leather pouch out and spilled some of the contents across the table.

"What the hell?" Ceil picked up one of the earrings and turned it over in her hands. "I remember these. And this!" She reached for the ring, tears in her eyes. "Oh my God, I know this ring."

Roe took the earring from Ceil's hand, then shook the pouch and the other one fell out. She was speechless. Maybe for the first time in her life.

Then the two of them burst forth with a million questions at the same time.

"Stop. Please." I held my head. Now I really was on the verge of a migraine.

Ceil turned to me. "So they tracked you down to return the jewelry? How did they get their hands on it?"

"Max said that when Gran was sick and knew she didn't have much time, she returned it to friends in Saint Gilbert."

"There has to be an endgame." This from Roe.

"I'm getting to that. Here's the history in a nutshell. The Gilbertis ruled this little country for a very long time—like, hundreds and hundreds of years—and it is little, it's only about twelve hundred square miles according to the internet. Think Rhode Island. When the Nazis invaded the country, they killed Gran's parents and her brother and one of her sisters and some other assorted relatives, but Gran escaped, along with her sister Amelia, and made it to England, where they stayed until the war was over. Gran was only fifteen. She and her sister were the only members of the Gilberti family to survive."

"Oh my God, just like Anastasia," Roe gasped.

"Wow, she was just a little older than Juliette," Ceil said, ignoring Roe. "Can you imagine losing your entire family that way and being forced to flee your country? Poor Gran."

Roe and I both nodded. Poor Gran indeed. We'd never had a clue what she'd gone through.

"Anyway," I said after a moment's silence, "after the war, the Soviets 'liberated' the country from the Germans and made the country communist. When the Soviet Union was dissolved back in the 1990s, a lot of the small countries were gradually released and permitted to go back to self-rule."

"Saint Gilbert was one of them?" Ceil asked.

I nodded. "So over the past years, there was a lot of dissention and dialogue about what kind of government they should have. According to Max, they actually tried several—communism, socialism. Some wanted a democratic monarchy, like they have in the UK, some wanted a straight democracy. Some wanted a return to the monarchy because many of the citizens were old enough to remember that things were very good when the Gilbertis were in charge. Some even wanted to go back to being part of Russia. So earlier this year there was an election to settle things once and for all."

"And . . ." Roe gestured for me to hurry up.

"The people of Saint Gilbert voted to restore the monarchy."

"But there is no monarchy. Gran is dead, her siblings are dead . . ."

"So they looked for and found Gran's surviving family." Ceil always was quicker than Roe, bless her. "And with Mom and her brother gone, they found you. What do they want?"

"They want me to go back to Saint Gilbert with them and—well, reestablish the monarchy. And, ah . . . be the grand duchess."

In my mind's eye, I saw a sort of *poof* where this latest bombshell hit the table and exploded.

"Why you? Why not me? Or Ceil?" Roe asked bluntly.

"Because tradition called for the oldest daughter to inherit the throne. That would be me."

"What if there was no daughter?" Ceil asked.

"According to Max, that never happened. There was always at least one daughter per generation."

Another long silence.

"I call bullshit." Roe sneered. A real, honest to God sneer. You don't see many of those. "It's a scam."

"For what purpose? What could these people possibly want from me? I work my ass off to pay the mortgage on this little three-bedroom row house. I get child support but trust me, Ralphie eats through a month's worth in three days. What do I have that anyone could possibly want?"

I stared at Roe. Like I said, if anyone was going to be a pain in the ass, it would always be Roe. Only this time I didn't blame her. Not entirely, anyway.

Ceil reached across the table for the laptop and spun it around. I already had pulled up everything I could find related to Saint Gilbert, and she began to read through it.

"Saint Gilbert, the former Grand Duchy of Saint Gilbert, ruled for generations by the Gilberti family." Ceil looked up. "That's us, all right. Tucked into a corner between Italy, France, and Switzerland. Roughly the size of Rhode Island, like Annie said. Population about six hundred thousand." She read silently for another minute or two. "So far everything these guys told you about the history of the place checks out."

"Let me see that thing." Roe leaned over her and reached for it, and Ceil batted her hand away.

"Wait till I'm done."

"There isn't much here about the country's financial status," Ceil continued. "Doesn't seem like there's much going on there. No mention of manufacturing, nothing about agriculture, tourism, mining— nothing. Oh, wait, they do export wine and cheese—both cow and goat—mostly to neighboring countries." Ceil scanned the screen. "So how are the people supporting themselves? They can't all have cows, goats, and vineyards. Maybe the information wasn't available when this was written since the country was going through an upheaval of sorts." She looked at me over the laptop. "What are you going to do?"

"What am I going to do? You mean, what are *we* going to do? This is a family thing. It isn't just about me," I said.

"Annie, they didn't come here looking for Queen Cecilia. They sought you out to be their queen."

"Actually, there's no queen. It's grand duchess. That was the title Grandmere inherited. Max said her mother abdicated in her favor right before they sent Gran and her sister to flee the country." I was a little shaky on some of the details.

Silence again.

"Well, that explains a lot about her, doesn't it?" Ceil said. "Her bearing. Her elegance. Her . . . *presence*."

"Why aren't you jumping up and down and screaming?" Roe's eyes narrowed. "Why are you so calm?"

"I'm finding it hard to believe." I answered as honestly as I could. "How do you react to something like this? It's just too bizarre. Besides, this is serious stuff. This is life-changing. For real." I looked at Roe, who also wasn't jumping up and down screaming. In fact, none of us were. Which means we were all in shock and disbelieving, and/or we'd all watched *The Princess Diaries* three times the night before and had a call into the last video store in South Philly for a copy of *Roman Holiday*. Okay, that last part was probably just me. No one does *royal* like Audrey Hepburn. I figured I could learn a thing or two from her.

"Like I said. Crazy shit." Roe reached for the leather pouch and put the jewelry back in, pausing over the necklace. "I don't recognize this."

"I don't either." I looked at Ceil. "You?"

She shook her head.

"Well, it's too fancy for her to have worn on casual occasions, and we never saw her get dressed up. Those red stones are crazy big, though."

Roe held the necklace up to her throat. "Can you imagine if these stones were real? I bet they'd be worth a fortune."

"They're rubies, Roe, and they are real," Ceil told her.

"How do you know?" Roe held it up as if assessing its value.

"Remember after I graduated from Rosemont and I didn't know what I wanted to do? And Mom said the rule was you either went to work or—"

"Or you went to school. No exceptions." I repeated one of Mom's hard-and-fasts.

"Right. So she asked me what I was interested in, and I said jewelry, and she said to find out what I had to do to get a good job in that field. I talked to someone down on Jewelers' Row, and he said I needed to earn a certificate from the Gemological Institute of America. So I started taking the courses online. I only finished three of them." One by one, Ceil held up three fingers. "Diamonds. Colored stones. Gem identification. Trust me, little sister. Those are rubies, and they are flawless. And," she added, "they are undoubtedly worth a fortune."

"Wow." Roe's eyes widened. "We could sell them, and we could . . ."

"Over my dead body." I snatched the leather pouch from her. "They don't belong to us. They belong to the people."

"What people?" Roe made a face. "*Us* people. He gave them to you."

"They belong to the people of Saint Gilbert. And he didn't give them to me to personally own. He gave them to me to . . ." I hesitated while I thought it through. "To convince me to go there—to Saint Gilbert—and bring these with me."

Roe rolled her eyes.

Ceil ignored her. "Annie, did you tell the kids?"

"I wanted to talk to you first."

"Why?"

"Because it involves all of us. We're the granddaughters of the last grand duchess of the Grand Duchy of Saint Gilbert." My turn for a little eye rolling. "It even sounds goofy to say. It sounds so *Disney*, or like a Hallmark movie. But the point of this discussion is, what do I do now?"

"Did they invite all of us, or just you?" Ceil asked.

"Well, just me, I guess. It was more like, please come for a week or two or however long you want to stay and meet the people. See the country before you decide."

"Decide what?" Roe asked.

"Before she decides if she wants to be the grand duchess." Ceil, as always, went right to the heart of it. "And you're going, right?"

"Maybe. I don't know. I wanted to see what you guys think."

Roe grabbed the laptop, paused for a moment while she stared at the screen Ceil had been looking at, then turned it to face me. "This is a castle. A real castle. It's enormous. It has one hundred and ninety-seven rooms." She looked up. "That's even bigger than Caesars Hotel and Casino where I stayed in Atlantic City last year." She went back to the laptop. "It says this castle is where they lived. If nothing else, you should go for a vacation, check it out. Hey, maybe the stables where Gran kept her ponies are still there."

"I always thought that was something Mom made up. I never thought that was real." Ceil propped her elbow on the table, her chin resting in the palm of her hand. I felt her studying my face. "You're very solemn about this, Annie."

"It's solemn stuff. I almost feel as if I'm in shock."

"I could slap you a couple of times if you think it would help," Roe offered. I'm pretty sure she was kidding.

"Thanks, but another cup of coffee would be just as effective. Honestly, I don't know how I feel. This is about more than us. This is about six hundred thousand people who live in that country. So yeah, I'm waiting to have my 'yahoo' moment." Maybe because part of me still didn't believe any of it. Or maybe I'd hallucinated the whole thing. Except for Max, who I know is real.

Maybe I'd touched his arm a time or two last night, just to be sure.

"So what are you going to tell the kids?" Ceil asked.

"Just what I told you."

"How do you think they'll take it?" Roe scrolled through the pages she'd pulled up on the laptop. "Wow, there are some real high mountains there. And beautiful lakes. Oh, and here's another view of the castle. It looks like Cinderella's.

"'Built in 1740 of local white stone,'" Roe read aloud. "'The Gilberti family ruled Saint Gilbert from Castle Blanc, seen here in a recent photograph, until 1941, when the small duchy was overtaken,' yada yada. 'The last of the grand duchesses, Annaliese Emelie Sophia Elizabet'—that was Gran—'inherited the title upon the death of her mother,' blah blah. 'Immediately smuggled out of the country by a loyalist following the German invasion. Eventually she settled in the United States, where she lived quietly and raised a family, the details of which are not available.'" Roe looked up. "I wonder why she thought she had to keep it a secret."

"Maybe there are people in Saint Gilbert who didn't like the monarchy to begin with. Rebels, anarchists, socialists, whatever," Ceil said. "Maybe someone else who thought they should be on the throne. If there ever was to be a throne again."

"Then why didn't she change her name?" I wondered aloud. "She could have taken Grampa's name, but she didn't."

"Maybe because she was one of the last surviving members of the family, and she wanted to keep the name alive," Roe said. "Then again, I'll bet there are hundreds of people named Gilberti in this country. But why would anyone care? The country was in Russian hands for fifty years, or thereabouts, and she wasn't trying to make a comeback. Seems to me she was content to leave well enough alone." She tapped her fingers on the table. "It looks like this confirms everything they told you. Of course, they could have read the same Wikipedia page we did. Or written it."

"But what would their motive be?" Ceil bit the inside of her mouth, a habit she had when she was thinking what we used to tease were deep thoughts. "How can we find out what the political situation is there?"

"Google 'newspapers in Saint Gilbert,'" I suggested.

Ceil reclaimed the laptop and typed something.

"Doesn't look like much of a newspaper." She read for a few seconds. "But it does reference the January elections and the result. More than sixty-five percent of the voters want the monarchy brought back." She read for a few more seconds. "And it says a search is being conducted to locate living relatives of the last grand duchess." She looked up. "So there you go. Your three buddies were telling you the truth."

We sat in silence for a moment. Then Ceil said, "I think you should go and see for yourself. Check out the country, see what's what. They invited you and you should go. I would."

"It's hard to say no at this point. I mean, it could be real, and it could be a good thing." I wished I could be more decisive. Honestly, I'm usually not so wishy-washy, but this—this was different. It wasn't like choosing between basic black heels and slutty red ones.

"You could be walking into a trap," Roe warned.

"Right. A trap set by sex traffickers." I felt like Juliette, rolling my eyes as she does when she's invited to spend the night with a girlfriend and I call the girl's parents to make sure they're going to be home—even though sex traffickers had been my first thought, too. "Because there aren't enough middle-aged women in Europe to keep the traffickers happy."

"You need to go," Ceil announced. "Think of it as sort of a reconnaissance trip. You'll know if this is on the up-and-up. It could be very exciting and wonderful." She reached for my hand. "Whether it's worth uprooting your family, totally changing your life—all our lives, really—only you can decide. But I feel very strongly faced with the same decision, Mom would have gone."

She was right about that. Mom wouldn't have had to confer with anyone. She'd have had her bags packed and been out the door faster than you can say Annaliese Emelie Sophia Elizabet Gilberti.

"I think it's pretty clear Mom knew more about Gran's family than she let on," Ceil added.

I was thinking she was right about that, too. Why Mom chose not to share what she knew with us, I'll never know. But I do know she would have embraced this situation. I was starting to think I should, too. As Ceil said, it could be exciting and wonderful.

Or I could find myself in a large metal crate on my way to an auction somewhere to be sold to the highest bidder. If not sex slavers, maybe organ dealers.

"Ceil, is there any chance you could spend a week here, stay with the kids while I'm gone?"

"Sure. I can operate my business from here as well as I can from home. When do you want to leave?" she asked.

"I need to talk to the kids, and I'll need to talk to my boss. I have vacation time coming, so taking a week off isn't going to be a problem. I'll call the men I spoke with last night. Max gave me a card with his name on it." It was still in the pocket of my sweater.

"We need to go through your closet," Ceil said. "I bet you don't have a lot to wear in a castle."

"True. Mostly skirts, pants, a few dresses, and a couple of suits for big meetings or for those times when a judge orders me into court to make me face him during settlement negotiations." It was a tactic a few judges used to get the plaintiff money when the judge knew there was no coverage or no liability on our insured's part but they wanted to make sure everyone left their chambers happy. Well, everyone but the Philadelphia Fire, Casualty, and Liability Insurance Company. "I guess I could do some shopping."

Ceil nodded. "Saturday. I'll pick you up. We'll go to the King of Prussia Mall."

"Okay." I hoped Ralph Senior wasn't late with the child support payment this month.

"I think you should think it over a little more." This from Roe. Of course.

"I plan to. But I don't see any advantage in putting this off too long."

"I think you're crazy to go off alone with not one but three men you don't know. Why would you even consider that?" Roe asked. "You won't walk from here to that little neighborhood market by yourself at night."

"I want to see the country Grandmere came from. I want to see where she grew up." Even as I said it, I knew that deep inside, my decision had been made last night when I saw those rubies tumble from their pouch.

"It could be dangerous," Roe said.

"I'm pretty sure I'm willing to take that chance," I assured her in my calmest voice.

"I'd go with you if you didn't need me to stay with the kids," Ceil offered. "I think it sounds like an adventure."

"You can go." Roe turned to her. "I don't mind staying here."

I considered it for a moment before the thought of Roe spending a week in my house with my children, teaching them things I've tried hard to wean them from. Like whining. Like being afraid to try new things. Like not trusting your gut. Indoctrinating them with her religion—Negativity—and taking them to her chosen place of worship, the Temple of No.

I decided to go for mature and gracious and tried to sound sincere. "Thanks, Roe, I appreciate the offer, but Ceil can make her own hours, which you can't do."

"True." Roe reached for the laptop. "I want to take another look at that castle."

Ceil got up and headed for the stairs. "I want to see what's in your closet. Then we'll make a list of what we're going to buy."

"Easy does it, sissy. I'm not a duchess yet."

~

I told the kids when they got home from school in the afternoon. Neither believed me until I showed them the pages on my laptop and pointed out their great-grandmother's name right there on the screen.

Juliette sat up straight, her eyes shining. "Oh my God! Oh my God! We're royalty." She poked her brother. "You can call me Princess Juliette."

"Prince Ralphie." He stood and preened in the mirror over the sideboard. "Damn. That has a ring." He turned to face me. "Prince Ralph. I'll make the name cool again."

"As if it ever was," Jules muttered.

"I honestly don't know what your titles would be. Or if you even would have one." No point in feeding that fantasy just yet.

"This is the craziest shit I ever heard." Juliette dissolved into laughter that bordered on the hysterical.

"Language, please."

Ralphie demonstrated his best gangsta strut around the dining room. "We're going to *bring* it to that place," he told his sister.

I momentarily considered going to Saint Gilbert and staying there until they both graduated from college.

"Ralph, enough with that . . . whatever you call that . . ." I waved my hand in his direction.

Juliette got up and began to rush from the room, her phone in her hand, her thumbs moving wildly. "OMG, I can't wait to tell everyone! They're going to be so jealous! The look on snotty Tiffany Stout's face is going to be epic!"

I stood, both hands held up in front of me. "No! No! You will not tell anyone, do you hear me?"

My daughter stopped in her tracks.

"Huh? Why not? If it's true, then . . ."

"We need to confirm a few things. In the meantime, you are not to tell anyone—I mean *anyone*—about this. Do you understand?" I looked from one of my children to the other. They were both clearly still in fantasy land. "Promise me."

"I promise," Ralph muttered.

"Promise what?"

"I promise not to tell anyone."

"Juliette?"

My daughter bit the inside of her lip on the right side, and I could tell she was getting ready to plead her case.

"Can I just tell Marisa?" She folded her hands in supplication. "Please?"

"No. Marisa's mother has the biggest mouth in South Philly. Besides"—I knew this part would hit both my kids where they lived—"suppose there's been a mistake. Are you willing to look like the world's biggest loser in front of all your friends?"

They both turned white.

"So what are we going to do?" Juliette put the phone down.

"I am taking a week to go to Saint Gilbert and check things out. You are staying here with Aunt Ceil. If you want to talk to anyone about all this, feel free to discuss it with her or Aunt Roe. But no one else. Got it?"

My children nodded.

"Now go do your homework."

"Why can't we go with you?" Jules asked.

"Because I have no idea what I'm going to find when I get there."

Jules frowned, but nodded. She gathered her book bag and turned to leave the room. "Do you think there's a castle?"

"There is. There's a picture of it on the internet. Look up Castle Blanc, Saint Gilbert."

"Ohmygod." Jules looked about to hyperventilate as she and her brother headed for the stairs. "I'm going to be a princess! My family owns a castle! Top that, Tiffany Stout!"

I could hear them excitedly discussing the news as they climbed the steps. I waited until I heard their respective bedroom doors close, then I took the card from my pocket and dialed the number Max had given me the night before.

Chapter Four

"I still don't understand why I can't go with you." Juliette sat on the end of my unmade bed and pouted, ready to plead her case for about the fiftieth time.

"Because you have school, and last time I looked, you weren't doing so well in algebra." I stood in front of my (very small) closet and debated over whether I should take another pair of shoes. I'd already packed walking shoes—a.k.a. white tennis sneakers—my favorite ballet flats, a wear-with-just-about-anything pair of strappy heeled sandals, a fun pair of leopard-print flats, and of course, those fancy very high heels Ceil talked me into at Nordstrom. I'd also picked up a little black dress à la Audrey Hepburn (*Breakfast at Tiffany's*) and two sundresses since I read the summer temperatures in Saint Gilbert averaged in the eighties, and I'd hit up Chico's for some of their knit things that don't wrinkle even if you roll them up and stomp on them, so for the first time in my life, I wouldn't have to overpack. "And you have that big history test next week, am I correct?"

Juliette rolled her eyes.

"Jules? History test next week?" I closed the suitcase.

"Yes. Test next week. But if I'm going to be a princess—or whatever they call the daughter of the grand duchess over there—why would I need to know American history? I already know a lot. I know all about the Civil War and the Revolution."

"But right now you're studying the Second World War. Which, I might remind you, was when the Germans invaded Saint Gilbert and killed our ancestors and forced my grandmother to flee." I hoped by looping in some family history, she'd become a little more interested.

"Yeah, well, we won't be reading about that."

"History is history. And you know what they say. Those who fail to learn from history are doomed to repeat it."

"I want to see the castle." Jules was still pouting like a cranky three-year-old. At least Ralph had a baseball game after school—we'd said goodbye this morning—so I didn't have them both leaning on me. Ralphie does well in every sport, and even though my Wildcat heart would love nothing more than to eventually see him in Villanova blue and white on the basketball court, his heart is on the soccer field. He's really very good, if I may brag on him for a moment, but they don't play soccer in the spring here, and the boy needs to run off all that energy—and hormones—so baseball it is.

"I'll take pictures." I hoisted the suitcase off the bed and set it on the floor next to my carry-on bag, which held the necessities of life in case my suitcase went to Iceland as I was heading to Switzerland: toothbrush, toothpaste, underwear, the little black dress I'd bought on Saturday, two belts, two Chico's tops, their basic black sheath, and those strappy heeled sandals. If the worst happens, I won't have to be out and about for a couple of days in the outfit I'm wearing on the plane: a black pencil skirt, a long-sleeved rose silk shirt, a black tunic-length knitted cardigan, and the basic black heels I'd bought to replace the ones I'd been wearing to work every day for the past gazillion years. I carried the new black leather bag Ceil had bought me for the occasion. I'd wanted to wear pants, but Ceil reminded me I'd probably be arriving at the castle in whatever I wore on the plane, so I should go for the skirt.

Did I mention we were landing in Switzerland? Yes, Switzerland. Because Saint Gilbert doesn't have its own airport. What kind of country doesn't have an airport?

"Annie?" Ceil called from the bottom of the steps. "A car just pulled up out front."

"Okay, I'm coming," I called back. I ducked into the bathroom with the bag containing my makeup to touch up my face. I pulled out the face wash, my favorite moisturizer, and my all-in-one shampoo and conditioner and set them on the counter while I searched for my lipstick.

"And a man is walking up to the door . . . and, oh my . . ." Her voice trailed off.

Must be Max. I stuffed the lipstick back into the bag, tossed it into my carry-on, and grabbed my suitcase from my room.

I made it downstairs, dragging my suitcase—okay, Ceil's suitcase, since mine is a wreck having spent the last sixteen years schlepping kids' things back and forth to the Jersey Shore—and stopped next to the newel post to take a deep breath.

"You okay, Toots?" Ceil tore her gaze from the front window, through which Max could be seen approaching the front door.

"I'm good." I wasn't good. I was a nervous wreck. This was happening too quickly. I wasn't ready. I might never be ready. I'd been awake all night thinking about the potential consequences of this trip, and I was pretty sure I hadn't yet thought of everything that could go wrong.

Dear God, I was starting to sound like Roe.

The doorbell rang, and both Ceil and I lunged for it.

She got there first.

"Hi. I'm Ceil. Annie's sister. You must be . . ."

"Maximilien Belleme at your service, madam." He didn't exactly bow, but he did almost bend at the waist just a teeny bit when he dipped his head slightly.

Ceil sighed.

I'm pretty sure I know what kind of service my sister was imagining Max could perform for her.

"And I'm Juliette." Jules stepped forward, stars clearly dancing in her eyes. "Annaliese's daughter."

"Ah yes, Juliette, Her Highness's only daughter." Max, born to charm, took her hand and planted just the whisper of a kiss on her knuckles. Jules visibly swooned, and I admit I almost did as well. "And as such, second in line to the throne."

"What?" Juliette's eyes grew wide. "What?" She turned to me. "You never said . . ."

I shrugged. It had never occurred to me there'd be a second to the throne, since I wasn't sure I was going to be first.

Jules turned back to Max. "What will I be called when my mom is crowned—"

I cleared my throat.

"*If* my mom is crowned grand duchess?"

Max smiled. "You would be Her Royal Highness Princess Juliette Elizabet Terese."

"How do you know my middle name and my confirmation name?" Jules asked. Then the effect of what he'd said seemed to hit her all at once. "Wait—princess? Ohmygod, *princess*? I *knew* it! Princess Juliette. For real? Ohmygod . . ."

Max smiled again, then turned to me.

"Allow me to carry your things, Your Grace." I should point out here that he said those words without cracking a smile.

I'd asked him not to call me that—just Annie or Annaliese, but so far, it's been "Your Highness" or "Your Grace."

He gathered my bags and headed for the front door. He stopped halfway there and asked, "Shall we?"

"Wouldn't have to ask me twice." Ceil's eyes were fixed on Max, and they said it all.

That's right, my normally sensible, no-nonsense sister Cecilia was practically drooling over my new best friend, Max.

"Would you listen to yourself? He's at least ten years younger than you are," I whispered as I followed Max out the door.

"I can't help it. Besides, who cares how old he is? He looks like a young George Clooney. Only better."

"I know, right? Just like I told you," I said in total agreement, then I reminded myself this was a serious excursion I was embarking on. Depending on the outcome, this next week could change our lives forever. I needed to take it seriously, and I needed everyone else to take it seriously as well. I hugged my sister. "Thank you for staying with the kids. There's no one else I'd trust to stay with them."

"There's always Roe." Ceil hugged me back.

I smacked her lightly on the backside. "Not funny."

Max and the Fireplug were loading my bags into the trunk of the Lincoln Town Car. Dead Man Walking opened the rear passenger door and stood next to it as if he were standing at attention in front of Buckingham Palace.

"Mom, you have a *driver*." Juliette had followed me outside.

"I see that." The trunk lid slammed, and I turned to take my baby girl in my arms. "Be good for Aunt Ceil, hear?" She nodded. "I'll call or text every day. You'd better respond. Like, within five minutes unless you're in class."

"Why would you text me when I'm in class?" Jules hugged me tight.

"Because I'm not sure of the time difference over there. I'll figure it out and I'll try not to call when you're in school." I held on to her for as long as I could.

"And why do I even have to go to class since I'm going to be a princess?" she whined.

"Hey, you're not a princess yet. Don't count your tiaras before they're on your head."

"Mom?" she whispered in my ear.

"What, sweet pea?" God, I was going to miss this kid. And I was only going away for a week.

"Don't take this the wrong way, okay? I mean, I love you and I hope you live forever." She took a deep breath. "But when you die, will I really be the grand duchess?"

~

The plane took off on time, and by on time, I mean only forty minutes after its scheduled departure. I sat next to Max, and his compadres—who I now knew were John-Paul Laurent (Fireplug) and Marcel Barsotti (Dead Man Walking)—were directly behind us. I kept trying to think of something to say, but my mind was swirling. For one thing, I hate to fly, though I had to admit flying first class was way better than any other option. Except for maybe a private jet. That would be pretty great, too. For another, I still had to pinch myself to be sure this was all really happening. And then there was the matter of whether I'd lost my mind by agreeing to do this. I still wasn't sure. I kept telling myself it wasn't too late to change my mind—until it was because we were on the plane and it was headed down the runway.

I sat back and closed my eyes until we were in the air. Did I mention flying terrifies me?

"I'm so very glad you decided to return to Saint Gilbert, Your . . . ," Max began.

I jabbed him with my elbow.

"*Annaliese.* Your arrival is anxiously awaited at the castle."

"One, you can't return to a place you've never been. And two"—I sat up and opened my eyes, and whispered—"I thought we agreed there wasn't going to be any kind of announcement."

"There hasn't been. But arrangements had to be made for your stay, and certain protocols have to be in place."

"Why? Why can't you just put me up in a nice little B and B for the week and let me sightsee, if the purpose of this visit is for me to see the country?"

"I don't believe there are any bed-and-breakfasts in Saint Gilbert. There's very little need for them since tourism is nonexistent." He lowered his voice. "And there's the matter of your safety to be considered."

"What 'matter of my safety' are we talking about?" I turned to look him full in the face. Which under other circumstances I might have enjoyed. Did I mention how beautiful his eyes are, or that he has these long, dark lashes?

"There is a faction—a very small faction, I assure you—that opposes the return of the monarchy. We simply want to make certain you are . . . *well insulated* from them." He added hastily, "Few though they may be."

"I don't have a problem with a difference of opinion. Maybe they're right. Maybe the monarchy is yesterday's news. Maybe there's a better way for the country to be governed." I still couldn't believe anyone in their right mind would consider me suitable for governing an entire country. Have they met the man I'd married? That alone should speak to my decision-making abilities. "Maybe I should talk to them and find out what their objections are."

"That would be ill-advised, Your . . . Annaliese. Especially at this time."

"What do you mean, *at this time?*"

"Feelings are still running somewhat high so soon after the election."

"I thought you said the election was in January. It's the end of April. That's four months."

Max shrugged.

"Well, at some time, someone should have an open dialogue with these people. Me or whoever ends up, you know, taking charge." I could not bring myself to say the R word: *rule.*

"Perhaps in time," he conceded. "After things have settled down a bit and the country is on the right track."

"What track is it on now?"

"Things are a bit . . . muddled."

"Muddled," I repeat blankly.

"Politically."

"You said the country voted for the return of the monarchy." I thought for a moment. "But there must be some sort of governing body already in place. A council, or a parliament, or something."

"It's called the Duke's Council, yes."

"Even though there's no grand duke?"

"There was when it was first convened in 1682, and up until 1941. There are still some who inherited titles that ensure them a seat on the council."

"So what do they do? Make laws? Pass tariffs? Appoint judges? Aren't there diplomats who interact with other countries? Ambassadors? Are they in charge right now?" If I sounded exasperated, well, I was.

"Yes, the Duke's Council does those things and is in charge."

"So why don't they just stay in charge? Why do they need a grand duchess, whether it's me or someone else?"

"Because they cannot agree on anything." He sighed deeply, and it was apparent that this was of real concern to him. "Since 1993, the council has been comprised of hereditarily titled dukes. Some of those factions I mentioned have been at odds with each other before, during, and since the election. It is sad to say, but we are dealing with a tangle of egos. They will never agree on what's best for the people in our country because they're all concerned with their own interests."

Like so many in our Congress, I could have said, but did not. "So what makes you think I can talk them into agreement?"

"You don't have to. If there's a dispute, the monarch makes the final decision. In the absence of a monarch, majority rules."

"Which explains why certain factions might not be happy to see me arrive in Saint Gilbert." I couldn't believe I allowed myself to be put in this position, that I'd allowed myself to be talked into coming on this trip. "And wait . . . aren't dukes always men?"

Max nodded.

"So this council is comprised of all men? No women?"

He nodded again.

"Well, that's going to have to change," I muttered.

"That would be difficult to accomplish, madam. That would involve changing the Duke's Council to . . . something else. There would be resistance."

Of course there would be.

"What kind of resistance? Is anyone going to be, like, you know, *shooting* at me?"

"One would hope not, madam." Max's face was serious. "But you will always be well guarded. As royals should be. We are even now recruiting a new class of guards in anticipation of the restoration."

Right then and there, I decided I'd spend my week getting to know the land of my grandmother's birth before heading back to Philly after having given my final answer—thanks but no thanks—and waved buh-bye.

"You needn't be concerned about your safety. But you do need to know that the most important reason we need a grand duchess is that the majority of the country's assets are in a bank in Switzerland, not to be released until a rightful heir is coronated."

"So in other words, I—theoretically—hold the key to the vault?"

"In so many words, yes." Max sighed heavily. "Saint Gilbert needs help moving forward. It's not a rich country. We have few natural resources and, as I mentioned, no tourism to speak of."

"Why is that?" I wondered aloud. "Every European country has tourists."

"Where there are commercial attractions, yes." He tilted his head toward mine slightly. "Saint Gilbert has very little in the way of commercial attractions."

Swell. I'm being offered the chance to rule a country that has no prospects, a dueling council, and all its money stashed in a Swiss bank that only I—or someone like me—can access.

"You have a castle, right? Everyone wants to see a castle," I said.

"We have more than one, actually. However, some are not readily accessible, and others are in need of some . . . repair," he said cagily.

"But you have mountains, don't you? I mean, you're right there next to Switzerland. People go there to ski, right?"

He sort of half nodded his head.

"What, people don't ski in Saint Gilbert?"

"Yes," he said. "But mostly to get from one place to another in the winter."

"Meaning what, you don't have roads?"

"Some of the more remote areas . . . not exactly."

"Are you kidding me?" I shook my head in disbelief. "Gosh, this place sounds better and better all the time. Why aren't there roads?"

He hesitated for a moment. "There were roads once, roads that connected rural areas to the capital city, Beauchesne—that's where you'll be living—"

"Staying," I corrected him.

"Yes, yes, of course. Many of the roads to the rural villages were destroyed during the war, and after the invasion, while the Soviets promised to repair them, nothing was done to improve the infrastructure. They left the country with very little to work with, to put it mildly."

"What exactly do you expect of me?"

"The people of Saint Gilbert look to America as . . . how did your former president say it, 'the shining city on a hill'? When it was made known that the rightful heir to the throne was American, the idea to return the country to its monarchal state spread like wildfire. Everyone knows when the going gets tough, the Americans roll up their sleeves and get tougher. We all have heard of American ingenuity."

Dear God. He said it all with a straight face.

Then he added, almost apologetically, "I believe the people are looking to you to help them move forward into the twenty-first century."

My jaw dropped open as far as it would go, and it was all I could do not to laugh. Was he kidding?

"Look, I am not Joan of Arc or Mother Teresa or Indira Gandhi or . . . crap. I have no experience ruling anything. It sounds like you're all looking for someone to perform some sort of miracle. The only miracle I've ever performed was getting myself out of a bad marriage with my sanity. I'm a middle-aged single mother who's working her ass off to raise a couple of kids and keep them out of trouble and keep my head above water financially. I can balance my own budget, but barely. What makes you or anyone else think I can make a difference in Saint Gilbert?"

"Ah, but you know how to work hard. You're intelligent, as proven by your school transcripts. You graduated with honors from the esteemed Villanova University. We know of their excellent basketball."

I frowned. "How did you get my transcripts?"

Ignoring me, he continued. "Americans are known to be innovative problem solvers. Add the indisputable fact you are the heir to the throne, and there was no need for further discussion."

I started to protest, but he held up one hand.

"Don't overthink this. Please. Just visit our country. Stay in the city. Drive through the hills. Meet our people." He paused. "They're your people, too."

"Max . . ."

"Please. All I ask for now is you give yourself a chance to get to know us. Bring a fresh eye to the table, as you Americans like to say. See the country. Keep an open mind." He smiled. "And if nothing else, you're going to be spending a week in a European castle."

"There is that." I tried to force a smile, too, but I think the result may have been more like a grimace.

We sat quietly for a few long moments. Finally, I asked, "How are you involved in this?"

"I told you my grandfather was the man who brought your grandmother and great-aunt to safety after the Nazis came through Saint Gilbert."

"How did that happen?"

"They set out through Switzerland into Italy; however, I am not certain of the exact route they took."

"No, no. I meant, how did it happen that he was the one to help them?"

"He was the captain of the castle guard. It was his duty to protect the royal family."

"I see." After another moment passed, I asked, "And what is your duty, Max?"

"The same as his, madam," Max said. "The position is hereditary."

So the too-hot guy with the gorgeous eyes was my bodyguard. I could live with that for a week.

Chapter Five

We landed in Geneva, Switzerland, and oh, the view from the plane took my breath away. First of all, flying over the Alps is an experience this city girl could never have imagined. The mountain peaks actually went through the clouds in places! And Lake Geneva! It positively glittered in the morning sunlight. Looking out the window of the plane before we landed, I thought of the pictures of the castle in Saint Gilbert, which showed a lake.

I asked Max, "Does the lake in Saint Gilbert sparkle as much as Lake Geneva?"

"I would say more, but then you would think I was speaking from prejudice. So let me say only that soon you will be able to judge for yourself."

A car was there waiting for us. The four of us—Max, John-Paul, Marcel, and I—piled in. John-Paul took the wheel and Marcel rode shotgun, leaving Max to share the back seat with me. After several hours of driving, we stopped in a picturesque town for lunch, but I was so nervous I don't remember what I ate. Even though several weeks had passed between my first meeting with Max and company and getting off the plane in Geneva, it all seemed to rush toward me like an Amtrak commuter. I had a feeling in the pit of my stomach that grew more uncomfortable with every passing mile. Fight or flight was only valid if there was an option for one or the other. I had neither.

Okay, so maybe another little bit of confession is in order: I'm a little bit of a controlling person. I'm a Leo, so I don't feel I should be held responsible for it, but that's the truth. I try hard to keep it from getting out of hand, but sometimes my natural diva takes over, and then you just need to stand back and watch a master at work. Which is one of the reasons it's so hard for me to understand why I didn't take command of this situation from day one and be more decisive. Like Ceil had said, Mom would have been on the first plane out of Philly—and Mom was a Gemini. Maybe it was because my kids were still young, or maybe I was afraid it was all true, what Max had told me at that first meeting.

If it were true, I'd have to change my entire life. And imperfect as it was, I liked my life. Routine in some ways, sure, but they were routines because I'd chosen them. I had money problems at times, and my kids were far from perfect, and sometimes, yeah, I admit I missed the company of a great guy. I loved my friends—Marianne was like my sister from an Irish mother—and I liked my job. I'd been rolling along at my own sweet speed since I divorced Ralph Senior, and I was fine with the pace I set for myself. So all the hemming and hawing I'd been doing was so not like me.

Finding out there were some factions that might not be too happy to see me on Saint Gilbert soil added a whole new level to my anxiety.

Yes, I could have said no right from the beginning and let the boys go looking for someone else. Surely they could shake another branch of the Gilberti tree to find a suitable heir. My mom's late brother, my uncle Theo, had a daughter, Beth, who was three years younger than Roe. I haven't seen her in years, because Uncle Theo moved to Wyoming when he married his second wife. So I don't know what Beth's been doing since she was convicted of embezzlement—before he died two years ago, Uncle Theo said that whole thing had been a setup—but as far as I know she's still alive and out there, so if need be, there's a backup, right, once she's served her time?

And then there's always Ceil, I guess. I mean, if the oldest can't or won't accept the job, maybe it could fall to the next oldest, right? And there was that comment Max had made to Juliette about being "next in line." I obviously hadn't asked enough questions.

But here I was, in the back seat of a shiny black car that was speeding around corkscrew curves, John-Paul driving as if it were his last shot to qualify for a spot on the Formula 1 circuit.

The scenery, however, was to die for. Huge white snow-clad mountains slid down into deep green valleys, and when I say huge, I mean don't think the Poconos. These mountains totally dominated the landscape. The lakes reflected the highest peaks and the sky. And oh, the sky! It was bigger than I'd ever seen, even bigger than the sky hanging over the ocean in Margate, New Jersey, on a clear summer night. There were mountain passes that took my breath away—literally, since some of them were guarded from the steep slopes only by ropes tied onto posts. I hadn't been that scared since Ralphie shamed me into going with him on the roller coaster at Great Adventure (referred to as Six Flags by everyone except New Jerseyans and those in adjacent states).

We passed streams that ran alongside the road and meadows where cows the color of rich cream grazed. Now, I'm a city girl, and to me, cows are brown and white, maybe black and white. But I never saw white cows like these. I turned in my seat to look at them as we drove by, and Max must have noticed my curiosity.

"Charolais." He pointed to the white cows.

"Is that French? I don't speak French." Actually, I don't speak any language other than English. I've never even been outside the USA. "I don't know what Charolais means. Wait, do they only speak French in Saint Gilbert?"

"English is the official language," Max told me. Still looking out the window, he said, "Charolais is the breed of cow. Originally from Charolles, in Burgundy, in eastern France. Now they're bred in America and other countries as well," he explained. "There are several herds in

Saint Gilbert, but also there are other breeds as well. Montbéliarde, Abondance, Aubrac, Tarentaise, and of course, the Rouge, which are found only in Saint Gilbert."

"They're all kinds of cows?"

"Yes. Breeds."

"Right. Breeds of cows. You mentioned that cheese was an important export."

Max nodded. "There are certain cheeses made *only* in Saint Gilbert. You will, of course, be introduced to them."

"But they're sold in America, right?"

"We cannot sell our cheeses in America, madam. They're made from unpasteurized milk, the import of which your laws prohibit."

"Then why don't you pasteurize the milk if it would open a large market for the farmers?" I asked.

He looked at me as if I were speaking in tongues. His expression read *blasphemy*.

"It would alter the character of the cheese, Annaliese," he said kindly, as if speaking to a three-year-old. "Also, we could not produce enough to export to America. Our cheeses are made the exact way they were made generations ago. The cheese from each village has its own particular flavor. Heating the milk to pasteurize it would alter the flavor."

Chastised, I looked out the window and watched the mountains fly by.

We drove for almost two hours before John-Paul slowly pulled the car to the side of the road and turned off the ignition. Why stop now?

"Why are we stopping?" I asked.

John-Paul turned and looked at Max, who nodded, then opened the back door of the car, got out, and walked around the vehicle to open the door on my side. He leaned in slightly, his hand extended to me. It was clear he wanted me to get out.

"What?" I asked, confused.

"Please. Come." His hand hung in midair, and when I looked toward the front seat, both John-Paul and Marcel had turned to face the windshield.

It occurred to me then that I could have totally misread this situation from the start. For once in her negativity-filled life, could Roe have been right? My overactive imagination—fueled most likely by fatigue and nerves—caused my blood to freeze in my veins. I had visions of a painful departure from this world à la *Goodfellas*.

Had I been played big-time? Were the three of them members of the faction that had not wanted to restore the monarchy but to make certain it would never be restored? Starting with eliminating the next in line, which would be me.

I swallowed hard and took Max's hand and allowed him to lead me from the car. We walked a few steps into an open field studded with blue and yellow flowers. I squeezed my eyes closed tightly. When I'd thought about how I'd leave this earth, I never pictured myself standing in a field of wildflowers in Switzerland next to a gorgeous man who possibly was about to hasten my departure.

"Open your eyes, Annaliese," Max said. "I want you to see the exact spot where your grandmother left her homeland and entered Switzerland as she fled the German army."

My eyes flew open. "Huh?"

"This is the border between Saint Gilbert and Switzerland, the very place where the grand duchess and her sister made their way to freedom. From here they traveled to Italy, and from there, eventually, to England. But this is where their journey began."

I was so relieved I almost passed out. I was all but hyperventilating, and my knees barely held me upright.

"We thought perhaps you would like to make part of that journey in reverse," he continued, "by walking from Switzerland into Saint Gilbert."

"Oh. Of course. Yes." Hysterical laughter was barely under control at this point. "Yes. I'd love that. Thank you. So thoughtful."

He took my arm, and after several steps, he paused on the edge of a large, flat rock and gestured to the valley below us.

"Welcome to Saint Gilbert, Your Highness," he said softly.

Honestly, I don't know where it came from, but I had a lump in my throat almost as big as the boulder we stood on. I guess that was for Grandmere's sake, should she be watching. I had a powerful feeling she might be. She should have been able to come home, and while I'm pretty sure I'm no substitute for her, I resolve to do her proud with every step I take from here on out.

I looked down upon green hills and valleys where small stone farmhouses and barns stood along the roadside and tiny villages dotted the landscape. There were white cows like the ones we'd seen in Switzerland—the Charolais—and sheep and goats in nearby fields enclosed by ancient stone walls. The sky here was the clearest, brightest blue I'd ever seen, the mountains high and snow covered, and in the far distance, there was a lake of sparkly blue water kissed by sunlight, and ohmygod, as Jules would say, there was the castle, white and turreted and straight out of a fairy tale, next to the lake.

"It's . . ." I tried to find words, but I had none. I actually had to fight back tears.

"Indeed it is, madam." Max nodded as if he understood. "Shall we return to the car now?"

"Could we walk for a little? We've been sitting so long, first in the plane, then in the car, and the countryside here is breathtaking." Reasons enough to walk, I told myself, but deep inside, I knew what I was feeling went deeper than merely a need to stretch my legs. I still couldn't put my finger on it, but moments later, it came to me.

I felt my grandmother there with me then, as deeply as I'd ever felt the presence of anyone. Her light touch on the back of my head, once so familiar, and the scent of violets that always surrounded her were not products of my imagination. She was there. More than wanting to walk where she had walked, I wanted to walk her home.

And I did—well, part of the way. We started down the mountain road, and while I didn't know how far we walked, I held out as long as I could before I had to wave the white flag. I was exhausted, I'm not gonna lie. I was sweating and my feet were killing me since I'd talked myself into wearing the new plain black heels I'd picked up at Neiman Marcus when I made a super-quick dash at lunchtime on Thursday for a few last-minute things. I hated that I felt I had to dodge my best friend—Marianne and I always shopped together at lunchtime—but I just couldn't bring myself to talk about Gran and Saint Gilbert. I'll tell her when the time comes, and she'll understand. I hope.

Max and I barely spoke as we walked except when he would point out something he thought I might like to be aware of: the lonely ruins of a farm where the Nazis had torched the house and barn; a small village known for its particularly fine wine, the sunlit vineyards scrambling up the hillside; and the weathered remains of an old stone chateau where relatives of mine, long gone now, had once lived. They'd been routed by the Soviets, their vineyards destroyed. I wanted to ask Max if he knew what had happened to them, but the lump in my throat was too big for words to slide past. Gran must have known, though, because I felt a wave of sadness pass from her to me. Whatever had happened there hadn't been good.

When I finally had enough, I practically crawled onto the back seat. And just like that, I knew Gran was gone. I guess she just wanted to see my first reaction to her homeland, and she was satisfied.

Chapter Six

By the time we reached the outskirts of Beauchesne, I was having an out of body experience. I asked John-Paul to stop for a moment. We were on a hill outside the city, the castle and the lake below, and I rolled down the window for a better look. Ancient oak trees lined the road that led into the town square. From the square, the cobbled street led to the castle, which dazzled from any angle. Something fluttered inside me, like something coming to life.

"Beauchesne." Max nodded toward the city that lay before us. "It means 'beautiful oak.'"

Now I should put it right out there that I did, in fact, pretend to be a princess when I was little, like around four or five. (You too? I mean is there even a girl who never did? Never once?) I told everyone I lived in a castle that was surrounded by a dark forest of twisted thorn trees and a moat. I saw that scene in a book once, and obviously that picture made a lasting impression on my young mind. The castle I gazed upon was nothing like that. This castle was made of white stone, and it had real turrets that soared toward the sky and wings that led in different directions. There was no moat, but the beautiful crystal-clear lake met a stone wall behind the castle. From an arched opening in the wall, steps led down to the water. And yes, the lake *did* sparkle more brilliantly than Lake Geneva.

"What do you think?" Max asked as I stared wide-eyed.

"It's beautiful. I saw a picture online, but it was nothing like this. This is . . ." I threw up my hands. I couldn't even put it into words.

"Would you like to continue on to the castle now?"

I nodded and the car began to ease slowly down the hill and into the city, where the street narrowed. On either side were shops in a row of Tudor-style half-timber buildings. There was a bakery with piles of bread and displays of pastries and cakes in the window, a dressmaker, a bookshop, a restaurant, a chocolate shop, a pub, a hairdresser, and a café with small tables set outside on the cobbled sidewalk where a small group gathered and chatted in soft voices. If our passing was noticed, I saw no sign of it. A square complete with a fountain lay just ahead. There was a statue in its center but because of the trees, I couldn't really tell what it was. All I could see from the car was what looked like a huge fish tail.

Opposite one side of the square stood a large church made of the same white stone as the castle, its spires rising into the sky. Next to the church the road led to the white fantasy castle. John-Paul waved at a man in uniform who stood at one side of the tall stone pillars marking the entrance to the castle grounds, and my heart was pounding so hard I was afraid I'd pass out. We drove past the pillars and through a gate that opened for us, then along a winding road lined with neatly trimmed boxwood. I wondered if the view had changed much since my gran lived here, if this was the same as what she'd seen when she'd looked over her shoulder as she fled her home.

The castle was at the end of that road, and because of all the twists and turns, I'd been able to see it from different perspectives. It was so much bigger than I'd imagined, much more beautiful and imposing. I swear, I felt like I'd just stepped into the pages of a fairy tale. John-Paul stopped close to a square tower that jutted slightly from the front, in the middle of which was a very tall and wide arched wooden door. I was so turned around I wasn't even sure this was the front of the castle. Max held the car door for me, and when I got out and stared up at that magnificent structure, my breath caught in my throat as I tried to take it in.

This was no fairy tale. While the past few weeks had held the air of a daydream, the building in front of me was very, very real. Its size diminished me and for a moment, I was seven years old standing on the steps of the Philadelphia Museum of Art for the first time and feeling very small indeed.

When I tell you my knees shook and my hands began to sweat a little, you'll understand, right? It's not every day you get to stand before a castle from which your family once ruled an entire country. Even if that country was no bigger than Rhode Island, still, I was looking at hundreds of years of my family history. It was humbling, even a little intimidating. If not for the war, my mother would likely have grown up here, my sisters and I possibly as well.

I heard my mother whisper, *Annaliese, stand up straight. And don't forget your manners.*

And Gran: *Smile, child. Be gracious.*

I straightened my back, and together the four of us approached the enormous arched door, which swept open as we drew near. A call had obviously been made to alert whoever was inside that we were on our way, because the man who opened the door wore what looked like a military-style coat complete with all sorts of brass and ribbon badges and a red sash that went from his right shoulder to his left hip. Behind him stood a gathering of people who peered anxiously around him, apparently to get a good look at me.

"Your Highness." He bowed from the waist, his bald head nodding once. "We have waited for a very long time to welcome you."

I turned to Max and silently begged for help.

"Your Grace, permit me to introduce you to Vincens DellaVecchio, grand chancellor of Saint Gilbert and a ranking member of our council." Max touched my elbow. "Chancellor, it is my honor to present

Her Royal Highness, the Grand Duchess, Annaliese Jacqueline Terese Gilberti."

I wanted to remind him I was not the grand duchess yet and I didn't know if I ever would be, but I didn't want to embarrass Max—or incur the wrath of Mom—so I said, "How do you do." Something I never said—let's face it, where I come from a good *Yo* or *How you doin'* can mean pretty much the same thing—but it seemed right under the circumstances, considering the fact that I had no idea what a grand chancellor did, but he was obviously important enough that he wore a red sash and gold braid on his jacket, and he was the one who got to open the door.

"Your Highness, I cannot adequately express the joy your visit brings. You are the answer to our prayers." His voice was warm, smooth as silk, his words well chosen. He looked to be around midfifties and cut quite the fancy figure in his finery, I had to admit. I wondered how old that jacket was—did they even have an army here?—and how he'd managed to preserve the brass and the gold fringe.

I was about to set the record straight about my visit—I've never been the answer to anyone's prayers—when Max stepped forward.

"Her Highness has agreed to visit with us for a brief time," Max said, and there was something in the way he tilted his head and looked down into the face of Vincens the Grand that gave me the feeling he wasn't all that fond of the chancellor. My gut was telling me the chancellor returned the feeling.

Interesting. I tucked that away for another time.

"We are grateful for however long you will honor us with your presence." Again, a half bow from Vincens. "But I'm sure Your Grace is tired from her journey. Perhaps you'd like to freshen up, rest a bit, then join us later in the drawing room?"

"I would like that, yes, thank you. But my bags . . ."

"Are already on their way to your room," Max said, his tone more formal now that we were in the castle and surrounded by others. He turned to a woman who stood tall amid the crowd gathered in the wide entry. "Madam, if you'd be so kind as to show Her Highness to her quarters."

"Of course. If you would come with me, my lady." A beautiful woman with a gracious smile who looked to be around fifty stepped forward and bowed slightly from her waist, a sort of non-curtsy curtsy. She wore a shirtwaist dress the color of the spring grass we'd seen on the mountainside, and her white hair sat atop her head in a neat bun. She had the liveliest blue eyes and gorgeous skin, flawless and just the right amount of natural color to her cheeks.

Well, the curtsying—the curtsy is so yesterday—was going to have to stop. It made me uncomfortable, along with all the Your Highness-ing and Your Grace-ing. I needed to speak to Max about that. Again.

I glanced over my shoulder at Max, John-Paul, and Marcel, who stood watching me. Max nodded his head, and I turned to go with the woman to whom I'd been handed over.

Now that I'd made it past the gathering in the entry—smiling whenever someone's eyes met mine—I stopped to take in my surroundings. The large foyer—easily five times the size of the first floor of my row house—opened into a long, wide hallway that seemed to stretch forever. The floor was made of black and white squares—marble?—set in a checkerboard pattern, and the walls were the softest shade of almost but not quite yellow imaginable. There were tall arched windows that reached almost to the ceiling along the inside wall that looked out onto a huge courtyard, and in the spaces between the windows I noticed the telltale discoloration where paintings had once hung. I wondered what had happened to them.

"Madam." I stopped for a moment and addressed her as Max had.

"Claudette is my name," she said.

"Claudette, what do they call this . . ." I waved my hand around to indicate the hall.

"It's known as the gallery, my lady."

"Thank you." I resumed my steps, so she did as well.

We passed a series of closed rooms on the left. As if sensing my curiosity, my companion said, "Most of the rooms in the castle have been closed for many years. We've just begun to reopen them. We'd hoped to have them all refurbished before your arrival, but there wasn't quite enough time."

"Why were they closed?"

She paused in the center of the hall. "You know of course our history, how the German army came and took over the country."

"1941," I said. "The year my grandmother and her sister left Saint Gilbert after her family was killed."

Claudette nodded. "The Nazis had the reputation of confiscating anything of value. We didn't have time to hide everything, so some things that hadn't been hidden away were destroyed or stolen by the invaders. When the Russians arrived, they drove out the Germans, and the commander of the troops who came through Saint Gilbert liked the castle very much." She smiled wryly. "So much so that he made this his headquarters, which meant we had the enemy with us every day. The upside was that no further physical damage was done, but again, many of our treasures that hadn't been hidden away went with him when he left."

"Hidden away where?"

She smiled. "There are many secret places in a castle as old and as large as this one, places that came in quite handy during the war. I'll take you on a tour while you're here if you like." She resumed walking.

"What sort of things were hidden?"

"Those with the most value. Furniture that had been in the castle for generations. Some jewelry. The best silver and china services. Crystal. Artwork. Many portraits." She gestured to the empty walls. "Many very valuable paintings once hung on our walls. Of course, we knew we would lose part of our heritage to the invaders, but I will say we were successful in saving more than we lost—certainly the very best of our art and antiques—and that was and still is a consolation. When the Germans came and asked about the blank places on the walls, we told them we'd been hit by a rogue band of Russians. When the Russians came, we blamed the Germans."

We? Did she say we?

But that would imply Claudette had been alive back in the 1940s, and that was impossible. She couldn't have been more than midfifties at the very most, a contemporary of the chancellor, perhaps, though the years had certainly been kinder to her. But if she were in her fifties, that meant she wasn't born until the mid-1960s. She must have meant the collective *we*.

"Ah, here we are."

The hall flowed through a wide arched doorway into another hall that turned to the right and led to a stairwell that was straight out of a fairy-tale castle. Wide enough for six to eight people to descend side by side, it rose majestically to the second floor, framed by balusters, also of white stone, like the steps. My head was spinning like Regan's in *The Exorcist*. There was too much to see, too much to take note of, too many questions buzzing around in my head, but I had no idea where to begin. There were double doors to the left, and I supposed if you were coming down this set of stairs, you might be headed there.

"What's through those doors?" I asked.

"Oh, that would be the throne room." Claudette turned and took ten steps, pushed the doors open, then beckoned me to step inside. With one hand, she flipped some switches, and the dozen or so crystal chandeliers overhead and the sconces that lined the walls came to life. The effect was breathtaking.

The floor here was parqueted wood and stretched all the way to a dais at the opposite end of the long, wide room. There, two oversize chairs with high backs sat side by side, their seats and backs covered in deep-blue velvet.

"The thrones, my lady." She beckoned me to continue on to the end of the room. "They're quite interesting. The carvings are exquisite. Do look."

Have I mentioned how bizarre this all was?

"Ahhh, no, thanks. I think I'll save that for later. Right now, I'd like to freshen up." I was tired, and I felt as if I hadn't washed my hands or face since last week. I was so thirsty my tongue was starting to stick to the roof of my mouth, and to tell you the truth, I wasn't ready for the whole throne experience just yet.

"Of course." She closed the doors and proceeded to the stairwell.

"I read online there are almost two hundred rooms in this castle." We began to make the climb. I should note the ceilings in this place are about twenty feet high, which made for a long climb when you're tired.

"One hundred ninety-seven, counting all the different dining rooms and their anterooms, the drawing rooms, the many bedrooms, the—"

"Stop, please." I shook my head. "I grew up in a house that had seven rooms. I live now in a house that has six. The largest house I'd ever been in was my grandmother's. It had five bedrooms and a bunch of rooms downstairs, maybe six or seven, and I thought that house was enormous. This is overwhelming. I'll never learn where everything is in this place."

"Then you might be pleased to know you won't have to, at least not currently. Only this section and the east wing are accessible at this time. The entire west wing is closed, all floors. The roof has damage and it's leaked into the rooms on the third floor, and because the house was unoccupied for so many years after the Russians left, the damage went unnoticed for far too long. The floor is soft in some sections." She paused at the top of the steps. I was breathing hard from the climb, but my companion was cool as could be. "We'd hoped to have repaired it before someone from the royal family returned, but there weren't sufficient funds."

I nodded. Anything I said would have sounded weird. Even a simple "I'm sorry" could have been interpreted as, "I'm sorry your country is poor and I'm therefore sorry to have come here."

"This way, my lady." She paused and nodded in the direction of another long hallway.

"What's over there?" I'd stopped on the landing and pointed to the right.

"That would be the east wing. There are guest suites, a smaller library than the one on the first floor, a small kitchen, a billiards room, a small drawing room . . ."

"I got it. Much the same as downstairs only with bedrooms for visitors."

"More or less, yes."

"You said 'smaller library than the one on the first floor'? There are two libraries?"

Smiling, she nodded.

I might enjoy this visit more than I'd thought.

I followed Claudette along the hallway. There were more empty spaces on the wall similar to those in the gallery below, where something had hung long enough for the wallpaper around it to have faded.

"There were more paintings here," I heard myself say.

"We'd thought of hanging them, but I thought perhaps you should have the honor of selecting the works you most liked."

She paused outside double doors painted white with gold trim, her hands on the doorknobs. "This was the suite the last grand duchess occupied, your great-grandmother. We've restored it as best we could, but of course, should you decide to stay, you may change whatever you like."

She threw open the doors to the suite. I glanced inside at what I guessed would be a sitting room and stifled a gasp.

My first impression was that the room was all gold, but in actuality, the walls were a rich shade of cream made vibrant by the sunlight that burst through the casement windows and made everything in the room glow. A sofa upholstered in white-on-white damask faced a fireplace of more white stone and was flanked by armchairs also in white. Several more chairs stood near the fireplace, all in damask but gold rather than white, and there was an Oriental rug in shades of rose and pale blue on the floor. Tapestries hung from the ceiling to almost the floor and covered two walls, and there were several doors leading who knew where on both sides. An enormous vase of dark-pink roses stood on a side table.

"The bedchamber is through here, madam." Claudette opened a door on the left and stood to the side.

The bedroom was something else. It was enormous and high-ceilinged and luxurious in the way you'd see in *National Geographic* magazines featuring centuries-old European castles. There were gilded mirrors and a dressing table with a gold lamp that had a fringed silk shade. More vases holding colorful flowers were set here and there about the room. The bed was some sort of dark wood and had posters that had to have been seven or eight feet tall on the four corners. Atop the posters perched birds in various stages of flight.

"What are those birds?" I asked.

"Falcons, my lady. The Gilbertis were great falconers," she explained with a smile. "And please, I would be honored if you would call me Claudette."

"Only if you call me Annaliese." I returned the smile and waited for her response, which seemed to be a long time coming.

"I couldn't . . ."

"Of course you could."

"I wouldn't feel comfortable."

"What is your position here, may I ask?"

"I'll be your—what did my son call it?—your right hand. I'd been granted the privilege of overseeing the preparations for your arrival and your stay. My official title is senior lady-in-waiting, but think of me as your 'go-to' person."

"So you'll be the person I'll be spending the most time with. The person who'll answer my questions—that sort of thing?" Is that what a lady-in-waiting actually did?

"Yes. More or less."

"Then you absolutely need to call me Annaliese." I held up my hand when she began to protest again. "I am not comfortable being called 'Your Highness' or 'my lady' or any of those other titles. I don't know if I'm ever going to be those things. I'm here because I thought in all fairness I should come and see for myself where my grandmother was born and see where she lived and where her parents died. But I don't know that I'm going to be staying. I'm asking you to please call me Annaliese."

"Shall we compromise, then? 'Your Highness' when we are in company with others, 'Annaliese' at other times," she suggested.

"Deal. Thank you." It was progress. "Oh, and please—spread the word that I don't want to see anyone curtsying."

"Consider it done."

I walked around the room suppressing the urge to pinch myself. I just couldn't take it all in. I opened each of the closed doors and peered into the spaces beyond. Behind one was what I suspect had been a huge closet the size of a room. Behind another, a room with yet another fireplace that I assumed was a more private sitting room. The others . . . I have no idea.

What in the name of all that's holy was I doing here?

In times like this, when I felt unsure of myself, I found it eased my anxiety to get the person I was with to talk about themselves.

"You mentioned your son said you'd be my companion," I asked as I made my way around the room. "Have I met your son?" Hopefully not a member of one of the factions Max warned me about. The ones who *hopefully* wouldn't be shooting at me.

"Yes, my lady. Maximilien is my son." She smiled apologetically and tried again. "Annaliese."

"Maximilien who?" Had I met another Maximilien? There'd been so many people milling about downstairs, I wasn't sure.

"Maximilien Belleme." Claudette laughed. "Please don't tell me my son has left so little an impression on you that you have forgotten him already."

I'm guessing the *WTF* look on my face gave me away, because Claudette laughed good-naturedly. "I am his mother."

"What? How is that even possible? You're way too young to be his mother. Did you have him when you were about five?"

She laughed again. "Maximilien is my youngest. I was thirty-six years old when he was born."

"But he's in his, what, late twenties? Thirties at most?" I paused. Math had never been my strong suit, but that would make her in her sixties.

No freaking way.

"My son is forty-two, madam."

My head began to swim. "But that would make you . . ." The numbers didn't compute. And in what world did Max look to be in his forties? Not the world I've been living in.

"Seventy-eight on my next birthday, yes." She nodded and moved to open a door to the left of the bed.

When I finally shook off my disbelief, I followed her, still trying to figure out how a woman who was almost eighty could look—and move—like she was thirty years younger.

A special diet consisting of foraged greens from the forest floor? Long walks in the mountain air? Bathing in the milk of the Charolais? A strict diet of unpasteurized cheese and wine?

She opened the last of the doors. "Your bathroom, my . . . Annaliese."

I probably said something like *thank you*, but I can't be sure. I was stuck on the fact that she looked years—*decades*—younger than she claimed to be. There wasn't a wrinkle on her face, nor an age spot anywhere I could see. The skin on her hands was as luminous as the skin on her face.

Whatever else I might learn about the home of my ancestors over the week I'd be here, the secret of Madam Belleme's youthful beauty had just earned a spot high atop the list.

Chapter Seven

Minutes after she left my room, Claudette had tea sent. It was hot and arrived in a silver carafe and was accompanied by a delicate cup and saucer, a small china bowl of honey, several sugar cubes in a silver bowl, some small sandwiches, and a plate of the same little cakes my grandmother had baked with me so long ago. Looking at that plate took me back almost forty years, and unexpectedly, my eyes began to tear. Someone had once made these exact cakes for Gran here in this very castle, and she'd brought the recipe with her to America via what must have been, for a fifteen-year-old who'd lived a life of luxury, a tortuous and scary route through the rugged Swiss mountains.

Much as I tried, I could not wrap my head around the ordeal my family had endured. Thinking about her flight had me wondering about the assassinations of her parents, her brother, one of her sisters, and who knows who else. That line of thought made me wonder where the assassinations had taken place. In the castle? In the woods? Where were they buried, and by whom? Are their graves marked, or are they lost forever?

Macabre thoughts for sure, but that was my mood. This was all so new to me, and I had so much going through my head at the same time I thought it might explode.

I poured myself a cup of tea and sipped it as I walked around the bedroom, trying to convince myself this was no different from any room in any upscale hotel. I was doing okay with this line of thinking until

I sat on the stool in front of the dressing table and saw the hairbrush and hand mirror there. They were made of gold-colored metal, and for all I knew, it could have been real gold, considering where I was. On the back of both the brush and the mirror was a stylized *G* set with red stones. More rubies? Ceil would know. I wish I had her eye for gems.

I made the mistake of picking up the brush and turning it over. There amid the bristles several thin strands of hair were entwined. Few though they were, I could tell the hair was the same cinnamon brown as my own. Suddenly everything made me sad—the castle that was partially boarded up, the room, the hair in the brush, my murdered relatives, my exiled grandmother. Everything made me want to weep.

One thing I learned about myself when I was a kid was that when I wanted to cry, I should just let it rip. So I did. I sobbed. I wept buckets. I moved to the sofa and cried my eyes out. I stood at a window and looked out at the lake and the fields and the woods that stretched for as far as the eye could see, and the mountains, all things that hadn't been visible from the front of the castle. I went to the window on the other side of the room and took in the vast gardens that went on forever and the courtyard—I bet you could fit half of Lincoln Financial Field in there—and the outbuildings that I supposed were stables and who knew what else, and I cried until I stopped.

Then I took a deep breath, and I felt one hundred percent better. I was still sad for my ancestors who were murdered or exiled, but the pain wasn't as overwhelming as it had felt twenty minutes before. And now I had to remove the telltale signs of my sob-fest. Some cold water, some eye drops, some concealer, and I'd be good as new. I grabbed my carry-on and went into the bathroom to repair the damage.

The bathroom was charmingly old-fashioned, with a large tub set into the floor like a pool surrounded on two sides by walls tiled in blue and white and pastoral scenes that reminded me of some old porcelain vases my mother had. The tub was clearly large enough for more than one person, which made me wonder if the last duchess had entertained in her tubbie, and if so, who. Several large towels the color of just-fallen snow sat on the wide ledge around the tub alongside bowls of soap. The fixtures, by the way, were copper—so trendy these days, right?—and the sink was round, the pedestal on which it sat fancy, like a Greek column. The large oval bowl was a painted woodland scene depicting a variety of wildlife: rabbits, deer, fox, and birds. The birds all had rounded heads. Marked by yellow beaks that were short but curved, with yellow circles around the eyes, they all looked alike to me. The tops of their heads were reddish, their chests were white with dark spots, and the backs and wings were brown on some, more like gray on others. Falcons, Claudette had told me. I'd never seen one, though I'd read they were nesting on some window ledges in Center City, Philadelphia, where hopes were high they'd help control the pigeon population. If ever a bird looked as if it meant business, it was the falcon with its sharp eyes and talons.

Behind a half wall—also tiled in blue and white—I found the toilet. The area was set off to itself, and as toilets go, it was pretty fancy and much more contemporary than I'd expected. I pushed the handle to make sure it worked, and a rush of water flowed into the bowl, so no problem there.

The entire bathroom was way bigger than my bedroom back home, and it was so beautiful, with the colored tiles and the painted sink. But my favorite thing was the shower. It was set into a deep niche in the wall, like the one that held a life-size statue of the Virgin Mary I saw in a church I was in once at the Jersey Shore. The niche was so far into the wall, when I stepped inside my entire body was beneath the overhead shower. The whole thing was made of marble, and it was so cool I wondered why we didn't have these things back in the States, though maybe some people do. I couldn't wait to use it. I was tired and I felt travel weary. I'd been on a plane for hours, then in a car for several more, and I felt dusty and dingy from the walk I'd taken with Max. I didn't want to meet whoever was going to be downstairs later in the condition I was in. Actually, I didn't want to meet anyone downstairs, period, but that was apparently beside the point.

I went back into the bedroom and struggled to get the suitcase onto the bed. The thing weighed about sixty pounds. I opened it and took out my hair dryer and the adapter Ceil bought me to make sure I'd have power to use it. I tested it in an outlet and it seemed okay, so I could wash my hair without worrying that I'd look like a drowned rat for the rest of the day. I took a minute and laid out the dresses I'd brought with me on the bed. I'd hang them up later.

I was annoyed more than I can tell you that I couldn't find my face wash and shampoo. I couldn't believe I'd left all that plus my moisturizer at home, but I must have forgotten to tuck them back into my bag after I'd used them early that morning. I had seen soaps in the bathroom, and I supposed I could get by with those, but I'd miss my moisturizer. (What woman over the age of twenty-five leaves home without it?)

The shower was perfect in every way. The water temperature adjusted to my preference, and even the soap was lovely, creamy taupe in color with streaks of purple. It smelled beautiful, like violets after the rain, which of course made me think of Gran, which made me wonder if she'd stood in this same shower once upon a time. The soap lathered like a dream and was so rich I didn't even miss my shampoo and conditioner when I washed my hair. The fragrance surrounded me completely to the point I was almost drunk with the scent. When I finished and dried myself, I was so refreshed, I felt I was ready for anything.

First things first. I plugged in the hair dryer and proceeded to blow my hair out straight. The air in Saint Gilbert was dry, which meant there was no frizz, which was a big win for me. Next, makeup, which THANK GOD was in my bag. I'd blown a bundle at Sephora in the mall, and I'd be really pissed if every last piece hadn't made it to Saint Gilbert with me. But it was all there, right down to the cream eye shadow and the concealer. I stood in front of a full-length mirror in the bathroom while I put on what I hoped would pass as a happy face.

I hung clothes that needed hanging in the massive closet and tried to decide what to wear. My gut told me to go with black. I went back and forth between two black dresses—I'd brought several with me, but how to know which would be more appropriate for this afternoon's get-together? I held up first one, then the other before placing them side by side on the bed and asking myself, what would Audrey wear?

There was a knock at the door, and before I opened it, I put on the robe (pure silk, I was positive) that had been left in the bathroom.

"I thought perhaps you might need some assistance, Annaliese," Claudette said kindly.

She wore a beautiful dress with a round neck, long, sheer sleeves, and a chiffon skirt in shades of blue and green on white, and it flowed around her hips like a cloud. The stones in her ears were clear but sparkly as all get-out, and they matched the large round stone in the ring on her left ring finger. I hadn't been a GIA student like Ceil, but I'd have bet my next year's mortgage payments those suckers were diamonds, and I don't mean the fake stuff like they sell on TV. Her hair was white, but the kind of white that women want—if they *had* to go white, if you know what I mean. Her skin was luminous—there's no other word for it—and her smile radiant. I know I said it before, but I still couldn't get past the fact that she claimed to be seventy-eight years old. Honest to God, she looked like she was in her midfifties. *Barely* in her fifties.

How in the name of all that's holy could this woman be Max's mother?

"You look gorgeous," I told her, still marveling at that flawless face. "You look more like a duchess than I do."

She dismissed my comment with a wave of her hand, but I could tell she enjoyed the compliment all the same.

"I would love your assistance, Claudette. I can't decide what to wear. I don't know exactly what type of get-together this is supposed to be." I stepped back, and she went straight to the bed where I'd left the dresses.

"This will be very informal," she said. "I would have preferred putting off any such reception until tomorrow, but everyone was so excited about your arrival, it was decided it would be best to have a very small gathering with members of the Duke's Council as well as some old friends of the monarchy in attendance in a very relaxed setting." She turned back to the more immediate issue. "Either of these dresses would be perfectly appropriate."

I'd started to feel a little overwhelmed, and it must have shown on my face, because Claudette assured me, "My son and I will be there to introduce you to everyone, and I promise, the reception will not last more than ninety minutes at the very most. The people you will meet today are dedicated to the Gilberti family and are thrilled that you are here." Before I could protest, she added, "Whether or not you decide to stay, your great-grandparents were very popular, and your grandmother had many friends who are delighted at the opportunity to meet her granddaughter."

Right. But no pressure, Annie.

"So you think maybe this dress?" I held up the short-sleeved sheath with the scoop neck I'd bought on a whim at Chico's during my fly-by shopping at the mall last week.

"Absolutely, yes. We can dress it up with a bit of jewelry, and it will be perfect."

"I don't have any jewelry," I told her. "Maybe one of the scarves I brought might work." I searched in my suitcase for a scarf that looked summery in pinks and white and black and draped it around my neck.

"Perhaps," she said.

I could see she wasn't down with the scarf idea, but she picked up the dress we'd agreed on, and when I took off the robe she slid the dress over my head. Just that quickly Claudette reached for the robe and hung it on one of the padded hangers.

"Whose robe is that?" I asked.

"Yours, now, if you'd like. It was made for your great-grandmother, but we found it with your grandmother's things, so I suppose she'd borrowed it from time to time. But like so many of her lovely things, it was left behind the day she fled the country."

I slipped into my shoes—I'd been debating between the leopard-print flats, which were my favorites, and the smooth black leather heels I'd been wearing that day and decided the black ones would probably be best for this first outing. Everyone knows you only got one chance to make a first impression. My sisters had an argument once about who first said that. Roe said it was Will Rogers and Ceil said it was Oscar Wilde. We looked it up and found out neither had actually said it, but it had been used in an ad for men's suits back in the 1960s.

"Annaliese." I'd been almost to the door when Claudette stopped me. "You need jewelry."

I started to repeat what I'd said earlier—that I didn't have any— when I remembered the pieces that had been returned to me. I dug in my bag for the leather pouch.

"Max brought these to me when we met in Philadelphia," I said as I emptied the pouch onto the bed's white coverlet. "I remember my grandmother wearing these earrings."

"They're lovely. Rubies have always been a favorite of the royal family. But perhaps you'd like a choice now that you're here."

She picked up a long white box from the dressing table. I hadn't seen it before, so I suspect she'd placed it there when she came in and I simply hadn't noticed.

I stared at the box for a long time, almost afraid to open it, so Claudette did. She appeared nonchalant as she dipped into it.

"You should always wear earrings, especially when you wear your hair tucked behind your ears. It looks lovely pulled back." She handed me a pair of gold earrings similar to the ones my grandmother had always worn, but these were much larger, and the centers of the roses held oval-shaped rubies. My jaw dropped.

Oh, they'd make an impression all right.

"As I said, rubies have long been favorites of our royals. Your great-great-great grandfather brought many pieces with him as gifts for his bride when he came to Saint Gilbert from France to marry the grand duchess of the day." She stood back while I fastened them in my ears with shaking hands. The last time I bought a pair of earrings for myself, they were from Macy's. The year Ralphie was born, my ex bought me a pair of silver knots from Tiffany's in the mall for Christmas, but they disappeared when we divorced. I figured he took them with him when he left, and I suspected that wife number two was the new proud owner. Not that I cared.

"They are perfect on you. Now, for around your neck." She lifted a strand of pearls as big as pigeon eggs from the box. And yes, I have so seen pigeon eggs. My ex's fool brother used to raise them on the roof of his row house in South Philly before the neighbors complained.

Before I could say a word, she'd fastened the pearls around my neck.

"For your wrist . . . I think . . . yes, this is perfect." She held up a gold bracelet that reminded me of the necklace I'd left on the bed. The strands of gold wound around my left arm from my wrist to three or four inches above it, but unlike Gran's necklace, the bracelet had no stones.

"Last piece." She smiled and opened her right hand. On her palm sat several rings. "You choose."

I stood there staring for what seemed like forever. I think I may even have pinched myself. Like I said, I didn't own a lot of jewelry. Not that I didn't love it. I just hadn't been able to afford anything that even came close to what Claudette held in her hand. I didn't think I could even afford reproductions. That each piece was solid gold and the gemstones real was a given. There was an oval ruby solitaire that could put out someone's eye (the royal equivalent of brass knuckles?), a large pure-white pearl surrounded by rubies, a pearl surrounded by smaller pearls, and a hefty piece of gold that looked like twisted rope. I liked the rope, but it didn't seem to go with the other things I was wearing, so I chose the ruby solitaire and put it on my right-hand ring finger, but it was too big. I switched it on to the middle, and it was perfect.

"Excellent choice," Claudette assured me. "You look very much a Gilberti, Your Highness."

She steered me toward the floor-to-ceiling mirror on the wall opposite the windows and stood back to allow me to look at myself. I barely recognized my own reflection, mostly because I couldn't look away from those big honking rubies in my earlobes. Seriously, though—I had to admit I looked good. If not like royalty, at the very least an heiress. Or a debutante. Okay, maybe a former debutante.

"Oh my God" was the only thing I could think of to say as I touched the pearls that hung around my neck. "I thought you said this would be very informal. Where I come from, the only people who wear this much bling are Mummers, and only on New Year's Day."

Claudette smiled.

"Are you really sure I should wear all this?" I turned my head again to check out the earrings. "It's all so . . . fancy. So . . . so . . . *regal*."

"These are a very small part of the collection that makes up the crown jewels, the majority of which rest in a Swiss bank."

I stared at the pearls for a moment, then touched the huge earrings. "These are beyond gorgeous, Claudette, and I would love to wear them." I unhooked the pearls and handed them to her. "But another time. I think today I'd like to wear the pieces that I brought with me."

I took the earrings from my ears and placed them in the box she still held. I went to the bed and picked up the smaller pair and slipped them into my ears. I put on the necklace, and it fit perfectly within the scoop of my neckline.

"The bracelet is part of that set, Annaliese," Claudette told me. "You should wear it."

I smiled and returned to the mirror. I liked what I saw much better. The pieces Claudette had brought in for me were gorgeous. Seriously, a king's ransom in rubies and pearls. But I knew these earrings. I remember these gracing Gran's ears. I never saw her without them, and if I'd ever really thought about it, I might have guessed she'd been buried wearing them. Now, in her castle among her people, I wanted to wear them for her. I feel pretty sure that somewhere she is smiling and nodding in agreement.

I'll try not to embarrass you, Gran.

I left the ring with the big stone on my right hand and slipped Gran's ring onto my left. I know she would have approved.

"I know these pieces. They feel right to me."

"They belong to you, Annaliese."

I shook my head. "Only if I stay."

"Which we're all hoping you will decide to do."

"You don't know me. I could be a dud." I held up my hand to admire the ring and immediately regretted canceling the mani appointment Ceil had made for me.

She laughed. "I seriously doubt that. My son is an excellent judge of character. He is totally convinced that you are the right person to lead this country and—"

"Please," I interrupted her. I didn't want to hear it. "I appreciate Max's faith in me, but please let's wait to see how things go."

"As you wish, of course." She opened the door and held it for me.

"My grandmother wore these"—I touched the earrings and held up the finger where her ring sat, big and bold—"for as long as I can remember. So how did they end up with Max?"

"My father, and later my brother, Emile, had been in contact with your grandmother from the day she settled in Pennsylvania. When she knew her time was coming to an end, she asked that we take the jewels back here, to save them for the next duchess."

"Did she think that would be me?"

"I believe she hoped it would be your mother first, then you."

"I see." I felt a little let down that Gran's wish for Mom hadn't come true. "I don't think my grandmother had all those other jewels with her. So where have they been since 1941?" I asked as I walked toward the door.

"A story for another time. The guests have arrived, and they're gathering in the drawing room. Many have waited years for this day." She took my elbow and guided me in the direction of the stairwell. "Shall we?"

As we went through the hall on our way to the steps, I remembered I hadn't taken any photos to send back to the kids. Maybe Claudette could take a few for me on my phone. I know my sisters would die when they saw me wearing Gran's jewels, not to mention that ring with the gigundo stone. I almost did.

Chapter Eight

When we entered what Claudette referred to as the main drawing room, every conversation stopped and every eye in the room turned to look at me. I channeled my best Audrey Hepburn (and maybe a little of my homegirl, Grace Kelly) and told myself I had Gran's royal blood in my veins, and if for no other reason, I belonged here.

Stand up straight, Annaliese, I swear I heard my mother and grandmother whisper at the same time.

Do me proud, child, Gran added. I blinked back a tear and silently promised her I'd do my best.

There was a harpist playing in front of the enormous fireplace, a young woman in her twenties, I guessed. Her fingers never missed a string even when the entire room went silent.

Claudette nodded to Max, who stepped away from the group he'd been chatting with and came forward to take my hand. He bent at the waist and brushed his lips over my knuckles, and I admit I felt a tingle up my spine.

"Your Grace, if I may be so bold as to present you to your—"

I cleared my throat. If he said *subjects* or anything that even sounded like that, I was ready to bolt, royal jewels or not.

But he'd gotten the message.

"To friends of the crown who have been waiting to meet you."

I nodded because I didn't know what was appropriate to say, and I allowed him to lead me around the room.

We were in the castle's main drawing room, a long rectangle with windows from which I could see the lake. The walls were paneled floor to ceiling in a dark wood, and here and there a portrait hung. Relatives, no doubt. There were little private seating areas with lovely furniture that struck me as being sort of French in style and tables adorned with vases filled with peonies, which are my favorite flower. When I mentioned this to Claudette, she smiled. "A favorite of your great-grandmother's as well."

"Is she in any one of those?" I asked, nodding toward the portraits.

"No. But there are many portraits of her in the castle. I'll be happy to show you." She gestured to a server, who produced a tray holding several different wines.

"What is your preference?" Claudette asked.

"I don't know. I don't know the choices."

"What wine do you fancy when you are home?" she asked. "What do you buy when you buy wine for yourself?"

"Pinot grigio," I told her. No need to tell her the stuff I bought usually came in a box or that for me, a splurge was when I ordered from one of the TV shopping channels.

She looked over the tray before selecting a glass and handing it to me, saying, "I think you might enjoy this one."

I took a sip. The wine tasted pure and perfect, the flavor magical, and was unlike anything I'd ever tasted. I wished my bestie, Marianne, was here to share it with me. That girl did love a good glass of wine. I know back home she must be pissed at me, that I'd taken "vacation" without even telling her I was going. She would have wanted to come with me, regardless of where I was going. I didn't want to have to lie to her, and I didn't want to tell her the truth, so I figured I'd just have to deal with her hurt feelings when I got home. Once I knew what I was going to do, I'd tell her everything.

Overall, the reception was an experience I'll never forget. I wish I'd brought a little notebook to write things down, because I didn't trust myself to remember every detail and every face. It was the most memorable ninety minutes of my life. Unbelievably, I met people who actually knew my grandmother. I knew she was fifteen in 1941, which meant she was born in 1926. Which means she'd be ninety-seven years old if she were still alive, right? There were women who'd grown up with her, who got into mischief with her and played with her as a child. They shared stories of first crushes and first kisses. These were women who knew her strengths as well as her insecurities and her secrets.

And there were those who were with her when she found out her parents and her older brother and sister had been arrested, who understood if she didn't leave the country that day, that *hour*, she'd quickly be arrested as well. I swear I could feel her anguish and her fear at having to flee into the mountains, knowing her family would be dead before she reached the Swiss border.

Oh, Gran . . .

I promised myself before my visit here was over, I would speak with every one of those beautiful ladies. And beautiful they were, by the way. Barely a wrinkle on any of their faces, no sign of that nasty crepiness that comes with age, no little brown spots on their faces or their hands. Oh, sure, the oldest in the group—the ones who had been Gran's compatriots—had a touch of crow's-feet and just the slightest bit of laugh lines, but I'm telling you, most of these ladies had skin better than mine.

"Do you mind if I ask what you use on your face?" I asked Francine, whose last name I never did catch but she claimed to be in her mid-nineties. Looked maybe sixty, and by sixty, I mean good sixty. Like Jane Seymour sixty. Like Christie Brinkley sixty. Yeah. That good.

She stared at me before shrugging. "I don't understand. Use on my face?"

Maybe start with the basics, I thought. "What do you wash your face with?"

She frowned as if she thought the question was either rude or stupid so maybe she did mind, but I couldn't help myself. I had to know, and since the person asking her was either the next grand duchess or merely the granddaughter of the last one, she felt compelled to answer.

"Soap," she said as if there could be no other answer.

"Soap? That's all?" I was incredulous. "What kind of soap? Dove? Ivory? Aveeno? Something made in France?"

"Just . . . soap." Francine looked increasingly confused. "I don't know those other things you said."

"What kind of soap?"

"Just the soap we make here."

"You make your own soap?" I pondered this for a moment. "What do you put in it?"

"Just the usual. Goat milk and a few violet petals, as we've always done. Nothing special."

"So it's just soap and water?"

"Of course with water." At this point, I'm sure she thought I was not worthy to call myself a Gilberti.

"I'm sorry, I don't mean to be personal." Oh, but yes, I did! "It's just that your skin is absolutely beautiful." I glanced around the room. Actually, everyone there had really great skin. Even the men. Everyone simply glowed.

"Oh. Thank you. I apologize for hesitating, but the question caught me off guard. I never think about it, you see."

"You never think about how your skin looks?" She had to be kidding. If I had skin like that, I'd be looking at myself in the mirror twenty-four seven. I'd probably never stop looking at myself.

She shook her head. "It's just *skin*, my lady."

Right. And the *Mona Lisa* was just a painting.

I'm sure I made an odd impression—not to mention a lasting one—on each of the ladies I quizzed about their skin. To a woman, they all seemed to have the same attitude: "It's just skin." Skin that hasn't sagged, lined, wrinkled, or creped in seventy, eighty, ninety, close to one hundred years? How is that ever *just*? How is that even possible?

Of course I met everyone in the room—Claudette and Max saw to that. If one didn't have me by the arm, the other did. Vincens DellaVecchio was there with his son, Philippe, a balding middle-aged man a little on the paunchy side who seemed a bit too interested in the fact that I was wearing my great-grandmother's rubies. If he wasn't staring at my boobs, he was staring at my ears, my neck, or the middle fingers of both my hands. I made the mistake of asking him if his wife was in attendance. He smiled waaaaay too brightly when he told me she was deceased. As if I were interested in his status. Ugh.

Anyway, I met the other dukes who made up the Duke's Council and their wives and children. My head was starting to spin. I couldn't keep them all straight.

I did meet several charming people I wouldn't mind seeing again. A sweet man named Louis confided he'd been in love with Gran from the time they were five years old and had been heartbroken when he found out she was gone. He assured me he'd had a happy life with his wife, Antoinette (who I met later when I'd made the rounds of the room and who—surprise, surprise—had skin like a baby). They'd had five children together and lived at the far end of the city.

"You must come for tea," Antoinette said after we'd been introduced.

"I would be honored," I assured her. It sounded like the sort of thing a grand duchess would say, doesn't it? I was discovering there's a lot to be said about role-playing. I was beginning to like it.

I met a woman named Marguerite who claimed to have been a distant cousin of Gran's and a daughter of one of my great-grandmother's attendants. She professed to be in her nineties. I was hoping to spend some time with her since I knew absolutely nothing about Gran's mother, but I was whisked away to meet someone else on the council whose name I can't even recall at this point. There were so many people, so many names. I did find it interesting, though, that the older generations in Saint

Gilbert seemed to be a melting pot for most of Europe. This one was of Italian descent, that one of German, this one Belgian, that one French, another was Swiss. I was grateful the official language was English and taught in the schools.

I made my way around the room, sampling different varieties of local cheeses that I can say without prejudice were hands down beyond delicious. There was a soft ivory-colored cheese that looked like brie and was to die for, creamy and mild and topped with sour cherries. The South Philly in me wanted to snatch the entire tray and sneak off with it to the back porch, or as they say here in Saint Gilbert, the south veranda. Oh, and they served a cheese that was sort of like a baby Swiss that was luscious with the thinly sliced dark bread it topped. There were several others, all served on pretty silver trays passed by good-looking young men in white shirts open at the neck and plain black pants. I don't know who they were, but I guarantee Juliette would have been taking pictures with her phone and sending them back to her friends.

And okay, I admit I covertly took some pictures to send home when I got back to my room. Which I was hoping would be soon because I was dead on my feet.

By the way, each of the wines I sampled were as exceptional as the cheeses, and I could see where these two products could have carried the country through difficult times. They needed a wider distribution of both, though, and something more to bring them into this century. The castle wasn't going to get fixed and the roads weren't going to be repaired without another product, and whatever that was going to be, it would have to be available on an international level. I made a mental note to mention that to Max later. Whether or not I stayed, someone needed to take matters into their own hands and make something happen.

I wanted to remember everyone's name, but it wasn't going to be possible. As fascinating as the company was, I was fading fast. Thank God, Claudette appeared at my elbow at the exact moment I realized I'd had enough, and she escorted me from the room, leaving Max behind to close out the reception.

"You are exhausted," Claudette said as she saw me to my room. "I'd thought perhaps we'd have a private, quiet dinner with you this evening, but that's clearly out of the question. I'll have dinner brought to you whenever you like. All you have to do is open your door and tell Sebastian."

"Sebastian?" I asked as we rounded the corner in the hall.

"The guard outside your room. Whatever you need, whenever you need it, tell him or whichever guard is on duty, and it will be arranged."

"Do I really need a guard outside my room?" I whispered as we drew close to the man who stood like a sentry, straight and tall and staring directly ahead. He wore crisply pressed white pants and a navy jacket that looked like a military uniform, with some of that gold braid on the cuffs and shoulders and a large sword hanging from his waist.

"The guard is ceremonial, of course, but he's also your means of communicating with me or Max or whomever it is you need or want."

"Is that real?" Pointing to the sword, I addressed him directly when we arrived at the door to my room.

"Yes, Your Grace," Sebastian replied.

"And you know how to use it?"

"Yes, Your Grace." Sebastian was apparently a man of few words.

"Well, what would you do if someone came running up the hall brandishing a gun?" I said, thinking of the old *don't bring a sword to a gunfight* trope. "What good would a sword be?"

"None at all, Your Grace." To his credit, he remained stoically still. "In such case, I would shoot him." He patted his left side.

"Good answer." I opened the door and an amused Claudette followed me into my room.

"I'm a little confused about the communication chain around here," I said after the door closed behind us. "I have Max's cell number, but that's all."

"Sebastian and his morning replacement have access to everyone in the castle." She closed the heavy drapes to darken the room. "Is there something you need?"

"Not at the moment. I guess the only thing I need right now is a nap." She began to turn down the bed.

"Oh, I can do that," I began to protest, but she was done in a flash.

"Is there anything else I can do for you?" she asked as she smoothed the pillow cover.

"No, thank you." I watched her walk toward the door. "Oh, wait. There is one thing. If I could have a glass in case I need a drink of water . . ."

"I'll have it sent up immediately."

"Thank you." I walked back to the bed and touched the pillowcases. They were soft as silk and just as cool to the touch.

Claudette left the room before I remembered I was wearing all this jewelry, and I wondered if I should have given it to her for safekeeping. But apparently she trusted me and the armed guard at my door. I took it all off, piece by piece, studying each before returning it to the leather pouch. I took off my dress, and if I'd been home in my own house, I'd probably have dropped it where I stood and fallen face forward onto the bed, I was that tired. But being in the castle, I hung it in the closet on one of those silk-padded hangers someone had brought in just in case Gran was still watching.

I went into the bathroom and washed off my makeup. I was tired, but I wasn't about to smear my face all over those lovely pillowcases on the bed. I was still annoyed with myself for leaving my face wash and moisturizer in Philly, but I had to admit, the soap in the bathroom removed every trace—even the mascara—and my skin still didn't feel dried out. *Hmmm*, I thought. Twice today I'd washed my face with soap—something I hadn't done since I was about twelve and found the stuff Mom used—and I'd gone without any sort of face cream, and yet my skin felt as if I'd been to a spa, without a trace of that tight masklike pucker it would get when I washed it with even a mild cleanser. Curious.

When I came out of the bathroom, I found a carafe and a crystal glass on a pretty tray on the bedside table, though I hadn't heard anyone come or go. I slipped into the robe before opening the door. I peered out, but there was no one in the hall except Sebastian. I gave him a thumbs-up and went back into the room.

I draped the robe over a chair, then pulled a nightshirt over my head before I crawled under the sheet and sank into that soft mattress. I'm pretty sure I sighed with pleasure. I closed my eyes, and for a few moments I started to drift away. I smiled and waited to sail off into la-la land.

But no. The questions that had been building up since I walked into Castle Blanc started popping inside my brain like dried corn in a closed container over high heat and ran the gamut from how did all the furniture and fixtures inside the castle survive not one but two invasions to how is it that the crown jewels weren't stolen? How did they get into a vault in a Swiss bank? Max said something about the country's money being tied up in a Swiss bank, too. How did that happen? The castle seemed well staffed—but if no one has lived here in decades, who are all these people and where did they come from? Who is cooking and cleaning and baking and bringing me water? How is there a castle guard when there's been no one to guard for all these years? And now that I'm here, what exactly do these people expect me to do? How will I tell my friends from my foes? Max gave me the impression he was on it, but how do I know Max isn't going to turn out to be the bad guy after all? If he isn't at my elbow, his mother is. Are they really trying to assist me, or are they just trying to keep an eye on me and control who I come in contact with, who I speak with, where I go? Who should I trust?

Fatigue plus uncertainty equals confusion and paranoia.

It was pretty clear I wasn't falling asleep anytime soon, so I got up and looked for my phone. I took pictures around the suite—the bed, the fireplace, the bathroom, the sitting room with its fancy wood-carved fireplace surround. I was tempted to take pictures of the jewels but decided that could be asking for trouble. I was on a group text conversation with my kids and my sisters, so I sent the photos to everyone at the same time. My accommodations this week, I typed over the images from the bedroom. Just call me Your Highness, I jested when I sent the photos from the reception.

Moments later, I had a slew of return comments.

From Juliette: OMG, Mom! That party looks AWEsome! I wish I was there! What did you wear?

From Ralphie: Cool. Who's the cute chick in the blue dress?

From Ceil: Oh, man, that bed looks amazing! The bathroom looks fabulous! Are you having a good time? How's Max?

From Roe: I hope you don't have to make that bed and clean that bathroom before you leave. Or is there maid service? Don't leave your wallet laying around.

We all texted back and forth for about twenty minutes. It seemed my family had as many questions as I did. Finally, I signed off after promising to send photos of inside and outside the castle, the gardens (for Ceil), the city (for Juliette), and any cute girls Ralphie's age (for—duh—Ralphie).

I leaned on the window ledge and looked out across the lake and wondered if the last person who'd called this room hers—my great-grandmother—had looked out at this same view in those dark days when the country was being invaded. Had she known what was coming?

Thinking about it made me so sad. I tried to turn it off, but I couldn't. I felt surrounded by something I can't explain. I'm not gonna say *ghosts* because I don't believe in them, so let's just say some energy I wasn't familiar with and leave it at that. It was odd to be filled with so much sorrow for people you've never met, but I guess there's a connection there, one I'd never been aware of. If I do nothing else while I'm here, I'm going to find out what happened to them—my great-grand-mother, my great-grandfather, my great-uncle and aunt, and whoever else met their fate at the hands of the Nazis.

That was my last coherent thought. I went back to bed and closed my eyes, and bam! Gone till morning.

Chapter Nine

When I woke up my first morning in Saint Gilbert, I pinched myself about eighty times. Had I really spent the night in a castle? And not just any castle. This was Castle Blanc, in Beauchesne, the capital of Saint Gilbert. Home of my ancestors. The place where my grandmother was born. I'm pretty sure my expression was just like Roe's *WTF* face.

I got up and took care of business. I washed my face with the taupe-y soap again—still missing my face wash—and I was ready to take on the world. Except I was so hungry I could eat one of those beautiful white cows we saw on the drive in yesterday.

Was that really only yesterday? I'd completely lost track of time. So much had happened since I left my house and got into the Lincoln and headed for the airport.

I stood inside the closet debating what to wear. The sun was out, and if yesterday was any indication of what a sunny day felt like around here, it was going to be warm. Maybe not South-Philly-in-April warm, but warm enough. I decided on a blue cotton knit tank dress and a blue-and-white-striped linen shirt to wear over it. I could tie the shirt at my waist and roll up the sleeves. My only other decision was what to put on my feet. I stared at the shoes I'd brought with me until I realized I couldn't make a big decision like that without coffee. There was a reason coffee was known in our house as the elixir of awareness.

I opened the door to the hall, but instead of Sebastian, another tall man in a navy-blue-and-white uniform stood at attention outside the door.

"Good morning," I said as cheerfully as I was able.

He nodded. "Your Grace."

I needed coffee too badly to get into the whole *Call me Annaliese* thing, so I asked if he could arrange somehow for a tray to be brought up.

"Of course, Your Grace."

I thanked him and went back into my room and stared at my shoes trying to choose until there was a knock at the door.

"Please come in," I said.

A pretty young blonde woman wearing a white shirt and black pants came in carrying a tray.

"Where would you like this, my lady?" she asked.

I looked around, then pointed to the table in front of the sofa. "There would be fine, thank you . . ."

In my ear I heard my mother's voice: *How many times have I told you not to point?*

"Andrea," she replied with a shy smile.

"Thank you, Andrea."

"You're most welcome, my lady." She carried the tray to where I'd requested. "Would you like me to pour your coffee?"

Being a mom, I'm used to waiting on others but not the reverse. It makes me uncomfortable to feel as if people are fawning over me. So I simply tell her, "Oh, no thank you. I can do that."

"Will there be anything else?"

"No, thank you . . . oh. One thing. Do you know the name of the man outside the door?"

"It's Hans, my lady."

"Thank you. There won't be anything else."

She left quietly, and I sat down to pour myself a cup of coffee. There was cream in a small china pitcher and tiny dark cubes of sugar in a little matching bowl. Once I'd doctored my coffee to my satisfaction, I sat back, tasted, and sighed, content. Best coffee on the planet. After a few delicious reviving sips, I lifted the silver domes that covered the other items on the tray. I found a pretty pale-blue plate with tiny white flowers painted around the edge, in the middle of which a pat of butter shaped like a flower was nestled next to a croissant. There was also a small bowl of honey and another containing some of the same sour cherry compote that had been served with cheese at yesterday's meet and greet. Another dome hid a bowl of strawberries that were half the size of my fist. I am not exaggerating. I could have eaten my weight in them.

I drank my coffee and nibbled at the croissant—first plain, which was delish, but then I decided to go for broke and slathered on the butter and the cherries, and wow. I never tasted anything so amazing. Those cherries were from God, I swear. By the time I finished, there was nothing left, not a crumb. But in my defense, I hadn't eaten since snacking on bites of cheese late yesterday afternoon, so I wrote off any calories I might have ingested.

I have to admit there's a part of me that could easily get used to living like this. Just having someone else figure out meals on a daily basis was almost enough for me to pledge my allegiance to the flag of Saint Gilbert.

So there I was, well fed and happy and on my way to being suitably caffeinated, when there was another knock on the door. I opened it and Claudette stood in the hall.

"Did you enjoy your breakfast?" she asked pleasantly after I'd invited her in.

"Every bite. If you're responsible for what was on that tray, I can't thank you enough. The coffee was amazing, and the croissant was baked by angels and the fruit was delicious." I gestured for her to sit; then I realized she was waiting for me to sit first, so I did. "But I have to know: Where did you find the strawberries?"

"In the castle garden. I'm so glad you enjoyed them. Starting the garden was an act of optimism on our part that you would be joining us. The plants were originally in a garden at one of the farms outside the city," she explained, "but after the vote in January, when we realized we were going to need a source of fresh food at the castle, we decided to move some of the plants here once spring arrived."

"Who tends the garden?"

"There is a full-time gardener but also several volunteers, men and women who were more than willing to lend their time and their expertise to ensure that you and your family had the very best Saint Gilbert had to offer. If you look out the window you will see the garden inside the stone wall."

"I did see it, last night and again this morning. I hope I get to meet the gardeners while I'm here."

"They would be honored, I am sure."

I finished my coffee, all the things I wanted to ask and wanted to know swirling around inside me.

"You look troubled, Annaliese," Claudette said.

"It's frustrating to have so many questions, I don't even know where to begin."

"What's the very first thing that comes to mind right now?" she asked. "The most immediate question?"

"Who are all the people inside the castle and how did they get here and who trained them? Who got the farmers together, and how did they know someone—if not me then someone else—might be living here?"

"Ah, those are easy questions. Once the election was over, there were a number of meetings organized by the Duke's Council."

"Would you tell me again who is on the Duke's Council?" I know I met them all yesterday, but I could remember only one or two. Whether I stayed beyond this week or not, I should know who these people are.

"Of course. Currently, Vincens DellaVecchio, Dominic Altrusi, Pierre Belloque, my brother Emile Rossi, my son Maximilien, Andre

DiGiacoma, and Jacques Gilberti, a distant cousin of yours. Vito Benocci passed away earlier this year. His position has yet to be replaced."

"So your family has been in Saint Gilbert for a long time," I said. "Max said his grandfather had been with the castle guards before him."

"Captain of the guards, as was my brother in his youth, as is my son now," she said proudly. "My family has been closely aligned with the Gilbertis since the country was founded hundreds of years ago. We've always played a prominent role. My mother, as I may have mentioned, was the principal lady-in-waiting to your great-grandmother. Had things turned out differently, I would have done the same for your grandmother and possibly your mother as well. My mother had trained me for the position, but sadly, it was not to be."

"And now you're my—you're the principal lady."

"I am at your service. And if you fear that I am perhaps too old"— she smiled in a self-deprecating way—"my granddaughter Madeleine is being trained to take over the duties one day. She has been invaluable in getting the castle ready for your arrival. As I'm sure you understand, there were many roles to be filled."

"How did you manage to find people for the kitchen, to clean, to do laundry, to serve, to . . . to do all those things I've seen happening here? The guards at the door. The girl who brought me coffee this morning."

"Our challenge was to find the best people for the positions, regardless of their age or family connections. There was no shortage of applications once it was made known that we were actively seeking to bring you here. That many new jobs would be available. Many of our young people have left the country, and we were hoping to convince more of them to stay."

"Any particular reason they left?"

"University in other parts of Europe or in America, mostly. They go away to school, they make lives for themselves, they decide not to come home. There are admittedly more opportunities for them elsewhere, I cannot argue the reality. We would like to change that, but I'm not sure how that will happen. My oldest son Andre, my daughter Felice, and several of my grandchildren are gone and come back only for holidays." She shrugged. "So it will remain until we can offer them a reason to stay. I'm hoping we can find such reason over time."

"Where does the money come from to pay them?" I'd been wondering where the money came from to do *anything* around here—restoring the castle being the most significant, though they had a long way to go before that project was completed.

"The country still has some revenues." Claudette smiled. "But mostly from the Grand Duchess and Duke of Saint Gilbert."

I believe my expression went from merely curious to *say what* in less time than it takes for a heart to beat.

"When the certainty of German aggression was recognized, your great-grandparents transferred the country's wealth, along with the crown jewels, to a Swiss bank, where it remained safe through the years. While it is true that the bulk of the funds can only be released once the monarchy is fully restored, the bank officials recognized our plight. They advanced some in good faith after the January vote and with the assurance from the Duke's Council that every effort was being made to place the proper heir on the throne, which is what your great-grandparents not only envisioned but assumed, which is why the funds were held until such time as one of their descendants took the throne. I believe they thought in time your grandmother would return to rule the country, but of course, they had no way of seeing into the future, no way of knowing the Soviets would prove to be as great a threat as the Germans." She smiled sadly. "It is very difficult for a very small country such as ours to maintain our sovereignty."

"And if no proper heir agreed to sit on that throne, what would happen to those funds?"

"I imagine they would stay in the bank and continue to amass interest, as they have since 1941, until such time as an heir was crowned."

"That's a lot of interest."

"It is indeed, Annaliese."

"But there are other branches of the family who could be tapped to be grand duchess or duke, right?" Please. The last thing I needed was to carry the weight of guilt that I'd deprived future generations of Saint Gilbertians of their country's wealth if I decided not to stay, which was a distinct possibility.

"Not especially suitable, but I suppose if we had to make do, we could. For a time, anyway." I swear her nose partially lifted as if in disdain of any of those other Gilbertis. I wondered who they might be. Which left me to question if I were the pick of the litter, what must *they* be like?

"So who are these relatives, and will I meet them?"

"I believe you met your grandmother's cousin Marguerite yesterday. And then there's Vincens DellaVecchio."

"The grand chancellor is a relative?" Something about that possibility made me recoil in a sort of horror. Maybe it had something to do with the way his son tried to look down the top of my dress.

"No, but there is a small amount of shared blood. Vincens's grandfather and your great-grandfather were brothers." She averted her eyes and glanced out the nearest window.

"Claudette, is there something about the chancellor I should know?"

"I am hesitant to say something that might be construed as gossip or would appear to be mean-spirited or in any way give you reason to think there might be ulterior motives on my part."

"I'd like your opinion anyway." I really did. So far, she seemed like a straight shooter.

"It is my opinion and that of my brother and my son and some others that he is not to be completely trusted, Annaliese."

I remembered the mutual stink eye exchanged between Max and Vincens the day before. "Do I need to know why?"

"There are some who believe he would attempt to exert undue influence over you if given the chance. He is well aware that any road to the throne, to legitimacy of his family, goes through you." She took a deep breath. "It is thought he harbors certain . . . aspirations. His son, Philippe, is a widower and you are a divorcée. His younger son is also divorced."

"You mean he thinks I might be interested in . . . oh God no." I laughed at the very thought of touching Philippe beyond a simple—and quick—handshake. The other son, even sight unseen, was a definite no. "That will never happen."

"You have two sisters and a daughter. He has a grandson a few years older than your Juliette. Philippe's son is seventeen."

"And that *definitely* ain't happening." My daughter and the spawn of paunchy Philippe? The very thought brought out the South Philly mama in me.

And my sisters? Almost as funny. Ceil would eat him alive, and Roe would have him running from the castle screaming like an overtired two-year-old who lost his blankie. It's Roe's superpower. There's a reason she's still single.

"So he thinks there's a potential to marry up, so to speak, and that would get him closer to the throne?"

Again, she appeared to choose her words carefully. "It has been rumored he has such aspirations."

"Then the chancellor will find himself very disappointed."

I stood, dismissing the thought of anyone named DellaVecchio getting chummy with anyone named Gilberti, and Claudette stood as well. Apparently we were both of the same mind as far as *that* family was concerned.

"What would you like to do today?" she asked.

"I'd like to see the city. Maybe poke into a few shops and visit sights a tourist might see." If of course Saint Gilberti had tourists. "And I would like to see the church." I paused. "Were my great-grandparents found after . . . you know? Were they properly buried?"

Claudette nodded. "They are buried in the churchyard."

"They are?" I smiled. That they'd been respectfully treated in death made me happy.

"They are there along with the others."

"The others who died with them?" I asked.

"Your great-uncle, your great-aunt. Several members of the royal household."

"Do you know where it happened?"

"They were taken two by two to the opposite side of the lake and into the woods, where they were blindfolded and shot." Her face was rigid. The telling was obviously unpleasant. "But even aware their deaths were imminent, they took care to provide for their country. To preserve as best they could for generations to come, abdicating in favor of their daughter and planning her escape, in addition to protecting the country's assets, as we've discussed. That your grandmother survived was due solely to their foresight. They sent her away uncertain if she'd escape alive, but they knew she would surely die with them if she remained in Saint Gilbert, so they trusted her fate to God. She resisted and fought leaving them and her siblings, but in the end, she conceded to her parents' wishes and left before the sun came up. By noon on that same day, her entire family had been murdered."

"They must have been very brave and very wise."

"They are the heroes of our country, madam."

"As was your father."

She smiled and nodded. "Yes. He led them to safety. My mother accompanied them so they appeared as a family."

"Why weren't my grandmother's brother and her other sister—Jacqueline—sent away with her?"

"Her brother was eighteen and felt a duty to remain with his parents. Jacqueline was younger—eight or nine—and refused to leave her mother. Trying to convince her to go with her sisters only served to delay their departure, as the story was told by my father. In the end, the grand duchess was forced to permit her older two daughters to escape, knowing her youngest would be killed along with her."

We both reflected silently for a long moment. Then, because I sensed she was hoping we'd put that topic aside, I looked over the row of shoes I'd left in front of the armoire. "So I guess if I'm sightseeing today, tennis-type sneakers would be the best bet. I mean, given the selection."

"Undoubtedly they would." Her light mood returned as she watched me tie on my white Keds.

"Not very royal," I muttered.

I'd worn this same type of sneaker since I was three, and they were still my favorite. You can keep your walking and running shoes with those big ugly soles and the flashing lights and their promises to make you run faster and stronger, lose weight, and help you meet your daily minimum number of steps, thank you very much. I go old school, and I'm okay with that despite the fact that my children would mock me unmercifully if they saw me tying them on.

"Is Max around?" I asked casually.

"I'm not sure what his schedule is this morning, but if you'd like to speak with him, I'd be happy to call him."

"I thought maybe he'd be a good person to show me around Beauchesne."

"I'm sure he would be happy to, Annaliese. I'll have him come for you." She began to make her way to the door.

"Oh, I can meet him downstairs. I thought I'd check out the garden."

"As you wish." She opened the door and waited to see if I was ready to leave. I was, so I grabbed my bag and followed her out the door.

I still had the feeling of being in a very luxe hotel as I accompanied Claudette down the stairs.

We reached the bottom of the stairs, and I looked back over my shoulder. The steps rose behind us, and I felt like pinching myself again. I'd fallen into someone else's life, and I wasn't sure what was going to happen when that someone showed up and wanted it back.

Chapter Ten

Claudette left me alone in the drawing room while she contacted Max. I wandered around the room, studying the faces in the portraits. Some, I supposed, were my ancestors who'd ruled this country. I wondered what kind of ruler my gran would have been. In my heart, I knew she—or my mom if it had come to that—would have been great, that they both would have done good things. Which of course led me to wonder what I might be like if I had wealth and power, what kind of a ruler I'd be.

Then I reminded myself where I'd come from and what I'd left behind. Growing up, our house was governed by the Golden Rule: do unto others as you would have them do unto you. My mother believed that with her whole being. That was the most important moral lesson my sisters and I received from Mom, and she made it cover a lot of ground. There were few situations she couldn't apply it to. It was right up there with "stand up / sit up straight / stop slouching" and "mind your manners."

The double doors opened, and Max walked in, tall and handsome (I know I've said it a million times, but it bears repeating: the man was *fine*) and totally regal in his bearing. He was casually dressed in tailored slacks and a light-blue button-down shirt with the sleeves rolled to the elbow much like mine were. The difference between us was that he looked like he belonged in a castle drawing room. I looked down at my tank dress that I'd bought off the rack on sale at H&M and my white tennis shoes, and it was glaringly obvious where I belonged. It occurred to me then that I should've called on my patron saint of fashion, Saint Audrey, before I ventured out of my room. I momentarily tried to picture myself in the outfit she wore in *Roman Holiday* when she set off to explore the city—that white shirt with the little scarf tied around her neck, the belted cotton skirt—and I sighed. Not with these hips.

I guess it's true what they say: you can take the girl out of South Philly . . .

"You wished to see the city, Annaliese. It would be my pleasure to accompany you. Is there any place in particular you'd like to see?"

Just looking at him made me smile.

"I'd like to see the church, and a few of the shops. I should think about souvenirs for the kids and my sisters."

"It's an excellent day for an excursion." He walked to the door and held it open for me.

"Could we stop in the garden before we leave?" I asked as I went into the hall.

Max paused for a moment. "Might I suggest we save the garden for last?"

"Sure." I shrugged. It really didn't matter whether we started or ended there. I just wanted to see the flowers that grew here. Maybe even pick a few for my room. I thought of the garden I strolled through with Gran during my solo visits to her home, and I wanted to know if she'd planted certain flowers because they reminded her of the gardens here. I know all I had to do was ask, and someone would pick them for me. But I'm a city girl, so when I have the chance to pick flowers on a sunny day in a beautiful garden, that's what I want to do.

Max and I followed the hall into the gallery I'd come through the day before and out to the reception area. I glanced up at the fancy staircase.

"Why are there two fancy staircases?" I asked, thinking of the one Claudette and I had used earlier.

"The one you generally use leads to the back of the castle, where the private rooms are located. This one"—he nodded at the stairs in front of us—"leads to more public rooms. The ballroom, for example."

"There's a ballroom?"

"Of course." He smiled as he took my elbow. "Every castle has a ballroom."

"Have you ever been to a ball here?"

He shook his head. "There have been none since 1941."

I had this insane vision of me in a light-blue Cinderella ball gown being spun around the ballroom floor by Max in a military uniform dripping with gold braid and medals, sort of like the one Vincens wears. There's an orchestra playing and . . . okay, we all have our fantasies, right?

"Shall we go?" Max stood at the doorway.

Today there was no gathering of the castle staff, but when we stepped outside, there were guards at the exterior door. Two on each side of the entrance, all four wearing the blue-and-white uniforms I'd seen on Hans that morning. They all nodded formally as I passed by, and I wondered if they were supposed to keep silent, like the guards outside Buckingham Palace. Three cars were awaiting us in the drive directly in front of the castle, and Max accompanied me to the passenger side of the one in the middle.

"I took the liberty of assuming you'd not want an official royal escort this morning," he said as he opened the door for me. "But an unofficial one is in order."

I glanced at the car ahead of ours, then turned to look at the one at our rear.

"Why?"

"It is required anytime a royal leaves the castle, madam."

"I'm just like any other visitor to Saint Gilbert," I protested.

He laughed as he closed the door. "Any other visitor upon whose head we might place the crown."

The crown? I hadn't thought about a crown. I hadn't even thought about tiaras except to tease Juliette. I wondered what the crown looked like. Would it look like that fancy number Queen Elizabeth II wore, dripping with jewels and sporting fur? (Was it ermine?) I'd bet that sucker had been heavy, though. Maybe Saint Gilbert's crown was more like the fat-free yogurt of crowns, the same basic look but lighter.

I got into the car—a very cool dark-green Jaguar that would have brought out all the neighbors on my block back home to take a closer look—and fastened my seat belt.

"Is that really necessary?" I was turned in my seat looking over my shoulder. "The guards?"

"Necessary in the sense that you are under my protection, and I take that responsibility very seriously."

"Because you think one of those people who didn't want the monarchy to return is going to take shots at me?"

"I don't rule out anything when it comes to your safety, Your Grace. But don't worry. When we get into the city, you won't even know the guards are there." He put his arm out the window and signaled to the car ahead of us.

"But if I walk around with half a dozen guards, everyone will know I'm not just another tourist."

"No one will know they're there," he repeated. "Relax, Your—"

"Annaliese," I snapped. "Enough with that 'Your Grace' stuff."

Max settled behind the steering wheel while I tried to settle my nerves. I rolled down my window and looked straight up at the top of the castle wall, where flags swayed in the light breeze.

"Is one of those the flag of Saint Gilbert?" I asked.

Max leaned over me slightly. He smelled of the same soap I'd been using, and I wondered if there was some sort of law that prohibited use of any other. I'd caught the same scent from his mother and the young girl who'd brought my breakfast earlier that day.

"Our national flag is the one in the middle, the blue-and-white one. The others represent various houses that had married into our royal family over the centuries."

"Families have their own flags?" I wondered what ours would look like back home. Probably a large pizza—pepperoni and extra cheese—on a background that looked like our kitchen counters, which unfortunately are still the same faded red Formica that was there when I bought the house. Kitchen reno was on the list of things to do after paying off my college loans and getting my kids through school without taking out a second mortgage.

"Some families do. Or did."

"So the country's flag has . . . that looks like the castle's tower in the center." The breeze folded the flag in several places.

"It is the tower. It's the symbol of our nation. It stands for strength and the fact that we will defend our sovereignty."

"Is there an army, then?"

"Not at the present."

I nodded and thought it wise not to ask how a country without an army defended itself. Instead, I tilted my head to watch a bird that flew past the tower at a high rate of speed.

"Wow, did you see that?" I leaned out the window hoping to follow its flight, but it was gone already.

Max smiled. "Ah, that is a falcon. Our national bird."

"Your mother mentioned that the Gilbertis were falconers."

He nodded as he turned the key in the ignition. "Every generation since the country was established, so they say. My grandfather told me the last grand duchess took her falcon to hunt every morning and again later in the afternoon. She was most fond of that bird, he said."

"I wonder what happened to it."

"It's said that when the duchess realized her fate, she let her falcon fly free, but the bird circled the castle for days, calling for her, before it finally gave up and flew off into the forest." He put the car in gear and made a U-turn in the drive, then drove through the stone tunnel. "So that bird we just saw could be a descendant of the duchess's falcon."

I thought about that for a moment, wondering how it might feel to have a bird like that land on my arm. I thought I might like it. If I were to stay in Saint Gilbert, I'd definitely bring back the practice. Not that I was planning on staying, but if I did, I'd do the falcon thing.

At the end of the lane, Max waited while the gate opened for the first car in line. He nodded to the gatekeeper—that word always makes me think of *Ghostbusters*—and drove past the gates and onto the cobbled street. A short distance from the castle, he pulled to the curb and stopped the car. The other two cars stopped as well.

"The church is just around that bend in the road, but there's no place to park there. We should walk from here," he said.

"That's fine. I could use a good walk." Without waiting, I unhooked my seat belt, opened the door, and hopped out. When Max met me in front of the car, he looked amused.

"What?" I asked.

"I would have expected you to have waited for me to open the door for you."

"Where I come from, girls learn at an early age to open their own doors."

I meant that figuratively as well as literally. I always knew if I wanted something, I should figure it out for myself. Mom said we each needed to choose our own path, make a plan, then follow it through. I followed that advice all my life, and it never failed to get me where I wanted to go. Okay, there was that marriage to Ralph Senior, but everyone's entitled to stumble once in a while, right? And besides, I wouldn't have my children if I hadn't married him, so no harm, no foul.

I watched, but so far no one had exited the other two cars. Maybe they were just supposed to do surveillance from the front seats.

We walked along a cobbled sidewalk, and it seemed the farther we walked, the steeper the path. I was glad I'd worn my Keds, because those stones were round and uneven, and if I'd had anything else on my feet, I'd have taken a header and it wouldn't have been pretty.

We rounded a bend and the church came into view. It was shining clean and white, like the castle, and the stained-glass windows sparkled.

It was glorious, and I thought being buried in its shadow wouldn't be such a bad thing. I mean, if you had to be buried, and eventually we all would be. Unless we opted for cremation. As if dying wasn't a scary-enough thought.

A black iron fence enclosed the churchyard, and the closer we got, the faster my heart beat. There were only a dozen steps leading to the church's front doors, grand arched things of highly polished wood.

"Would you like to go inside?" Max asked, and I nodded.

"Yes, please."

I should explain here that I am a highly emotional person. I cry at weddings, funerals, christenings, Hallmark commercials, those Budweiser beer commercials with the Clydesdales, Ray Charles singing "America the Beautiful," Louis Armstrong's "What a Wonderful World," and every play or musical event either of my kids had ever been in. I have even been known to shed a tear at presidential inaugurations (depending on the president, of course). I had a lump in my throat while Max was telling me the story about my great-grandmother and her falcon. So it shouldn't surprise anyone that I walked up those steps with my eyes stinging and my bottom lip trembling (and I really do cry ugly). I can't even describe the feelings that swept through me when Max opened one of the doors and led me inside.

It took my eyes a moment to adjust to the lower light, but I could see the ends of the pews were beautifully carved, the seats themselves hewn of thick, dark wood. The altar was white marble, and the statues that stood on either side—the Virgin Mary with another woman on one side of the altar, Christ on the other—were life-size and lifelike. The stained-glass windows told the story of Jesus from birth to his death and were stunning in their design and color. I'd been in a lot of churches, but I'd never seen anything like this one. It was so beautiful and so serene and felt so holy, it would make a believer out of just about anyone. Okay, maybe not, say, Arlene Mulroney, the meanest of mean girls from my sorority, but probably everyone else.

"The saint with her arm around Mary . . . ?" I asked. I felt I should know, but I couldn't remember who she could be.

"Saint Ann. The patron saint of Saint Gilbert and the mother of the Virgin. Grandmother of Christ," Max whispered. Even though there was no service going on, it still felt right to whisper. "The first duchess was named Ann."

I should have realized it was Saint Ann. Who else could have been so familiar with the mother of the savior than the woman who'd given birth to her?

I walked all around the perimeter of the nave, studying the stained glass. I became increasingly aware of Gran's presence as a slight pressure on my right arm.

It's okay, Gran. Lean on me . . .

After I completed my round with Gran and cleared my throat of the emotions that had been building up, I asked Max, "How was this all preserved during the war?"

"The windows were removed and hidden in a number of secret places. Then the openings were covered over with wood."

"And the Germans never asked where the original windows were?"

"Of course. They were told the Russians took them."

"And they believed that?"

Max shrugged. "The Germans believed the Russian were barbarians and vice versa. When the Russians came, we told them the Germans destroyed them."

I could swear I felt the warmth of Gran's smiling approval.

"Where were the windows hidden?"

"I will show you sometime before you leave. I think it might amuse you." He glanced at his watch, and I wondered what other obligations he'd put off from the morning to usher me around the city. "Is there anything else you'd like to see here?"

"Your mother said my great-grandparents and some other relatives are buried in the churchyard. I'd like to see their graves."

"Of course." He took my elbow and led me through a side door near the altar that opened onto the peaceful fence-enclosed churchyard.

My great-grandparents rested beneath a huge black obelisk upon which stood an angel of snow-white marble. She looked down on the graves, wings fully unfurled. She was beautifully carved, her face both earthly and ethereal.

Their names—Grand Duchess Elizabet Maria Jacqueline, the Grand Duke Theodore Philippe Emile—were carved into humble flat white stones level with the ground. I walked around the obelisk and found the graves of their son, Prince Theodore William, and a daughter, Princess Jacqueline Cecilia, side by side. Gran's brother and sister. The moment was surreal. Just weeks ago their names were only echoes of something I'd heard as a child—and yet here I stood, feeling a connection so strong and so real.

The pressure on my arm increased, and I felt Gran's smile fade.

I couldn't explain why, but at that moment I wanted my sisters with me. I wished my kids were here. I felt a sadness I honestly hadn't expected, a bond I couldn't explain, as if strands of DNA were twining like vines from beyond the grave. I wondered what *they* thought of me, if they thought me worthy to bear their name, to follow in their footsteps.

I wondered if right then Gran was thinking about how she'd been sent away, spared by the love of her parents and the loyalty of their subjects from certain assassination. If she, like me, might be wondering how, had it not been for the insistence of the former and the diligence of the latter, I wouldn't be standing there, my children would never have been born. I hadn't expected the emotions—the gratitude and respect and the love—that washed through me for these people I'd never met and, up until a month or so ago, had never even heard of.

And because my grandmother had never gotten to do so, in her honor I knelt next to the graves of her parents and prayed for their brave and good souls. When I'd finished, and stood, I realized the pressure I'd felt on my arm was gone, and so was she.

Chapter Eleven

"Where would you like to go next?" Max held open the smaller of the two gates that fronted the graveyard.

"I think I'd like to check out the shops we passed yesterday when we drove into the city."

"We can cut through the square," Max said as we crossed the street. "There are several places that might be of interest to you."

It was cooler under the high canopy of the oaks for which Beauchesne was named. Two black squirrels ran across our path, and birds flew from one branch to another. Were they the same birds as back home? I didn't know, and was just about to ask, when I heard splashing water.

"The fountain?" I tilted my head to one side, listening, the birds forgotten.

Max nodded.

"All I could see from the car was the tail of a really large fish." I walked a little faster as we drew closer, then called back over my shoulder. "In Philly, there's a fountain on the Ben Franklin Parkway right in the middle of a traffic circle, Eakins Oval. It's named for Thomas Eakins, a famous painter. It's by the art museum. You know, where the *Rocky* statue is?"

Max smiled but didn't comment as he followed along, his hands in his pockets, dark glasses covering his eyes.

"There are actually three fountains," I went on as I drew closer to the sound of water. "The one in the middle is George Washington on his horse, and all around him are—"

The fountain came into sight and I stopped in my tracks. "Oh."

Max smiled. "As you can see, there's only half a fish. The other half is . . ."

"A mermaid." I walked closer, mesmerized.

She was lovely, even in stone, exquisitely carved, with hair that curled around her face and fell all the way to her waist, covering all but a glimpse of cleavage. Her face was so lifelike, I could almost believe a real mermaid had sat for the artist. Her arms were stretched upward gracefully, and water flowed from her fingertips like offerings.

"She's beautiful," I said, awestruck.

"Serafina," Max addressed the mermaid, "I am pleased to present Grand Duchess Annaliese Jacqueline Terese Gilberti."

"Not yet," I reminded him.

He folded his arms over his chest as he addressed the fountain in a mock whisper. "We're doing our best to convince her to stay."

I pretended not to hear.

"Tell me about Serafina."

"She's been a fixture in Saint Gilbert since the duchy was established. The legend is that a farmer and his wife came into the city to sell their cheese. The wife wandered away, got lost, and in the dark, she stumbled into the lake. From the courtyard, the duchess witnessed the fall and rushed as fast as she could to the water to save the farmer's wife, but she was too late. The woman had drowned. The duchess sat by the water and wept with guilt that she'd been unable to save her. But the spirits who lived in the lake heard the duchess weeping and took pity on her. They changed the drowned woman into a mermaid who would live in the lake for as long as there were Gilbertis living in the castle."

"So I guess Serafina's been gone for a long time."

"Close to eighty years." He glanced down at me, a hint of mischief in his eyes. "But maybe she'll be back now that you're here. Once word of her return spreads, the streets will be jammed with flocks of tourists hoping to see her. The restaurants will be filled, and the shops will—"

"Ha! Don't even try to put that kind of guilt on me; it won't work." I walked around the fountain, admiring Serafina from every angle. I didn't believe in mermaids, of course, and despite the attitude I was throwing at Max, I was touched by the story. "I'm a mother. I know guilt. I know how to inflict it and I know how to deflect it."

He stood on the opposite side of the fountain, looking up at the statue, his hands palms up. "I tried, Serafina. I tried."

"Very funny, you." I arrived back where I'd started. "Let's go see this city of yours."

"This city of *yours*, madam." He fell in step next to me, guiding me toward the path that led to the shops.

"You're really pushing this today, aren't you? I have no idea what I'm going to do, so could we please put all that aside?"

"As you wish."

I laughed. The line always made me think of *The Princess Bride*. It had been one of my favorite movies forever. I watched it at least once a year with my sisters and Juliette.

We emerged from the park onto a street so narrow, I wondered aloud how two cars could pass without sideswiping each other.

"This is the oldest section of the city," he explained. "When it was built, people traveled by horse, or by carriage."

"Late fifteen, early sixteen hundreds."

"Someone's done her homework." A smile tugged at the corners of Max's mouth.

"Don't read anything into it. I looked it up on Wikipedia." I glanced around as we headed up the street. "Where do people park their cars around here?"

"It's a problem," he acknowledged.

"One of the first things I'd do if I were in charge would be to build a parking lot somewhere."

He raised an eyebrow but didn't say anything.

"Don't read anything into that, either. I just mean, if you want tourist business, you need to be able to accommodate them."

He started to say something, but I cut him off. "Could we stop here?" I paused in front of a coffee shop. I couldn't stop thinking about the delicious brew I'd had that morning.

"Of course." Max opened the door of the shop and we both went inside.

The coffee shops back in Philly varied greatly from dingy neighborhood deli-type places with worn linoleum floors to modest like the one at the end of my street, with its polished hardwood floor and antique wooden counters, to upscale cafés. Of course we had Starbucks, and we had Wawa—whose coffee I preferred—and we had donut shops that serve coffee and any number of little places dotted throughout the city. But this coffee shop in Beauchesne had them all beat when it came to ambience—and to the coffee.

There was an ancient-looking glass case displaying several varieties of croissants and scones that looked like a spread in *Martha Stewart Living*, and little plates of tea cakes that had been iced in pastel colors, also very Martha, and therefore were almost too pretty to eat. Almost.

While Max placed our orders and chatted with the woman behind the counter, I looked around the room. Dark wood, a small fireplace with a white mantel, some tiny tables each with a vase holding one or two spring flowers, a well-worn wood floor. There were paintings on the wall, and while I did not recognize the name of the artist, I could tell they were originals. I could imagine sitting there near the fire on a chilly morning, sipping coffee and eating a scone or two.

Max introduced me as a friend to the woman who was preparing our coffee, Clothilde. After I'd admired the shop, I asked about the paintings.

"Ah, those." She waved a hand as if to dismiss their importance. "My son fancies himself an artist, so to humor him, my husband began to hang his work here in the shop. We should probably replace them now that he's moved to London."

"They're very lovely," I said. They were. Gentle landscapes and scenes from nature. I paused in front of a painting of a falcon in flight. It arced over the castle tower and flew toward the woods much like the real one we'd seen earlier. I thought perhaps at the end of my stay I might return and buy it if Clothilde was willing to sell it and I could afford it.

Max and I took our coffees, his croissant, and my scone, and we sat outside at a table shaded by a red-and-white awning. I tasted the coffee and grinned.

"I will say this. The coffee in Saint Gilbert just might be the best in the world. Not that I've had coffee from everywhere in the world, but I can't imagine any better."

"Ah, something in our favor. I'll take it."

Max took a bite of his croissant and I attacked my scone. You'd think that after the breakfast I'd eaten, I'd be good for most of the day, but nope. The scone was delicious, every bit as yummy as it had looked in the case, and I said so.

"Two things in our favor. Things are looking up," Max said. "I'd say our prospects are improving."

"And I'd say this is still only my second day, and there are so many unanswered questions."

"Ask, then."

"How is it that so much survived not one but two invasions? All the beautiful furniture in the castle, and the artwork, even the jewelry your mother showed me last night. Why isn't it all in Russia, or Germany?"

Max took a sip of coffee and nodded his head as if he'd been expecting those questions.

"We'd had word that the Germans were on the move and likely headed this way. We are a very small country, but we were not without our riches. Knowing what was likely to happen—not only to herself, but to her family, her country, her castle—your great-grandmother had the rooms stripped of as much as could be hidden. Furniture, tapestries, art—everything that could be moved quickly, in anticipation of the invasion, leaving just enough that the castle did not appear barren."

"I get that. But where could you hide so many things?" I knew I was making a face, but I couldn't help myself. "There's one hundred ninety-seven rooms in the castle. That's a whole heap of chairs and settees and fancy tables, my friend. Where did they go?"

"Have you seen the castle's dungeon, madam? It's most interesting, not just because of its size, but it's said there's a labyrinth of secret rooms." That little bit of mischief was back in his eyes again.

I found myself whispering, though I wasn't sure why. "They hid stuff in the dungeon?"

"There are sections that are quite dry and suitable for storage. There are also hidden rooms within the upper floors of the castle where artwork was stashed. Much of the china, silver, many of the accoutrements of castle life found a place behind this wall or that."

"Stuff was hidden in the dungeon. Huh." I thought about this for a moment. Pretty clever. Especially since it worked.

I remembered then that we'd been accompanied into the city by two cars. I looked around but didn't see any guys hanging around. "Where are your men? The ones that are supposedly guarding me?"

"Ahhh, Annaliese. You assume."

"Assume what?"

"Assume that all of my men," he said as he picked up our plates and cups to return them to the shop, "are men."

I looked up and down both sides of the street. Here and there were couples walking along or pausing in front of this shop or that. Across the street, a pair of women stood, their arms around each other, admiring something in a shop window. Next to where I stood was a butcher shop where a man and woman were discussing whether to have beef or lamb for dinner that night.

"Are they . . . ?" I whispered to Max when he returned.

"If I told you our secrets, they wouldn't be secrets anymore." He held his arm out to me. "Now, which shop would you like to go into?"

I looked up and down the street. "All of them."

The doors to all the places I'd noticed on our way into the city yesterday stood open. I couldn't wait to see inside each and every one.

And that's what we did. It was hard to take it all in, so I snapped a whole bunch of pictures on my phone. Everyone was so friendly and so proud of their shops and their wares. Having Max as my guide made the day seem even more special. I could almost imagine that we were . . . ah, never mind. It would never happen. For one thing, if I declined the opportunity to put *duchess* before my name, I'd never see him again. For another, he was so out of my league it wasn't even worth fantasizing. Even though I did.

I met a dressmaker whose displays made me wish I were twenty pounds thinner and five inches taller, because her work was truly showroom quality. I wasn't personally familiar with haute couture showrooms, but I'd watched enough award shows on TV to know perfection in design when I saw it. The woman, Gisele, was young—maybe midtwenties—and said she'd inherited the shop from her parents, her father who'd been an excellent tailor, her mother a clever designer. It was clear she'd inherited gifts in equal measure from both. She'd designed and made everything in her shop, and most items were one of a kind. There were sheaths made of wools so light and fine they almost felt like cashmere, and finely tailored suits. Dresses and blouses in silks that floated through your fingers like a soft breeze when you touched them.

Boy, this woman would clean up on Philly's Main Line, in Gladwyne or Bryn Mawr, or in one of those little boutiques on Chestnut Street in Center City. But here business was slow, she explained, since she'd just started out, but she was sure things would pick up after the American duchess came to Saint Gilbert.

I couldn't even look Max in the eye.

"Who told her there might be an American coming to Saint Gilbert, eh?" I asked Max after we'd left Gisele's shop.

"After the vote in January, it was well known that we were exploring that option," he said.

"Thank God she didn't know it was me," I said, then paused, wondering how many American women in the company of a member of the Duke's Council—the captain of the castle guard, no less—had dropped into her shop this week.

She might well have suspected. If she did, I'm pleased she didn't ask. If I ever do become the duchess, she was going to be my go-to for clothes.

We heard much the same optimism from other shopkeepers about business prospects looking up now that there'd be a Gilberti on the throne again: "After the American comes," or "After the monarchy has been restored," or "When our duchess has been crowned." I was seriously glad Max did most of the talking, lest my American accent be detected. Which it would have been since it was hard to disguise I was from South Philly.

Anyway, I had to admit I found the oldest section of Beauchesne truly charming. There was a cheese shop that sold only local cheeses and a wine shop across the street that sold local wines. I wish I could recall exactly which cheeses I'd eaten and which wines I'd drank the day before because I'd love to take home some of each. A market displayed the most beautiful produce next door to a bakery I recognized from our drive through the previous day. We also passed a stationery store that sold books and newspapers, and a candy shop whose owner claimed to be a sixth-generation Swiss chocolatier and where I picked up some goodies for the kids. There were several restaurants that didn't appear particularly busy at that hour, though an outside table or two had patrons. Each posted their menu in their front window, and while they each offered different items, I had to note there wasn't a Philly cheesesteak on any of them. If I were the duchess, that would change. Of course, the baker would have to duplicate the rolls so they're like the ones from Amoroso's or Liscio's, because everyone knows it isn't a Philly cheesesteak if the roll isn't right.

All things considered, the town had definite tourist appeal, and when I mentioned that to Max, he reminded me there were no places that offered accommodations that he knew of, and there were few attractions that would make people want to spend their money in Saint Gilbert as opposed to Italy or France or the UK.

"There has to be something," I murmured.

"We're hoping those fresh American eyes of yours will come up with it." Max was only half kidding. "Something that would make Saint Gilbert a destination. Something that sets us apart from those other places where people go to spend their vacation money."

"I'll let you know if anything occurs to me." The half of him that wasn't kidding was starting to get under my skin. I didn't appreciate having the onus put on me. It was a burden I didn't want and didn't feel I deserved. But since this could be my only visit to Saint Gilbert, I let Max dwell on his little fantasy of me flying in to save the day before he realized they'd have to move on to plan B. Assuming there was a plan B.

Then, because I didn't want to discuss it further, I took a quick right into a tiny gift shop, and after I picked up some beautifully wrapped soaps to take home for Ceil, Roe, and my bestie, Marianne, assuming she was still speaking to me, I was ready to go back to the castle.

We walked back to the car and because the street was too narrow to make a U-turn, Max drove straight up the hill past the church. This section of the city was residential, and while I didn't let on to Max, I fell in love with the rows of attached houses. Max called them town houses, but in Philly, we said row houses (tomato, tomahto). They were, like the shops, half-timbered and looked Tudorish, with casement windows and arched doors and little front gardens that were longer and wider the farther we drove up the hill. The front yards were all in bloom, and there were roses and other flowers I couldn't identify from a distance, and window boxes that overflowed with trails of color. All in all, Beauchesne looked exactly the way I pictured an old European town to look. The effect was totally enchanting, and in spite of myself, my mind immediately began to envision ways to market the city to attract visitors before I shut that exercise down. Totally unlikely, I reminded myself, and at best, premature.

Even so, God forbid Max knew what I was thinking.

Chapter Twelve

"Tomorrow the tour of the countryside, yes?" Max parked the car and left it in front of the castle door where we'd picked it up that morning.

"Yes, but right now, I want that garden tour."

"Of course."

Max laughed when he saw me get out of the car. We met up at the hood.

"You know, there may come a time when someone will always be there to open your door for you," he teased.

"Only if I let them."

We went into the castle, and I followed Max into the gallery and through French doors I'd originally thought were windows that opened onto the courtyard. Flowers grew in neat beds around the perimeter of the courtyard, so the area was awash in color—red, purple, cream, rose, yellow, pink, orange. The grass was carefully trimmed, and the cobblestone walkways were pristine.

"What is this area used for?" I asked.

"What would you like it used for, Your Grace?" Max asked with a straight face, but his smiling eyes gave him away.

"Flogging annoying members of the Duke's Council comes to mind."

"There are some on the council who might enjoy it."

I held up a hand. "Please. Don't tell me who."

"My lips are sealed, madam."

I laughed in spite of myself. "So what is this area used for?"

"At one time, outdoor entertaining. Garden parties and such. Perhaps one day . . ."

I could imagine beautiful women in light summer dresses from another era gracing the grounds. It would be lovely. "And where do we find the garden?"

"Around to the left, Your Grace."

"What happened to 'Annaliese'? I thought we had an agreement," I said.

"Apologies. Here at the castle I'm inclined toward formality. I'll try to be more mindful."

We walked around the side of the castle and found the garden I'd seen from my windows, which was even more spectacular when you were right there in it. The rose garden alone was breathtaking, and I said so.

Max smiled that half smile that I have to admit was growing on me. Maybe a little too much so.

I walked through the rows of blooms, stopping to—yes, smell the roses.

"Do you have a favorite?" Max walked behind me, slowing his pace to match mine.

"They're all beautiful, though this pale-pink one is lovely, and it's incredibly fragrant." I took another sniff, then stood back and gestured for Max to smell a particularly large bloom.

"Some of the bushes are original. I understand that some cuttings have been made over the years. The gardeners have been vigilant, as you can see, and have taken excellent care."

"Original? You mean from when the garden was first planted?"

"Yes. But don't ask me the year. I know it was long before my mother was born, because the rose garden was well established when she was a child."

"I had no idea rosebushes could live so long." I walked around the rest of the garden, admiring flowers I didn't even recognize.

I stood in the midst of all that color watching butterflies hover and flit, and I felt like I should be wearing a straw hat and pair of dusty overalls like Rebecca of Sunnybrook Farm. "Do you think I could cut some for my room?"

"Of course." Max held up a finger. "One moment, if you would . . ."

He disappeared behind the corner of the castle wall, and I wandered through the entire area a second time. I thought maybe once I got back to Philly, I'd check out some of the famous gardens in and around the city, like Bartram Gardens and Longwood Gardens, neither of which I'd ever been to.

Max appeared at the corner he'd rounded a few minutes earlier, a pair of clippers in one hand and a bucket in the other.

"Roberto said he'd be happy to cut a bouquet for you, but I told him I believe you wished this pleasure for yourself," he was saying as he came closer.

"You believe correctly."

I watched him stride on those long legs across the lawn and into the garden. The sun played off his dark hair and . . . damn.

Just . . . damn.

He was saying something else, but for a moment all my attention was elsewhere.

". . . and they'll stay fresh longer." He handed the clippers to me.

I should have asked him what he'd said, but then I'd have to own up to being one of those shallow women who get distracted by a really great-looking guy, so I just said okay. Most of the time I could control myself, but every once in a while, his handsomeness struck me all over again.

I'd been wondering about his relationship status, and while I hadn't wanted to appear, you know, predatory, I really wanted to know. It was inconceivable to me that a man as fine as Max would be unattached. So I took a deep breath and asked, "Are you married?"

"I was. My wife died six years ago."

I hadn't expected that.

"I'm so sorry." I was. Really. I don't wish death on anyone, even someone whose husband makes me sweat just looking at him. He looked mildly uncomfortable, so I didn't ask him the question on the tip of my tongue: How did she die?

"Do you have children?" I asked.

"A daughter. Remy." He added, "I believe she's Juliette's age."

I wondered if she was one of the young girls I'd seen around the castle. I wondered if she looked like him, then I wondered what his wife had looked like. Probably a supermodel.

I spent the next ten or fifteen minutes pondering the private life of Maximilien Belleme while cutting flowers and plunking them into the bucket. When I finished cutting, the bucket was jam-packed with flowers of every color, size, and shape.

"Do you think I overdid it?" I asked.

"Do they make you happy?"

"They do." I looked up at him and smiled. For a moment I almost forgot who I was: a forty-four-year-old divorcée living out my six-year-old self's princess fantasy, complete with a handsome—if not a prince—duke. Then I tapped myself on the shoulder to reel myself back in. Annie? Anyone home? Bueller?

"Permit me to carry those for you." Max held out both hands, and I passed over the bucket. "Would you like to see the kitchen garden while we're here?"

"Is that where the strawberries are grown?"

He nodded and gestured for me to follow him through a gate beyond which all I saw were trees. But once we stepped through it, there were rows and rows of green growing.

"My mind is spinning," I told him. "It's hard to take this all in."

"The orchard has been here for many years, but the garden is new. We tried to prepare for the event that you and your family would be living here," Max said. "And of course, it follows you'd be entertaining."

"So what happens to all this if there is no duchess, no royal family living in the castle?"

A cloud passed over his face. "I imagine we'd take it to the market while we explored other options," he said.

"So you do have a plan B."

Off to the left lay the lake, which I'd yet to see up close. I started off in that direction, and Max fell in step with me. We walked in silence until we reached the waist-high stone wall that separated the castle grounds from the water. I leaned on the wall and peered into the lake.

"Serafina's children?" I pointed at the water below, where a school of small fish swam in a sort of zigzag pattern.

"Perhaps." He placed the bucket on the ground.

I watched the fish for a few minutes. They looked like minnows to me, but then, where I come from, we call all tiny fish minnows.

"I can't rule a country I know nothing about," I said, finally understanding why I felt so much inner confusion and, yes, frustration. "Even the most basic things. I don't know your birds or animals or fish or flowers. Except for how it pertains to my family, I don't know your history. I don't know your heritage, your culture, your legends."

"We're happy to teach you."

"No, you don't get it. When you grow up in a country, you learn those things gradually, starting from the time you're little. Like, I don't know, Betsy Ross. George Washington and the cherry tree. Johnny Appleseed. Paul Bunyan. Pecos Bill. Bigfoot. The Jersey Devil." Which my cousin Frank swears he saw one night in the Jersey Pine Barrens, but I'm pretty sure he was drunk at the time. "Trying to learn someone else's legends seems like trying to learn the words to a song long after everyone else did, you know?"

"Does it matter who learned first, as long as you learn?"

"I don't know. It seems sort of . . . phony. Like trying to be a Saint Gilbertian when you're not really."

"With my most sincere apologies, I cannot agree. If someone comes into your country and is granted citizenship, is he any less American than you when he pledges his allegiance to your flag? Should he feel like a 'phony' because he wasn't born there? Should he be less proud, feel less devoted?"

I thought it over for a moment, acutely aware right then that I was the granddaughter of more than one immigrant. "No. He should feel proud of his citizenship."

"Well, then." He turned his back to the lake so he was facing the castle. "The things you mentioned are all easily learned. Our birds? Much like those in America. Golden orioles, cranes, ducks, geese. You already know we have falcons, but we have other raptors as well— hawks, owls, eagles. Here at the lake, we get ducks and geese, like any lake in America. We have the great blue heron, thrush, larks, pipits, sparrows. Nothing unusual there. Fish? The same as your freshwater lakes and ponds and streams. Pike, bass, trout, perch. Flowers? Again, the same. Roses, iris, peonies, daisies, lilies, as you have seen—and of course, violets."

I thought about this for a moment. I had to admit that even back in Philly, I doubted I'd be able to identify any of those fish if I saw them in a stream, though the birds I probably knew. The flowers, I knew the common ones. So maybe not so different. So I did feel a little less like a—ha!—fish out of water.

God, I sounded like my father, the great jokester of the family, a man who never met a pun he wouldn't repeat. He was such a happy soul, right up to the minute he had an out-of-the-blue, totally unexpected widow-maker of a heart attack and died on the spot. I wondered if he was aware of my mother's heritage, that his mother-in-law had been royalty. Until, that is, the world swept away her family and her country and her friends and everything else she knew and loved.

I hated thinking about that. Best to ignore the past and focus on the present, as my dad's Italian mother, my nonna Rose, used to say. She was one whose eyes were always clearly on the path ahead. I decided to channel Nonna Rose for a change and stay in the moment.

"What are those little fish swimming down there in the lake? Those tiny silvery ones," I asked.

"Sunbleaks." Max looked pleased that I'd asked. "We're keeping an eye on their population because somehow a fish that originated in Asia called the topmouth gudgeon was introduced into some streams in France. They eat the sunbleak's eggs, and they also pass on a parasite that renders sunbleaks unable to spawn."

"Who brought them here?" I asked, annoyed at the thought of interlopers interfering with the native fish. Cheeky buggers, those damned topmouth gudgeons! Like the pythons that some idiot let go in the Florida Everglades that ended up destroying the habitat by eating the native animals. Were people really that clueless, that thoughtless?

Never mind. We all know the answer.

"It's not known how they first moved into European waters," Max was saying, "and at this point it's almost immaterial. What matters is that we destroy the ones we find."

"Is anyone actually looking for them? I mean, does Saint Gilbert have a—I don't know what you'd call it—a fish and stream department?" I thought for a moment. "Fish and game? Wildlife conservation?"

"Nothing formal, but it's an excellent idea. When the Duke's Council meets next week, I'll propose that such a post be established."

"Is there a lot of sportfishing in Saint Gilbert?" I asked as we started back toward the castle, Max carrying the bucket of flowers.

"We have several picturesque lakes and streams, and fishing is popular here in the city," Max said thoughtfully. "The areas further from the city aren't as . . . accessible."

"Ah yes. The old the-Russians-were-supposed-to-fix-the-roads-but-didn't story." I recalled he'd mentioned that before. "Can't the Duke's Council vote on doing something about that?"

"There has been discussion but no consensus, but since the funds have been lacking, the arguments were moot. And there are other issues, madam."

"We must be close to the castle. I'm 'madam' again," I teased, but Max didn't smile. "So what other issues, besides the fact that your country only has two exports and you can't sell either in America."

"We could probably sell the wine, if we had a wine merchant who isn't married to the vineyards in France and Italy. Unfortunately, that is a hereditary post, and the man has singular vision. If he sold our wines on a broader international scale, he'd sell less from his family's vineyards."

"That's a clear conflict of interest. He should be removed." Something else to add to the list of things I'd change if in fact I were grand duchess. The thought had come quickly, and just as quickly, I swatted it away. "So what else? Infrastructure? Tourism? Other ways for people to make a living?"

He nodded slowly. "All those, yes."

"And by the way, you have a massive PR problem in that no one outside my family or who took a wrong turn at the Alps has ever heard of Saint Gilbert."

"That too." He nodded glumly.

"Maybe what you need isn't a duchess, Max. Maybe what you need is a good PR firm."

And quick access to those funds that have been collecting interest since 1941.

Chapter Thirteen

I had dinner that night with Max, Claudette, and several loyalists who'd been key supporters of the movement to return to the monarchy. We ate in a formal dining room—the smallest of several—and I had to admit, the food was every bit as good as the best I'd had back home. Actually, in some cases—as in the salmon and the vegetables—it was better. Dessert was better, too—some chocolaty thing that had layers of something that tasted like shortbread cookies covered with raspberries before the chocolate was artfully poured on.

If they kept feeding me like this, I'd be lucky if any of my clothes still fit by the end of the week. Then again, I might not care. Besides the fact that everything I'd tasted was delicious, there was something so decadently wonderful about having someone grow your food for you and someone else preparing fit-for-a-king meals. Or in my case, fit for a duchess. Part of me could totally get used to it.

The other part of me was still very conflicted.

I loved the good old US of A. If I moved to Saint Gilbert, I'd miss my friends and my life, my city, my job. Did I really want to leave everything behind to make a new life in a foreign country? Even if they do speak English here, and even if my family's roots are here, it's still foreign to me, right?

Of course, if this had happened right after my divorce, I might have jumped at it. Timing is everything.

Anyway, it was quite an experience, sitting at the head of the table in that beautiful room. The walls were papered with little gold crowns on a dark-blue background, and there was a rug on the floor that looked like it was older than God. The colors were faded, but even so, the blues and reds and creams were pretty. The table was covered in ivory damask and set with beautifully painted china—creamy white with a dark-blue border set with a gold crown. (BTW, the plates were set so the crown was at the top. Every time I looked down, I was staring at that crown. Subtle.) The flatware was ornate and heavy silver, each piece topped with, yep, that crown. A large round bowl in the center held a mass of peonies flanked by silver candelabras that looked like they could knock someone out, or at the very least raise a good-size goose egg. The overall effect was elegant, and I have to admit, it humbled me to think they'd gone through all that trouble for me. I'd never been treated like royalty before in my life. No one was royalty in South Philly, except maybe our sports heroes.

Like I said—conflicted.

The evening had been formal and a bit stilted, and I can't say I enjoyed the company since everyone was on their best behavior and the conversations were very dry and lacked animation. I understand it was a political necessity—these were descendants of the people who'd contributed to my grandmother's support and kept the fire of the monarchy burning all these years. Sort of like a White House dinner to thank the big donors who helped the president du jour get elected. But I still felt a little let down. At the end of the meal, we walked the guests to the reception area to see them off, but as soon as they'd departed, as if he'd read my mind, Max offered to show me the dungeon.

Now, back home, if a guy asked me if I wanted to see his dungeon, I'd run like hell. I heard there's a house somewhere on Catharine Street that had something kinky in the basement. It was supposedly owned by a guy who tended bar in Queen Village, but I personally had never met him. At least, I didn't think I had, so I cannot confirm the rumor.

Anyway, so there I was. It was dark outside, and the lighting in the castle wasn't all that great, and Max handed me a flashlight. He left the room and came back with a second light and said, "Just in case." Though he didn't say just in case what. I trusted him, so I followed him through the castle. We walked through an arch that led into the kitchen, where the basement stairs were located. Max turned on the overhead light, but he was wise to bring flashlights. We went down fairly wide stone steps that ended far below the first floor. The room at the bottom of the stairwell was wide and windowless and had—yes—chains bolted to the wall. I'm not making this up. I was thinking about how my kids would love to have a Halloween party down there.

All of a sudden, I started to giggle. Now, normally, I'm not a giggly woman, but can't you picture it? Me, following Max through some darkened rooms, flashlights in hand, down into the depths of the castle dungeon where chains are hanging from the walls?

"What?" Max asked.

"Sorry," I whispered, "but I feel like we're in an episode of *Scooby-Doo*."

"Who?" He stopped and turned around.

"*Scooby-Doo*. It's a cartoon dog, like a Great Dane? My kids used to love it." Max still looked blank, so I said, "Never mind." I gestured for him to keep going. How did you describe Scooby to someone who'd never had the experience?

"Was anyone ever . . ." I pointed to the chains dangling from the stone wall.

"Not in my lifetime, but I always thought they must have been put there for a reason, so who knows?"

I walked around the large room trying not to imagine some poor sucker suspended from those chains when I noticed there were several doorways leading off to the left and a dark hall to the right. "I guess those don't lead directly to the secret rooms."

"Correct, madam. Otherwise, they wouldn't be . . . ," Max teased.

"Secret. Right." I rolled my eyes à la Juliette. "So where are these hidden rooms that were large enough to store a castle full of furniture and other goodies?"

"Well, they didn't hide everything. That would have been too obvious. They had to leave some furnishings and some trappings of a royal home lest the Nazis become suspicious."

I followed Max down the dark hall into a rabbit's warren of tiny rooms.

"Cells?"

Max nodded, so I asked, "Were prisoners kept here? For real?"

"Some, but I doubt there was much real torture involved, if that's what you're wondering. I think at one time the castle dungeon was used more or less as the city jail. There would have been thieves, the random highwayman, probably the occasional murderer kept down here."

He opened the door to one of the cells and walked in and appeared to be scanning the stone walls. He stepped closer and ran his hand over a course of irregularly shaped stones, then said, "Ah, here we are."

With a push against the corner of one stone, a portion of the wall began to open inward.

"Oh my God. It's just like in the movies!" came out of my mouth before I had time to realize how goofy that must have sounded.

Max laughed and swept an arm forward. "After you, Your Grace."

I stepped inside and for a moment wondered if there was a safeguard in case there was a glitch and the wall closed by itself.

"Anyone ever get stuck in here?" I imagined some poor soul weeping inconsolably when they realized they were locked in.

"Once or twice, but their bodies were found before they decomposed so they could have decent burials."

At my look of horror, Max laughed again. "Just kidding, Annaliese. There is a way to both close and open from the inside."

He showed me the lever, and I was able to exhale.

I was seriously relieved. I doubted there was a cell phone in the world that got reception down here, so far underground and surrounded by thick walls of solid stone.

Of course, getting locked in with Max for a while could have its perks. Heh.

I chastised myself—but not too much—for letting my mind go there. I mean, it was inevitable. The guy was just about everything any woman would want. And he was within arm's reach every day. A girl could dream, right?

I brought myself back to reality. "So this is the secret place where the castle stuff was stashed." I walked around the room, which was large but maybe not large enough for an entire castle's worth.

"One of several." Max leaned against the wall, his hands in his pockets, one foot crossed over the other.

Damn. I really did like a casual guy.

"Would you like to see the others?"

"How many others? And are they all as empty as this one?"

"Several others. And yes. All empty now."

"Not much point in going from one empty room to another." I walked back out into the cell. "Didn't the Germans or the Russians wonder why there was so little space down here? I mean, it's a huge castle with an enormous footprint. Even I would expect the basement to be much bigger."

"There are many halls that lead to other halls, and altogether, they effectively create a sort of maze. Each hall has any number of cells, but to go from one hall to another can be confusing. The hall leading into the next hall can appear to go on forever to one who isn't familiar with the design. I doubt either of our invaders thought this was anything other than what it appeared. A prison with different . . . cellblocks, I believe you'd call them."

Max pushed the stone back in and the wall closed up. When the opening was completely closed, I couldn't tell where it had been. Whoever had designed and built it had been extremely clever.

We started to walk, and while I wasn't sure where we were in relation to where we began, we found our way back to the stairwell in no time. We went up the steps, guided by our flashlights.

At the top of the steps, Max asked, "Where to next?"

"I think I'd like to turn in. I am exhausted." Jet lag had finally gotten its teeth into me, and suddenly it was all I could do to keep my eyes open.

"Of course. I'll see you to your room."

"No, that's all right. I remember the way."

"I'm sure you do but still, you should not be unaccompanied."

I started to ask what he thought could possibly happen to me between the first and second floors, but I remembered there could be people around who might not be happy with my presence in the country, who *hopefully* wouldn't be shooting at me. So instead of taking off, I allowed him to walk me to my door.

"Thanks for everything today, Max. Taking me to the church, the tour of the town." I smiled. "For showing me the dungeon."

"You're most welcome, Your Grace," he said, adding that last part, no doubt, for the benefit of Sebastian, who'd taken up his post outside my door again. "It was my pleasure."

"Good night, then. And good night, Sebastian." The guard nodded his head in acknowledgment, and I went into my room and closed the door behind me.

I heard them talking while I toed off my heels and pulled my dress over my head, glad I'd had time for a shower before dinner so all I had to do now was wash my face and fall onto the pillow. And that's exactly what I did.

Chapter Fourteen

I called Ceil when I awoke the morning after my excursion to the dungeon. While we chatted, I sat on the little sofa in my sitting room, my bare feet resting on the table in front of me, the phone nestled on my shoulder. I rubbed my temples with the fingers of both hands, hoping to make the headache go away. It felt like a hangover headache, but I didn't think I'd had that much to drink the night before. Sure, wine with dinner and a nightcap of something—I don't remember what—but I felt fine until I got up this morning and I swear, there was a tiny elf sitting behind my eyes tapping teensy nails into the heels of little elf-shoes with his tiny hammer. It could have been the combination of everything: the flight and the subsequent jet lag, the wine, the overwhelming experiences of the past few days. All that.

"The cemetery is very quiet and dignified, and oh man, the emotions standing right there where our murdered great-grandparents and great-uncle and aunt are buried. I really wish you'd been with me, Ceil. It was such a *moment*."

"I can't even imagine. Maybe I can go back with you sometime and you can show me," Ceil said. "The town sounds wonderful, and all those little shops sound so charming. I'm really sorry I didn't go with you."

"Next time you will come with me, and we'll bring the kids. Roe, too, if she wants to come."

"Think there'll be a next time? Crap, I just spilled my coffee." I could hear Ceil's footsteps as she went from the dining room into the kitchen for paper towels.

I waited, giving her a minute while she cleaned up. I used almost all of that minute to wonder if there would be a next time.

"Annie? You there?" Ceil came back on the line. After I assured her I was still there, she said, "It all sounds so magical, like the real Magic Kingdom. We should all go, even if we're not going to be the royal family."

"We will. I really want you to see this place. You'll love it, I know you will."

"Sounds like you're warming to it."

"Oh, I'm warming. I really do like it here. Does that mean I'm staying?" I sighed. "I'm not there yet, Ceil. There's too much to sift through before I even start to think about what that even means."

"I get it. So how'd they let you out to roam around the country without security? Do they have a Secret Service there?"

"Well, I'm not a prisoner, ya know. And they have the castle guards. But yes, there's security, and I was never alone." I told her about the two cars that accompanied us yesterday. "There were a few times when out of the corner of my eye, I'd see Max looking off somewhere, almost as if he'd made eye contact with someone, but there didn't seem to be anyone there. Of course, if you're in a sort of Secret Service, you'd know how to remain secret. And there were other people in the city, looking at the shops or sitting outside one of the restaurants. But no one overt or all dressed in black."

"It sounds like a movie," Ceil said. "It all sounds so dreamy."

"I wish we'd known about all this when we were kids so we could have talked to Gran about, well, all of it." I didn't want to share the fact that I was pretty sure Gran was here with me. Probably Mom, too. I wasn't sure if the woo-woo factor would intrigue her or have her question my sanity.

"Maybe she wouldn't have wanted to. I bet it was all too painful for her. Mom didn't even talk about it, so the pain must have gone really deep."

"I'm sure it did. Ceil, have you ever driven past Gran's old house? The one we used to visit when we were kids?"

"A couple of times," she admitted. "That black iron fence that surrounded the property is gone, and it looks like the neighborhood has gone downhill. A couple of the houses on her street looked kind of shabby. Like they were in need of attention. It made me so sad. Did you ever go?"

"When the kids were little, yeah. One time, I parked in front—the fence was still there then—and just . . . remembered. I thought it would be nice to tell the kids about her, you know? Show them the house she lived in, the house Mom grew up in. Tell them a little about how we used to go visit."

"How'd that go?"

I snorted. "The two of them were beating the crap out of each other in the back seat and never heard a word I said." My nostalgic moment ruined, I'd driven away, wondering why I'd thought three- and six-year-olds would rather look at an old house through the car windows than beat up on each other.

I hung up after texting her the photos I'd taken the day before, thinking how everyone in the family would find something to love here. I thought briefly about using "the REAL Magic Kingdom" in a hypothetical marketing campaign intended to introduce Saint Gilbert to the rest of the world, but I think Disney had "the Magic Kingdom" in a lock. A country that couldn't afford to fix its roads couldn't afford to take on Disney.

I looked out the window that faced the lake and thought about Serafina. The water was perfectly calm and so blue, the scene so inviting, that I couldn't resist. If there really was a mermaid, I was pretty sure she'd show herself on a morning like this.

Not that I believed there really *was* one. Besides, she'd been gone since 1941. Not that I believed she'd ever been there for real, of course. I opened the door and found Hans at his station.

"Any chance I could have my morning coffee down near the lake? Like around the arch?" I asked.

"Of course, madam." He maintained that stiff upper back thing, standing ramrod straight and staring directly ahead. "I shall arrange it immediately."

"Thank you." Believe me, no matter how this whole thing worked out, I would cherish those three little words—*of course* and *immediately*— till my last day.

I'd thought about my plans before I got dressed, so I was appropriately attired for seeking hidden rooms and exploring the countryside with Max. The breeze blowing into my room was a little cooler than yesterday, so I'd put on a long-sleeved shirt that was a sort of sea-glass green—one of my favorite colors—and a white pencil skirt. I had become conscious of how I looked when I was going to be with Max. He always looked so *GQ*, and I always felt so like the losing side of *Who Wore It Better?* when I was with him. So I brushed my hair out straight and tucked it behind my ears (Claudette said it looked best that way) and proceeded to walk that fine line when I put on my makeup. You know, the line between making yourself look naturally good and looking made up.

I noticed the lines around my eyes seemed to be softening a bit. My job must be more stressful than I realized if four days out of the office made the crow's-feet less noticeable. Then again, it was probably just the lighting.

Sadly, my shoe choices were the same as they'd been yesterday. I sighed, going once again with my Keds. If we were going to be out in the countryside, I might be called upon to walk around on uneven ground, and since I already knew what it felt like to walk those country roads in heels, this time I went for comfort.

By the time I got outside, a small table had been set up in precisely the spot I'd envisioned. There was a tray much like I'd had for breakfast my first morning, and a small vase filled with wildflowers. I sat in a comfy chair and poured myself a cup of coffee and just felt like, *Ahhhhh*. You know that feeling, right? When things are just the way you wanted them to be, and it makes you happy? Like kicking off tight shoes or taking off your underwire bra after a long day? That's how I felt. I sat in the morning sunshine and gazed out at the beautiful lake and nibbled my scone and ate more of those incredible berries and drank my coffee and just . . . *ahhhhh*.

For just those few moments, I felt like a duchess at home in her world, where all was well and good.

Then I saw Max walking toward me from the castle, and the morning got even better.

"Good morning," he called as he drew closer.

"Morning to you." I sat a little straighter as he approached, and I didn't even need Mom to remind me. I'd been slightly hunched in the chair before I saw him, and slouching wasn't a good look for anyone. "Want to join me?"

I looked at the tray and realized there was no extra coffee cup.

"Well, I'd invite you to share my coffee, but . . ." I pointed at the table. "Only one cup."

"Thank you, but I've had my morning limit." He stood with his hands on his hips looking down at me.

Be still, my flip-flopping heart.

"Almost ready for that drive about I promised you?" he asked.

"Sure. I just have to run back up to my room for a minute." What I wanted to do was check to make sure there were no little strawberry bits or seeds in my teeth.

"Of course. I'm not rushing you."

"I'm finished here." I touched the corners of my mouth with the napkin—surely the softest linen on the planet—and stood.

Walking back up to the castle, I had the opportunity to see that structure in all its magnificence.

"Whoever designed this place was a genius," I said.

Max nodded. "It is quite the castle."

"And you're quite the master of understatement. It's the most beautiful building I've ever seen."

Max smiled, no doubt hoping I was about to say I'd like to live here for the rest of my days, but I was nowhere near making that sort of decision.

I finished upstairs—teeth, makeup, hair—and was back downstairs with the escort who'd been waiting outside the door to my suite. I guess they were taking this guard-the-potential-duchess thing more seriously than I was.

But once again, outside there were three cars waiting. And once again, Max took my arm and led me to the middle of the three.

"Security detail in place?" I teased after he'd opened the passenger door for me and I slid across that cushy leather seat.

He wasn't amused.

Max got in behind the wheel and started the car. "Security is not a joke, Annaliese. It's a responsibility I take very seriously."

Chastised, I said, "I'm sorry. I'm just not used to having anyone worry about me."

"You'll get used to it."

"Only if I come back."

He ignored my remark and instead said, "I thought today we'd do a tour of the southern part of the country. You saw much of what the north is like on our drive from the airport the other day."

"What will we see in the south?" I asked.

"Villages, farms, a few vineyards. Lots of mountains, especially as we get closer to Italy."

"You said my grandmother's escape route went into Italy." I recalled the story, every detail I'd been told. But I knew I hadn't heard it all.

"Unfortunately, I don't know exactly where they crossed from Switzerland into Italy. I doubt if anyone knows the exact place." So apparently Max hadn't heard it all, either.

We drove along winding roads, some more narrow than others, and I could see where a little roadwork would make the travel from one village to another much more pleasant. It was uncomfortably bumpy in many places.

"Whoa!" The car hit a rut, and I was jarred in spite of the seat belt. I recovered my composure enough to say, "Well, that was impressive."

"One of the many roads that need improvement." Max swerved to the right to avoid another deep rut.

"Why haven't they been fixed? Surely there's been plenty of time to repair the roads."

"Plenty of time, but insufficient funds. Remember, most of the country's wealth is sitting in a bank in Switzerland." He slowed a little and glanced over at me. "Just waiting for the duchess to unlock that vault."

"I hate feeling responsible for all of Saint Gilbert's problems." I know I was whining, but I couldn't help it. "Don't think I'm not aware of what I could do *if*. . ."

"You shouldn't feel it's all on you. Even once the funds are returned, the council will have to agree to the repairs."

"But I—theoretically—would have the final say, right?"

"I'm fairly certain, yes. But remember, we haven't had a duchess ruling our country since 1941. The Duke's Council has made all decisions unopposed since the 1990s when the Soviet Union broke up. I don't know what precedents applied before that."

"So they—this group of all men—have never been challenged."

Max's smile was barely detectable, but I didn't miss it. "You'd be the first. Theoretically."

"How do you even learn to rule a country? How do you know what to do when you're asked to make decisions that will affect the lives of several hundred thousand people?"

"I admit our situation would be a challenge since there's no one in place to show you everything you need to know. So in that respect, yes, I agree it would not be easy. But there are those with whom you can consult. There's the council, of course. Some members may be more helpful than others."

"The chancellor?"

Max shrugged. "His position is traditionally that of a principal advisor. There are some areas in which he could be invaluable. Diplomacy, for example. He's very good at that sort of thing. He's known to heads of state outside Saint Gilbert, and well liked, from all I've heard."

I made a mental note of that.

"But not in the everyday running of the country?"

"In those matters, I would rely on my instincts." He cleared his throat. "Your instincts are quite good, Annaliese. My best advice to you is that you trust yourself."

"What makes you think my instincts are worth trusting?"

"You followed them to Saint Gilbert, didn't you?"

I guess he had me there.

"What if I want to do something but the council doesn't agree?"

"You would have to find a way to convince them to want what you want." He smiled again. "I have no doubt you are well capable of getting your way once you set your mind to it."

Well, there is that . . .

"There's a very pretty village less than a mile from here," Max said without segue. I guess he felt he'd made his point. "We could stop and have lunch, if you like."

"I'd like," I told him, then looked out the window to the mountains up ahead. "Are those the Alps?"

"Yes. That's Italy in the distance. The Alps run through Italy, France, Switzerland, Liechtenstein, Austria, Germany, and Slovenia, as well as Saint Gilbert."

I nodded. I remembered those mountains. "So there should be ski lodges and slopes for tourists."

"I agree. I'm sure the next duchess will find a way to bring tourists to Saint Gilbert." He reduced the speed as we entered a small village.

I frowned. "Stop dumping everything on the duchess."

"I'm not dumping on her, as you say. I'm challenging her. My instincts tell me she's a woman who enjoys a challenge." He parked the car along a tree-lined street and unhooked his seat belt. "I doubt she's one to back down."

I refused to pick up that gauntlet, though I had to admit, apparently he, too, had damned good instincts.

We had a terrific lunch in a beautiful café, and afterward we popped into a few of the little shops. But we avoided any further discussion of why I'd come to Saint Gilbert and just enjoyed the rest of the day. On the way back to the city, we took a side road that led to a castle that had a moat without water, and since no one lived there we couldn't watch the drawbridge come down, but it would have been fun. The hillsides were dotted with chateaus, and we drove through a number of perfectly picturesque villages. We stopped at several farms where Max knew the farmers, and as a city girl, I have to say I was loving the countryside and all the people we met. But by the time we arrived home—that is, back at the castle—I was ready for a nap and an early evening. I was in my room for the night by nine, in bed by ten.

When I closed my eyes, I could still see the faces of the farmers we'd met. They'd offered me wine and cheeses, and one even gave me a basket of wool he'd shorn from his sheep.

It was really thick and, frankly, didn't smell all that great, but I was gracious and accepted the gift with a smile. After we left, Max told me the wool from the local sheep is highly prized, but when I asked if any of it was made into yarn and exported, he said, "Not to my knowledge." Another opportunity lost, like the wine and the cheeses, if you ask me. He said he doubted the sheep farmers have the start-up money for anything more than what they're doing, which is basically selling their wool to a woman in the city who makes it into yarn. He wasn't sure where it goes from there. I told him that knitting is huge in the States, and he just said, "Hmmmm."

I was starting to get frustrated with all the opportunities wasted here. I realized people didn't have a lot of disposable cash—neither did the government, apparently, since my great-grandparents spirited away most of it into a bank in another country for safekeeping. Which was a better idea than letting an invader or some unscrupulous Saint Gilbertian loot the coffers, but it wasn't doing anyone any good where it was. Yes, I was increasingly aware that I could solve that little problem for them, but at what cost to me? To my family? It was one of those things I didn't want to think about right now.

I turned over and went to sleep thinking about American tourists oohing and ahhing over skeins of brightly colored yarn displayed in the window of one of those cute shops in Beauchesne.

Chapter Fifteen

"You'd asked about the portraits of your family," Claudette said the next morning when she'd come to check in with me after breakfast. "Perhaps you'd like to take a walk with me?"

"I would." Especially after having eaten several of those yummy croissants. This morning's were filled with a soft cheese and strawberries. So delicious.

I followed Claudette around the hallway to the main stairwell. At the top of the steps was a huge open area that I assumed was some sort of reception hall.

"Indeed it is, Annaliese. Guests would wait here before being announced to enter the ballroom." Claudette kept walking, then flung open a set of huge—I mean *huge*—double doors.

The ballroom was immense, the biggest room I'd ever been in, bigger than a basketball court.

"They must have had really fancy balls here," I murmured.

"Oh, most certainly. Your great-grandmother loved nothing more than a grand party. There'd be a full orchestra and the room would be filled with flowers, and everyone would wear their most fabulous gowns and jewels. Not just the local lords and ladies, but others as well. From France and Italy and Germany and the British Isles. India, even. At one time, Saint Gilbert was known for its excellent hospitality." She sighed. "It must have been a sight to see."

I raised an eyebrow, and she laughed.

"My mother told me how the music would play and couples would dance. And how, as a child, she had a little secret place above the ballroom." She pointed upward to where there were what looked like those box seats you see at the opera were located. "She would hide and imagine the scenes her mother described to her."

I knew without asking that as a child, my grandmother also had hidden in that secret perch and listened to the music, watched her parents and their guests swirl around the ballroom floor. To a little girl, it all must have seemed like . . .

"Magic," I said aloud. I suspected Gran was there with us, a smile on her face.

"Oh yes, in my mother's day, everything seemed touched by magic. It must have been a wonderful time to live in Saint Gilbert." She turned to me, her eyes still shining from a memory of a long-ago night. "My mother always went to Paris for her gowns—Paris, of course, came to the duchess—and she'd wear her best jewels. My father would wear his uniform. As captain of the castle guard, he must have been quite a sight, all those medals and gold braid. They tell me it was a time like no other. A time of peace and prosperity."

"No wonder the vote came in on the side of the monarchy," I said, not for the first time my mind darting to the vision of Max in one of those fancy uniforms. Most definitely a sigh-worthy sight.

"No wonder at all." She took one last look around, then turned back to me. "But we're here to look at portraits. If you'll follow me . . ."

I reluctantly left Max in the ballroom wearing his gold braid as we walked out to the reception area and took a left. Three doors down, the hall overlooked the first floor on one side. Claudette unlocked a door, opened it, and stepped inside. She turned on the light and I followed her into the room. She pushed on the head of a falcon carved into the mantel, and the wall next to it silently slid open.

My jaw dropped. There were paintings *everywhere*. I mean, stacks leaning against every inch of wall, and lining the walls.

"Oh my God." I stood in the doorway trying to take it all in.

"I admit it's a bit much, but I thought you'd like to see them all while you're here."

"It's almost spooky that the builders of the castle had the prescience to include these secret rooms. It's almost as if they expected something dire to happen," I said.

"Actually, the story is that the secret rooms were built for the sons of the first duke and duchess. They had seven sons and one daughter, who were apparently a rowdy bunch. When the castle was built, the duchess requested a series of rooms such as this hoping her children would be kept occupied playing hiding and finding games," Claudette explained.

"We call that hide-and-seek back home, though we never had secret hidden rooms. Mostly we'd play outside and hide behind parked cars." I walked around the room for a moment, imagining my kids and their cousins playing such a game. "I wonder how many times one brother locked another inside."

"There's a safety latch in every room," she said, pointing out the lever on the wall. "You couldn't get stuck inside unless you chose to." She paused in front of a large painting, then stepped aside. "This is a portrait of your grandmother as an infant in the arms of her mother. I think it's particularly lovely."

"Oh. Oh . . ." I walked over to the painting for a better look. It was maybe four feet wide and more than twice as tall, and it took my breath away. Baby Gran was wrapped in a white blanket, her eyes closed, nestled in the arms of her mother, who smiled at her sleeping dark-haired daughter with undeniable love and pride. My great-grandmother wore what looked like a wrap or robe, crimson in color and trimmed in gray fur, and she wore gold earrings and a gold cuff studded with red stones. On her head sat the most gorgeous crown.

"I'm betting those are real diamonds in her crown," I said.

"Not a crown, Annaliese, but her favorite tiara. And yes, of course the diamonds are real."

"Wow, if that's her tiara, I can't even imagine what the crown must look like."

Claudette smiled as she went through a stack of several large paintings that stood against the wall. "Here you can see what the crown looked like as it sat on your great-grandmother's head."

I helped her extract the painting from the stack and took a few steps back to take it in.

"Jesus, Mary, and Edna," I said, my mother's late next-door neighbor's favorite expletive escaping from my mouth without me realizing it had.

The portrait was life-size, and the woman portrayed was stunning. She stood against a backdrop of perfect blue—not baby blue, not marine blue, but something in between. At her feet, a small brown-and-white dog sat at attention, and on her head sat the crown. It was gold, studded with rubies and diamonds, and looked like it weighed a ton. It was beyond what I could have imagined, and my great-gran wore it proudly. Her dark-brown hair was gathered from her face and held up at the back of her head, and she wore the most gorgeous white dress I'd ever seen. The neckline was a deep V and hung slightly off her shoulders. The sleeves were caught up on each side of the bodice by a gorgeous diamond, ruby, and pearl pin. The skirt that flowed from the sashed waist draped beautifully, perfectly, to the floor. She was exquisite, and I said so.

"Oh yes, she was quite beautiful. Even after her marriage to your great-grandfather, nobles from all over Europe tried to woo her." Claudette said this with a smile on her face.

"Do you suppose she ever succumbed to their, you know . . ."

"Not that I ever heard. She was totally devoted to her husband. They were very much in love, soulmates, it was said."

I stepped closer to the portrait. "She was so tall, and her eyes are so green."

"As were your grandmother's." She added, "As are yours. But she wasn't tall. I don't think she was more than two inches past five feet."

"Juliette's height." I stared at the image expertly done in oils. "Actually, Juliette looks a bit like her. The eyes and the mouth are very similar."

"So my son told me. He saw a resemblance immediately upon meeting your daughter. It is our hope she will see the portrait for herself one day, madam." She rested the painting back against the wall.

I recalled all the empty spaces on the walls where paintings had once hung. "It would be nice if the walls were filled again. But the one of Gran and her mother—could that be hung in the room where I'm staying? Just for now?"

The portrait was so intimate, such a beautiful moment between mother and child, I didn't feel it belonged on display for just anyone coming into the castle to see. Maybe I'd change my mind, or maybe whoever was going to be in charge under plan B would feel differently, but for now, I would love for Gran and her mama to stay with me.

"The dog in the painting," I asked. "What breed is that?"

"That's a Gilberti spaniel, Annaliese. Very rare. They were bred here, but the Russians took many with them when they left and interbred them with something else. For a while, it seemed the breed had died out. However, with the newly resurrected sense of nationalism, I've noticed a few around the city. Perhaps the breed was kept alive in the villages or the countryside. Whatever, the dogs, too, are enjoying a slight comeback." She gazed out the window and said with a hint of pride, "Just like our city. Our country."

I didn't want to dwell on the reason for the comeback.

"It's a very cute little dog." It reminded me of a cross between a Cavalier King Charles spaniel and an English spaniel.

"That was Josephine, Her Majesty's favorite. The duchess had her portrait painted with her several times. Would you like me to procure one for you? Perhaps a pup?"

I had a fleeting vision of myself seated in a fancy chair surrounded by any number of Gilberti spaniels, like the late Queen Elizabeth II with her corgis.

I have to stop thinking like that.

"Oh no. But thank you." I sort of hated to pass, but I'd never had a dog and I wouldn't know what to do with it. I worked during the day, and the kids would be at school. Still, it was damn cute, and the kids would love it.

For the next several hours we went through all the paintings, Claudette making notes in a black notebook as she recalled as much as she could about who was depicted and where each had originally been hung. When we'd finished, every piece of art had been cataloged, and she and I had discussed potential places where each might hang. It had been a fun exercise, and besides learning who was who in my family tree, helping her made me feel I'd accomplished something for the first time since I arrived.

My eyes kept going back to the white dress in the first painting I'd looked at. I couldn't even begin to imagine what such a thing might cost today, and I had to ask. "Was the dress stolen?"

"Oh no. Great pains were taken to preserve it and the many others."

"Where . . . ?"

"This way, madam." Claudette secured the secret chamber, then escorted me into the outer room, where she turned off the light and locked the door behind us.

Across the hall and almost to where it met another hallway was a room comfortably furnished with a small sofa, several chairs, a bookcase full of books.

"When the castle was endangered, many of your great-grand-mother's gowns along with her mother's and her grandmother's were hidden away lest they be stolen or destroyed." She pulled a book from the shelf, and the wall spun around to reveal a room. "As you can see, much was saved."

Oh, how I loved all these hidden rooms! It was like living inside a treasure hunt!

"Holy crap," I muttered as I followed Claudette into the room, my head feeling as if it were spinning out of control. There were gowns everywhere I looked. One thing I could tell for certain: my great-grandmother—and apparently her mother, and *her* mother— loved having jewels sewed onto her clothes. There had to be a fortune just in the rubies alone, and I said so.

"Yes, the Gilberti women have always been fond of pretty stones." She adjusted what appeared to be a ball gown on its hanger. "Some of these gowns and day dresses go back more than a hundred years, Annaliese."

"They've obviously been well preserved. Why weren't these sold and the money used for the things the country needs?"

"Everything you see here was personal property. All will remain under lock and key until the rightful heir is crowned. She may do whatever she wishes with them."

"You mean me."

"Should you decide to be that person, yes."

And with that, my head finally exploded. I looked around the room at the racks of clothes, the glorious colors, and all the finery, and I just couldn't take it anymore. The responsibility was too great. Did it make me shallow that I didn't reach my tipping point until I was faced with a room full of jewel-encrusted gowns?

"I think I've had enough for one day," I told Claudette as I headed for the hallway. "I think I'd like to go to my room for a bit."

"Of course." Claudette locked the door behind us. "There is a dinner scheduled for tonight, but if you're too tired, we can simply cancel it."

I admit I did think about bailing, but in the end, I shook my head. "No, we'll do it. I know I said I'd meet with all of Gran's friends who wished to come."

I was really tired, but since I might not have this opportunity again, I couldn't bring myself to back out. I'd take a little nap and a shower, and I'd be good to go to meet Gran's friends. I was looking forward to it.

~

The dinner was lovely, though I only made it downstairs with seconds to spare. I dressed in black—because everything I'd brought with me was casual or black—and Claudette draped my neck with a mile-long string of pearls that, honest to God, I could have used as a jump rope. She wound it around my neck several times, then let it fall until the longest loop hit right around my waist. Pearls and diamonds in my ears, and then for a change, diamonds and emeralds on my fingers. I had to say, this much bling made my very simple black dress look glamorous. I took as many pictures as I could, because I will probably never look like this again.

And what's that, you ask? How did I look? I looked *royal*. Truly royal. I walked into that dining room feeling like a million bucks. Well, yeah, since I was probably wearing a million bucks worth of jewels.

Like I said before, I didn't own any real jewelry, and I wasn't the fancy type. But I don't care how plainly you think you like to dress—let someone wrap you in sparklies like the ones I had on, and trust me, you will like it. A lot.

This dinner was the polar opposite of the dinner with the donors, as I liked to think of that first formal event. Gran's friends—such delightful ladies!—had all dressed for the occasion, and I found it very touching that they'd taken such care with their appearance. I made an effort to speak with everyone and used my phone to have Claudette take my photo with each individually. I promised to send them a copy, but I'd really taken them for myself so I could show my sisters Gran's beautiful friends. The cocktail hour had been a bit subdued, but once we were seated in the dining room, the ladies began to reminisce, and I could feel Gran's bittersweet emotions.

"Oh, Princess Annaliese was such a devil when she was younger," a giggling Martine said. "She loved to move things around from room to room so as to confuse the adults. She would make us help her, then we'd get in trouble, but she always admitted that she was behind the mischief."

"Remember when she moved all the furniture around in the drawing room and Her Highness came into the room and wasn't watching where she was going and almost tripped over a footstool?" Alma tried to hide her own giggles behind her hands.

"And when she dyed one side of her sister Jacqueline's hair with beet juice? It was such a horrible shade of maroon." Marguerite laughed.

"Oh, she got into such trouble for that," Louisa said.

"Her hands were stained from the beets so she couldn't even deny it had been she who'd done the deed," Edwina said, her eyes dancing with the memory.

"Oh, and when she put salt in the sugar bowls and sugar in the salters," Alma reminded them.

"The kitchen was in a tizzy that time," someone added, and they all laughed heartily.

And so it went throughout the meal, the ladies sharing their fondest memories of life in the castle in those days. The laughter sounded as if it had been bottled up inside them for a very long time, and they were happy to let it out.

Until Louisa said, "And the way she used to fly across the fields on her big black mare. Like she was chasing the very wind." She paused as her eyes filled with tears.

"Katrinka," a subdued Elena said. "The horse's name was Katrinka. Her Highness used to admonish the princess that she rode too fast, that she was too reckless, but the princess never failed to give Katrinka her head and let her fly. She said it was good for the horse and good for her." She dabbed at her eyes with her napkin. "I often wondered what became of that horse."

"Taken by the Germans," tall, noble Patrice declared as if still angered by the memory. "My father told me they'd emptied the stables and took all the horses. The best went to the officers, so I imagine Katrinka was spoken for by someone who ranked high."

"Hopefully someone who appreciated her and took good care of her," Elena said softly.

For a moment, the dining room fell into silence as the ladies sat with their sad memories surrounding them.

Hoping to lighten their mood, I raised my wineglass. "I'd like to propose we drink to Katrinka and my grandmother. Perhaps they've been reunited in the hereafter and are, at this moment, racing across the fields."

"That's a lovely thought, Your Grace." Louisa raised her glass, and the others followed. "To our beautiful friend, long gone now, and the beautiful memories she left us."

"We were blessed to have lived in that time, and to have known her. She was a bright soul even then," Alma added. "I'm grateful to have shared a childhood with her." She turned to me and placed a hand on my arm. "As I'm grateful to be sharing this time with you. Seeing you has been a reminder of the good times we shared with her, before the bad times came and she was forced to leave us. Thank you for bringing us together again, here in this place where we spent so many happy days with the friend we loved so dearly and missed so much."

"Still miss," Marguerite said.

"Here, here," someone added.

The ladies all tilted their glasses in my direction, and I murmured a thank-you. It was all the lump in my throat would allow.

I closed my eyes and imagined I could see Gran on that beautiful black mare jumping over clouds and flying toward the horizon. I wondered if in fact she had been able to see her horse again since she'd left this life, but who the heck knows what happens after we pass. It was enough for me to know that Gran was finding some peace in the company of her beloved childhood friends and in their remembrances of her.

~

I slept late again the next morning, and I was pretty sure everyone in the castle must be gossiping about the lazy American who did nothing but eat, drink, ride around with Max, and sleep. When I left my room for breakfast—I thought I'd dine in the small morning room that overlooked the castle grounds for a change—I found my great-grandmother's picture hanging between the large arched windows. It was one of the portraits that had caught my eye the day before, one of the many where she'd been painted in a white dress, though not the same as *the* white dress. Judging from the number of paintings I'd seen the day before, white was a favorite of hers. In this one, she wore lots of emeralds. I mean, she dripped in big, fat green stones.

"Gifts," Claudette told me when she joined me, "from an Italian count who'd courted her when she was younger, before she met and fell in love with your great-grandfather."

"And I guess they're in the Swiss bank with the crown and the tiaras and the ropes of pearls."

She nodded. "The duchess wanted those most valuable and sentimental pieces secured for her daughter."

"Who never got to wear them."

She patted me on the arm. "But perhaps a great-granddaughter—perhaps someday even a great-great-granddaughter will wear them. I believe that would please her."

I sighed at the thought of having that emerald-and-diamond necklace around my neck and that emerald crown—excuse me, tiara—on my head, then pushed the thought away. I couldn't let my decision be influenced by the fortune in jewels awaiting me in Switzerland, as lovely a fantasy as that was shaping up to be.

Later that day, Max took me on a complete tour of Castle Blanc from the first floor to the third—except for the west wing—and I have to say, my ancestors had their priorities straight. I'd never even dreamed of a time where I might have two libraries. I'd peeked into the small one on the second floor one morning and found it charming and cozy. But the one on the first floor! Now that was a library! When I opened the door and found those sky-high shelves packed with books, I almost fainted. There was so much history contained in that one spacious room, and in so many languages: not just English but French, Italian, German, and several I didn't recognize. I wanted to see a fire blazing in its two—*two!*—fireplaces, one at each end of the room. I wanted deep, cushy chairs and good reading lamps and something to prop my feet on. Oh, and soft, warm throws, the plushy kind. I could have spent an entire day there exploring the shelves. If I decided to become the duchess, I would have a library hour every day. One hour, in here, discovering the books my gran and the other Gilbertis read.

The music room was at the end of the hall, and it, too, was spacious with a high ceiling. I could easily imagine little concerts here back in the day when there'd probably been a piano and maybe a harp and some other instruments. Now it was just a large empty space with a dusty floor. I wondered if I listened very carefully I'd hear echoes of music from long ago, but I couldn't stand still long enough to find out, and besides, that's a little too woo-woo for me.

I remembered my mother talking about how she'd taken piano lessons when she was young. She'd wanted us three girls to play as well, but none of us wanted to. Along with that memory came the image of Gran playing for me once when I'd spent the day with her. I'd watched the way her hands seemed to float over the keys, spinning music from her fingertips. I remember thinking I'd been a bit hasty in my refusal to learn. I wondered if it was too late now.

I fantasized for a moment, about being the duchess and taking lessons on that same piano my gran played, but I quickly brushed the thought away. Gran had had beautiful hands, with long, gracious fingers. I looked at my stubby fingers with gnawed nails that my ex used to call peasant hands, a stark reminder of who I was and who I was not.

Was it possible to step out of myself and become something more? I really didn't know.

There was only one way to find out, but in my heart, I was further from making that decision than I was when I got here. What had at first seemed *big* now was more than big, more than life-changing. It was *world* changing, for me and my family, and would alter the course of our lives—our collective history—forever. It was frightening to hold that kind of power. Was I worthy to make that decision for my children, my sisters, even for myself?

The truth was, I was afraid to take the chance to find out.

Chapter Sixteen

The night before I left for home there was yet another dinner, and many of the people I'd met during the week had been invited. It was held in the gallery, which had been lit with hundreds of white candles in silver candleholders. Paintings had been hung on the walls—Claudette's doing, for sure—and there were flowers everywhere. We drank local wines, and there were toasts and well-wishes from around the table. I knew that I'd look back on that night when I got home and wish I'd said more, but my heart was in my mouth when I'd been asked to speak.

"I'm trying to find the words to tell you what this week has meant to me. I can honestly say I've loved every minute I've spent in Saint Gilbert. The country is beautiful beyond what I could have imagined, and you are all so gracious and kind and welcoming. I've made memories that I know will last my lifetime. It's been wonderful to see where my grandmother was born and grew up, to meet her friends who knew and loved her and who kept her alive in their memories even after her time here was cut short. I'm grateful to you for teaching me about my family, my heritage, things I never would have known or even suspected before I came here, and I thank you from the bottom of my heart. I only wish my mother was alive to have come with me, but I can say without embarrassment that I have felt her here with me, just as I have felt my gran—your last duchess—around me every day. So for them, and for my family, I thank you for inviting me to come as your guest to this wonderful place. Thank you for opening your country to me."

I guess I could have said more—maybe there were those at the table who'd been waiting for me to make an announcement—but I was so close to tears I couldn't have said another word. After I'd finished, everyone present stood and applauded, and I had to bite my lip to keep from out-and-out bawling.

I'd been made to feel such a part of this place all week that it felt almost like leaving home. I don't know how else to explain it. When I went to bed that night, it was with a thousand voices, sights, and sounds in my head, and I was still awake in the morning.

So I got up with the sun and attended an early-morning service at Saint Ann's in the city, after which I stopped in the churchyard for one last visit with Gran's parents and siblings before I left. I wanted them to know that even if I never came back, I would never forget them. No way could I have left Saint Gilbert without saying goodbye. I could feel the presence of my mother and grandmother—both overwhelmingly sad—and hoped that there'd been a reunion of spirits, so to speak.

I'd invited Max and Claudette to have breakfast with me by the lake, and when I asked Max to tell the castle guards to see we were not disturbed, he smiled and said, "Tell them yourself, why don't you. You're still the heir to the throne for as long as you're here."

So I asked that our party remain private, and I had to say, I enjoyed my last chance to be waited on for probably the rest of my life.

It was another glorious morning. The lake was sparkly like it had been the day I arrived. We made small talk and I sipped my delicious coffee (I was *so* going to miss my coffee!), but I noticed Max glanced at his watch several times, so I knew it was time to leave. I secretly waved goodbye to Serafina, then we walked back to the castle without saying much. I went up to my room to make sure I hadn't left anything behind, and moments later Claudette knocked on the door.

"Is there anything else I can do for you?" she asked.

"No, but thank you. You've been so wonderful, Claudette. I'm so grateful to you for all you did for me this past week. I don't know how I would have survived without you. I'd have been lost every day." I swallowed the now-familiar lump in my throat.

"It was my pleasure to assist you, but more, it was the greatest honor to have met you. You are truly a daughter of Saint Gilbert, and everyone who's met you hopes—*prays*—for your return." She handed me a package wrapped in white tissue and tied with a simple yellow ribbon. "Soap to take with you. I heard you say last night that you'd bought some but had hoped to buy more before you left because you enjoyed it so much." She smiled. "The duchess should never have to buy soap in her own country."

"Thank you, Claudette." I think I surprised her by hugging her, I was so touched by her thoughtfulness. I couldn't imagine leaving here without a hug for the woman who'd been so kind—almost motherly—to me.

"You're most welcome." For just a second she dropped her guard and returned the hug. Then, "I believe your car and driver are ready, Your Grace."

On the way out of the room, I stopped to say goodbye to Hans, who acknowledged me with a little smile and nod of his head. Claudette and I walked the now portrait-lined hall to the landing, then down the steps and through the gallery. The tables and chairs and candelabra from the night before were gone, so our footsteps echoed as we walked through the long, empty space.

As on the day I arrived, the castle staff assembled in the grand entrance, and I took a few seconds to say goodbye and thank each of them for their part in welcoming me and taking care of me. Then I was in the car, with John-Paul and Marcel in the front seat and Max next to me, one black car in front and another behind us, and we were moving toward the drive. I turned back to the castle and watched the blue-and-white flag snap in the breeze at the top of the tower. Then I saw a dark flash across the sky from the woods to the castle.

"Max, I think I saw the falcon."

"Come to say goodbye, no doubt." He looked over his shoulder as the bird disappeared around the castle wall.

"Well, *I* doubt, but it's a nice sentiment." We paused as the gate was being opened, and the cars passed through before heading out of the city the same way we'd entered a week ago. When I looked back, I could see the tip of the spire on the Church of Saint Ann above the treetops in the park.

"Which reminds me." Max reached into the pocket of his suit coat—a luscious dark-blue jacket that was soft as silk—and brought out a small box. "Something to remember us by."

"Max, you didn't have to . . ."

"Open it." He leaned back as if watching for my reaction, so I knew whatever was in the box had meaning.

I pulled off the leather cord that wrapped around the box several times and raised the lid.

"Oh . . ." I lifted the silver falcon pin from the box and held it up. The workmanship was incredible. "It's gorgeous. Just . . . perfect." I leaned back looking for a place to pin it and decided on the collar of the white short-sleeved blouse I'd worn with the same black pencil skirt I'd worn on the trip over.

"Here, permit me." Max smiled and took the pin from my suddenly inept fingers and secured it to my collar. His fingers brushed soft as a whisper against the side of my neck, and I felt it in every part of my being. I mean, like, body and soul. If circumstances had been different I'd have kissed him, a for-real kiss that would never happen. I guess he was just part of the big fantasy. You know, single, middle-aged mom inherits a crown and moves to the castle where she meets a handsome . . . oh, you know the rest. It's a favorite trope. Except of course no one fantasizes about being middle-aged.

"I love it, Max." I touched the pin with the tip of my right index finger. "Thank you."

"You are most welcome. I hope you will think of us whenever you wear it."

As if I needed anything to remind me of Saint Gilbert—or Max.

Too choked up to respond, I merely nodded. The words that were on the tip of my tongue stayed stubbornly where they were.

I tried to settle into my seat as John-Paul drove on through the countryside, a silent Marcel in the passenger seat lost in his thoughts. We passed the old farms with their stone houses and barns, their fields full of goats or cows. The little villages Max and I had driven through a few days ago, and the kind and gracious people I'd met there, went by in a blur, along with the chateaus and castles perched on distant hilltops. I regretted not having visited them all and learning their stories. Before I knew it, we'd passed the boulder from which I'd taken my first step into Saint Gilbert, and from there, it seemed we flew into Switzerland.

Why is it that the ride *from* always seems shorter than the ride *to*?

Soon we were at the airport, and then blink! I was on the plane heading home, my entourage of three in attendance, seated as we'd been on the flight over the week before: Max at my side, John-Paul and Marcel in the seats in front of us. I closed my eyes during the takeoff and didn't open them again until Lake Geneva was growing smaller by the minute in the distance. I watched from my window seat as the lake, then the mountains faded into the distance.

I knew Max had questions, but I still had no answers. He'd brought me to Saint Gilbert for one purpose, and I sensed that my leaving without having committed to the country must be making him feel as if he'd failed. I wanted to assure him it wasn't him, it was me, but that was what you said when you broke off a relationship with someone you were never really into in the first place. I felt conflicted and emotional and just a little guilty that I hadn't been able to be what they all hoped. There was nothing I could say, so I pretended to sleep, and eventually,

I did. I woke up just as the movie he'd selected began, so for the rest of the flight, we had something neutral to talk about—*Aquaman*, and the visual splendor of Jason Momoa.

There was a three-hour delay due to some mechanical problem when we stopped at Heathrow and another delay landing in Philly, so with all that and changing planes and sitting around, it was midafternoon by the time I arrived at my house. Jean-Paul parked the long black rental car in the middle of the street because there was no other place to put it, and he and Marcel stood guard and waved cars around it while Max got my luggage out of the trunk. I stood on the sidewalk waiting for him and noticed Mrs. Santangelo two houses down trying not to look at us as she washed her front stoop. It was white marble, like so many of the others on our street, and like so many of the residents around here, washing the front steps was an obligation only a little less sacred than Mass on Sunday. I waved to her, but she pretended not to see me. Just like she pretended she didn't see Max gather up my luggage and follow me into my house.

"That you, Annie?" Ceil called from the dining room after I shut the front door behind us.

"It is." I turned to Max. "You can leave my bags here. Thank you for bringing them in for me."

"Well, it wouldn't do to have tossed them onto the sidewalk as we drove by, Your Grace."

"Stop with that. We're not in Saint Gilbert, and I'm not your grace." My words came out sounding more harshly than I'd intended. "I'm sorry. This whole thing, the past week, has been . . ." I didn't even have words.

"I understand, Annaliese." His voice was soft and, I don't know, so sincere that I felt tears forming in my eyes. "You know what I and so many others are hoping, but I will not press you. I know there are many factors to be considered, and I trust you to make your decision, whatever it may be, for the right reasons. Take what time you need. Let me just say that I hope you enjoyed your stay with us as much as we enjoyed having you. You know how to contact me once you know what you want to do. I would ask only that you give serious consideration to what we've offered you. And if your desire is to decline, you let us know in order we might begin our search for an alternative. But whatever you do, know you have earned our respect and our deepest regard, and that you were always our plan A."

I barely trusted my voice, but I was able to squeak out, "I'll do my best not to make you wait too long. I promise."

"That is all we ask." His eyes were locked on mine the entire conversation, and sensing there was little more to say, Max took my hand. He brushed his lips across my knuckles, lingering several beats longer than was most likely necessary. "Goodbye, Annaliese."

"Thank you for everything, Max. No matter what happens, I'll never forget my time in Saint Gilbert." I took a deep breath. "I'll never forget you."

"Nor I, you." He smiled—somewhat reluctantly, I thought, but maybe that was just me wanting him to feel the same things I was feeling. He bowed slightly from his waist, then turned and left. I watched him get into the car and raised my hand to wave goodbye to John-Paul and Marcel, who took one look back at me. We'd said our goodbyes in the car, but honestly, I was going to miss them, too. They always came off like a couple of big lugs, but they'd grown on me.

"Well, that was some sweet sorrow." Ceil joined me at the front door and waved at the car as it pulled away. The windows were tinted, so it was hard to tell if anyone saw her or waved back.

Long after there was nothing left to see, I closed the door and slumped against it.

Chapter Seventeen

"You look like crap," Ceil told me. "Come into the kitchen. I'll make coffee, and you can unload it all on me."

"It's too soon to unload," I said, my back still to the door. "And no offense, but the coffee in Saint Gilbert has ruined me for the bargain brand I buy."

"Too bad." She grabbed me by the arm, walked me into the dining room, and deposited me in a chair. "You're back to reality, duchess. But I brought my coffee with me, and it's a hell of a lot better than yours."

"Okay, then." My elbows were on the table, and without Mom there to chastise me, I didn't care. "Where are the kids?"

"I made them go to school today since we weren't sure what time you'd be back. They have exams next week, and I didn't want to give them an excuse if they don't do well." Ceil walked into the kitchen.

"Excellent move. Are you sure you never had kids?" I called after her.

"Positive, but I have a sister who has two firecrackers, and I learn fast." I could hear Ceil pouring water into the coffee maker.

"How were they? Did they give you a hard time?"

"Nah. They save that for you."

The water was dripping into the pot, and I could smell the coffee as it began to brew. If I'd had more energy, I'd have gotten up and dug through my suitcase to find the bags of coffee I'd brought home with me.

Minutes later, Ceil came into the dining room carrying a tray that held two mugs of coffee, two spoons, a container of half-and-half, and a couple of pink packs of sweetener.

"Now spill." She handed me a mug and a spoon. "Start wherever you want, but start."

I spilled as I sipped. I told her everything, showing her pictures on my phone to illustrate a point now and then. I talked and cried and laughed and remembered. Even knowing I was going to have to repeat it all to Roe and the kids, I spilled it all.

"There's something different about you." Ceil studied my face and poured a second round of coffee into our mugs. "Not sure what it is. But your face . . ."

"Fatigue? Stress? By the way, this coffee is better than mine, thank you. Still not Saint Gilbert phenomenal, but better. I did bring home some of the great stuff, but it's buried in the suitcase."

"I can't wait to try it, but don't change the subject. You were stressed before you left."

I shrugged. "Stress is stress. Oh, I have something for you."

I went into the living room and opened my carry-on bag and took out the soaps in the pretty wrappings I bought in the gift shop in Beauchesne.

"This is the coolest soap," I told her. "They make it in Saint Gilbert with goat milk. Like an idiot, I left my face wash and moisturizer at home, but after a day or so, I didn't miss them. This soap didn't dry my skin at all."

"It's pretty." She sniffed it. "And it has such a nice light fragrance. Sort of like . . ." I waited to see if she picked up the same scent I did. "Violets. Like Gran's violets."

"I thought so, too. See the little flecks of purple in the soap?"

"I do." She sniffed it again, and she smiled. "It smells like Gran. Funny, isn't it, how scents can stay with you so long and bring back so many memories?"

"It's been scientifically proven. The sense of smell is the strongest link to memory of all the senses. Memory and emotion. Both can give you that ping of recognition from smelling something. Like the way tuna sandwiches always take me back to the lunchroom in grade school. And the smell of lilies always take me back to Dad's viewing and the grief I felt standing next to his casket." I choked back tears.

Ceil nodded. "Me too. Same memory. Every time I smell lilies I have that same overwhelming urge to vomit I felt that night. Gross but true."

We each took a moment to remember our dad and to compose ourselves.

After a moment, Ceil cleared her throat. "Anyway, I find it hard to believe you haven't used anything on your face but this soap. Your skin looks really good. *Really* good. Way better than when you left." She leaned closer. "Your crow's-feet are almost gone."

"I know. I guess I smile more at the office than I knew."

Just then the front door blew open and the hurricanes that were my children blew in.

"Mom's home! Mom!"

"Mom! Where are you?"

"Dining room." I got up and braced myself for the onslaught of my children. Say what you will, there's no feeling like having your kids so happy to see you that they damn near drive you into a wall.

And nothing will make your head explode quite like having them throw questions at you like fast pitches. The noise level in the room rose about a thousand percent.

Finally, "Okay, guys, I missed you both, too. So much! But let's slow down. You're going to give me a heart attack. Plus I can't talk that fast."

They each pulled up a chair and sat, and their interrogation began.

"So what was it like? Is the castle really huge and fancy? Like Cinderella's?" This from Juliette.

"What's the city like? Are there a lot of hot girls? Is there a soccer team?" This from guess who. "All countries have soccer teams, right? Can I try out if I'm the prince?"

And so on until it was time for dinner, which Roe was bringing. Once she arrived, we started all over yet again. My jaws and mouth were tired from so much talking and laughing. After we ate, Ralphie took my phone upstairs to print out my photos while he studied for his math exam. Juliette was almost in tears when she was denied the pleasure of sending photos of the castle around to all her friends.

"I'll send it anonymously, I promise!" she insisted.

"Nope. Not till I know what we're going to do," I reminded her. I'd only told them eighty-five times over dinner that I didn't know what that was going to be.

"But . . ."

"Stop. Let it go for now."

"But, Mom, you have to say yes. We have to live in that castle." She draped her arms around my shoulders and whispered, "I really, really, really want to be a princess."

"I know, sweet pea. But there are other factors that have to go into my decision."

"Like what?" My son came back downstairs and raised an eyebrow, like there could be any decision other than *Yes! We're going to Saint Gilbert to live in a castle!*

"For one thing, you won't see your father except maybe for visits on holidays," I began.

My son blew that off with a snort. "Which is different from when we see him now how?"

The boy had me there. "Okay, but your friends . . ."

"Will all be going to different colleges in another year anyway." He smirked devilishly. "But none of them will be a prince."

"I'd have to give up my job, which is a position I've had to work long and hard for."

I had. That old saying, a woman has to work twice as hard to be thought half as good as a man? Yeah. Alive and well.

"Your job gives you migraines, Mom," Juliette added. "You always say if you won the lottery, you'd quit in a Broad Street minute."

"Do you mean Broadway minute?" Ceil asked.

"Philly style, Aunt Ceil." Juliette kissed me and both aunts and picked up her book bag, which she'd dropped on the floor. She started out of the room, then turned and asked, "Is there a high school in Saint Gilbert, or will we have a private tutor?"

"Go study for your exams." I pointed toward the steps, and the two of them headed upstairs, whispering to each other. I turned to my sisters and said, "They're plotting a full-out attack. They think they can wear me down."

"Will they?" Roe asked. "'Cause it sounds to me like you really liked the place."

"I did," I admitted. "Actually, I loved it. It's impossible not to. The country is beautiful, the people are charming and friendly and welcoming, and the accommodations were out of this world. I never expected to be treated the way they treated me there, not even in my wildest imagination. The food was fabulous and the wine delicious. Then there was the matter of our family. The history. Our great-grandparents' tragic story. How they knew they were going to be murdered and how they plotted to secure the throne for their family. They were so brave and so smart. Roe, you stand there on their graves and you feel so *connected*."

"You stood on their graves?" Roe wrinkled her nose. "That's kinda crass, don't you think? And I'm pretty sure it's bad luck."

Ceil and I both rolled our eyes at the same time.

"I guess you had to be there to appreciate it," I said, dismissing her comments.

"I'm sure they were happy that one of their descendants made a point to seek out their graves and acknowledge them. Annie"—Ceil turned to me—"did you pray for them?"

I nodded. "I did."

"On your knees?" Roe asked.

"Of course."

"There you go." Ceil threw up her hands. "I bet they were thrilled. Assuming they were someplace where they knew what was happening."

"True," Roe conceded. "I'll bet no one even thinks about them anymore."

"Au contraire. They are well remembered. Revered," I told her. "And I even met people who remembered Gran and shared their wonderful memories of her."

I repeated all the stories my jet-lagged brain could remember, and when Ralphie came downstairs with a stack of photos in hand, I took them on a photo tour of Saint Gilbert and the castle. I showed them the portraits, explaining who everyone was as best as I could recall. I admit after a while my brain and my mouth weren't synced as well as they could have been, but they got the idea. They pored over the photos, and seeing their reactions to the gowns and the jewels was epic. Like, jaws-dropped epic.

"Wow!" Roe's eyes were wide and round. "The crown jewels! Did you get to try them on?"

"No, those are still in a vault in Switzerland." I explained our great-grandparents' plan to keep the country's wealth from being plundered, which everyone agreed had been brilliantly clever. "I don't think they ever imagined it would be so many years before there'd be an heir." I tapped the photos. "They hid furniture and paintings and other valuables in secret rooms in the castle."

"Secret rooms? That's so cool! Mom, you have to say yes." Juliette, who'd followed her brother downstairs, pulled a photo from the pile. "I need to wear this tiara to my prom."

"Baby, there is no freshman prom," I reminded her.

"Oh. Right." Her expression darkened, then a moment later brightened again. "I could come back for junior prom with my class, right? I could wear it then. Or I could wear it for a prom there, in Saint Gilbert. There has to be a school there. They must have . . ."

My head began to split open, and what was left of my brain started to leak out onto the table. "Enough for tonight. Guys, I have to go to bed. I can't even think anymore." I kissed everyone good night, then went into the living room to head for the stairs. My suitcase still stood in the middle of the room, another reminder I'd been away and now was home. I called the kids and gave them the chocolates I'd brought back, and Ralphie carried my suitcase upstairs. Roe left, and Ceil decided she'd stay over and leave the next day. We argued over who got to sleep in my bed—where she'd been sleeping all week—and who would sleep on the sofa. She insisted the sofa was fine—it was a sleeper sofa, but we rarely opened it. I gave up and went upstairs, undressed, and went straight to bed.

I was so happy to be in my own bed again, I barely had time to appreciate the feeling before I fell into a deep sleep. I didn't bother to set an alarm. After all, I got up with the kids every morning like clockwork, right? Not this time. It was almost eleven when I woke the next day. Thank God Ceil was still there to get the kids off to school, though they probably would have been okay on their own. They might have balked at having to spend their own money for lunch, though. When I finally got my act together, I went downstairs and found Ceil working on one of her design projects at the dining room table.

"I made scones," she said without looking up. "They're on the pan on top of the stove."

"Thank you, God," I said. "Oh, yum! Cranberry-orange! My fave. Thank you, Ceil." I poured a cup of the coffee she'd made, placed two scones on a small plate, and stood in the doorway between the kitchen and dining room. "Let me know when you want to take a break."

"Two minutes. I just want to . . ." She was shaking her head, looking at the room she'd been designing. "Oh, yeah. The black-and-white check for the window treatments. Definitely."

A few minutes later she looked up. "I can break now for a few."

"Come in and talk to me." I sat at the kitchen table, and after she poured herself a fresh mug of coffee, she sat across from me. "I can never repay you for staying with the kids, Ceil. If I'd had to worry about them with everything else that was going on . . ."

"You've already thanked me. It was my pleasure. It really was. I'll stay with them anytime."

"So bring me back to reality. Tell me what's been going on around here while I was gone. What did I miss?" I hadn't heard any local gossip in a week, and I was pretty sure I was entering a state of withdrawal.

"There was one thing." Ceil's eyes had a wicked sparkle, a sure sign that something of note had happened. "The day after you left, Karen Bustamonte died."

"She *died*?" My chin all but hit the table.

"Yeah, not to be confused with *dyed*."

Ceil. The punster. A chip off the old block.

Karen Bustamonte owned a local hair salon, Do Me, Do My Roots, on Broad Street. I have it on good authority that she was doing Ralph Senior within six months after we'd said "I do," but I guess that was old news. Everyone in the neighborhood knew she'd been a . . . how to put this delicately? She'd been paid for her "companionship," which is how she earned the money for the down payment on her shop. She'd been married . . . I dunno, five times? I'd lost track.

"How did she die?"

"She was hit by a garbage truck that was backing up while she was crossing Broad Street at seven in the morning. Tied up traffic for hours while they picked all the trash off her."

After a long moment of silence during which time both of us, I'm sure, were mentally picturing the scene, I asked, "So did you go to the viewing?"

"I wasn't going to, but Ralphie said he went to grade school with Karen's son Joey, and how he felt bad about it, and how he was pretty sure Joey'd show up if that had happened to you, so yeah, I took Ralphie." She took a sip of coffee. "I thought it would be okay with you."

"Yeah, it's okay." It was nice of Ralphie, who always did have a soft spot for his old friends. "Thanks for taking him. I'm sure Joey appreciated it."

"Everyone asked where you were," she said. "I told them you were away for a week on business. Technically, not a lie. Family business is business."

I nodded and took a bite of a scone. "True enough. And this is delicious, by the way."

"Thanks. So what do you think you're going to do?"

"I don't know. I really liked it there."

"Duh. Castle life."

"That was part of it, I'm not gonna lie. But it was everything. The history, the church, the lake, the shops, the countryside. And oh, Ceil, there are castles just waiting to be renovated. Right up your alley. And the hillsides—a chateau here, a farm there. And the food! I drool every time I think about the food. The wine . . . dear Lord, the wine. And the people . . . so friendly, so open and kind. So . . . patiently waiting for the American to come and turn things around." This last was a downer for me. "I'm damned if I don't go, and I'll be damned if I do go and I can't make anything good happen."

I took a few more bites of the scone. "Except of course I'd bring back a lot of money that's been sitting in a Swiss bank since 1941."

"I know I said it last night when you talked about that, but that really was pretty clever. At least it couldn't be stolen."

"Yeah, but if I don't go back and get crowned, the money stays there until they can find someone else. Honestly, I'm between a rock and a hard place." The scone went down in one last bite. I eyed the second one hungrily.

"You don't have to make a decision right now. Take some time and think it over. What's going to make you happy? What's best for the kids? What's best for the people of Saint Gilbert?"

"Well, obviously, it's best for them if I go back and make sure all that money's returned. It would mean new roads, schools, a bigger hospital. Crap, maybe even an airport. And I'm still not convinced there isn't some way to market the country to bring in tourists. It's a beautiful place that no one's ever heard of. I think once people find out about it, they'll want to go."

"Where are the photos Ralphie printed out?" Ceil asked. "I want to look again."

I went upstairs and retrieved the stack of pictures and handed them to Ceil when I went back down. She went slowly through the pack, paying closest attention to the countryside scenes.

"I could see marketing destination weddings at those castles once they're renovated." Ceil got a faraway look in her eyes, and I could see the wheels start to turn. "Think of what *that* could bring into the country. We could do an entire campaign around weddings alone. What starry-eyed girl wouldn't want to get married in a castle? We also could market the castle as a B&B to groups—corporate retreats, girl getaways, family reunions—and offer wine and cheese tours as part of a package."

She sat quietly, tapping her finger on the side of her mug, and I knew what that meant: she had something she wanted to say, but she didn't really want to say it.

"Okay, enough of the tapping already. Spill."

"I know it's strictly your choice, and I will respect whatever you decide to do, I swear it. But . . ."

"But . . ." Honest to God, sometimes it was like pulling teeth.

"But I was just thinking. You have the chance to do something that will change people's lives probably for generations. How often does that happen? Even if the only thing you do there is fix the roads, that's still making the place better than you found it."

I broke the second scone in half and put both pieces on the plate before I looked up at my sister.

"If I give up my life here to go there, I'm damn well going to do more than build a couple of roads."

Chapter Eighteen

On Monday, it was back to the salt mine we call PFCLIC. Getting up and dressed for work, driving out of the city via the expressway and into the county, it felt as if my week in Saint Gilbert had never happened. Like the trip, the castle, the people. Max—like none of it had been real at all. Like I'd stepped out of my life for a little while, and now I was stepping back in.

I pulled into a parking place in front of the building and turned off the radio and that morning's discussion of the latest Eagles trade and last night's Phillies game. I grabbed my coffee and my bag, and got out of the car, as I'd done a thousand times before. Walked into the building, past the reception desk, grateful that Debbie wasn't in yet so I didn't have to stop and talk. I loved her, but I just wasn't ready for the whole "how was your vacation" chitchat.

On to my cubicle where I found stacks of files on my desk, some with notes, some with bills that needed my authorization to pay. I sat down and within minutes my phone rang, and it was the same old, same old, like I'd never left. Nothing had changed at all. I glanced at the pile of phone messages and pushed them to the side of my desk. There was no one I really wanted to talk to.

It really was depressing. I'd pinned the falcon Max had given me onto the collar of my blouse that morning, and every once in a while, my fingers found it.

Around ten thirty, Marianne came into my cube. While I finished up the call I was on, she moved the files from my visitor's chair, sat, and waited for me to hang up.

"So, what, you couldn't tell me you were taking vacation?" she asked the second the call disconnected.

"It was a spur of the moment thing. But you're right. I should have told you. I'm sorry I didn't." Actually, I was sorry I couldn't, but that wasn't the same thing.

"So how'd you spend your week? I tried calling you a few times, but for some reason the calls wouldn't go through. I thought you'd have called at least once while you were off." She pulled her chair closer to my desk. "Tell me you didn't have a secret rendezvous with some tall, dark, and handsome someone."

Close, but not exactly the type of rendezvous she had in mind.

I forced a laugh. "No, just some R and R. You know."

She narrowed her eyes and stared at my face. "R and R my ass. You went to a spa. Dammit, why didn't you tell me? I'd have gone with you."

"What? No! Like I could afford a week at a spa."

"Annie, the lines around your eyes are gone. So are the elevens between your eyes. So you had Botox. You can admit it. No judgment."

"Mare, I didn't have work done on my face." My fingers went to the space where my eleven-lines used to be. I say used to be because I couldn't feel them, which was odd because they'd been so deep, I'd started referring to them as the Mariana Trench. "And you know I'm such a wuss; the last thing I'd let someone do is stick needles in my face."

Marianne pulled a small mirror from her bag and handed it to me. I took a good, long look.

"I guess I should take more time off. Just one week away from all the stress around here . . ." From the cubicle next to mine, my fellow examiner was screaming at someone on the phone. I nodded in that direction. "Point proven. You're in underwriting, Mare. You don't deal with the assholes we have to deal with."

"You know, you've taken time off before, and you didn't come back looking this good. You look almost . . . radiant." She was staring again. "Actually, you look like you've been having really good sex. A *lot* of really good sex."

Nothing forced about my laugh after that.

"No. *Hell* no. No surgery. No Botox. No spa. And definitely no sex, good, bad, or otherwise."

"So where did you go? What were you doing that you couldn't get a phone call?"

I debated whether to tell her the truth—I was dying to tell her the truth—but the phone rang, and I was literally saved by the bell. "We'll catch up later," I told her. "Let me take this call . . ."

I managed to avoid her through lunch by not taking the allotted hour, for which I had a legit excuse (all those files and phone calls to catch up on), and I was on the phone when she stuck her head into my cubicle at five. She whispered, "Call me," and I nodded. I still hadn't figured out what I'd tell her, but I knew I had to tell her something.

Driving home, all I could think about was the decision I had to make. I'd talked to Ceil again that morning before I left the house, and it was clear what she thought I should do. Ceil is always thinking about the other guy, so of course the first thing she'd think of is how I had an opportunity to impact an entire country and do good things for the people living there.

It felt strange returning to the routine of work, eat, sleep, and repeat, but that's how the next couple of weeks felt, except I had to come up with a story to tell Marianne. So I told her I'd gone to see some family of my mom's in Nebraska I hadn't met before who I'd just learned about—sort of the truth—and she seemed okay with that. I hated lying, but when the time came I could tell her the truth, she'd be okay with it.

While I still loved everything about my life I'd loved before I went to Saint Gilbert, it was pretty hard not to see that my time was spent focused on myself and my kids and little else. What was I going to focus on a few years from now when the kids were off to college? It wouldn't be too long before my nest was empty.

And then there was the fact that I was missing Max more than I expected—a fact I didn't feel I could discuss with anyone, not even Ceil. I'd spent so much time with the man, we'd developed what I'd thought of as, at best, a special relationship, and at the least, a good rapport. I wondered if he thought of me, too. I'd never felt that deep a connection to any man, not even—here I am tempted to make a joke, but I'll let it go—the one I married.

"You know, you've been at work for two weeks, and the lines you used to have on your face—the ones you attributed to work stress—still haven't come back," Ceil observed on Friday night while we waited for Roe to arrive with dinner. Both kids were out—the all-grades dance at the high school. They'd left the house arguing over whether Juliette's friends were too young for Ralphie and if his friends were too old for Jules.

"It's just a matter of time before they do." I looked closer at her face. "But are you using something new on your skin?"

She shook her head. "Just the soap you brought me. Why?"

"You skin looks . . ." I thought back to what Marianne had said to me, then got up and looked in the mirror hanging over the sideboard. My eyes met Ceil's in the glass. "Radiant. Like you've been having a lot of great sex."

"Ah no. Regrettably, no. Just your soap." She got up and stood next to me in front of the mirror. "Although we do both look . . ."

"Pretty damned good."

"Younger."

The front door opened and closed with a slam. "I'm here and I brought dinner," Roe called from the front room. She came into the dining room with a large white bag. "Capellini with spring vegetables and ham. The sauce is to die for. And yes, I made it myself because Albert was . . ." She paused and glanced from Ceil to me and back again. "Why are you two standing in front of the mirror? That's so weird."

Ceil and I stared at Roe, then looked at each other.

"Roe, come here," Ceil beckoned her.

"I have to put this down in the kitchen, then I'll . . . ," Roe began, and Ceil cut her off.

"Put the bag on the table and come here," Ceil told her.

For once, Roe did as she was told. "What?" she asked when she joined us.

Ceil and I studied her face.

I took a step closer. "You've been using the soap I brought you."

"Well, yeah. Wasn't that the idea?" Roe backed away from our scrutiny.

"Have you taken a good look at your face recently?" I asked.

"Like I have time to stand around and stare at my face?" she scoffed. "Unlike some of us."

"Roe, take a good look at yourself." I pointed to the mirror.

Roe exhaled loudly and frowned, but she looked in the mirror anyway. She stared for a very long moment before touching her reflection. "Something's different."

"There's hardly a line on your face," Ceil pointed out.

Roe continued to stare. She looked at Ceil, then at me. "You two as well." She leaned almost into my face to get closer. "You had those lines like Mom had. Huh." She touched the space between my eyes. "But they're gone. And the lines at the corners of Ceil's mouth . . ."

"The soap," Ceil and I said at the same time.

"That has to be it," I said, "if none of us has had Botox or some other treatment."

They both shook their heads.

"There has to be something in it," Ceil said. "Maybe it's the violets."

"I don't know what they put in it, other than goat milk and violets," I admitted. "But I told you I didn't see one single person in Saint Gilbert who had so much as a frown line." I turned away from the mirror. "I mean, even old people. Like in their eighties and better. Everyone there has this gorgeous skin, men and women, and looked years—*decades*—younger than they were. And the funny thing was, everyone acted like it was no big deal. Like the women I talked to hadn't even noticed how fabulous their skin looked. When I asked them what they used on their faces, they said just soap."

"If that's it—if it's something in the soap you brought back . . ." Ceil's eyes went wide as she grabbed my arm. "They're sitting on a gold mine."

Ceil and Roe started talking excitedly at the same time, and I covered my ears. I hadn't seen much of any industry in Saint Gilbert, but this could be a turning point in the country's fortunes. If this soap could erase lines in my forty-four-year-old face in a week, imagine what it could do for women—and men—in their sixties, seventies, and beyond.

Wait. I'd already seen what it could do.

"Maybe we're jumping the gun. Maybe we're just imagining this," Ceil said.

"Yeah. Maybe this is sort of like mob hysteria." Roe.

"So maybe we need to test it out a little more." I sat at the table and thought how best to do that. "I still have the bars Claudette gave me. Maybe if we get a few other people to try it . . ."

My sisters nodded.

"I'll give a bar to Marianne. She commented on my skin the first day I was back." I bit the inside of my cheek while I thought this through. "She has those lines from her nose to the side of her mouth." I traced an invisible line to make my point. "If they go away, we'll have to agree, we could have something."

"If you have extra, I'll give a bar to my landlady. She's about ninety." Roe had a tendency to exaggerate. I'd met her landlady. She was twelve years older than me.

"I can give a bar to my assistant, if you have enough," Ceil offered. "She's your age, Annie, but she looks a lot older."

"I have enough to go around. I'd bought some and Claudette gave me some before I left. I think I'll call Marianne and see if she's planning on going to the market tomorrow and if we could meet up for lunch."

"Will you tell her where the soap came from?" Ceil asked.

"I think I'm going to have to. She's my best friend, and I've been holding out on her and it's killing me."

"So tell her. She'll be excited for you," Ceil said.

And dear God, was she ever!

I was so glad I was smart enough to not have that conversation in the office. She squealed so loudly the woman in the booth behind us dropped her fork on the floor.

"Shhh." I looked around to see who'd turned to look at us. Enough that I knew we had to lower our voices. "Mare, listen to me. I don't want anyone to know about this. At least until there's some decision made. It's a secret, okay? We can't talk about it at work. Which is why we're having this conversation now."

"Okay. Okay. I'm good. I'm calm. But honest to God, Annie . . ." She patted one hand over her heart. "This is the wildest thing I ever heard."

"Believe me, I know."

"Did you take pictures?"

"I did." I pulled out the few I'd stuck in my bag that morning and put them on the table. "See, this is—"

"Oh my God." The words came out in a whisper of reverence. "It's a castle. It's a real castle." She glanced from the photo to me. "This is the place where your grandmother was born? You stayed here?"

I nodded. We went through each of the photos, and when we finished, she wanted to see them again. Then she stacked them like you'd stack a pack of playing cards and said, "I don't understand why you're even hesitating."

"A number of reasons." I reached out for the photos, and she pulled them back.

"Is this where the spa was?" she asked.

I laughed and she handed over the pictures. "No spa." Not yet, anyway. "Which reminds me. I brought you a little present from Saint Gilbert." I found the bar of soap in my bag and handed it to her. "This is made there. This is all I had to use the entire time I was there because I'd left my face wash home."

"You used soap on your face? Every woman over the age of twenty knows that's a no-no."

I returned the photos to the zippered compartment in my bag. "Did I come back looking wrinkled and dried?"

"No," she admitted. "You looked pretty good." She narrowed her gaze. "Still do, actually."

"What you said was I looked like I'd had a lot of really good sex," I reminded her.

"And this was all you used? You swear it, Annie?"

I crossed my heart. "I swear."

"Huh." She sniffed the soap. "Smells pretty good."

"Just use it. Promise. Nothing else but this. No face wash, no creams, no serums." I reached across the table and tapped the soap. "Just this."

She studied my face for a minute before nodding. "Okay. Yeah, I promise. What the hell? At least I'll smell good."

~

Within five days there was a noticeable difference on Marianne's face, and trust me, I looked carefully every single day. By Thursday morning, it was pretty clear that the soap was doing its thing for Mare. That night, when Ceil and Roe both reported in that the women they'd given the soap to had the same results—nothing dramatic in that short amount of time, but diminished facial lines—we knew we were onto something. I wasn't sure what was in that soap, but it was powerful.

I thought of Claudette and her flawless face, and I immediately thought of a spa where all the products were made from . . . whatever it is the soap is made from. I imagined women—and men—from all over the world opting for a few weeks in Saint Gilbert instead of a surgeon's knife or an injection of something into their faces. Ceil was right: Saint Gilbert was sitting on gold. And I was pretty sure I knew how to mine it.

Which was the moment I decided to trade my South Philly row house for a castle in Saint Gilbert.

~

In fairness to my kids, I had to wait until the school year had ended to even tell them what I'd decided. I thought they should finish taking their exams and Ralphie should go to his prom. Who knew what would happen in the long run? If we ended up coming back to Philly for whatever reason, I wanted to make sure everything was smooth for them with school. But on the day after our soap revelation, I called Max on my cell from my car.

"I hope this call brings good news," he said after we'd finished our initial greetings.

I couldn't even put into words how good it was to hear his voice again.

"I hope so. I mean, I hope it works out well for everyone." I took a deep breath. "I'd like to come back if you still want me. I mean, if the council or the country or . . ."

He fell silent for a moment, and I wondered if they'd started a search for someone else and came up with a better candidate.

"Annaliese, are you sure?"

"As sure as I can be. I think."

I could feel his smile through the phone, and it made me want to weep. "You've no idea how happy you have made me." He added quickly, "And of course everyone who's been waiting to hear from you, Your Grace."

"Don't start with that already."

He laughed. "You'll get used to it, I promise. But only, as you wish, in public. I'll try to remember. So when can we come for you?"

I explained to him about the kids' school schedule and that I wasn't telling them until after school was out for the summer in a few weeks, but I thought we could probably wrap things up here by the end of May.

"Please, can we keep this between us? Just for a little while longer? I don't want it to become public and somehow get back to the kids until I tell them."

"I will need to tell the members of the Duke's Council," he said, "but I will ask them to consider your situation and to respect your wishes. I feel certain they'll be more than happy to comply. Our country's been without our royal family for so many years, another few weeks should not matter."

We talked about dates and logistics and I don't even remember what, because my heart was pounding so loudly in my ears, I missed half of what he was saying. After we'd hung up, all I knew was the date of our departure had been set and I'd promised Max I'd talk to my sisters about making the trip with me. I couldn't imagine either of them would decline the invitation.

Neither did.

Ceil had just enough time to finish up work she was doing for a client, and Roe had time to help her boss find a replacement for her.

I'd planned on keeping the whole thing under wraps so we could make our departure as quietly as possible. But as the saying goes, man plans, God laughs.

I planned to meet with my boss at the end of the week, at which time I'd hand him my resignation along with my two weeks' notice. I was still rehearsing what I was going to say when my cell rang.

"Oh my God! Mom!" Juliette was shrieking. "We were in English class and Mr. Porterfield read news from his phone, and it said that you're the duchess and that we're going to live there in the castle and . . ."

Off she went, breathless and babbling. I leaned against the wall, wondering what had happened. Who'd released the story to the press? I felt certain it wasn't Max, but apparently someone on the council couldn't keep his mouth shut. "And now everyone knows I'm a princess, and OMG you should have seen the look on Tiffany Stout's face. It was . . . it was . . . *awesome*. It was the best moment of my *life*."

A click on my phone indicated a call was waiting. Ralphie. I hung up with Jules and listened to more of the same from my son. No, I didn't know how the story got out. There was no way to deny it, so I told Ralphie we'd talk about it when he got home but, in the meantime, for him to downplay it as much as possible. As if.

I walked into Lenny Scott's office and sat on one of the two chairs that had been placed directly in front of his desk in such a way that you had to look him straight in the eye. Yuck. Anyway, the news had preceded me, even here.

He held up his phone and said, "This really you?"

I didn't need to see what was on the screen to know what he was referring to. Reluctantly, I nodded.

"Really? Wow. Is that crazy or what? How long have you known?" And off he went on a stream of questions, none of which I got to answer because he was talking so fast. Easily as fast as Ralphie, though Juliette still had them both beat when it came to speed-speech.

"So I guess you'll be leaving us. Damn. Who'd ever have guessed you were a *royal duchess?*"

After he came back to earth, we agreed on a last day for me—that would be that very day, since we both knew the interest generated locally if not nationally soon would prohibit any work from being done in any department, so I might as well leave right then before the television crews started showing up.

A glance out the window behind him proved we were already late on that score.

I went back to my cube to gather my things, still feeling jumbled. I packed my personal belongings—the pictures of my kids, my philodendron and Boston fern, both of which were doing supremely well, an old pair of running shoes from when Marianne and I were walking the parking lot at morning and afternoon break times to try to drop a few winter pounds—then I picked up the phone and called Marianne to tell her I'd been publicly outed on social media.

But too late. She'd just walked into my office.

"I'm so happy for you. You're going to be such a kick-ass duchess." She gave me one big squeeze, then held me at arm's length. "Do I get to come to the coronation, and where can I get some more of that soap?"

Chapter Nineteen

The sheer act of getting everyone and everything ready to travel from Philly to Saint Gilbert with my sanity intact was a feat I would not like to repeat. There were so many decisions to make and things to do before we left. Like what to do about my house. Maybe we'd be back in six months. Maybe we'd never live here again. The truth is I couldn't bear to sell it. I bought that place all by myself, and I was crazy proud of that fact. I decided the way to go was to find a renter until I had a better feel for what was going to happen. So we left it furnished, packed up our clothes and personal items, and shipped it all to Saint Gilbert.

Juliette reminded me we needed to go shopping, since none of us—least of all her—had what could be described as a wardrobe fit for a princess. Or a duchess, come to think of it. But it wasn't as easy as it sounded. There were reporters camped out across the street from our house. I'd started having my groceries delivered because I couldn't step outside without having microphones shoved in my face. Cameras followed Ceil and Roe everywhere, and the kids were getting accosted wherever they went. And just try keeping a kid in the house when the weather was great and school was out for the summer. Max, Jean-Paul, and Marcel returned to Philly to act as both security and runners and drove us into Center City and out to King of Prussia to get in some necessary shopping. They'd brought a small cadre of guards with them, several of whom accompanied my kids and my sisters wherever they went, which thrilled the kids beyond reason that they had their own security detail, but my sisters, not so much. Ceil found it cumbersome to have people trailing her whenever she left her apartment, and Roe found it annoying.

"Get used to it," I told them all. "This is nothing compared to the security you're going to have in Saint Gilbert."

Max handled a lot of the interviews early on but finally convinced me that I had to face the cameras myself at least once before leaving the country. So I did. I stood on my front steps and answered questions as best I could. It seems I wasn't the only one who'd had those princess fantasies as a little girl, because almost every woman reporter I spoke with confessed on the sly that I was living her dream.

At the last minute, I reluctantly agreed to make a few trips to New York to appear on all the morning television shows. The interviews were all easier and more pleasant than I'd expected. I really hadn't wanted to do any of them—I was nervous, and I was afraid I'd come off looking like a tongue-tied dork, but Ceil and Roe both watched and said I came across as being very relatable. Which I suppose meant almost the same thing as dorky, but okay. I tried to be as pleasant as I could, because it occurred to me that once we started marketing Saint Gilbert—and that fabulous soap—I'd want *GMA* and all the others on my side. So I went and I faked being relaxed and told the story over and over and over. Everyone wanted to hear it.

The kids were especially happy about the spread in *People* magazine because they were in it. And every interview, I talked about how beautiful Saint Gilbert was and how everyone would have to plan a visit so they could see the castle and the city and the countryside. Ceil was already planning on selling Saint Gilbert as the most romantic spot on earth for a wedding. We'd have to see how that played out, but she was pretty convincing.

Keep in mind all this happened in less than two weeks. Was it any wonder I was eager to leave once the decision was made? Not to mention the kids were antsy to get there and see everything. I suspected Juliette couldn't wait to take pictures of herself in the castle to send back home to her friends. Ralphie had cute Saint Gilbertian girls and soccer on his mind.

On the day we were to leave for Saint Gilbert, the long black car pulled up in front of the house, and this time Marcel accompanied Max to the door. Between the two of them, they managed to fit all our travel luggage into the trunk. We were traveling light since most of our things had been sent ahead, but still, there were five of us making the trip this time. We'd had a few friends over the night before to say goodbye and promised invitations to the coronation—should there be one—to everyone except Ralph Senior and his missus. Truth be told, if I never had to look at him again, I'd be happy.

He'd come into my house—invited by our son—slapped me on the back, and said, "I always thought your mother was stuck up. Now I know why."

Before I could respond, he went on. "Look, I don't mind you making Juliette into a princess—girls love that stuff, I know—but I'm not so sure I like the idea of you taking Ralphie to another country. Like, away from my influence, surrounded by a bunch of women. I don't want you turning my son into some pansy prince. Wearing tights. That kind of shit."

You should know I'd always tried to maintain a respectful attitude toward the father of my children—only because he was their father and because I never wanted them to feel torn between us. But it took me a moment to compose myself and get past the ugliness of his remark. Honest to God, who still thought like that? It's 2023! In my job and sometimes in my neighborhood I heard rough talk. Often profanity. I could deal with that. But stupid talk like that crossed my personal line between tolerance and intolerance. I was glad Ralphie was in the kitchen.

"You're an idiot, you know that, Ralph? An insensitive idiot. Our son is who he is, and I thank God he hasn't been under your influence these past few years. As a result, he's growing into a kind, caring person who doesn't judge anyone. Yes, he'll be a prince, and whether he wears tights, soccer shorts, or a tiara, I'm good with it. As I've always been good with whoever those kids are or who they choose to be."

It could have been the fire in my eyes—or maybe the growling undertone my voice takes on when I'm really pissed off—but he backed up a few steps. Then his wife—the ever-lovely Lorraine—appeared and took him by the arm and reminded him that their twelve-year-old next-door neighbor was watching their kids and the babysitter had a curfew.

"Go say goodbye to your kids, Ralph." I started to walk away. "And don't expect an invitation to the coronation."

"Really?" Lorraine looked genuinely surprised. "Huh. I thought as parent and stepparent, we'd be invited for sure."

"Not gonna happen." I had to bite my tongue to keep from making a crack about those silver Tiffany earrings she was wearing—the ones that had disappeared from my jewelry box right about the time Ralph had started dating her—but I refrained. I made my way through the crowd to the kitchen and out the back door. I needed a few minutes to myself. I was trying to remember what I had seen in Ralph that had made me want to marry him. Nothing came to mind except the reasons why I'd wanted to unmarry him. I wondered if there was a woman alive who didn't look back on that one guy who made her ask herself, *What the hell was I thinking?*

My backyard wasn't exactly what you might think of when you think *yard*. There was no grass to speak of, and the majority of the space was a concrete pad that served as a patio. I had a small table with four chairs, and that was about it. The year we moved in, I planted perennials in the few areas that had dirt—mostly around the fence—because someone told me you could stick perennials in the ground and you didn't have to do much else except water them and they'd come back every year, and that sounded like a pretty good deal to me. Maybe I was remembering the beautiful flower beds at Gran's house. But not having much of a green thumb myself, I planted some iris and a couple of peonies and some black-eyed Susans that a friend at work gave me, and that was pretty much it. It wasn't exactly a botanical garden, but it was mine.

I sat on one of the chairs and thought about what I'd done, quitting my job and going on record as the new grand duchess. I kept going back and forth between knowing I was going to kick butt in Saint Gilbert and do a lot of great things for the people there and utter despair, fearing I'd totally overstepped and would sooner or later step in it big-time and I'd be a ginormous disappointment to everyone—my kids, my sisters, the people who held my great-grandparents in such esteem. And Max, because most of all, I felt he really believed in me, in my ability to do what needed to be done. To roll up my shirtsleeves and dig in, as he'd once said.

"Second thoughts?" Ceil said as she stepped outside.

"Yes. No." I shrugged. "I don't know."

She stood behind me and massaged my shoulders. "You're going to be the best thing that happened to Saint Gilbert since our great-grandparents stashed the cash in a Swiss bank."

"Or its biggest disaster."

"Not a chance, sister. You're going to be great. Just remember where you heard it first."

I put one of my hands over hers and squeezed it. Even though I was two years older, Ceil has always been my champion, and I knew I'd never thanked her as much as I should have. I wanted to then, but the words logjammed in my mouth, and I just couldn't say what I wanted to.

But in true sisterly fashion, Ceil squeezed my hand in return and simply said, "I know." She kissed the top of my head. "I know, sis."

Then she pulled me out of my chair, saying, "Go back inside and thank everyone for coming. We have an early flight, and it's going to be hard enough to sleep with the trip tomorrow and everything."

And that's what I did. I thanked everyone and, with Ceil's help, sort of ushered them all to the front door. Which, upon opening, revealed Ralphie sitting between two girls on the front steps and two more sitting on the step below him. At each side of the bottom step stood a member of the black-clad castle guard. I wondered how they were managing to keep straight faces, just from the little bit of conversation I heard.

"It's so exciting to know a real prince," one of the girls cooed. "Do you think you'll come back for prom next year?"

"Well, since I won't be going to school with you guys, I guess not." He paused before adding, "Unless someone invites me."

Four voices piped up at the same time with an invitation.

"Sorry, girls, I hate to interrupt your prom plans, but I'm afraid I'm going to have to send you all home. The party's over, all these nice people behind me want to go home, and we have to be at the airport early." I stood on the top step, my arms crossed over my chest, so they all knew I meant business. Ralphie didn't bother to protest, so I figured he must be tired. "Say good night, Ralph."

The steps cleared and the adults left. It was nice that so many of our friends and friends of Mom took the time to stop over. I wished I'd had more time to chat with people, but I was exhausted. Ceil and the kids and I did a quick cleanup, loaded the dishwasher, took out the trash, and went to bed. Marianne had promised to come over on the weekend to get the house ready to be rented, which was just one of many reasons why I loved that woman like another sister. Plus the lease was up on her apartment in six weeks, and she said she'd move into the house if we hadn't found a renter by then.

One less thing to worry about, I thought as I pulled the light blanket up to my chin and started counting sheep. In an Alpine meadow. Next to a vineyard. On a hill just slightly below a chateau that my sister has big plans for, a hunky Saint Gilbertian by my side . . .

Chapter Twenty

How to describe what awaited us in Beauchesne? If I said everything but a marching band, would you get the picture? It was like the Mummers Parade on New Year's Day in Philly—without the Mummers. People actually lined the city streets to see our car arrive. Since there were five of us Max had arranged for a limo, so the ride got a little hairy on those tight mountain turns. The windows were tinted dark, but Ralphie—ever the ham—rolled down the one closest to him so he could wave to the crowd. His smiling face appeared on the front page of the city's only newspaper, and I swear he'd frame it and hang it on the wall if I let him. He was hoping someone would leak it to *People* magazine so everyone—meaning the girls from school—would see it. Eventually that did happen, and I'd never seen him so happy.

There was the drive through the castle gates and the kids and my sisters trying to take it all in at once, as I had done. Then the entry into the castle, where once again the staff lined up to greet us. But this time around, there were familiar faces in the crowd, and I greeted those I remembered and introduced myself to the ones I hadn't met, then I introduced my sisters and kids to everyone. There were a few curtsies here and there, but I was going to leave that conversation to Claudette. I couldn't help but notice there seemed to be more people gathered in the reception area than last time. Just like I couldn't help but notice the stars in my children's eyes.

Claudette was, as always, in control. She'd had our things taken to our rooms as they arrived. She'd made sure our rooms were all in the same hall so I could be close to my kids and my sisters. There was dinner in one of the smallish dining rooms, and while I remember thinking how delicious everything was, I was so jet-lagged and there was so much chatter, by the time our entrées were served, my head was spinning like one of my mom's old 45s. Shortly after dinner, I said good night to both kids in their rooms and I went to bed. I think the deliberations of the past month had taken a toll on me, and now that I'd made a decision and was actually here, in the castle, with my family, I just wanted to sleep.

Early the next morning, there was banging on my door. I wondered why Hans or Sebastian or whomever was on duty in the hallway was permitting it. Finally the door opened just a crack.

"Mom?"

"Yes, Juliette?" I sighed.

"Are you up?"

"I am now. Come on in."

Jules flitted into the room, already dressed in jeans and a nice top. She flopped onto the bed next to me.

"Mom, pinch me."

I gave her a tiny tweak.

"We're really here," she said, wide-eyed. "We slept all night in a castle."

"We are and we did." I pushed myself up onto my elbows. "Did you sleep well? Was your bed comfortable?"

"Like sleeping on a cloud." She snuggled next to me. "Don't you wonder if maybe this is an alternative reality? Like we're still back in Philly, doing our normal thing, and yet we're here at the same time?"

"Um, no. I barely have enough energy for one reality, and this is it." I smoothed her hair back from her face. "I'm going to get up and take a shower. Maybe you could ask whoever is at the door if he'll order a light breakfast for us. Berries, croissants, scones, coffee . . . you know."

"I can do that." She started toward the door, then glanced over her head. "I'm a princess. I can give orders."

"No, no," I corrected her. "Not *orders*. A princess never gives orders. She requests nicely. Politely. A princess would say something like, 'Good morning. Do you think perhaps we might have a light breakfast brought up for my mother and me?"

She nodded. "A princess is polite. Not rude. Doesn't order people around. Got it."

When I came out of the bathroom dressed for my day, the tray had already arrived, and my sisters had arrived as well. They were seated in front of the fireplace in the front room, and I joined them.

"I hope you don't mind that we crashed the party," Roe said. "But Ceil and I thought it might be nice to have a few minutes to catch our breath with you."

"I'm glad you're here." I noticed there were more coffee cups and plates than there would have been for just Juliette and me.

"When Aunt Roe and Aunt Ceil came in, I asked the guard if he would please request another tray," my daughter announced proudly. "I was very gracious."

"I'm so proud." I could feel the approval of Mom and Gran. I guess they understand how hard it is to raise polite kids in today's world.

I patted Jules's shoulder and sat next to her on the settee and poured myself a cup of that amazing Saint Gilbert coffee. I took a sip and sighed. "Oh, how I missed you," I murmured to my cup.

"I totally understand why," Ceil said. "The coffee, the fruit, the croissants—all delectable. You did not oversell any of it."

"I hope this place has a gym." Roe helped herself to what might have been her second scone. Maybe more than second since I was late coming to the party.

"I don't recall you ever going to a gym." I piled strawberries onto my plate along with a dollop of whipped cream. Heaven.

Roe shrugged. "I could never afford a membership."

"Well, I don't know if there's one now, but if not, maybe we can find some room in the budget to bring in some equipment."

Roe and Jules stared at me blankly. Finally, Roe said, "What budget? You're the duchess. You rule this place."

"Ah, I think we need to get a few things straight right off the bat." I poured a second cup of coffee while I got my thoughts in order. "The treasury is not my personal bank account. And I don't know that there's much in it right now. Frankly, I don't know the extent of the country's finances, but I intend to learn. Do we get an allowance? Do we own anything outright? I have no idea. In the meantime, please mind your best manners and treat everyone kindly and gently. Pretend Mom is looking over your shoulder." It wouldn't surprise me if she was. "We're not here to steamroll over the country or the people. We are here to help. Got it?"

"You sound just like Mom when we went to Gran's house," Roe muttered.

"Well, we *are* in Gran's house," I reminded her, then watched her face as that reality sank in.

"So what's on the agenda today?" Ceil asked.

"I'm going to be in meetings most of the day, so you guys can do what you want." I paused. "What would you like to do?"

All three spoke at the same time.

"Okay, let me start over. Ceil, would you like to go sightseeing? Travel around the country to see what's here?"

"Yes. I can't wait to see those chateaus and those desperately-in-need-of-rehabbing castles you told me about."

"I want to see the vineyards and the farms where the cheeses are made." Roe, ever the food-hound.

"I want to see everything." Juliette. So easy to please, my girl.

I walked to the door and asked Hans to see if he could get in touch with Claudette. Within minutes she was at the door. I explained what my daughter and sisters were wanting to do, and she nodded.

"I will arrange for a car and a guide, and I will alert Max so he can order security for the day," she told them. "In, shall we say, thirty minutes?"

"Perfect." I thanked her and walked her to the door. "And thank you for sending up breakfast for all of us. We all appreciated it."

"Of course, Your Grace. Will there be anything else?"

I hesitated. I wanted to sit down with a few advisors, but I wasn't sure who they would be.

"If I could speak with Max in about a half hour? In that small sitting room on the first floor?"

"He is at your service, as are we all." She turned to the others, who were listening from their seats near the fireplace. "Your Highnesses, perhaps we could gather in the reception area where we met yesterday when you arrived?"

It took a few seconds for it to sink in she was addressing them.

"That would be fine. Thirty minutes, then." Ceil stood and smiled. Roe and Juliette were still processing the fact that someone had called them *highness*.

"All will be ready for you." Claudette acknowledged the arrangement with a slight nod of her head before she left the room.

"So you have a half hour to get yourselves pulled together." I turned to my daughter. "You might ask your aunt Ceil to help you pick out something that makes you look more like a princess." When she started to protest, I reminded myself she was only fourteen, so I added, "Maybe one of those cute sundresses you bought, but even your denim skirt with a cute top would be more appropriate than jeans. Until we figure out the protocol, let's confine the jeans to the castle."

"Not to hammer home the obvious, but I believe we'll set the protocol." Roe paused. "Well, you will. There hasn't been a monarch here since 1941, so I think it's safe to say there's no precedent."

"Good point. But remember, people will be watching what you wear as well as what you do and what you say, so I'd like us all to dress nicely when we leave the castle grounds. Agreed?"

They all nodded. "So go. Drive through the countryside. Spend some time in the city. Poke into the shops. Talk to people. Learn as much as you can. Smile and be gracious and let people know you are happy to be here and that you want to be one of them."

"Aren't you coming with us?" Roe asked from the doorway.

I shook my head. "I'll catch up with you later."

Juliette asked, "What are you going to do while we're gone?"

"What I came here to do." I opened the door and shooed them out.

∼

I dressed quickly—black dress, pretty scarf, comfortable but good heels—and grabbed my leather folder from the table. Maybe Max planned to have someone accompany me, but I wasn't waiting around. I left the room, nodded good morning at Hans as I passed. At the end of the hall, I went down the steps and right to the cozy room that I'd noticed the last time I was here. Between the large drawing room and one of the dining rooms, it was small enough to feel intimate but large enough to give me space, so it didn't feel *too* intimate. I'd decided to use it as my go-to meeting and planning room. My office, until I could arrange something better.

Max was waiting for me when I opened the door, and he stood as I entered the room.

"Your Grace." He bowed slightly at the waist. "You wished to see me."

"I did," I said. "I do."

Next to the windows that faced the lake stood a table. I dropped the folder on its top and gestured for Max to come over and take a seat, which he did after he held my chair. I sat and rested my arms on the folder.

"We have things to discuss," I told him.

"Where would you like to begin?" he asked.

"Well, I know in order to get the money released from Switzerland, I have to be crowned. So how does that happen? Crowning me, I mean."

He appeared momentarily stunned. Then, "I'm afraid I don't know what the process is. I am certain there's a protocol, a ceremony of some sort, but since I've never seen one, I can't say for sure." His mouth turned up at one side in a sort of half smile. "But we can find out. There has to be something written down. Perhaps my mother knows where."

"If you could find out what we have to do, I'd appreciate it." I took my notes from the folder. "Now, I think the first thing we need to do is look at the books."

"The books?"

"The accounts. Wherever we need to look to determine how much is in the country's treasury. And we need to know the correct manner in which to approach the Swiss bank. I want whatever belongs to Saint Gilbert to be returned as soon as possible. Does anyone know exactly how much is in that bank?"

Max was looking at me as if I'd sprouted a second head.

"What?" I stared back. "Am I going too fast for you?"

He looked slightly flustered. "I'm sorry, Your Grace, but I didn't expect you to . . . to . . . what am I trying to say?"

"Come out shooting? Hit the ground running?"

He nodded. "Like that, yes."

"I've given this a lot of thought. I decided if I were to come here, it was going to be for the best reasons. And the best reason I can see is—in your words—to get this country moving. You have no international profile because you have no businesses that deal on an international level. There is no reason for tourists to come here. You have a—pardon me—crappy infrastructure. You need new roads. Your hospital looks like it's from the Middle Ages. And what condition are your schools in? We need to make people want to come here, to visit, to stay. To invest in the country, maybe even buy a first or second home. We have something they can't get anywhere else, but we'll talk about that later."

"Everything you said is true. Sad but true." He did look sad. "All that and more."

"We'll talk about the 'more' some other time. Right now, I want to go over my agenda with you so you can tell me what my first moves need to be. I have a plan, Max. We will bring this country into the twenty-first century, and we can do it in a relatively short period of time."

He raised one questioning eyebrow.

"So tell me, where do I begin?" I asked.

"I think you should first meet with the Duke's Council. Tell them you are looking forward to your coronation. That should make it official, and plans can be made."

"And the coronation itself? How soon can we do that?"

He'd taken a pen from his jacket pocket and tapped it against the palm of his left hand. "Again, speak with my mother. If she doesn't know, she can find out. She will be more than happy to assist you in organizing the coronation and whatever that entails."

"I will do that. We clearly need an event planner, and I don't know anyone else who knows more about the monarchy than your mother." I made a note on the pad I took from my folder: talk to Claudette re. coronation. And a hairdresser. One who can tend to my roots. I'd had them done before I left Philly, but those suckers grow out fast.

"You mentioned you had an agenda. A plan . . ."

I shared the details with him—*all* the details—and when I finished, he sat back in his chair, silent for a moment. Then a smile spread across his face.

"Remarkable. Ambitious. Certainly challenging. But quite possibly all doable."

"I thought so." Yes, I did feel smug. "So let's begin. Will you ask the other dukes to meet with me?"

"Generally, the chancellor is charged with convening the council. Under the circumstances, it might be best if you handwrite a letter to him yourself and ask him to call for a meeting at the earliest possible time."

"That's Vincens?"

"Yes. One of his official duties is to be one of your chief advisors."

"Okay, then. Vincens it is." I thought for a moment. While I had—for the moment, anyway—chosen Max as my primary counsel, I had to leave the door open to consider other options should it turn out that he had an agenda of his own. Was I wrong to put my trust in one man? My gut told me I could trust him, but still, how well did I know him? He was the first person I met, and the one who'd been sent to find me and convince me to come to Saint Gilbert. I really didn't know anyone else on the council other than Vincens DellaVecchio. Could I trust him? I didn't think so, chancellor or not. Maybe in time he would prove me wrong, or someone else might step up, but right now, Max was all I had. "Could you give me a list of everyone who's on the council? Your mother mentioned names to me once, but I don't remember them."

"If you have something upon which I could write . . ."

I took a yellow legal pad from the folder and handed it to him. While Max wrote, I got up and looked out the window. The distance to the lake was at least a football field. The water was almost the same blue as the sky, and it looked so peaceful. I still couldn't believe I was here, that I was doing what I was doing. In for a dime, in for a dollar, my dad used to say. Well, I was in, all right.

Max completed the list in a remarkably short time.

I looked over his shoulder at what he'd written. "Why are there only seven people on the Duke's Council?"

"There's been attrition over the past few years. We lost several senior members due to . . . well, old age, basically. In past years, before my time, perhaps there'd been more. How many do you think there should be?"

"I don't know. More than seven, I would think." I frowned as I scanned the names.

"There had been eight, but we lost our most senior member to pneumonia earlier in the year, right after the referendum."

"So there's at least one vacancy," I noted. "Can you tell me about these people? Whatever you know? I know I've met a few, but I don't know them."

"Of course." I sat down and pulled my chair closer to his, and he ran down the list while I made notes. This one was ancient and ornery. That one was affable but not very bright. This next one argued with everyone for any reason. And so on. I had to admit, by the time he'd finished, I was uneasy. This group didn't bode well for the future I had envisioned for Saint Gilbert, but maybe I was overreacting.

"Why hasn't the deceased member been replaced?" I asked.

"There hasn't seemed to be a sense of urgency. Also, I suspect there are certain members of the council who are quite content with seven."

"Why? Wouldn't spreading around the authority make it easier to get things done?"

Max smiled. "Ah, Annaliese, you think with such logic. I'm afraid when it comes to our council members, seven is an ideal number."

I must have looked puzzled because he added, "It's an odd number. An odd number means there's never going to be a tie. When it comes time to vote, one side will always have at least one more vote."

I wrinkled my nose. Talk about stacking the deck.

"Who decides how many members should be on the council?" I asked.

He appeared to think for a moment. "I believe it may have been done by charter. If so, there should be a copy in the library. Would you like me to look?"

"I would. Thank you."

Max stood as he prepared to leave the room, but before he could take two steps, I asked, "Tell me again, why are there no women on the council?"

"Because it's the *Duke's* Council, my lady."

"That stinks. Some of the smartest people I know are women."

"Agreed, Your Grace." He paused. "But perhaps a full reading of the charter is in order. There may have been other provisions that might open the door for inclusion of a woman other than the duchess."

"We should check the document," I said.

Five minutes later, we were doing exactly that.

"Where does it deal with vacancies?" I was looking for a place where it might spell out how to replace members who died without a natural replacement.

"Ahhh, here. Article thirty-five." Max tapped the section with his index finger.

I read the paragraph several times just to be certain I understood, then sat back in my seat and smiled. I was pretty sure I knew how to get around the fact that up until now, the Duke's Council had been a men's-only club. I just needed to practice a little patience.

Chapter Twenty-One

Things moved pretty quickly after that. I wrote the letter to Vincens, and he wrote back inviting me to address the Duke's Council. Three days later, I met with them and formally announced I was accepting my role of grand duchess. I was careful to watch the faces of the men around the table when I did so, hoping to gauge the level of enthusiasm or lack thereof. But everyone appeared to think it was a swell idea, and they were all cheerfully on board. Of course, the thought of all that lovely money coming back into the country's treasury probably inspired their delight at the prospect of having a grand duchess again. Research had concluded that the ceremony itself should take place in the Church of Saint Ann, which made me happy since I figured my ancestors were right there out back and maybe would be watching somehow. As my first official act, I put Claudette in charge of the festivities.

"I am honored, Your Grace." She bowed at the waist when I asked her if she would take on that project. While she'd never attended a coronation herself, she'd heard tales from her mother and had a pretty good sense of what was proper. "Somewhere, perhaps in the library, there should be notes on past coronations."

We agreed she'd have someone search for any documentation that could be found but also that the ceremony wouldn't be crazy lavish and should focus on the country more than on me. I wanted the foreign press invited and wanted tours of the city offered to them. I wanted to reach out to the TV shows that had interviewed me recently and invite certain of their hosts to attend. We made list after list of who should receive invitations and how many events there should be. An A list to attend everything, a B list to attend the celebration Claudette said would be held in the streets of the city. What foods to serve, which tiara to wear to which event, and what activities should lead up to the actual day and what should follow, e.g., should there be a ball afterward (I nixed this, tempted though I was by thoughts of swirling around the dance floor in the arms of a certain handsome captain), a day of activities on the lake, things like that.

Claudette would definitely need an assistant. I was certain she'd have a few people in mind who could help out, but I wanted Ceil in the mix as well. And reluctantly, I conceded that Roe should be included when it came to planning what we'd be feeding the people who came to the castle.

Who knew becoming a duchess would be so exhausting?

After adding the names of a few select friends from home to the guest list, I left the details in Claudette's hands and agreed to meet every morning to go over her progress and to discuss any other issues that might arise from day to day. I did enjoy a good party—and had given a few over the years—but I'd never been to an event of this scale. Every meeting concluded with my head spinning, but Claudette was unflappable. In the archives she found an invitation to my great-great-great-grandmother's coronation, and she used that as a template. I had to admit I felt a bit of a thrill looking at the finished product. We'd decided to include a personal note of invitation from me to everyone who'd interviewed me or who'd asked for an interview. I was really starting to enjoy this.

Having everyone in my family under the same roof—especially if that roof sat atop a castle, even if it leaked in a few places—was alone worth the trip. I had breakfast with my daughter and sisters every morning—Ralphie was usually up and out by then since he'd started jogging early every day along with his personal security detail—and the five of us had dinner together every night when something official wasn't on the calendar. There were several events to introduce my children and sisters to the members of the council and their families, and I was surprised by the way my kids comported themselves. Of course, I reminded them before every dinner or party that their ancestors—especially my mother and grandmother—were watching from somewhere, so make them proud. And they did.

Claudette had given us all a quick tutorial on what was expected of us, from the order in which we should stand in the receiving line to which was the fish fork and which was the oyster fork. We made it through the first few dinners without too many screwups, so I was grateful for her help. The formal dinners were usually accompanied by music—a violinist or harpist or some soft piano playing—and the conversations were generally a bit stiff. But when it was just the five of us in the small breakfast room (we preferred it for our family dinners), it was almost like being back in Philly, with everyone talking at the same time.

"Mom, you're never going to believe what happened when I was jogging this morning." Ralphie's eyes were lit with a happy fire. "I met a guy who plays soccer and thinks we should have a team and compete with all the other national teams. He played in high school, like I did, and he knows some other guys who play. He said they're really good. But there's no stadium. Can we build a soccer stadium?"

"Oh my God, Annie, Ceil and I toured this castle today, and you would have died it was so gorgeous. Not nearly as big as this one, but it was pretty big. It belonged to . . ." Roe turned to Ceil. "Who did it belong to again?"

"It belonged to Princess Gabrielle Maria. Great-grandmother's cousin who married an Italian count. The castle was hers, though, so it stayed in the family. Our guide told us Gabrielle had three sons. Two died in a futile attempt to oust the Soviets, but the youngest survived, and he had two sons, both of whom are deceased and neither of whom left heirs. The castle needs some work, but it has elegant bones and overlooks beautiful meadows and streams, and there's an orchard and a vineyard." Ceil sighed. "It's just waiting to be rehabbed. It would make a perfect wedding venue."

"Oh, but tell her about the castle with the terraced fields and the rows of grapevines." Roe rested her elbow on the table and her chin in the palm of her hand, a faraway look in her eyes. "The wine here is spectacular, but imagine if we had a royal brand of wine. Can't you just see the label? Serafina sunning herself on one of those big rocks down near the lake with *Wines from the House of Gilberti* in script. Maybe with a falcon somewhere on the label."

"House wine indeed." I grinned. The idea appealed to me. I mentally added it to the list. Could I put Roe in charge of such a venture?

"Mom, I made a friend today," Juliette announced. "She's Claudette's granddaughter, Remy, and she's so fun. Her mom died in a car accident, so she stays with Claudette a lot. She goes to a private school just over the border in Switzerland. Mom, can I go to private school, too?"

And so it went every night. New experiences, new friends, new dreams for this new life of ours. Whether those dreams would become happy realities or haunting nightmares was anyone's guess.

Chapter Twenty-Two

The frenzy at the castle before the coronation began days before the event was to occur. The steady hum of vehicles driving up the long lane seemed to go on nonstop for hours. Imagine the biggest party you've ever been to and all the work that went into it, all the people who were involved in the preparation, and multiply that by about, oh, maybe five hundred.

I'd had trouble falling asleep the night before the big day: the clock read two fifteen the last time I'd looked at it, and I'd barely gotten three hours of sleep. I finally got out of bed and showered, taking my time to inhale the now-familiar subtle scent of the soap that always had a calming effect on me. I would forever associate that gentle scent—Gran's violets—with my first days in Saint Gilbert. I slipped into my silk robe and waited for Claudette, who'd promised to take care of everything I would need for the day. Honest to God, I don't know what I'd have done without her. She'd become like my fairy godmother, and while she directly tended only to me, she'd found and trained the appropriate personnel to tend to each member of my family. Ladies-in-waiting for my daughter and sisters and a butler for Ralphie, who might never get over having a butler of his own.

Surreal.

But then again, that entire day was like walking through a dream.

Breakfast was served with the usual crew joining me in my room as they had every morning since we'd arrived. The conversation was more subdued, though, and ran the gamut from clothes to who was to stand where when the official photographs were taken.

"How excited are you, Annie?" Ceil asked.

"About five seconds away from hyperventilating."

"You might want to get over that before we get to the church," Roe suggested.

"Yeah, Mom," Jules chimed in. "Passing out at the altar would not be a good look."

Ralphie nodded. "No way to gain the confidence of your subjects."

We all sort of half laughed.

"Speaking of your subjects," Ceil said, "people have been lining up around the church, through the park, around the square—however close they can get to the church—since yesterday."

"Like they were lining up for rock tickets," Ralph said with a grin.

"How would you know this?" I asked Ceil.

"I heard the guards talking about it in the hallway this morning. They were right outside my door."

"Were they concerned about anything in particular?" I tried to sound as nonchalant as I could. Me passing out at the altar would be far better than someone else blowing up the church.

"No. Just that they were calling in guards from other places to make sure they had enough." She nibbled a croissant. "Oh, and they were talking about the need to hire more."

More guards? Hadn't they just brought in a new class of guards? Why would they need more? I need to ask Max if something was going on I should know about.

We were all finishing up breakfast, and while I would have loved to have prolonged the time with my family on this momentous day, I knew we needed to get moving. Reading my mind, Ceil finished her coffee, stood, stretched, and said, "It's almost showtime, ladies. And Ralphie. Time for all the royal Gilbertis to prepare for the main event."

Ralphie was the first out the door, and my sisters were about to follow him when I grabbed each of them by their arms.

"Tell me the truth. Would you rather you were being crowned today instead of me?" I asked. The question had been nagging at me since the morning after I'd first met with Max and company.

"Would I still be able to renovate the castles and plan weddings there?" Ceil asked.

"Would I still be able to be the chef for Ceil's castle weddings?" This from Roe, who doesn't know that I know she's made the acquaintance of the castle chef and has ventured downstairs to cook with him on more than one occasion.

"Probably not," I told them both. "There's too much other business the duchess has to take care of."

"Then no," Ceil said.

Roe shook her head. "Me either."

"Okay," I said and kissed them each on the cheek. "I just had to ask."

"Go get gorgeous." Ceil gave me a quick hug, which was followed by a hug from Roe as they left the room.

"Mom, your gown is the most beautiful dress I have ever seen. I hope I get to wear it one day at my coronation." Jules hastily added, "I mean, when you don't want to be duchess anymore."

I hugged my daughter to me, then pushed her out the door and closed it behind her.

I maybe forgot to mention the Dress.

When it came time to discuss what we'd all be wearing for the occasion, I mentioned that I'd met the dressmaker in the city, been greatly impressed with her work, and thought she should be given an opportunity to work with us rather than bring in a foreign designer. Claudette agreed immediately and we called Gisele, who'd about fainted when we told her why we wanted to speak with her. When she realized we were serious, she asked first if photographs of any gowns from previous coronations were available. Claudette and I exchanged a smile and led the young woman to the room where clothing from other eras had been stored. After her initial shock, we left her alone to inspect and sketch. When we returned an hour later, she'd pulled out several gowns that had caught her eye.

"These are classic gowns, one a Worth, and it's beyond perfection. And perfectly preserved." Gisele gestured to three gowns, each a shade of white but different in style as befitted each era. "I could re-create any of these—with enough time, of course—or I could possibly alter one to fit you. Whatever is your pleasure, Your Grace."

I studied each dress carefully, then glanced at Claudette. She was standing still, watching me, debating, I sensed, as I was, the propriety of wearing a gown once worn by a former grand duchess as opposed to spending a bit of a fortune to have one made.

I touched the sweetheart neckline of one, the satin skirt of another, the silken bodice of a third. Any one of them could be altered to fit me. Although the Duke's Council had obtained some funds for the coronation from the Swiss bank, I didn't want to spend too much of that money on myself. There were so many other things to consider.

"Claudette, what do you think? Is it sacrilege to alter one of these historic gowns?"

"I think it would be lovely, Your Grace. Perhaps afterward we could open a small museum in the city where these vintage gowns and uniforms could be displayed. It would make a most interesting tableau to have photographs of you wearing one of these gowns hanging next to a portrait of the first duchess who wore it, whichever you choose. Tourists would love it as much as Saint Gilbertians." She hastened to add, "Of course, it's up to you."

"Perhaps Your Grace should try on all three and see if one pleases you." Gisele's suggestion was spot-on, and so that's what I did, and that's how I chose the gown I'd be coronated in.

Which did I choose? Why, the one that looked best from the back, of course. You really didn't think I'd pick a dress that made my butt look big, did you?

~

The procession from the castle to the church was led by a prancing white riderless horse decked out in colorful fashion. Why riderless, since that generally implies that someone has died? Well, of course, someone had, but that was years ago. As explained to me, the presence of the horse was the Saint Gilbertian equivalent of the Brits declaring, "The queen is dead. Long live the king." After the coronation, a member of the castle guard would ride the horse back to the castle.

Since there were no antique carriages available—no one knew what had happened to those that had once been housed in the carriage house next to the royal stables—I and my family arrived separately in white Mercedes limousines. I had no idea where those cars had come from, but there was an entire fleet of them in front of the castle when I walked out through the front doors into the glare of the morning sun. I hoped they were leased and not purchased.

As head of the castle guard and therefore my personal security—not to mention a senior member of the Duke's Council—Max accompanied me in my car, for which I was grateful beyond words. I was nervous and felt like a total imposter, or a really bad actor about to step onto the stage in front of the entire world. Max wore his uniform, replete with medals and ribbons. I was never particularly attracted to men in uniform, but damn, that man looked good. I ignored the sudden jump in my libido—*so* inappropriate under the circumstances!—and asked what the medals signified, and he took his time explaining each one, maybe to take my mind off what would come once the ride ended. Max being Max, I doubt he'd suspect the flush on my face was due to his proximity, which I told myself I could think about later because right now there were other more pressing matters.

Due to the deep curve in the road leading from the castle to the church, the long cars had to circle the city and approach Saint Ann's from the opposite direction. I was surprised to see how many people lined the streets and shouted and waved as the cars passed by. Was I supposed to wave in return?

As if he'd read my mind, Max said, "After the coronation, you might want to greet the onlookers as we drive by. But on the way to the church, the windows should remain closed."

I nodded. I'd do that. I hope someone got the word to the others, particularly my son, who we recently discovered loved few things more than an open window and a cheering crowd.

I'd checked out Ralphie and the others earlier that morning before they left for the church. It had been decided that members of the royal family would arrive at the church in a specified order, with Ceil and Roe the first to leave the castle, followed by Ralphie, then Juliette, my presumptive heir. I'd asked them all to wait in the hall outside my room before they made their way ceremoniously down the grand stairwell. Ceil and Roe both wore gowns designed by Gisele and made by her trusted seamstresses, Ceil elegant—of course—in a dark-blue satin, Roe in a similar gown of a lighter shade looking pretty regal as well. They wore jewels at their necks and in their ears and tiaras on their heads, and both looked as royal as any of our ancestors whose portraits hung on the castle walls. Juliette was the picture of a young princess in her gown of peony pink, rubies at her throat and dangling from her earlobes. On her head she wore a tiara of diamonds and rubies and on her face, a look of disbelief that this was actually happening.

But the biggest transformation was that of my son. Ralphie had been dressed in a uniform that was a near replica of one worn by my great-grandfather in one of his portraits. There were ribbons and gold braid and medals and God only knew what all on that boy's chest. He stood tall and straight and, well, *manly*, and his face appeared so serious and mature, I had to blink to make sure it was really him.

Who says clothes don't make the man?

And this only days after Juliette showed me his Twitter account, where someone had started a page called @RealSPhillyGurlz and, using the hashtag #IKissedAPrinceAndILikedIt, invited all the girls Ralphie had dated through high school to share their memories of their special time with my son. I stopped reading after I got to the part where someone suggested a rating system. There are some things a mother didn't need to know.

Anyway, we got to the church and found the doors closed and no one standing on the steps except members of the castle guard. Everyone else who was to attend the ceremony had already been escorted inside, where they awaited my arrival. I've never been comfortable being the center of attention, so the panic attack that hit me at that moment was to have been expected, I guess. In any event, it took me a while to convince myself to exit the car, climb the church steps, and go inside and just get it all over with. After today, we could control the amount of pomp and circumstance, right? I'd only have to do the things I'd taken this job to do. New roads. Better schools. A modern hospital. Build a tourist industry. You know, save the country.

I took a deep breath and with Max's assistance, I started up the steps. Several young women wearing long dresses appeared from nowhere to lift the long train on the back of my cape to keep it from sweeping the ground. Did I mention the cape? Long, red velvet, and trimmed in fur? I laughed when I first saw it—it looked like something Ceil had worn to the Halloween party we went to one year at the Victorian Room at the hall owned by the South Philly Vikings, the Mummers band. The cape Claudette had placed over my shoulders before we left the castle was real, heavy, and hot as a bitch in that mid-August heat. Oh, and they'd pinned a red satin sash onto my dress, from one shoulder to my waist. The Order of the . . . I forget what it was, but Claudette said it was mandatory that I wear it, so I did.

Did I feel like I was playing dress-up? Did I want to make nervous jokes the entire time I was being outfitted? Did I hear Bert Parks singing "There She Is, Miss America"? Yes, yes, and yes.

The doors opened at my approach and organ music began to play and everyone stood and turned. As we'd rehearsed several times over the past week, I slowly walked the aisle to the altar, hoping I wouldn't trip. It took all my willpower not to bolt just to get there as quickly as possible. But I was okay. I knew I wasn't walking alone.

I stood as the ladies-in-waiting removed my cape and carried it off. I'd rehearsed with Claudette several times—thank goodness someone knew the protocol!—so I knelt when I had to, stood when I was sup- posed to, bowed my head when it was indicated. Father Francisco, the local priest, assisted Bishop Guardini, who'd arrived two days ago from Italy and who'd prayed for a long time before placing the ruby-and-di- amond crown on my head. That crown was beautiful beyond anything I could ever have imagined—red velvet with all those jewels on it. They told me it only weighed one and a half pounds, but sitting atop my head, it felt more like fifty. Now I know where the expression "heavy is the head that wears the crown" came from.

Imagine, if you can, being me on that day. It was as if I were playing a role in a historical drama. I mean, it was like something I'd seen in movies.

The altar had been covered in fragrant white roses, and I mean *covered*. Several times during the ceremony, a lone violin played. But there were moments I know I will never forget if I live to be a hundred: the wink of confidence from Ceil when I caught her eye; the look of pride on my son's face, the awe on my daughter's. Living in South Philly all our lives, nothing had prepared any of us for what was happening. The closest we'd ever come to any manner of pomp and circumstance was when, thanks to our father's army veteran brother who lived in Springfield, Roe was Poppy Queen at the American Legion Memorial Day Parade the year she turned ten. She rode on the float and waved to the crowd, "America the Beautiful" blasting from the speakers on the back of the truck. I remember her fingers were dyed red by the end of the day because she'd handed out so many red crepe paper flowers to the parade watchers lining the streets.

After what had seemed an eternity to me, a lone trumpet began to play, a choir of children began to sing, and the ceremony was over. It was done. I was officially the Grand Duchess Annaliese Jacqueline Terese of the Grand Duchy of Saint Gilbert. I went back down the aisle—the "no curtsy" memo apparently hadn't been widely circulated, because people actually curtsied as I passed by—and when the front doors opened, I stood on the top step as I'd been directed and waved to the cheering crowd that had gathered along the street and in the park waiting for my family to emerge. There were cameras everywhere. Television crews from various countries around the world had come to record what they'd called "a modern fairy tale come true." When my sisters and my children joined me, we stood together, all of us soaking up the good wishes along with the improbability of the moment.

The internet was awash with photos of all of us looking dignified, regal, and ready to rule. Apparently there was a worldwide fascination with this story, and it was repeated over and over in newspapers, magazines, and television reports, all basically the same story: "Middle-aged Single Philadelphia Mom Learns of Royal Heritage!" "From Divorcée to Duchess! How It Happened (see page 3)!" The Philadelphia papers were full of interviews with friends and coworkers and even, unfortunately, Ralph Senior, who at least didn't repeat the comment about my mother being snobby.

Again, it was surreal. But I welcomed the publicity because it worked along with my plans to give Saint Gilbert a higher profile. A *much* higher profile.

I should say right here that while I wasn't much for the pomp, I had to admit, I had tears in my eyes. Not for myself, but for Gran. She should have had the chance to stand there with that crown on her head; she was the Annaliese the people should have been calling for. It broke my heart to think about everything she'd been deprived of. And my mother . . . she would have been next in line after Gran. Mom would have been a kick-ass grand duchess. Those roads would have been repaired if she'd had to go out there and fill in the ruts herself or, at the very least, direct the road crews.

So I broke from the agenda, and the first thing I did was lead my immediate family through the gate into the graveyard. When we got to the place where our relatives were buried, I turned to my sisters and my kids and said, "I think it would be appropriate to say a prayer for our great-grandparents and our other relatives before the celebrations begin."

Everyone nodded silently.

We all bowed our heads and I told them I was sorry that things turned out the way they did so that my grandmother or my mother wasn't the one wearing the crown. I said I'd do the very best I could and for them not to be shy about offering advice if at all possible—like if they found a way to communicate, that would be good—and that I'd try to make them proud of me.

The rest of the day was a total blur. There was a reception in the castle organized by Claudette and her committee. Large potted plants— trees and flowering things I didn't recognize—were arranged through- out the gallery where local wines and cheeses were being served along with some very fancy goodies. There was music from a harpist. The guests consisted of Saint Gilbertian loyalists, members of the Duke's Council, those elderly friends of my grandmother, and heads of state from various countries. Every invited nation had sent dignitaries, the Brits even sending a prince, a princess, and a duke—ones I'd never heard of, but still, they were members of the royal family, albeit peripheral.

The French, Germans, and Italians had sent dukes and counts along with prime ministers and other civil representatives. I'd been schooled in protocol for greeting such visitors, but even so, the entire day had seemed so ridiculously implausible, I had moments when I couldn't believe this was actually my life. A whole contingent came from the States, including Marianne, but I didn't have much time to spend with her. We agreed she'd come back for a longer stay once everything settled down. The day was pleasant enough, but I have to say, one thing really got under my skin.

I took Ceil aside and said, "We have to talk."

"You betcha. God, you look so regal. So imposing." My sister's eyes were shining. "I can't believe we're here and all these people are—"

"Going to be leaving later to stay at a hotel in another country. We have to talk about hotels." I glanced around the room. "None of these people are staying in Saint Gilbert."

Ceil stared at me while she let that sink in. "Because there's no place for them to stay here."

"Tomorrow morning we talk about that castle you toured, the one that belonged to our great-grandmother's cousin, Gabrielle. We need to find a contractor to go out there and check it out, stem to stern."

"You're thinking hotel."

"I'm thinking it pisses me off that even if we get people to come here, they're going to be staying somewhere else unless we do something about it, and quick. This is not going to happen again."

Ceil nodded. "Right. Priorities. But . . ."

"But what?"

"I wanted that castle for the spa. You know, the place where we will wash away crow's-feet, marionette lines, and elevens."

That was important.

"Okay, there must be someplace else we could turn into a hotel. Make the spa a priority. I've already had visitors comment on the beauty of everyone's flawless, wrinkle-free skin. We need to strike while that iron is still hot."

It had been my plan to introduce those wrinkle-free ladies of a certain age to our guests who were decades younger.

"I'm finding the people of Saint Gilbert are so beautiful, so youthful," one of the ladies from the French contingent had commented. I'd judged her to be in her midsixties, and to say that time had not been kind to her skin would have been . . . kind. "Everyone I've met here has the most beautiful skin. And if you'll forgive me for mentioning it, Your Grace, you could pass easily for thirty or even less, though I've read you're . . . well, a tad bit older than that."

"Quite a few years older, yes." I smiled.

"What is your secret?" She returned the smile. "There must be a secret."

"Oh, there is." I'd leaned close to her to whisper as if sharing a strict confidence.

"Tell me," she'd begged.

"We're not ready to share, but we will, and soon. If you like, I will put your name on the list of first-to-knows."

She stared at me for a moment, then I raised an eyebrow.

She grabbed my arm. "You're serious, aren't you? There really is something . . ."

I nodded knowingly, if not smugly.

"Put my name on the very top of that list. I must be the first to know! I would be eternally grateful!"

I squeezed the hand of my new BFF and assured her I would do that.

Just as I'd assured dozens of other women with whom I'd had similar conversations. As long as all these obviously beauty-conscious aging women were here, I should take advantage of the situation, right? I mean, what else did we have to talk about after we got past the clichéd "Quite a change from your life in America, isn't it?" and "How does it feel to be royal after growing up in . . . where was it now, Baltimore?" So I decided to plant the seeds, as it were. Dangle a carrot. Ensure a certain number of people left this weekend with Saint Gilbert firmly in their minds and wondering about that secret I'd hinted at. They were going to think about Saint Gilbert every time they looked in the mirror. Of course, now that I had people interested, we'd have to deliver, but I was already working on that.

After the coronation reception, we'd moved on to a luncheon. Later there would be a tea, then a formal state dinner for select guests that would be held in the throne room. I got to sit on the throne, which I have to say, while a beautiful piece of antique furniture, was not very comfortable. I had taken a few minutes on rehearsal day to inspect the carvings of falcons, flowers, and Serafina and noticed then the presence of two chairs. Fortunately or unfortunately—depending on how you looked at the situation—this duchess had no duke to occupy the other.

Of course, we had to change clothes for every event. Now, I've never been much of a clotheshorse—honestly, I couldn't afford to be, what with the mortgage and two kids. But I had to admit, it was fun, like an all-day, all-night costume party.

I got to wear the most amazing clothes—and jewels! Dressing up at all was a new experience for me. Except for weddings and funerals and the occasional important meeting at work, I almost never wore anything fancier than a good blouse with a skirt or, if it was important, a suit. So to wear several couture-quality dresses and gowns in the same day, thanks to Gisele's clever designs and quick seamstresses, made my head spin. Ceil, Roe, and Juliette all found their wardrobes drastically changed as events were added to the agenda and proper outfitting was necessary. A tailor tended to Ralphie's needs as outlined by Claudette. It occurred to me on Monday afternoon watching the sailboats as they raced around the far end of the lake—the last of the scheduled activities that included visitors—that I hadn't seen either of my children dressed in jeans and T-shirts in almost a week.

But once the last luncheon had concluded, my family and I bid goodbye to our guests, and the gowns and jewels were put away, it was time to put on regular clothes and get down to work. I couldn't wait.

Chapter Twenty-Three

The morning after the last official event, Ceil, Roe, and I sat lazily around the table I'd had set up in my bedroom to use for small informal family meetings. We had pads of paper on the table, pens in our hands, coffee in our cups, and scones on a pretty blue plate with a raised gold crown on it. I thought we'd be all rough and ready to roll, but we were exhausted. I didn't expect to see either of my kids until later that day. So it was a drink coffee with the sisters, munch on goodies, and relax morning. I'd wanted it to feel more like an official meeting, but I was fried from the intensity of the past week. But I still wanted to feel productive.

"We need a plan," I told my sisters. "And it has to be smart, easily implemented, and not cost a fortune. And we need to start right away, while this 'fairy-tale story' is still fresh in everyone's minds. We need to put our little country on the world map, give people reasons to want to come here."

"Right. Let's start with something easy." Roe rolled her eyes.

Ignoring her, I continued. "We have to put the emphasis on what we have that no other country has. So write down 'the fountain of youth.'"

"Really? You think anyone's going to believe that the actual Fountain of Youth is located in Saint Gilbert?" Roe tapped her pen on the palm of her left hand.

"There are some who already do." I smiled smugly. "I already have a list of potential invitees, that is, ladies who are eager to know the secret of why everyone in Saint Gilbert has such beautiful skin. We're going to invite select high-profile women who could use a little facial and body magic to our spa and give them our secret treatment. It's a start."

"Wait, what spa?" Roe frowned. "What special treatment?"

"The one Ceil is going to open this fall. I understand the weather is lovely here in October and November." I turned to Ceil. "How much time do you think you'll need to get one of those castles or chateaus in shape?"

Ceil closed her eyes, and for a moment I thought she might be meditating. But it turned out she was putting the whole thing together in her head.

"Okay, we're going to need an actual spa area, a place where aestheticians can give 'facials' using the amazing soap," she said. "We'll need bedrooms for the guests with adjoining baths. A lounge or three. A pool. Patios or someplace really nice outside. A lovely dining area. Everything top of the line and luxurious."

"How long, Ceil?" I asked.

"Give me enough money, the right crew—and the right building, of course—and I'll give you your spa with five-star accommodations in maybe three months. Four at the most," she said in that cool, confident Ceil manner. "Depending, of course, on how much restoration and updating is necessary."

She paused, and I could see those wheels of hers turning.

"There's the castle that had belonged to Princess Gabrielle Maria. Oh, and the one that our great-uncle Theodore lived in—I haven't been inside, but the exterior looks pretty good. I'd have to go through it top to bottom to see if it's suitable, but it could be a contender."

I nodded. "So if our great-uncle had no heir, the ownership should have reverted to the family or the government. Either works for our purposes. I'll ask Max to check on that, but in the meantime, he can arrange for you to get inside. Do either of you have plans for the week?"

Ceil shrugged. "None. I'm available every day."

I turned to Roe. "I'd like you to go with her and check out the kitchen."

"Why?" she asked.

"Because if we're going to have people staying there, they're going to have to be fed. Which means there has to be working appliances." I sat back in my chair. "You're the only one in the family with experience cooking for a crowd, the only one who could tell me if we have what we need. If not, what do we need and how much will it cost? And then start thinking about hiring a top-notch staff. Emphasis on healthy meals."

"Oh, okay. Outfit a cooks' kitchen? Easy peasy. And I know lots of people who are really good in the kitchen." Roe's face brightened. "I can definitely do that." She paused. "Can I be the chef? I really want to be a chef."

"Fine, you can be the chef." I'd tasted her cooking and for all her faults, she really is a damned good cook.

"In that case, I'm free all week, too, so just let me know day and time and I'll be ready to go."

Ceil began making notes, as did Roe, who was making a list of things she wanted to check out in the castle's kitchen.

"So, one castle or two?" I asked. "Gabrielle's and Theodore's, or just one?"

"Both." For once, my sisters were in accord. "One for the spa, one for our first hotel."

I looked at Ceil. "You're going to have to pick one to start."

"I'll have to take a good look at both of them before I can make that decision."

"So that's step one of making Saint Gilbert a destination." I flipped to the page of notes I'd made while I was having my first cup of coffee earlier, before anyone drifted in to have breakfast with me.

"We're going to want local food and wine to be showcased when we start having tourists. We're going to need someone to oversee all that." My head began to spin, and I began to experience a rare moment of panic. I had no idea what I was doing. What in the name of God made me think I could do this? I tossed my pen on the table.

Sensing my frustration, Ceil said, "Let's just work on one thing at a time. First let's focus on getting the right building ready, get the spa up and running, and get people to come here and give them a lovely place to stay and an experience they'll never forget."

"That's not exactly one thing," I said. "And we'll still have to feed them."

"Next year we'll plan ahead and have lots of local produce. Imagine serving our guests those amazing strawberries. And we can talk to the baker in town and make sure she and her husband can produce more bread and croissants." Ceil was making a list of her own.

"And we'll need to make sure there's excellent wine to go along with all the delicious food I'm going to prepare," Roe said.

"Let's see what shape the vines are in at that chateau we passed the other day," Ceil said to Roe.

"I remember that one. It's on a hill, and the vineyard sort of flows down from it. So picturesque. We should find out who owns it. And we should look into producing our own wines." Roe repeated the thought she'd had when we first talked about the vineyards.

"Let us handle all this, Annie. The castles, the vineyards, everything. We can check in with you every week and let you know where we are, but right now, you have other things to deal with," Ceil pointed out.

"Like my meeting with the ladies who make the magic soap. Without them, there won't be any need for a spa." I closed my notebook and pushed back my chair. "And my first official meeting with the Duke's Council is Thursday morning." I blew out a long breath, making my cheeks billow the way I did when I was a kid and frustrated about something. "But first let me call Max and see what we can do about having you two get into those castles."

"I want to be with you when you speak to the soap ladies," Ceil said. "That way, I can be the point person on soap so you don't have to be."

And that's why most of the time, Ceil was my favorite sister.

~

Max knew right away who to call to help tick off a few things on the list. As soon as could be arranged, Ceil and Roe would tour the interiors of the castles in question with a man named Louis Bondersan, who owned one of the few contracting companies in Saint Gilbert. He was, Max assured me, an expert on restoring old buildings, very reliable, and his work was impeccable—he was the best the country had to offer. He also arranged for a farmer to check out the chateau Ceil had mentioned to see what shape the vineyard was in.

Later that day, Max and I were in the little room on the first floor that I liked to use as my private office and for meetings. It was cozy and filled with light, and I could picture it in the fall and winter with a nice fire going. For such an enormous building, it was filled with charming little rooms scattered throughout. I couldn't wait to see what was in the closed-off wing and show off its beauty. Maybe invite heads of state to come to Saint Gilbert and stay in the castle during their visit. I wondered how long it would take to get the castle repairs completed once the funds were available.

Which reminded me to speak with Andre DiGiacoma, who for years had been the liaison between Saint Gilbert and the Swiss bank holding our funds. I told Ceil to stay on Bondersan to get estimates as soon as they were available so I could have DiGiacoma put the request through to the bank once we decided which castle would best suit the spa. One more thing on my list.

"Perhaps it might best serve your purposes to . . ." Max had hesitated after I told him of my plans to add members to the Duke's Council and for the spa.

"To do what?"

"To slow down just a bit."

I frowned. "Slow down what?"

"Some of your efforts to—well, to take on everything at once."

"Why would I do that?" I put down the pen I'd been holding, looked him in the eye, and waited.

Finally, he said, "Because sometimes it might be better to accomplish one goal before attacking another."

"What, you think I can't walk and chew gum at the same time?" At his look of confusion, I added, "Do more than one thing at the same time."

Max sighed. "I think you are the most capable woman I've ever met, but if I may speak freely . . ."

"You already have, so you might as well just put it all out there." I crossed my arms over my chest, not sure of what he was going to say but suspecting I might not like it.

"I would hate to see you complete your research on all these many projects only to have the council not approve them."

"Why do I need their approval?"

Max shrugged. "It's always been so; the council controls the agenda."

"Only because since the Russians left, there hasn't been anyone else in charge. And it hasn't always been so. I've been reading up on the history of Saint Gilbert, Max. I've done my homework. So I have news for you and the other members of the council.

"The way the council functions today isn't the way it was intended. I understand why the council has made all the decisions for the past twenty-five years or so. There's been no duchess or duke, no head of state, since my great-grandparents. But here's the thing: originally, the

Duke's Council was established to *advise* the ruler, not to dictate to whomever was on the throne."

"Perhaps that's so, but this group has functioned for many years as the ruling body. You should be prepared for some to object to a return to the old ways." Max sighed and leaned forward. For a moment, I thought he was going to take my hands in his. "Put bluntly, the members of the council are not accustomed to having anyone tell them what to do or how to spend the country's funds, limited though they have been. Especially now with the influx of so much money from Switzerland in sight, there are some who will reject any oversight on your part, because more funds are at stake."

"I'll find a way to work around them."

We stared at each other for a long moment.

"So in other words . . ." I wasn't sure how I wanted to phrase this part, but it didn't matter. Max cut to the chase.

"Some might consider you a threat."

"Why would they vote for me in January but consider me a threat now?"

"Before they met you, some might have thought—erroneously, obviously—they could control you."

Swell. So in addition to the faction of the population who'd voted *against* bringing back the monarchy, now I had to worry about some of those who'd voted *for* the return of the old ways. Except now they were going to find out that some of the old ways weren't going to work for me, and the new ways might bring about changes they might not like. Eventually, I was going to have to come up with a way to make them want to walk my way.

I did have a few thoughts on that.

"You're saying I might have to watch my back."

Max nodded.

"But that's *your* job, right? You watch my back."

"I do. I and the members of the castle guard would lay down our lives for you."

"Take a bullet for me?" I was only half kidding.

"Without hesitation." He wasn't kidding at all.

It sounded so corny, but I knew he meant it. I felt humbled and maybe just a teensy bit scared inside. I mean, I'd be a fool to laugh off the fact that there might be some who wished that I'd stayed in Philly. The thought was sobering, not gonna lie. But I was raised by a woman whose mantra under adverse conditions was *never let them see you sweat*.

So I flashed my best smile for Max.

"Then I guess I don't have anything to worry about," I said with all the bravado I could muster, resolved to keep on the path I'd set for myself and for Saint Gilbert.

Chapter Twenty-Four

On Thursday I got up early and dressed in my I-mean-business clothes: a black linen dress and low-heeled shoes and the four strands of pearls Claudette produced and deemed necessary for what I wanted to accomplish. I spent the entire morning trying to decide which one of two bombs to set off at that afternoon's meeting of the Duke's Council. I was prepared either way, but I wanted to have my plan solid in my head before I walked through the door into that room. I was pretty sure I was going to upset more than one applecart whichever foot I led with (so to speak), so it was just a matter of me making up my mind.

When the time came, I was ready. I entered the room with a confident smile on my face.

After all the pleasantries had been exchanged, I jumped right into it. Gently, though.

"I'd like to thank each of you for the part you played in my coronation. It was a day I'll never forget, and I owe the success of it all largely to you. So thank you."

Smiles all around. Everyone likes to be acknowledged and thanked, right?

"I also want to thank the members of this council, past and present, individually and as a body, for running this country in the absence of a monarch. You've done an amazing job in the face of so many obstacles to keep the heart of Saint Gilbert beating. You and your predecessors are to be commended for the part you played in ensuring the country maintained its sovereignty. Every day I'm becoming more aware of the challenges the council faced over the years. I'd like to honor you all at a special dinner in November. You are the true heroes of Saint Gilbert."

Okay, that last part came flying out of my mouth before I'd really thought about it, but it was the right thing to do.

And the funny thing was, as I was speaking, I realized I actually meant every word. Facing the Germans, the Soviets, the political infighting, and the many factions that had tried to steer the country in a dozen different directions must have been hell at times for the men who'd had to deal with them, all to preserve the heritage their ancestors had established in this little bit of a country. Saint Gilbert was David in the face of many Goliaths, and it was important to acknowledge that struggle.

For a moment, there was silence. Then there was much chatter and congratulating each other on their successes over the years. I let them prattle on and talk about whose ancestors had sat on the council and whose ancestors had served Saint Gilbert in the dark days of occupation by two foreign countries. They'd come through it all intact, lost no territory, and had managed to keep the lights on—so to speak—and the bills paid with what little revenue they had. Yes, I did have the impression that some skimming off the top had occurred, but all things considered, that had been a small price to pay. Now the country was back on track, they had their duchess, and soon the money would flow in from Switzerland like manna from heaven.

"And now we will have all the funds we need to restore our beloved country." Vincens stood, his hands holding on to the lapels of his suit jacket.

Now the buzz began for real, everyone excitedly talking about how they were planning to spend the money. I heard everything from "buy a yacht" to "repair my villa" to "build up the army."

The vision of the bunch of them standing with their arms up as millions of euros fell into their smiling upturned faces flashed through my brain.

"I've been wanting a golf course here for years," someone was saying.

"We need the polo grounds refurbished," someone else said.

"What good are polo grounds without the horses? We need the stables rebuilt."

"And we must do something about renovating the ski lifts."

"May I remind you that it's impossible to get to the ski lifts? The roads are ridiculous, and the lodge is uninhabitable. No one's been down those slopes in years that I know of."

"Kids still go up there."

"They aren't supposed to. I doubt if it's safe. Why—"

I took this all in for a few moments, then said, "Okay, seriously? Yo. Slow your roll. A moment?"

I took a deep breath and reminded myself to be professional and duchess-like and not dis anyone, a challenge because I like to speak freely. I was having to learn to be a little more diplomatic than comes naturally. So instead of saying the first thing that came to my mind—*Golf course? Polo grounds? Yeah, those are top priorities*—I said, "A golf course and ski runs and polo grounds would be fine additions, of course. Excellent tourist attractions, to be sure. Someday." I paused to let that word sink in. "That day is not now."

Before the objections got out of hand, I continued. "You can drive only so far out of the city before the roads become rough and, in some places, impassable, as someone just pointed out. The roads are crap, so how does one get from one place to another? And where are these golfers and skiers and polo people going to stay? The players and the spectators? Right now, Saint Gilbert needs good roads and upscale accommodations for visitors, neither of which we currently have."

Blank looks were exchanged all around the table.

Finally, Vincens spoke up. "Your Grace, if I may . . . we've had no problem with our guests obtaining accommodations in Switzerland and in France, so I—"

"*I* have a problem with that. That's not going to happen again," I snapped more sharply than I'd intended, shocking him and everyone else. Possibly even me. "Why should we send our guests into another country where they will spend their money on rooms and dining and shopping and recreation? Why shouldn't we keep that money here? And think of the new jobs that would be created in and around the city and in the villages. I've heard that Saint Gilbert's children grow up and leave, to return only occasionally to visit family, because there are no jobs for them here."

More than one head nodded at this.

"Madam, surely with the money flowing into the country from the Swiss bank, we're no longer in need of funds. We can build that golf course, the polo grounds, and our visitors may stay wherever they please." Vincens made the mistake of chuckling as he looked around the room.

"Chancellor, in America, there are lotteries where you can buy a ticket and potentially win millions of dollars. Studies have shown that a good number of those lottery winners have gone bankrupt within years of winning. Why? Because they spend like drunken sailors and don't pay attention to where the money is going. They had no plan, no discipline. It was just spend, spend, spend, like the money was going to last forever." I fixed him with a stare that I hoped might make him squirm, though I saw no visible sign of that. "I do not intend for this country to be watching the funds dwindle down to nothing within a few years, and that's exactly what will happen if we are not careful handling what we have and find ways to bring new funds in. We need to invest our money cautiously." No one moved. "So yes, the funds my great-grandparents sent to Switzerland will be made available to us, and we will use them wisely. When they are made available. Eventually."

"Eventually?" someone spoke up. "Why not immediately? We've complied with the terms of the former duchess and duke, we have our duchess . . ."

"And where would those funds be sent, sir?" I asked.

"Why, to our bank, right here in Beauchesne, of course."

"Until Saint Gilbert has a financial institution stable enough to handle funds of this magnitude, I'm afraid the money will remain in Switzerland," I explained to them, as it had been explained to me earlier that morning on a call with the Swiss gentleman who'd been safeguarding our accounts. He'd clued me in on a number of things I hadn't been aware of. "We can request certain amounts to be transferred as needed, but I'm afraid until we have a trusted, experienced, competent system in place, we cannot put the entire fortune into the bank here in the city. The systems have not been updated in twenty years. It can't even handle the number of decimal points in the amount of money that will be coming our way. We need a first-rate financial consultant with a staff who knows what they're doing to set up our new system. I admit this is all beyond me. I don't know what we need, but I do know after speaking with the Swiss gentleman this morning and with the liaison between Saint Gilbert and the Swiss bankers"—I nodded in the direction of council member Andre DiGiacoma—"I became aware of certain . . . deficiencies in our systems. Sir, if you would . . . ?"

Andre nodded and stood. He was tall and thin and had a full head of bushy white hair and a beard that matched. "Her Highness is correct. As you know, as head of the state bank, I have had the privilege and the honor to serve as the liaison with our Swiss partners. I must say they have been excellent stewards of the money that had been passed to them by our late rulers. They have invested very well over the years. Our country is very sound financially. *Very* sound."

"Then what is the problem?" A visibly annoyed and frustrated Vincens spoke up.

"As Her Highness has said, our bank cannot handle the amount of money that is being held for us. There is a desperate need for the systems to be completely overhauled. I'm afraid until we have totally upgraded our technical systems and our digital capacity, the money will stay where it is."

There was an outbreak of protests—the bottom line being, *So how do we get our hands on the cash?*

"Guys, enough. Please." I turned and addressed Andre. "It's my understanding that your counterpart in Switzerland will make funds available as you request them for specific projects, correct?"

"Yes, my lady."

"So if we wanted money for our roads to be improved, say, and new roads to be built, how would we go about getting the money for that project?" I asked.

"We would submit a request for the funds, my lady."

"And just like that, they'd hand over the money?" I frowned. "So what would stop someone from requesting, say, ten million for roadwork that cost eight million and then pocketing two million for themselves?"

"Very little, madam," Andre admitted. "Only a strong moral character."

Swell. Best not to rely too heavily on that.

I cleared my throat.

"I would like to propose some safeguards. Any money that's requested should be accompanied by what in the States would be called backup. You want money for roads, submit an estimate from whoever is going to be building them showing how much it's going to cost, how much each piece of the project will cost. I worked in insurance for years, and if I wanted a bill paid, whether it was a doctor's bill or an attorney's, the request had to be submitted with the appropriate backup or it wouldn't be paid."

"Surely Her Highness isn't suggesting that our requests are broken down like grocery lists, with the cost of the milk, the bread, the meat itemized?" Vincens demanded.

"Actually, that is exactly what I'm suggesting." I turned to Andre. "Does that suit your purposes?"

"Oh yes, madam. More than enough." He nodded. "I would venture to say my counterpart in Switzerland would have no problem freeing up funds if the requests were made in such an organized, competent fashion."

"I would like to volunteer to assist Andre. As chancellor, I can surely be of service when it comes to budgeting and overseeing the transfer of funds," said Vincens the volunteer.

I wasn't sure if this would be the equivalent of putting the fox in charge of the henhouse.

I glanced at Andre, who appeared less than delighted. But Vincens was still the senior member of the council, so Andre merely nodded and said, "Of course, Chancellor. I would be honored to have you work with me."

"So that's how we're doing it." I glanced around to see if anyone was nodding now. No one was. I did see a lot of angry men who saw their plans to capitalize on the influx of funds disappear before their eyes, but I knew how to get them to walk my way.

"But our golf course . . . ," Pierre Belloque began.

"Do you have a site in mind?" I asked, clearly catching him off guard.

"We—that is, a few of us—have long thought that area to the south of the city proper would be appropriate."

"I agree." He was visibly surprised at my immediate concurrence. "Find us an expert on golf course design—someone recognized as one of the best, if not *the* best—and invite that person to come to Saint

Gilbert. If we're going to do this, we're going to have the best golf course in Europe. Have the property you have in mind assessed and see if it's feasible. If it isn't, find another site."

Belloque's face broke into a wide smile of joy. "Immediately, my lady. Thank you."

"Who owns that property, by the way?" I asked.

"Actually, my wife does," Belloque said somewhat sheepishly.

"Would she be willing to part with it at a fair price?" I asked.

"Yes, of course, madam."

"Then start the ball rolling." I smiled and pretended to be looking at something in my folder. "Oh, perhaps you could also look into the renovation of . . . what did you call it earlier, the polo grounds?"

He nodded. "They were quite popular back in the day. My grandfather played. He wore the colors of the last duchess." His chest swelled a little at this pronouncement. "People came from all over Europe to play here."

"Really?" This was news. My brain immediately added *polo grounds* to my list of things to do. "But if we're going to invite people here to enjoy recreational pursuits, we're going to need our roads repaired, so we're back to that again. And suitable accommodations." I looked directly at Vincens. "I repeat, I will not have visitors coming here and leaving for dining and overnight stays in Italy or France or wherever. If they come here, they will stay here. I am in total agreement that we need to offer a world-class golf course, for example. Anything we can do to promote the country and attract tourists should be on the table. But we cannot promote tourism until we have solid infrastructure in place. That means we will have five-star hotels with fine dining."

"Building new hotels will be an expensive proposition, my lady," Vincens reminded me. Why did he always look so damned *smug*?

"I'm aware, Chancellor. Which is why I'd like to propose that we utilize several old chateaus outside the city for this very purpose."

"Madam, with all due respect, I know for a fact that most of them lack indoor plumbing," Vincens said. "Even the Russians wouldn't stay there."

"The chancellor is correct, my lady," Dominic Altrusi spoke up. "I happen to own one of those ancient chateaus, but there are others. I've not been able to afford any of the necessary work."

"Might I then appoint you, sir, to head a committee to determine the feasibility of renovating some of those chateaus for use as hotels?" I asked Dominic as if I hadn't already thought of that. "Find out who owns them. See what it would cost for the country to buy, then renovate each one up to modern standards."

"Of course, Your Highness. I'd be pleased to," Altrusi said.

"If anyone knows of another chateau that might be considered, please let Dominic know so he can add it to his list. We would also be happy if the owners decided to renovate their properties and keep them privately owned. As long as we can count on a certain number of hotels or bed and breakfasts, I don't care who owns or runs them." I sighed deeply. "Of course, once again, there is the matter of the roads. We'll need someone to look into the possibility of having roads repaired or new ones created." I tapped my pen on my folder and waited to see if someone would step forward.

"My lady, if I may?" Jacques Gilberti stood. Up until the day of the coronation I hadn't even spoken to him, though I was told he was a distant cousin. He was an attractive gentleman in his fifties—I guessed at his age—and married to a lovely woman named Lorena. That was all I knew about him.

I nodded. "Of course."

"I would be happy to assume the responsibility of looking into the situation with our roads and our bridges. While I myself have no experience, I have a son who is an engineer. I could call upon his expertise to guide us if Your Highness agrees."

"Your son studied engineering?" I was so relieved that someone actually got my concern about the roads, I could have kissed the man right on the mouth, cousin or otherwise.

"He is a graduate of a fine school of engineering in America," Jacques said proudly. "Perhaps you have heard of the Massachusetts Institute of Technology."

I was momentarily stunned to think anyone I was related to—however distantly—got into MIT.

"Of course. Congratulations. It's one of the finest engineering schools in the world."

"So I've been told, my lady." Cousin Jacques was still beaming. "He's been working in America, but perhaps we can persuade him to come evaluate our needs."

"We'd be grateful for his input."

By the end of the meeting, every member of the council had agreed to take responsibility for something. One was going to look into what we would need to build a new hospital (his daughter was a doctor in Germany), another was going to look into promoting Saint Gilbert's products for export. Max's uncle, Emile Rossi, offered to look into ways of attracting new businesses to Saint Gilbert (once we get Operation Soap off the ground, he and I will talk). Someone else stepped forward to look into what the country's needs were as far as education was concerned. Soon I had more than half of what I mentally thought of as *Jobs to Assign* actually covered, and I hadn't had to twist one arm. I felt we were on our way to doing some serious business.

So perhaps now might be a good time to move along to step two of my agenda.

"You know . . ." I started looking thoughtfully at the contents of my folder, as if something were just occurring to me. "I'd been discouraged by everything I thought would be necessary to bring Saint Gilbert into this century, and I am so pleased that every member of this council has stepped up to offer his skills and creativity to ease some of my concerns. But I think perhaps some of these tasks are going to prove to be an eventual burden for one person to handle." I bit my bottom lip and tried to look pensive. "I did some reading up on the history of the Duke's Council." I looked across the table to my left and saw a *here we go* look cross Max's handsome face, and I inwardly smiled. "I was surprised to learn that originally, the council had many more members, and it wasn't unusual for some of those members to be women. In view of all that I and the council are tasked with doing, I think it is appropriate to add a few new members at this time. This is permitted by the charter."

There was some grumbling, not unexpected.

"Does Your Highness believe we're not up to the tasks?" someone asked with just a hint of indignation.

"I believe you are all very competent, very accomplished. And as I said earlier, the country would not have survived without your leadership. But"—here I made it a point to look every member of the council in the eye—"I'm also thinking it's unfair to ask the few of you to shoulder so many burdens. Obviously, there is much to be done, but the more people we have working on our concerns, the faster our goals will be met. There's an expression my mom used to say, something like 'many hands make light work.' Something like that. In that spirit, I want to propose that we add a few members to the council so that—"

There was more grumbling, louder this time. I let them go on for a few minutes before breaking it up.

"Sorry, but the more I've thought about it, the more I've come to understand the necessity. If you know someone you think would be a capable and hardworking addition, please speak up. You are seven now, I make eight. Let's shoot for a few more, shall we, keeping in mind that quality is more important than quantity?"

The griping immediately began anew, but Vincens spoke up over the din.

"I agree with Her Majesty. We have a huge responsibility before us. We are being tasked to rebuild this country. There is much work to be done before *all* our money is in our coffers. So in that regard, I would like to propose adding my son to the council."

Swell. I inwardly groaned. The thought of facing that leering mug once every week was enough to make me ill.

Max stood. He was wearing what I thought of as his Lord of the Castle Guard uniform, and may I say, he wore it exceptionally well. It's difficult sometimes to keep my inappropriate thoughts from getting the best of me.

"I agree, Your Grace." Max turned to the others. "The chancellor has suggested his son should join the council, and I heartily concur."

I tried to mind-meld with him from across the table. Mentally I was screaming, *Shut up! What are you doing? I can't stand that guy!*

But then Max continued. "I would be pleased to welcome Carlo DellaVecchio as the first new member of the Duke's Council."

I frowned. Carlo? Who's Carlo?

"But . . . no, no, I meant Philippe . . ." Vincens tried in vain to speak over the chorus of *yeas.*

As much as it pained me to agree to adding another DellaVecchio to our numbers, Max must have had a good reason to endorse him so readily.

I took my cue from him and said, "If there's a reason why Carlo DellaVecchio should not be invited to join the council, or if anyone feels he is unfit for any reason, now is the time to voice your objections." I glanced around the table. No nays. While Vincens clearly had preferred his other son, he could not very well say nay to the inclusion of any of his children.

"Very well, then." I turned to Vincens. "Would you care to deliver the news to your son yourself, or should we approach this in a more formal manner?"

"Perhaps a written invitation from Your Majesty . . . ," he said with some resignation.

"Consider it done." I waited a moment so Vincens could accept the congratulations from his peers.

When all the backslapping ended, I turned back to the table. "I'd like to suggest someone whose honesty and intelligence is well known to me personally, and hopefully will soon be to you as well. My sister, the Princess Cecilia Elizabet."

The room grew really quiet really quickly.

"Well, then," I said with a Cheshire-cat smile, "apparently there are no comments so we'll assume it's fine with everyone?" Heh.

Dominic Altrusi cleared his throat. "Your Grace, the princess is . . . a . . . well, she's a *woman*."

"Indeed she is, sir. As am I. Is that a problem?"

"Well, only because, well, as you know, this is the *Duke's* Council. Dukes are, traditionally, men," he said awkwardly.

"Actually, I've discovered something interesting about the council. It was established as the council the duke of the day could rely on to advise him, not necessarily a council comprised only of *dukes*, though it may have been so for years. You see the difference?"

I glanced at their confused faces.

"The council was mentioned in the charter as an advisory body to the first duke, though it was understood it would advise whomever would later sit on the throne. In the past there have been women on the council."

Deep breath, Annie, then lower the boom.

"And I should add that I also read that the members of the council serve at the pleasure of the sovereign." I waited a beat before I added, "That would be me."

Before anyone could object, Dominic said, "Her Grace is correct. It's all in the charter."

"I would most heartily welcome the princess to the council, Your Grace. It seems only fitting, does it not?" Emile Rossi looked around the table. No one was jumping up to agree with him, but no one apparently wanted to risk their position by telling me *thanks but no thanks*.

"Thank you, Emile. I'm sure she will serve the country well. Are there any objections to either of our proposed members?" The room was as quiet as a tomb. "Wonderful. We have our first new members. Anyone else want to propose someone?"

No one spoke.

"So maybe think about who you might want to see join us on the council and bring it up at next week's meeting. Otherwise, while I would really rather see twelve people, if ten is the best we can do for now, so be it." I closed my folder. "Is there anything else we need to discuss today?"

Andre stood. "There is one other thing I should perhaps mention in relation to the funds . . ."

"Yes?" I'd just picked up my pen and dropped it into my purse, ready to pull the plug on that day's meeting.

"As it had been explained to me years ago—and I confirmed anew with my liaison—before the balance of the funds can be returned, Saint Gilbert must be able to prove a means of ongoing self-sufficiency."

"Meaning what?" Jacques asked.

"We have to show that we have a sustainable economy. That this country can support itself without draining the funds once they are returned to us."

I nodded slowly and smiled. "I have a plan for that."

"And that would be?" Vincens asked.

"That would be on the agenda for next week's meeting. Thank you, Andre, for sharing that information. Will there be anything else? Anyone?"

Most of the men seated around the table looked confused. Others were busy with their phones doing whatever old men do on their phones.

"Very well, then." I channeled my best Sister Mary Camille, my tenth-grade history teacher. "Till next week."

Chapter Twenty-Five

Five men scrambled to be the first out of the room. When only Emile, Max, and I were left, I smiled. "Was it something I said?"

"I never would have believed that anyone on the council could have been persuaded to actually *work*," Emile said.

"It's the old carrot and stick thing. You want a golf course? Here's what you have to do to get it. It's amazing what people will do when the outcome is in their best interest."

"You played it perfectly, madam." Emile bent slightly at his waist. "I commend you."

"Thank you," I said just a bit smugly. "I was pretty smooth, wasn't I?"

"Indeed you were, madam." His eyes were deep brown like his nephew's, and they were smiling. "Well done."

We entered the hallway, and Emile bowed again before excusing himself, which left Max and me alone. He started walking in one direction and I in the other.

"May I ask where you are going?" he asked when he realized I was no longer beside him. "There's nothing over there except . . ."

"The library," I stage-whispered. "I love the library, and I love the idea of having a little bit of time to myself in a place where no one knows where I am when I need a break. Which means I won't have to speak to anyone or make any decisions. I can read, or I can just sit and gaze out at the lake and think my thoughts without having to share them. When I was living my old life, I drove an hour to work and an hour home, every day. That was two hours to myself to listen to music or sports talk radio, or think about something I wanted or needed to do at home, or think about the kids, or just think about myself. You know, my place in the world?

"Now my place is very different, but I still have times when I miss being alone. I've always loved libraries, and the books here!" I grinned. "Woo-hoo! Such a treasure trove of genealogy and history. And art. Did you know that at one time, Castle Blanc had collections of art that today would be worth . . . oh my God, millions. Maybe even billions. I mean, beyond the portraits of my ancestors."

"I do know that at one time there'd been an extensive collection, yes, but I don't believe it's ever been proven what happened to the paintings. My grandmother told me the story about how things disappeared, one by one, gradually, so at first no one noticed."

"How can that happen?" I frowned. "How can there be a Degas on the wall one day and not the next, but no one noticed?"

"The originals were replaced with reproductions, some of them not very good, but the eye often sees what it wants to see. By the time it was realized that only poor fakes hung on the castle walls, it was too late. They were gone, and there were no clues as to where they might have gone."

"Hmm. And here I was thinking they were sold off or something. Sounds like an inside job to me."

"Most likely, yes. But there was nothing that pointed to any one individual, so . . ." He shrugged.

"And when did this happen?"

"In the mid-1930s."

"Hmmm. Right before World War II began." I thought about that for a moment. "Almost as if someone knew what was coming. What do you think happened?" I mentally added *find the missing paintings and make whoever has them give them back* to my agenda.

Another shrug. "My best guess? Whoever took them sold them to private collectors who would agree to keep them out of sight."

"What's the purpose of having art that's out of sight? Isn't the idea that you look at it?"

"That's what normal people would do. But there are some people who like to have what no one else can. I suspect it would be people like that who ended up with our paintings."

We'd arrived at the library's double doors. "This is where you leave, my friend," I told him. "And where my hour of peace begins."

"I will have a guard posted immediately," he told me.

I made a face. "I don't need a guard. No one knows I'm here but you."

"You always need a guard and always will have one, as long as I am captain and responsible for your safety."

"But I'm the duchess, so I can overrule you."

"In all things but this, Your Highness. When it comes to your protection, I'm afraid I outrank you."

"Seriously?"

He nodded.

"That's written down somewhere, like a law?"

Another nod, this one accompanied by that half smile that makes my heart flip over backward.

"All right. Send someone. He can stand out here and guard the door. But tell him I'm to be left alone, that no one is to bother me."

"Understood, madam."

"Good. So go on, call someone." I turned to open the door, but Max reached past me, his arm grazing mine. Sigh. I didn't even want to put a name to what I felt when he was that close to me. "But I'm going to look up this 'captain of the castle guard trumps the duchess' thing."

"I would expect nothing less from you, Annaliese." His mouth was close to the side of my face, and don't think for one second that it did not occur to me that if I turned my head just a scootch, we'd be mouth to mouth. The temptation was overwhelming, and I could feel my face flush at the very thought of having that choice to make.

But he opened the doors and walked past me to turn on the lights and look around the room, no doubt to make sure there were no pirates or terrorists or other bad-deed doers lying in wait.

I went inside the large room with the tall glass windows and the two fireplaces, and I simply wandered.

"Marcel will be at the door momentarily." I could feel Max's eyes on me. "Do you have any instructions for him?"

"Yes. What I said before. No one is to bother me for the next hour."

"I'll pass that along to him. Good afternoon, Annaliese." Max left the room and closed the doors behind him.

For a moment I just stood in the middle of that grand space and soaked it in. Could there be a more wonderful dream than a library of your own? One filled with books from floor to ceiling on three sides, everything from fairy tales to history to memoirs and biographies and sciences? Oh, the joy of it! In those stacks I found books about the early rulers of Saint Gilbert, about noteworthy people who'd lived there. I read about alleged sightings of Serafina and the earliest families who settled in that corner of what had been originally part of France. Or what would now be France if it hadn't been carved out as a duchy by one of my ancestors. I met those ancestors—and others, most of whom ruled wisely, though there were a few duds in the lineage—and discovered my heritage. With all the responsibilities of being the GD (Grand Duchess), I totally appreciated that I could have one hour to myself when no one could get in my face about anything. I claimed that time as mine, and I was going to safeguard it—with a little help from Marcel.

I found a book that intrigued me and relocated a chair from next to the fireplace to the windows. I sat, kicked off my shoes, and pulled my legs up under me and opened the book and began reading about how Napoleon had made a request to my great-great-great grandparents for troops to reinforce his army, a request that apparently amused my G-threes greatly. Apparently Saint Gilbert has never had much of a military, and frankly, I'd say they'd managed to survive through the ages well enough without all that fighting other countries seemed to get off on. Even if they'd had an army with which to defend themselves in the 1930s and '40s, they'd have been no match for the Germans or the Soviets, so I guess there was some wisdom there.

There were several photos of my G-two grandfather in his uniform, the jacket of which was covered with ribbons signifying the Order of This or That and the whatever regiment and God only knows what else. Thinking about men in uniform, however, made me think of Max, and how amazing he looked in his Captain of the Castle Guard finery. Which made me think about how fine he looked in everything—his uniform, a three-piece suit, casual slacks and a shirt with the sleeves rolled to his elbows.

All of which made me think about Max in general. I knew it sounded corny, but besides being the most beautiful man it had ever been my pleasure to meet, he was also the *nicest* man I ever met. His quiet humor never failed to make me smile. He was thoughtful and kind, and he treated everyone with respect. Including his mother and me. Especially his mother and me. It made me think that his father must have been a nice guy, too, because I thought boys learned a lot from watching their fathers.

Fortunately, in the case of my son, his father wasn't around all that much during his formative years. Thank God.

I hesitated to describe Max as *nice*, because the word generally sounded so dull, so milquetoast-y, but when you really thought about it, the nice people were the ones you needed in your life. Nice was the friend who was always your port in the storm. The shoulder you cried on. The one who always told you the truth and helped you up when someone else had knocked you down.

That was Max. He was also one of those guys who could get away with being a bit of a jerk because he was so charming and sexy and handsome, but I'd never seen a sign of the jerk in him. He was always a gentleman.

Had I just called Max sexy? I did. I'd been trying really hard not to think of him in terms of sex for a number of reasons. A—I didn't know how he felt about me. B—I didn't know if he was seeing someone and couldn't bring myself to ask because I wasn't sure I wanted to know. C—maybe he was still in love with his late wife. D—and maybe most important, I was the duchess, so in a sense he worked for me—and that could be a problem.

For example, suppose I made an (ill-advised) advance and he felt pressured to comply. You know, like the movie guys used to do to young women who just wanted to act in a film and were made to feel there was a price to pay for their dreams. And that was sexual harassment, because like I said, I was the duchess and that could be seen as me coercing him into a relationship he really didn't want. I'd been on the other side of that scenario, and believe me, I would never want anyone to feel the way I was made to feel. I quit a job once because of it, and I couldn't even explain to my mother why I wanted to leave a good-paying position when I had nothing else lined up, though I knew I'd find something quickly (and I did). I know everyone doesn't have the luxury to walk out, but I was still living at home, so I didn't have to worry about being homeless or starving.

Here's the thing: I really liked Max. I would rather we never moved out of the friend zone than to have him feel he was being forced to want me *that* way. But if he ever gave me a sign he was interested, oh, mama—don't think for a minute I would . . .

My deep thoughts were interrupted by loud giggling. The library door swung open, and my daughter and two other young girls practically fell into the room.

"Excuse me? Did you not see the 'Do Not Disturb' sign on the door?" I asked.

"There's no sign on the door, Mom." Juliette was still giggling.

"Marcel is the sign. He was told not to let anyone in."

"Oh, yeah, that. He said that, but I said it wouldn't apply to me because I am your favorite child." Jules wrapped her arms around me and kissed me on the cheek.

"Not right now you're not," I grumbled. So much for me time.

"Mom, do you know Remy?" She stepped aside and pulled the taller of the two girls closer.

"Of course I know Remy." Max's daughter. Long, dark hair, beautiful long-lashed blue eyes. "I do remember her."

Remy dipped her head in acknowledgment.

"And this is Mila. I met her this morning. She goes to school with Remy."

"Your Majesty." Mila's smile was a mile wide, and she sort of half curtsied. She was shorter than Jules and Remy and carried a few extra pounds that somehow made her seem even cuter. Someone had apparently coached her on how to properly address the duchess.

"It's nice to meet you, Mila." I returned the smile, then looked up at my daughter, who was now draped over the back of my chair. "So what are you three up to this afternoon?"

"We just made a video," Jules announced proudly.

My eyes narrowed. "What kind of video, and for what purpose?"

"It's a sort of travelogue," Jules said excitedly. "I thought it would be fun to do a series of videos about Saint Gilbert and put them on YouTube? That way, my friends back home can see where I live and how beautiful the country is, and maybe they'll want to come here on vacation. You know, like you're always talking about making people want to see the country because nobody's ever heard of it?"

I thought this over for a minute. The kid might be onto something.

"Remy's helped a lot because she knows just about everything about Saint Gilbert, so she's like the travel guide." Jules nodded in the direction of Mila. "Mila's brother has lighting equipment, and he showed her how to use it so she's like our producer and camera person and technical director."

"What have you shot so far?"

"This morning we just walked through the castle—just a few rooms on the first floor. I think it would be cool to start each segment with just a little peek at the castle. And we shot it from outside, too. You know, so people can see how big and beautiful it is." The more excited Juliette got, the faster she spoke.

"People who have seen it compare it to Cinderella's castle in the books," Remy piped up.

"Then we walked into town and just showed some of the shops. The bakery. Gisele's shop. We had to tell the security guys to stay out of the picture. And tomorrow"—Jules's eyes were shining—"we're going to shoot Serafina and then walk down to the lake and tell people about the legend. That was my idea." She smiled with much self-satisfaction. "Everyone loves a good mermaid legend, right?"

"Well, I know I certainly do. And I can't wait to see what you've done. I'm intrigued." I really was. We might be able to use it when we start our big campaign vying for tourist dollars later this year.

"It's not ready for anyone to see yet," Mila spoke up. "We need to clean it up a bit."

"What needs to be cleaned up?" I felt my eyes starting to narrow again.

"Just, you know, bad lighting, or times when the camara got turned around and all you see is sky or grass. That sort of thing," she explained. "And I dropped the phone a couple of times."

"You shot it with your phone?" I asked.

Mila held up her cell. "My brother's going to show me how to upload it so I can edit it."

"Well, when you're finished doing all that, please let me be the first to see it."

Jules turned to her friends. "Mom wants to make sure there's nothing objectionable. Or that we didn't do anything stupid or that makes us look dorky."

"You make me sound like a professional critic."

"You are sometimes. You always say that it's part of your job." Jules leaned over and kissed the top of my head. "It's okay, Mom. I still love you."

"Of course you do. Now you three go. I have . . ." I glanced at my watch. "Twenty minutes left on my hour."

"Mom needs to keep one hour every day for herself," Jules told her friends. "She has to make up for the alone time she used to have when she drove to work and back every day."

I was taken aback by her insight. I didn't realize it was evident that I missed that drive time. Maybe those two hours alone had kept me sane between the people I had to deal with every day—demanding attorneys, misogynist coworkers, entitled claimants, indignant insureds—not to mention my ex. And then there was my family. If you think it's easy raising two teenagers by yourself these days, I invite you to try. It has its joys, of course—I think by now you know I would die for my kids—but I'd be lying if I said it was all fun and games. They are both pretty good, mostly, but man, they've both tested me to the limit at times. It was okay, though. We all survived.

Jules's friends said polite goodbyes, and my daughter led them out of the room. I tried to get back into the frame of mind I'd been in before the interruption, but my brain was soaring around in a dozen directions. I knew that popular videos could get a gazillion views and that the makers of those little gems could become quite influential. Did I want my daughter to become a media influencer? Not really. But what harm could it do if she and her friends spent some of their time introducing people to the beauty of this little country? So I mentally gave them my blessings and thought of a few more things they could video.

Ceil should take them to the castle she's going to be working on. It could be the first step in laying the groundwork for our spa. I leaned back and closed my eyes and imagined all those teenage girls showing their middle-aged mothers and older grandmothers the magical place where they could spend two weeks and leave their wrinkles behind. I was still toying with the idea of whether to use a reference to the fountain of youth when my phone's alarm told me my hour was up. I tucked my book back onto the shelf and went to my office to confirm that the plans were in place for me to sit down with the entire group of soap makers on the following day. I couldn't wait.

Chapter Twenty-Six

At breakfast the following morning, Jules showed off her finished video to me, her aunts, and her brother, who stopped in to see if we had eaten all our chocolate croissants (we had, to his disappointment). I had to admit those young girls did a damned fine job. If I didn't know better, I'd have thought I was looking at a professional production. While Juliette and Remy did get a little giggly at times, it was just enough to add a touch of sweet girlish charm.

The video started with Juliette standing in front of a portrait of my grandmother that hung in the upstairs hallway. She and Remy were both dressed in short black skirts and white button-down blouses, the sleeves rolled to the elbows, and looked like tour guides. Which, now that I think about it, was probably the intent.

"Hi," Juliette said brightly. "My name is Princess Juliette Elizabet Terese of the Grand Duchy of Saint Gilbert. Yes, I am a real princess." Eyes wide. Giggles. "Is that crazy cool or what? And this is my friend Remy," she said as Remy stepped into view. "She's not a princess, but her father *is* a duke. Remy grew up here in Saint Gilbert, and she knows all the cool places. So I thought it would be fun if we could show my friends back in my hometown of Philadelphia my new home and tell you all about the country that my mom inherited from her grand-mother. My mom's the grand duchess, which is sorta like queen if they had a queen here." Here she grinned. "I know, right? I wouldn't believe it myself if I didn't know for a fact it's all true! I mean, I'm living it!"

Another giggle.

"Oh, and you don't have to be from Philadelphia or one of my friends to take the tour with us. You just have to love a good fairy tale." She appeared to be thinking this over. "Or maybe you just want to learn about a beautiful place you've maybe never heard of."

Juliette stepped aside and pointed to the portrait she'd been standing in front of. "This is my great-grandmother. My grandma's mom. Her name was Her Royal Highness, Grand Duchess Annaliese Emelie Sophia Elizabet of the Grand Duchy of Saint Gilbert. She was twelve when this painting was made. Wasn't she beautiful? She was fifteen when she was forced to leave the country when . . . well, I'm saving *that* story for another day, but it's dramatic and scary and maybe just a little bit romantic. Well, just the part about how she met my great-granddad in London. It's so cool. Oh, and it's real history, like, the Second World War history? So it's educational! You'll love it, I promise . . ."

And so went the video. At the end, once more standing in front of the castle, she smiled for the camera and said, "Come back next time and you'll see more of the castle we live in. It's called Castle Blanc because it's white, and *blanc* is French for 'white.' See you!"

When it was over, I got up and gave her a hug. "That was amazing, sweetie. You did a great job leading the narration. I'm really impressed."

"Way to go, Juliette. You were adorable." Ceil, who'd been hanging over my shoulder, applauded. "The castle looks magical, and I love the way the shops all look like they're from another world."

"Well, they sort of are, Aunt Ceil," a beaming Jules told her. "They're, like, a thousand years old."

"Not quite a thousand, but they are pretty old," I pointed out.

Roe grabbed the phone and studied the images for a moment. "It sort of reminds me of Society Hill back in Philly."

"Yeah, if Society Hill had been built when Tudor architecture was the latest thing. Like, in the fifteen hundreds." I got up and tugged on a strand of my daughter's hair. I really was proud of her. When your teenager tells you she's made a YouTube video, you're at the mercy of the gods, so I'd been holding my breath until I'd seen what the girls had produced. "You and Remy nailed it on your first try. I hope you get a million hits."

"I love the flute music in the background," Ceil added.

"That's actually Remy playing the flute. It's from a recital she did at school last year. Her dad bought the video and we lifted the sound. Pretty cool, huh? It was my idea to add music." Jules was delighted with herself, the way almost-fifteen-year-olds are when they do something new and they are perfect the first time out.

"It almost looks professionally done," Roe said as she handed the phone back to Jules. "Like there are no stumbles or anything."

"That's 'cause Mila's brother edited it for us last night," Jules explained. "He's really good at that sort of thing. He's going to be a filmmaker."

"Let me see that." Ralphie reached for the phone. "What's your friend's brother's name? The guy I play soccer with in the afternoons is studying film."

"His name's Henri." Juliette turned to me. "Isn't that the coolest name? It's spelled like Henry but with an *I* instead of a *y* at the end, but they pronounce it like *On-ree*. Emphasis on the *ree*."

"Gotta be the same guy. Yeah, he's a cool dude. Good soccer player, too." Ralphie turned to face me. "He's the guy I told you wants to put together a team and maybe find someplace to make a field."

"I gotta go. I'm meeting Remy and Mila in an hour, and I have to get dressed." Juliette put out her hand, and her brother put her phone into her palm. "Thanks for letting me share your breakfast again, Mom."

"You're welcome. I love starting the morning with you." I stood and stretched, wondering if there was ever a day in my life when it took me a full hour to get dressed. My coronation maybe. I know I didn't take that long to dress for my wedding.

"A soccer team. That would be good." It was on my list, but now I started thinking about it for real. All the European nations have soccer teams, right? It's like the big sport, except they call it football. Which is not what people in the States think of when they think *football*. Still, soccer is pretty popular in the US. Ralphie and Jules both played from the time they were little. Jules dropped it in high school—lacrosse and field hockey are the "in" sports for girls at her school—but Ralphie was really good.

"Maybe you could put that on that list of things to do you're always talking about. I mean, you're the duchess. That should count for something." That son of mine. He's a study in subtlety.

"It's already there." When he started to pump his fist, I hastened to add, "Not at the top of the list, but it's on there."

"Wait till I tell Henri." Ralphie started toward the door.

"Nope. Not yet. I'll let you know when." He gave me a thumbs-up, which means he heard me but he wasn't making any promises. "Not kidding, Ralphie. Not for public consumption." But the door was already closing behind him. "And if you're going jogging, don't forget to tell your security people."

Not that the guards at the front door would let him leave the castle without someone with him.

"Good talk, son," I muttered. "Well, this has been a pleasant way to start the day, as always, but we all have things to do, places to go. I'm meeting with the soap ladies—"

"Don't leave without me. I'm coming along." Ceil drained her coffee cup and set it on the tray.

"I thought you were touring castles today."

"We'd hoped to. The contractor was busy, but he said he'd free up tomorrow for us. Of course he immediately offered to put off his work today to accommodate us, but I didn't want him to do that. I remember how pissed I'd get when a contractor I was working with didn't show up and set my entire job back, so I told him tomorrow was soon enough."

"Nice, Ceil." My sister always put herself in the other guy's shoes. I admire her for that. It was something I didn't always remember to do. I made a mental note: be more like Ceil.

"And Roe—what's on your agenda?" I finished the very last of my coffee.

"I thought I'd drive around and see a little more of the country," she told us. "Check out a few farms, see what's growing. That sort of thing."

"I'll ask Max to arrange for a driver." I searched my bag for my phone.

"Just a car. I can drive myself," Roe said.

"Um, no. They drive on the opposite side of the road here."

"So?" She was scrolling through her phone, smiling at something.

"So when was the last time you drove a car?"

Roe shrugged. "I dunno. Last year, maybe?"

"It was the week before Christmas, and you borrowed my car and you took out the trash cans Mrs. Girardi used to save her parking spot."

It's a South Philly thing. Parking on those narrow streets is a bitch. All those row houses, no garages, so little room out front to park a car. Residents will put anything out in the street in front of their houses—trash cans, folding beach chairs, whatever they can find—to mark their territory to reserve what they believe is their personal parking space. It's South Philly for *don't even think about parking here.* It's not legal, and the city's cracked down on it, but it still happens.

"I paid to replace them," she said archly.

"The dent in the front of my car is still there," I reminded her.

"Not my fault your insurance has a high deductible." She made a face at me. So mature.

"In any case, Annie's right, Roe," Ceil chimed in. "Back home, you can barely drive on the right side of the road. You're not driving here. Besides, I thought you said you wanted to see more of the countryside.

Which you cannot do if you're desperately trying to keep the car on the road."

Before Roe could argue the point further, I said, "Ceil's right. You can't drive and sightsee at the same time. Plus you can't leave the castle without security."

"Still not sure I see the point of that, but okay." Roe nodded. "See if you can get someone to drive me around and keep me safe. Let me know."

Ceil shoved our sister out the door. "I'll be back in twenty minutes to go meet the soap ladies," she said over her shoulder.

"Ceil," I called to her before she closed the door. "You said *back home.*"

"I did?"

"Yeah, you did. Do you think you'll ever feel like Saint Gilbert is really your home?"

She paused, and I could tell she was thinking. Finally, she said, "I don't know. I hope so. I want to. It's different, but it's a good place. I feel comfortable here. You?"

"Same."

"Do you ever miss the States? Philly? Your old life?" she asked, one hand on the elaborate brass doorknob.

"Yeah. Oh, yeah, I do sometimes. There's no place like home, Ceil."

"And yet, here we are."

I shrugged. "I think this is where we're supposed to be."

"Do you think you'll ever go back?"

"Definitely to visit. But to stay? I don't know. I kind of feel torn. I love the US of A. But I'm loving Saint Gilbert, too."

"We can have dual citizenship, though, right?"

"I'm pretty sure. I wouldn't give up my US citizenship."

She left the room, closing the door softly behind her. I sat for a moment, thinking about all that I'd left behind. My house, my friends, my neighborhood, my job, my coworkers. My old life, my old city. I was feeling a little nostalgic for Philly, to tell you the truth. It's a very unique place, Philly is. Oh, I know all the negative things people say about it, but it's not that bad.

Well, okay, sometimes it is. But I was born and raised there, had my kids there, worked hard to buy us a home there. It would make me very sad if I never saw the city again.

But right now there was another city on my mind, and I needed to get myself pulled together to deal with the needs of Beauchesne and the surrounding villages.

~

Roe was off and running with her driver and her guards by the time Max had our car waiting exactly at ten. Ceil and I left the castle with our little entourage of security. I likened them to the Secret Service but much lower key, though they did all dress in black. They accompanied me everywhere outside the castle walls. I still didn't see the need, but Max insisted, and since protecting me was his primary official function, I'd stopped questioning the need for the car in front and the car behind the one I rode in.

"This is so exciting," Ceil whispered as we both settled into the back seat of the car. "Aren't you excited, Annie? We're going to meet the ladies who make that lovely soap and see if we can talk them into making more and being part of our efforts to bring . . ." She paused. "What?"

"What what?"

"What are you thinking about? You're a zillion miles away and thinking about something else when you should be thinking about soap. What's going on?"

"There's something I've been needing to talk to you about, but I needed to wait until we were alone for more than five minutes, so I guess now's as good a time as any," I said.

Ceil poked me and drew my attention to her left hand, where her index finger pointed like a little arrow to the front seat, where Max sat behind the wheel.

"Not exactly alone," she whispered.

"Oh, Max already knows." I met his eyes in the rearview mirror, and for a moment I forgot what I'd wanted to discuss with her.

"He does?" Ceil frowned.

Might as well just toss it out there. "Ceil, I suggested to the Duke's Council that you be brought on as another member."

"What?" Her eyes went wide. "Why? I'm not a duke, and I'm not a man."

"True, but you don't have to be either." I explained to her what I'd found about the council through my research. "We need more responsible people tackling the problems we have to resolve, Ceil. I need someone I trust with my whole heart. Someone I know is smart and hardworking and . . ."

Ceil laughed. "Don't overplay your hand. I'm in if you need me."

As if there was ever a doubt. "Thank you. You're the best sister ever."

"Are you adding Roe as well?"

I shook my head. "I'm thinking two Gilberti women are all they're going to be able to handle. Besides, I don't think Roe's the council type."

"Don't sell her short. Granted, she's different in a lot of ways, but she's smart in her own right, and if you give her free rein with the kitchens for the castles and the chateaus, you will congratulate yourself for your brilliance. She's an amazing cook. I'm happy that she's going to have the chance to come into her own."

"All the more reason for letting her do her thing while we do ours." It wasn't so much that I doubted Roe's abilities or her intelligence or her work ethic. It was just that sometimes, I couldn't deal with the baggage, the drama, that Roe always seemed to drag around with her. In the end, though, she was my sister, and I did love her. Most of the time.

"Yeah, I know she can be tough." Ceil patted my hand.

"Right," I agreed. I mentally checked off *Ceil to council.* Which left about eight hundred other things to resolve by the end of the day. It was a depressing thought, and it was weighing me down. Most days I'm okay with all the responsibility—I actually *like* it, and I love being in charge. But some days—like today—I feel like I'm floating in a sea of giant cotton balls, getting nowhere and fighting off suffocation.

When I didn't say more, Ceil poked me again.

"What's going on with you?" she asked. I could feel her studying my face. A moment later, she said softly, "You're losing your mojo, Annie."

I shook my head. Suddenly even the thought of explaining how I felt exhausted me.

"I'm not going to stop asking, so you might as well spill."

"You know, like when you have one of those days when all of a sudden, it all seems like too much? Like, thinking about one more thing will make your head explode?" I forced a smile. "I'm sure it's only temporary."

"No, it's Annie syndrome. Must do all things. Must be all things to all people. High-achiever syndrome." She sighed. "It's a lifelong affliction for you. You're a people pleaser and a doer, a combination which could end up making you empress of the world or hiding in a small room somewhere clutching your blankie."

"Or the grand duchess of Saint Gilbert."

"There is that for real." Ceil took my hand. "What do you need, Annie? Let's figure this out. Your shine is slipping."

I gazed out the window and thought about that. What did I need? Finally, I whispered, "I need help."

"Okay."

"I have so much going on inside my head right now. All the things we need to accomplish. Everything that has to be done." I felt tears building behind my eyes, and I tried to hold them in. "It's overwhelming. I want it all and I want it all done right."

"And you want it all done right right now." Ceil knew me all too well. "So let's look at where we can get help. Maybe it's not necessary to do it all."

I shook my head again. "I've set out this whole agenda and committed to it, and now I have to do it. Fix it all. The roads to nowhere and the schools that don't function and having to go to Switzerland or France or Italy for everything we don't have here and that's most everything. I have to do it. All of it, or I've failed."

"That's ridiculous." Ceil swatted away the thought with her right hand. "You're trying to resurrect a country that's been dormant for years. Just the thought that you would attempt such a thing is mind-blowing."

"It's what I came here to do."

"And you've already set the wheels in motion for so much to happen. There is no failure here, girl. Especially on your part." She paused. "Want my advice?"

"Of course."

"Bring in people you trust to handle some of the load."

"Other than you, and sometimes Roe, I don't have anyone." I thought that over. "I have Max, and I have Claudette, both of whom are already overloaded with responsibilities."

"Who do you trust most in your life? Other than us."

I didn't have to think twice. "Marianne."

Ceil pulled my phone from my bag. "Call her. Right now. Offer her whatever she needs to come here and be your right hand."

I stared at the phone.

"You need a right hand," she told me.

"I have you."

"I have my own responsibilities here, Annie," Ceil said softly.

She was right. She has a whole spa / wedding destination / luxury stay-in-a-castle getaway industry to create, castles and chateaus to renovate and decorate, a PR plan for the country, marketing for the spa. I did need a right hand, but it couldn't be her.

"I'll call Marianne this afternoon when we get back. Maybe she'll consider it."

Ceil laughed. "Please. 'Come live in my castle and we'll do stuff together.' She'll be on the next plane."

I smiled. "She'll clear her decks and then she'll come. I don't know why I didn't think of it. Thanks, sis."

"Of course. That's why I'm here. To help you think."

We both laughed lightly. I did feel better. Ceil was spot-on, as always. I needed help, and I was too bogged down to realize that all I had to do was ask. There was no doubt in my mind that Marianne would be here by the end of the month.

"So does that about cover it?" Ceil asked.

I nodded. "Pretty much. Except for the apple thing."

Ceil frowned. "What apple thing?"

"Someone was telling me last night that in the southwest corner of Saint Gilbert, there's an orchard where they're growing heirloom apples. Some of the varieties are so rare, there's only one tree of its kind left. Can you imagine? How sad is that? One tree before that kind of apple disappears forever. So I need to . . ."

"No, you don't. Appoint someone minister of agriculture and turn it over." Ceil looked to the front seat. "Max, I'll bet you know someone who is really into agriculture who would love to take on such a project."

He nodded. "I do, indeed, Princess. Should I make a call?"

Ceil answered before I could open my mouth. "Yes, please."

"Consider it done, Princess." His smile lit up the mirror.

Ceil turned to me. "And that is how you handle the fate of the lone heirloom apple tree."

"Thanks, Ceil." I felt more than a little foolish for having forgotten how capable my sister is. I've always said she should have been the first-born. She's more like the older sister than the middle.

"Max," Ceil said to the face in the mirror. "What do you call my sister when you're alone, like, talking casually?"

He paused. "At her insistence, I call her Annaliese."

"At my insistence, under the same circumstances, please call me Ceil. Or Cecilia."

"As you wish."

Max followed the car in front of us as it made a right turn onto a lane that led to a pretty white building that had masses of flowers planted around the steps. It reminded me a little of the villas you see dotted through Southern Italy. Ceil leaned close to the window and gazed out. "Oh. Are we here?"

"Max?" I asked.

"Yes, Your Grace. This is where the soap makers' guild meets." He parked the car behind the first one, whose passengers had gotten out and headed up the steps into the building. Moments later they returned and signaled Max. Very James Bond. I'd gotten so used to it that I barely noticed them, but it was clear Ceil was intrigued.

I answered her unspoken question. "I don't know what they're doing, but it's what Max wants, and he's the chief."

"Captain," he good-naturedly corrected from the front seat as he opened the driver's side door and stepped out. "And it's just a precaution, Your Grace. We take the security of all our royals very seriously."

Chapter Twenty-Seven

The ladies of the guild—and yes, they were all ladies—were gathered in little clusters here and there throughout a large reception area. They were chattering when we entered the room, but our entrance caused a bit of a stir. I greeted the members I'd already met by name, and there were many of them, but I was surprised at just how many women in this twenty-first century were still making their own soap. I said as much after Ceil and I were formally introduced by the head of the guild, Louisa Allard, whom I'd met several times in the past. I took a few moments to explain why I was there, our thoughts about the soap, our plan to market it right there in Saint Gilbert, and how I thought the soap would be the *it* factor to put the country on the world stage. Where, I said with conviction as I closed, Saint Gilbert belonged.

There was silence. Then there was applause. Wild, happy applause.

"Your Highness, I believe you can see with your own eyes how delighted we are with your recognition of our humble product," Louisa began once the room began to settle. "We are deeply grateful for the opportunity to play so important a role in your strategy to improve the lives of the people of our country, and we are honored that you chose the women of Saint Gilbert to lead the way." She smiled broadly. "Because it is the women—only the women—who make the soap."

"I'd wondered about that when I realized there were no men in the room," I said, and light laughter followed.

"The men have always believed soapmaking is beneath them," someone said.

"It's the soap that will save Saint Gilbert," I told them, and I meant it. The golf courses and the ski slopes were all going to be solid tourist draws, but the salvation of Saint Gilbert would be the soap. Because if there was a woman alive who at fifty or sixty or seventy wouldn't love to shave a decade or three off her face, I haven't met her. Not that everyone had to look like they're twenty-five. My philosophy was you do you. But I know a lot of women don't like what they see in the mirror, and if something as natural as soap could make those ladies a little happier, why not? I say no judgment either way.

"The women have always been the backbone of this country." I knew that voice. It belonged to a woman I'd met during my first visit. Her name was Marguerite, and she was a contemporary of my grandmother's and her second cousin. She'd told me once that her mother had been an attendant of my great-grandmother. How's that for a legacy?

"Our times of greatest prosperity were those times a grand duchess sat on the throne. Our greatest monarchs were women." Turning to me, she continued. "It was your great-grandmother who devised the scheme to send our treasure to the Swiss for safekeeping. It was she who insisted that your grandmother be crowned and swept from the country even as the invaders were at our door and she knew for certain that her own death was but hours away. Even so, she kept a cool head and ensured the monarchy would continue, and with the monarchy would come prosperity once again. It has always been so." She smiled. "You are a worthy successor. We are fortunate that you have come home to us."

Well, choke me seven ways to Sunday. I had a lump in my throat the size of the Liberty Bell. Honestly, you want to shut me up, say something like that. Compare me to the women in my family who were heroes in their own right—call to mind the bravery of my grandmother, the wisdom and forethought of my great-grandmother—and I'm a puddle. It gets me every time.

"You are most gracious. Thank you for your kind words," I heard Ceil say when I'd fallen silent. "I speak for my sister—for both my sisters—when I tell you we are blessed to be here. We want nothing more than to see this country thrive. And to that end, let us get down to work. The duchess has told you what we're planning. Tell us what you will need to make those plans a reality. We need to speak specifically, ladies. What raw materials will you need, how much, and where will they come from? How much soap do you produce now? What could we count on to be produced in the future?"

And the excited chatter began again. I breathed a sigh of relief, stepped back, and let Ceil do her thing.

"What can I get you, Your Grace?" Claudette appeared out of nowhere as she sometimes seemed to do. "A coffee, perhaps?"

"I would kill for a cup, yes, thank you."

"No need to go to that extreme." Smiling, she led me to a settee near the front of the room, where I could watch and listen but not intrude upon the magic my sister was weaving among the ladies of the guild. With a gesture, Claudette had a tray holding several cups, a carafe, a sugar bowl, and a small pitcher set up before me on a small table.

I glanced up at Claudette. "You know me too well."

Still smiling, she poured a cup for me. "I know you often enjoy a little midmorning 'pick me up,' I believe you call it."

"I do. Thank you." I sipped the delicious liquid and sighed. The day was unfolding better than it had begun. I was happy for a few moments to sit back and listen to Ceil asking questions and discussing the viability of the type of spa she had in mind. It was a great relief to have someone else take the reins, and after all, the spa would be her baby.

That lasted for about five minutes. When I heard the word *lye* bandied about, I had to interject.

"Lye?" I stood, cup still in hand. "Did you say lye? You aren't talking about putting lye into the soap, are you? It's corrosive. It'll burn the skin right off your face."

"All soap contains lye, madam," Louisa explained kindly. "Soap is made when a fat—such as olive oil or coconut oil or lard—is combined with an alkaline, such as lye. A chemical reaction called saponification occurs. It takes time for the process to work, but through it, the lye is naturally removed from the mix, and what remains is ready to be worked into soap. I invite you both to watch the process sometime. You must take precautions, of course—protect your skin and eyes and clothing from the lye, which is in a flaky form—but the process is very safe when you adhere to the guidelines."

"When does the goat milk go in?" I asked.

"Ah, that is a different part of the process. We freeze the goat milk, add the lye to it, stir it until the lye has melted the frozen milk. Then we add the oil . . ."

"Do you use olive oil or . . ."

"Olive, sometimes, yes. Our climate is not suitable to grow the fruit, but my sister has a grove in Italy, and she sells only to us," someone said.

What followed was a lively discussion of who preferred one fat over another and why. Apparently there was no one way, no set recipe for the soap. So what was the magic ingredient that kept the skin of everyone who used it looking so many years younger?

I asked, and the room fell silent. I looked around at all the faces, waiting for someone. Anyone.

"If you don't all use the same recipe, why is the end effect always the same?" I asked. Still nothing.

Finally, I asked, "What are the common ingredients?"

"Goat milk," someone said.

"Violet petals," someone else offered.

"There are many soaps that smell of violets, some artificially, though. And there are lots of soaps on the market in America that contain goat milk," I told them. "None of them have the effect on the skin that yours does. Why is that? What's the difference between the goat milk in Saint Gilbert and everywhere else?"

Again, no response.

"Maybe there's something in the grass the goats eat," Ceil suggested.

"They eat other vegetation as well," someone noted. "Maybe there's something in the vines or the flowers. Goats eat what they eat. They're not very discriminating."

"Maybe it's in the water," Louisa suggested. " Forgive us for not having a definitive answer. None of us really thought about how the soap affected our skin until you began inquiring. It's simply been the way we've made soap in this country for hundreds of years. No one's questioned it before."

"It could be something in the water," Ceil agreed. "The water here is partly glacial runoff." She turned to me. "I read that somewhere."

"So it could be a mineral in the soil, or in the water, or in some way the goats metabolize whatever they eat or drink. Or somehow a combination of the water and the—whatever it is the goats are eating." I thought for a moment. "Are these everyday, common, anyone-can-buy-them-anywhere goats? Or are they special to Saint Gilbert?" Thinking about heirloom apples has a way of making your brain expand into other territories. Like heirloom goats.

"They're just goats, Duchess," a voice from the back volunteered. "The only kind of goats we've ever had."

Hmmm. I looked at Ceil and she looked at me. Maybe these were special goats that produce magic milk? We shrugged at each other. Maybe someone in the country knew, but it was clear no one in this room did.

Mental note to self: Where did the goats come from originally?

Then we talked about infusing the soaps with scent and adding flower petals to make it pretty. Everyone seemed to have their own idea of how the flowers should be prepared before dropping them into the soap, when, and how much. We spent an enlightening few hours with the ladies of the soap guild, including a delicious lunch prepared back at the castle and delivered and supervised by Claudette and her staff. Which explained why Claudette was there, but not why her staff was larger than mine.

I brought this up to Ceil when we arrived back at the castle, gift bars of soap in hand.

"Claudette is the most together person I've ever known," Ceil said. "She just figures out what has to happen and then she makes it work. What exactly is her position here?"

I had to think that over for a moment. "She's sort of like the major-domo, the person in charge of the castle."

"With your blessing?"

"Absolutely. No one—I mean, no one—knows this country or this castle the way that woman does. She's been in charge since the day I first set foot in Saint Gilbert, and I couldn't function without her. She has this network . . ." I shook my head in wonder at just how vast that network must be. "She knows everyone in the country, and she knows where to go to get what we need and who best to do whatever. I think she's been planning for this—the return of the duchess—her entire life." I pondered that thought. "She did say that her mother had been the head lady-in-waiting for our great-grandmother, so I guess she learned protocol and everything from her mother. I think they all thought that Gran would come back someday and she'd be the grand duchess and life would return to normal. So maybe Claudette's mother was training her so that when that happened, she'd know what to do."

I thought about what I'd just said. "So of course, she'd be the person for me to go to, to help develop a staff that could lighten the load. Someone to handle communications, someone to keep a calendar for me."

"Excellent idea," Ceil said. "Especially since there are days when you don't know what day it actually is."

"Right." I could see this working out for me.

"And someone to help you with your clothes," she added.

I felt my face draw into a frown. "What about my clothes?"

"You spend twenty minutes every morning standing in the closet, trying to remember where you're going that day, who you're going to meet, what you're going to do, and what you should wear to cover all the bases. And then you end up wearing one of your black dresses anyway."

"I like my black dresses," I muttered.

"Well, some events call for a little more pizazz. You could have someone who knows your schedule, knows what you need to wear, and has it ready for you."

When I started to protest, she talked right over me.

"And there are days when you have to change from something casual to more formal for a different meeting or whatever, and you waste another twenty minutes or so in the closet trying to decide what to change into. Someone else could have that change ready for you."

"I haven't needed anyone to dress me since I was three. It all sounds ridiculously indulgent, Ceil."

"It would be if you didn't have an image to create and maintain. You are now the face of this country, kiddo. You need to play the part. You shouldn't be wasting time trying to figure it out, and you shouldn't show up everywhere in the same dress."

Hmmm. As much as I hated to admit it, Ceil was right. I spent a lot of time trying to figure these things out. "Maybe I'll talk to Claudette."

Ceil held up her hands. "My work here is done. Look how much we've accomplished already today. Soap guild—check. Annie's agenda—check. New staffing—check." She nudged me with her shoulder. "Help is on the way, sister. Just hang in there."

"First thing when we get back to the castle, I'm calling Marianne," I told her. "Then I'm going to set a meeting with Claudette and figure out the rest of it."

By the end of the day, Marianne had promised to be here by next week at the earliest, the end of the month at the latest. As predicted, she was over the moon about joining us and said she'd been secretly hoping I'd need her. She was going to be the royal secretary—keeper of my calendar and scheduler, for starters. Claudette had offered to have Marianne more or less shadow her for the first few weeks after she arrived so she could see how the castle was run, and she'd also gone over official castle functions pertaining directly to me and offered her suggestions on not only positions but personnel to fill them ("For Her Grace's mistress of the wardrobe, I'd suggest Elaina Montrose. She has an excellent sense of style and protocol for one so young . . ."). And before the sun had set, we had a candidate for minister of agriculture. Max had personally suggested Carlo DellaVecchio, a name that sat uneasily with me, but Max had faith in him, and I was going to have to trust him.

Besides, Max had told me he believed Carlo would work very well with Ceil, and while I wasn't sure exactly what that meant—for Ceil or for the soap industry or for the goats we were going to try to track down—I gave Max the green light to offer the new position to Carlo. I could only hope it didn't turn out to bite me in the butt. I still hadn't met a DellaVecchio I trusted.

Chapter Twenty-Eight

With Ceil and Rosalie off early to check out possible spa venues with the contractors—in the end, Max had arranged for two: one who specialized in exteriors, the other interiors—I had a fairly quiet day. I suppose at some point, after all the repairs on Castle Blanc had been completed, we would be hosting social events, but right now weekends are low key. I spent most of the day in the little room I'd claimed as my own, located within the suite we'd designated as the castle offices. So far, mine was the only office in use other than the larger space I'd offered to Claudette, who, as our driving force, needed the most room. I was still writing thank-you notes to the visitors who'd attended the coronation, many of whom had brought gifts from their respective countries. My mom had always insisted on handwritten thank-yous, so I'd had plenty of practice over the years. At my request, Claudette had a list of visitors and gifts and their donors left on my desk so I didn't miss anyone. I especially enjoyed writing notes to the ladies who'd been so intrigued by the flawless, wrinkle-free faces of the people of Saint Gilbert. For them, I tossed out a cryptic line: I'll be in touch soon regarding your possible return to Saint Gilbert. Heh.

Sometime in the midafternoon, I thought I heard voices—lots of voices—coming from the front of the castle. I left the office and greeted the guard who was always stationed outside any room I was in, but as

I passed him, I realized I was not alone. Two guards accompanied me, silently falling into place, one on either side.

"I'm good," I assured them. "You don't need to walk me to the front door. I know the way, but thank you."

"Captain's orders, Your Grace."

"All righty, then." I didn't see the need, but there was no use protesting. These guys answered only to Max. I pointed toward the end of the hall and the front entrance to the castle. "Onward."

Of course there were uniformed guards to open the castle door, and our little trio walked out into the courtyard where what appeared to be a battalion of guards were assembled. At the front of the troop, Max stood in full uniform, speaking softly enough that those in the back had to lean forward to hear. All in all there were probably close to sixty or seventy, mostly men, but I was glad to see several young women in the group. As I and my two new best friends made our way across the wide courtyard, heads began to turn in our direction. When Max saw us, he said something I could not hear to the assembly before him and strode toward us.

"Your Grace," he said, stiffly half bowing from his waist.

"Captain Belleme," I said with more formality than usual. "What's going on here?"

"I was having an informal chat with our newest recruits," he said.

"Why are you recruiting more guards? You just added more right before the coronation. Is there something I should know?"

His hesitation was brief but still, I caught it. "Only that with the increase in the number of people coming and going from the castle every day and the efforts we know will be made to bring tourists into our country, it was thought best to prepare now for a time when we might better guard our castle, our city, the villages. And of course, our duchess and her family."

"How many new recruits are there?"

"Counting these, perhaps a hundred or more."

I felt an eyebrow raise. "To guard a castle in a country as small as this?"

"I believe in being prepared for any and all . . . situations, Your Grace."

"I think I'd like to hear more about those *situations*. Let's take a walk." I nodded in the direction of my two personal guards. "I don't think we need the extras."

Max dismissed the two guards, then gestured to another of his officers, who apparently picked up where Max had left off in his address to the recruits.

I wandered toward the far side of the castle in the direction of the lake, and Max followed, his hands clasped behind his back, his expression thoughtful. We walked in silence until we arrived at the grassy area that led down to the water. It was a beautiful afternoon, sunny, a clear blue sky and a soft breeze, and the lake sparkled. I'd have loved to kick off my shoes, grab Max by the hand, run down to the water's edge, and wade into the lake, but I felt eyes on me from every direction and figured it might not be cool if anyone took a picture. So unduchess-like. Then again, it would make me happy. Still, I reined myself in. I was curious about this effort to add to the number of castle guards. Max wasn't one to act without good cause.

"What's really going on, Max?" We'd reached the stone wall surrounding the lake, and I leaned against it. "What's with the troops?"

"Information has come my way relative to some rumors that are drifting around the city. No one seems to know where they're coming from."

"Rumors?" I couldn't help it. I rolled my eyes. "Rumors have you concerned enough to recruit additional guards?"

"You are aware there is a faction of the population who . . ."

"Right. Didn't want the monarchy returned. Wanted something else." I paused. "What do they want? Besides maybe or maybe not wanting to shoot me."

"They've not been very active lately, so we're still trying to determine that."

"They didn't want the monarchy back in January, so they probably still don't want it." I was trying hard not to pout. No one likes to hear that they are unpopular or unwanted, even if it's only by a small segment of the population. "Are these people credible? I mean, are they just rabble-rousers or do they have a point? Small group? Big group? Are there active protests?"

"Most likely a small faction, since they haven't been heard from since your coronation. Credible? I don't know."

"Why the concern now if you've known about them all year?"

"Someone's been chatting up people in the cafés and on the street, but we don't know if it's the same group. But that someone's been starting conversations with something along the lines of 'Who is Annaliese Gilberti?'"

"Seriously? Who *am* I?" I laughed out loud. "What is that supposed to mean?"

"That's one of the things we're trying to find out."

"Is this the first you heard about this?"

"I have only been recently informed," he said cryptically.

"Informed by whom?" I stopped and recalled something he'd said a moment ago. "And this information that 'came your way'? Where did it come from?"

He shrugged. "There are eyes and ears."

"Eyes and ears?" I grinned in spite of the seriousness of the conversation. "You mean, like *spies*?" Intrigued, I leaned a little closer and lowered my voice. "Are you telling me the captain of the castle guard has *spies*?"

He cleared his throat. "The castle guard is charged with protecting the realm in any way necessary. That often requires information to be gathered by whatever means is available."

"We have *spies*." I couldn't help it. The latent James Bond in me was tickled at the very idea of a network of spies operating in my castle. Yes, it may have been a little childish, but come on, it was just another part of the fairy tale I was living. "So do they have a name? Like MI6? CIA? KGB?"

He looked skyward. "I never should have said 'eyes and ears.'"

"Oh, come on. Don't stop now." I moved closer. "Max, are you the spymaster?" An image of Varys, the Master of Whisperers, the Spider from *Game of Thrones*, popped into my head.

"You are making entirely too much of this, Annaliese." It seemed he was trying to sound a little stern, but when you were Max, it was hard to pull off. His half smile was always the tell. "Suffice it to say that there are a few individuals in key places who keep their ears to the ground. And that is all I will say about that."

"Not even to tell me who . . ."

"No."

I sighed, and Varys disappeared in a cloud of smoke. "So where do we go from here?"

"We wait to see what the intelligence shows. And we will continue to search for the leader of the January opposition to see if they are involved."

I brushed off the back of my skirt where I'd been leaning against the wall. "Is there any danger right now?"

"None that I can see," Max assured me. "I would certainly alert you if I thought there was an imminent threat."

"Good. Because right now, my sisters are off somewhere with a couple of contractors looking at old buildings."

"A couple of contractors and a good number of guards, who have gone through each of those properties prior to the princesses arriving and have been stationed there while the chateaus are being evaluated."

"Thank you."

Max nodded, and together we started to make our way back up to the castle. Several times the backs of our hands glanced off each other, and I wanted nothing more than to take his hand and walk the rest of the way holding it. But I couldn't bring myself to do it. What if he pulled away? How embarrassing would that be? I've never been shy about approaching a man I was interested in, but this was different from flirting with a guy at a club in Philly. There was so much more at stake than whether he was going to buy me a drink or ask for my number and whether he'd turn out to be a nice guy or a jerk. This man literally held my life and that of my family in his hands. But even more important, I was afraid any overt action on my part that turned out to be unwanted might change our relationship—not in a good way—and I could not bear to have that happen. So I merely continued to let my hand brush against his a few more times all the way back to the castle.

$\sim$

If Saturdays at Castle Blanc were just another day at the office, the nights were no more exciting. We'd fallen into the habit of having a family dinner together in one of the small informal dining rooms, and we'd talk about the same sort of things we used to talk about at the table in Philly. News from the old neighborhood. What the kids' next year of school might look like. What everyone had planned for the coming week. Yes, of course, the details differed wildly from the past, but the essence remained the same. We were just a family talking about our lives. Then the kids would go up to the room on the second floor that we'd designated as a theater—really just a TV with a massive screen and some comfy chairs—so they could watch a movie. This weekend Juliette had asked if she could have Mila and Remy come to watch some favorite movies, so of course I said sure. The girls were going to spend the night, so Jules was looking forward to her first real sleepover since we moved to Saint Gilbert. I knew she missed having the kind of close friendships she had back in Philly, and I hoped these two girls would be the same kind of loyal and true friends as those she'd left behind. I knew she loved being here and loved being a princess, but I also knew she'd sacrificed a lot, as all of us had.

I went back to my office after dinner and rooted through my trash can—what, like you never did?—searching for that morning's newspaper. I found it under a bunch of discarded notes I'd made while I was writing thank-yous earlier in the day. I spread the paper out on my desk and started with the first page. The story I was looking for was on page 3:

Castle Guard Calling for Recruits

It sounded nonthreatening, and certainly gave no hint of an emergency. Just a callout to add to the numbers of guards charged with protecting Castle Blanc and the royal family. A list of requirements, age limits, who to contact, what to bring with you if you are called for an interview, what the training would consist of, what benefits were attached to the positions. I could see where some of the younger people in the city and the villages would respond favorably. At present, there were not a lot of options for employment. That would change in the coming months, but most of the population was unaware of what we were planning. Which made me think we should do a better job letting people know what we were going to be rolling out soon. I'll have to take that up with the council.

I turned off the light and closed up the suite of offices. A guard was outside in the hallway, and I noted he remained there even after the two others appeared to walk me to the second floor. I have no idea how they knew I was on the move, but they popped up like fly balls at Citizens Bank Park. When we reached the second-floor wing where I and my family had our private rooms, I noticed a little more activity than usual. There were two guards posted at the entrance to the wing, and two outside each of our rooms. The two who escorted me returned to the mouth of the wing and stood with the others. Max was being overly cautious, I was sure.

Chapter Twenty-Nine

Once in my suite, I toed off my shoes and called Ceil to tell her to come to my room when she and Roe got back. Over breakfast, we'd agreed to have a sisters' night like the ones we used to have in Philly on those Saturday nights when no one had a date (which was practically every weekend) or had to work late (mostly Roe, but sometimes Ceil was pushing to finish up a job). We planned on wine, snacks, and maybe a showing of our favorite movie, *A League of Their Own*. I took a shower—I loved that shower niche every time I stepped into it and couldn't get enough of that delicious soap (our spa-goers were in for a treat)—and by the time I'd dried my hair, my sisters had already made themselves comfortable in front of the fireplace in my cozy sitting room. Ceil wore a three-piece knit lounging set that could pass for daywear—long pants, a tank, and a cardigan that matched the pants. Roe wore Snoopy pj's and fluffy slippers.

"Did the guards have trouble keeping a straight face when you emerged from your room dressed like that?" I couldn't help but ask Roe.

In typical Roe fashion, she shrugged. "I didn't notice."

And I was certain she hadn't. I'd never known anyone who was less self-aware than my sister Rosalie. I can't remember her ever really caring about what anyone thought of her.

"So I want to hear all about these places you saw today," I said. "Between Ralphie and Jules chatting away at dinner about who they'd been texting from Philly—mostly Jules running on about who watched her video and who wanted to come to Saint Gilbert—I didn't get a chance to grill either one of you."

"So unlike you to miss an opportunity," Roe said.

"I know. Doesn't seem right." I sat on the settee next to her and eyed the tray of goodies that had been delivered while I was in the shower. A beautiful display of cheese, fruit, crackers, and some little pastries had been set up on a table near the fireplace. "So tell me everything."

Ceil spoke up enthusiastically. "Both contractors are terrific. I've worked with my share, and these two know their stuff. The exteriors of both the castle—that would be Gabrielle's—and the one belonging to our great-uncle Theodore are in good shape. His is actually more of a chateau than a castle—not fancy, no turrets or anything. Maybe add some downspouts to one, redo a patio on the other, some plaster repair, but for the most part, things look very good. We will need accessibility ramps added to both, and I'd like to see a terrace off the back of the chateau, but I've been told both are easy additions."

"And inside?" I asked.

"More work in there. First of all, we need all modern plumbing. All new electric systems. And I sketched out the interiors to show Gaspard—Gaspard Gauthier—where I wanted the actual spa area and how I wanted the private rooms set up. We also talked about a common room, which I doubt will get a whole lot of use—most of our ladies aren't going to be coming here to socialize with each other—but at the same time, we don't want to give the impression that we expect them to hide away the entire two weeks they're here, as if there's something wrong with going to a spa that's going to take years off your face and body."

"How long will all this take?" My stomach took a dip. It sounded like a lot of work. I'd wanted it all done *now now now* because I couldn't wait to get started and show off what we, as a country, had to offer. I was certain we would be the destination of the rich and famous (at least, the aging among the rich and famous) once the rest of the world caught up.

"When did you want it done?" Ceil asked, and I laughed.

"Is next weekend too soon?" I said.

"Realistically. And keep in mind I couldn't even get the promo ready by next weekend." She tapped the side of her wineglass. "However, I think a lot could be done in, oh, six or seven weeks."

"Mom always said it's not nice to tease." I gestured for her to pour some wine for me.

"Not teasing." She grabbed my glass by the stem and proceeded to pour. "The work inside is mostly cosmetic. Well, except for the plumbing and the electric work. Oh, and bathrooms, but the contractor said if he had free rein to hire he could get it done."

"Did he give you an estimate?"

"Just a ballpark." She sipped her wine, calm as always. "It's a big number. Stunning, actually. Guaranteed to get bigger if we give him 'free rein.'"

"Did you get it in writing?" I asked.

Ceil shook her head. "Not yet, but it's coming. He promised to have it to me no later than Tuesday. He has to check some prices first."

"A really big number?" I winced at the thought.

"Yup." Ceil smiled. "But if we want it done both fast and right, we don't have a lot of options."

"True enough. Give me a copy of the estimate as soon as you get it." I sipped my wine for a moment while I thought this over. I figured it would cost us a lot to renovate a couple of castles. "Tell him to make sure he gives us separate estimates for the two buildings."

"I already did. I figured if the number makes us gag, we do one building at a time." Before I could ask, Ceil added, "I'd go with Gabrielle's castle first. It needs the least amount of interior work."

"How do we know we can trust this guy?"

"Max suggested him, so he must know him. Ask him what he knows about his reputation. Though I have to say, going on my own experience with contractors, he did know what he was talking about. But oh—I almost forgot the most exciting part! The place is furnished! All this glorious furniture we can use! Someone had the foresight to cover everything so there's no dust, no fading fabric—thought that could be cool, you know, to give things an authentic antique vibe. But it's all there. You could almost believe someone was still living there."

"How is that possible? We know that during the occupations, furniture was stolen or destroyed."

"The story I heard from the guide who took us through was that Gabrielle fled the country right before the Germans arrived," Ceil said. "Remember, she was the first cousin of our great-grandmother, so she would have been aware of what had happened to the duchess and her family. Maybe when she fled Saint Gilbert, she managed to take some things with her, or bought a lot of stuff before she returned after the Soviets left. It's going to save us thousands."

"I wonder where she spent those years." I did wonder. So much of Europe was under German occupation during the 1940s.

"Maybe Switzerland? Maybe Italy, because she was married to an Italian count? They had a few kids, but the guide said there are no heirs, which is why we are able to get our hands on the castle. It belongs to the state now," Ceil reminded me. "I bet Claudette knows the whole story, though."

"The kitchens are going to kick ass." Roe hopped in the second Ceil paused for a breath. "Everything shiny and geared toward taking care of a crowd of pampered guests. Lots of refrigeration space for all the cheese and fruits and salads. It's going to be *gorgeous*. Our visitors are going to leave Saint Gilbert looking better and feeling better than they did when they arrived. The meals alone are going to be worth the price of the spa experience."

"We'll have to take that into consideration when it comes time to decide what we're going to be charging," I told them, even as I debated whether to tell my sisters about my conversation with Max that afternoon. Would they feel threatened? Frightened?

"Roe's drawn up a design for the tableware, and it's perfect," Ceil interjected. "Simple, elegant plates and cups and saucers—creamy white porcelain with only a sketch of the crown at the top. It all screams—albeit quietly—we're expensive and exclusive. Of course, they're pricey, too. We're thinking the promo should say something like, *You deserve to be treated like royalty. Come to Saint Gilbert and let the magic happen.*"

"I like it." I tapped Roe on the knee. "Good job."

"What, the dishes? Ha. The mere tip of my brilliance. Wait till you see the menus I'm drawing up. Oh, and Roberto was at the chateau checking his vines. He's working on a special wine that will be available only to the castle, but I'm thinking one special to the spa might be the way to go. Like, our visitors could take home a bottle or two, but it would only be available to those who have been 'guests' of the spa. And Roberto has the most amazing garden with a greenhouse where he can start vegetables early in the spring and keep the growing season going well into the fall."

"And Roberto is . . . ?" I leaned back and watched my youngest sister come to life.

"He's the son of the head gardener here at the castle—also Roberto—and he has the most amazing vision," she said, eyes shining. Not sure if the glow was there because of Roberto himself or his "vision," whatever that might be. "He's going to work with me to plant what I want to serve not only at the spa but here at home." She looked smug for a few seconds, then said, "Oh. I said *home.*"

"I guess you're feeling it," I said.

"I am, for sure. Oh, and you know, there should be a gift shop at the spa." Roe's eyes lit as inspiration struck. "We could sell the robes—Ceil and I were thinking dense white terry with the crown logo on the pocket—and the soap. Maybe the wine . . ."

"I don't think we should sell the soap for people to take with them," Ceil pointed out. "Maybe when they leave, a gift basket with a few bars to keep the magic going, but if we start selling the soap, won't it be easy for someone to analyze it and make it somewhere else and poof! So much for exclusivity."

"I don't think it would be that easy to re-create this stuff outside Saint Gilbert. I mean, we don't even know what's in it." I reminded them, "The ladies in the guild don't know what's in it and why it works the way it does. I'm not too worried, but I definitely would not want it sold outside Saint Gilbert. Giving our spa-goers a little parting gift is one thing. Letting someone else sell it alongside bars of Dove and Ivory in the supermarkets is something else." Thinking of protecting our exclusivity brought to mind something else. "And we need to make sure those goats don't leave the country."

"Right. We'll anoint them national treasures and make it a crime to sell the goats to anyone outside Saint Gilbert," Roe said.

I added, "A to-be-determined stay in the castle dungeon if you're caught."

"I agree," Ceil said, and Roe nodded her agreement just as there was a knock on the door.

Roe jumped up. "I'll get it."

Ceil was busy opening a bottle of wine, and I was scooping up some brie-like cheese onto a cracker that by itself was delicious. No wonder Roe was happy and felt so at home here. Saint Gilbert was foodie heaven, and, I realized, all her life, Roe had been all about the food.

"Here, I can take that. No, no, it's no trouble at all. Thank you so much for making this. We appreciate it."

I heard the door close and turned to see Rosalie carrying a large tray with a silver dome in the center.

"What in the world . . . ?" Ceil glanced up just as she was about to pour wine in each of our glasses.

"Nachos." Roe sat the tray on the ottoman in front of the chair Ceil was sitting in.

"Nachos?" Ceil and I said at the same time.

"In Saint Gilbert?" I leaned over and lifted the dome. "Those are sure enough nachos."

"I taught Emmeline, one of the cooks, how to make them. I thought the kids would like them, but I wanted us to try them first." The smug, happy smile was still on Roe's face.

The three of us dug in. For a few moments, the only sound in the room was the crunch of the tortilla chips and the occasional moan of joy as we indulged in salsa, guacamole, savory beef, sour cream, sharp cheddar . . . ahhhh.

"Am I the only one who's finding this"—I gestured at the plate of nachos—"almost sacrilegious? I mean, here we are in this luxurious room in this beautiful centuries-old castle, where since we arrived we've been served only the most elegant, sophisticated, glorious food . . . and we're eating nachos."

"Yes, and I'm happy for it." Roe scooped up another chip and bit into it. "The jalapeños aren't as hot as the ones back home, but these aren't bad."

Ceil nodded. "It did cross my mind to object on general principle, but the need for nachos has overwhelmed my better judgment and I can't help myself. But it is funny, now that you mention it, that we really haven't seen any junk food since we arrived."

"This is a country that understands food," Roe said between bites. "Even their snacks are beautiful and healthy and delicious. I don't understand why everyone here doesn't weigh about a thousand pounds, what with all the cheese and the sublime chocolate and the tortes. All of which make me deliriously happy, but still. Every once in a while, you need a little street food."

"Amen." I scooped up another beefy, cheesy chip, still trying to decide if I should tell them about my conversation with Max, when Roe piped up.

"We had double guards today," she said nonchalantly. "Because there's someone who's spreading rumors about us and what to do about us, I guess. Shoot us? Send us packing? Whatever."

My jaw dropped.

"Yeah, they're doubling security," Ceil added. "But I'm sure you know about that, Annie."

"Well, yeah." I tried to match their easy tone. "But who told you?"

"We overheard the guards talking when we were touring the castle. I asked them if they thought we were in any danger, and they said no, that they were there as a precaution." Ceil turned to me. "Were they right? There's no real danger?"

"That's what Max said, so I guess it's under control."

"Good, because we're having too damned much fun right now to have to worry about some yahoo trying to upend all this." Ceil took a sip of wine. "They did say that a bunch of new guards were being trained, so I guess that's a good thing, but I'm telling you, God help the yokel who tries to get between me and my castle. I have big plans for that place, and no malcontent had better get in my way."

"Are you sure you wouldn't want that place for your own? You don't have to spend the rest of your life living here, you know," I told her.

"I know. And I will find a place to call home. Right now, I can't focus on anything but getting the spa up and running. There are plenty of places in and around the city that I could happily live in. I'm in no hurry." She shrugged nonchalantly. "I'll know the right place when I see it. Gabrielle's castle doesn't feel like home to me."

I watched Ceil pick through the nachos in search of one with a lot of cheese and wondered why we'd reacted so differently to the same situation. Ceil was ready to kick anyone to the curb who got in the way of her fulfilling a lifetime dream of actually making over a castle.

I was seriously concerned about even a hint of unrest. Was it because I was the one who was being named in those rumors, questioning who I am, while she was the one having the time of her life, orchestrating a makeover of a beautiful and classic three-hundred-year-old building? After all, it was there that her responsibility ended. Or was it because, as the mom of two kids who at any given time could be anywhere in the country and therefore possibly at risk from a malcontent, I had a different stake in the stability of Saint Gilbert?

And then there was Roe, who seemed to totally dismiss the very thought of any threat. She had gardens to plan, exquisite dishes to concoct, and whole menus to write, and bless her heart, neither hell, high water, nor rebel factions were going to rock her world.

Wait—what? This behavior was so un-Roe-like. Who was this woman, and what had she done with my little sister? This woman was all dreams and joy for the moment. Her eyes sparkled as she spoke of her plans to create the most wonderful food on the planet.

Oh, she looked like Rosalie. Sounded like Rosalie. But I hadn't heard one negative word in . . . I couldn't remember the last time I'd heard her complain about anything. Maybe when we told her she couldn't drive in Saint Gilbert. But not so much as a contrary word since.

Huh.

Roe was seated on the floor, leaning back against the sofa. I poked her with my foot.

"What?" she asked without looking at me.

"You're in a pretty good mood," I said.

"Why wouldn't I be?"

"Nothing to complain about? Nothing to whine about?"

Roe shrugged but didn't respond. Ceil looked from me to Roe, then back again to me.

"Annie's got a point," Ceil said. "It's not like you to not find fault with something."

"What's to find fault with?" Roe picked up two of the last chips from the plate and took a sharp bite out of one of them.

"You usually find something." There. I said it. "And we're both wondering what's changed to make you so . . . oh, mellow might be the right word."

Roe ate the chips. Ceil and I waited for a response.

Finally, Roe said, "For the first time since Nonna Rose died, I don't feel as if I need to explain myself."

Huh?

"Roe, Nonna Rose died when you were . . ." I quickly calculated. I'd been eighteen, so Ceil had been sixteen. "You were fourteen when she died."

Roe nodded but didn't look at either of us. "November 9. Right after my fourteenth birthday."

"So I don't understand what you're saying."

Roe sighed a long, drawn-out sigh. "Nonna always made me feel . . . crap, I hate using 'hip' expressions, you know? Like, new clichés? But she always made me feel *seen*. Like she knew me and understood who I was. I never had to be anyone else when I was with her."

"Why did you ever feel you needed to be someone else?" I slid down to the floor to sit next to her.

"You're kidding, right?" She scoffed. "Daughter number three, coming in a distant third to you two." When I started to protest, she talked over me. "Sister number one, the pretty one, who also happened to be the smartest kid in her class. Sister number two, also pretty, athletic, smart, artistic. Where did that leave sister number three, who was neither pretty nor particularly smart compared to the first two. Not athletic, not artistic. Just—*average* in every way. Mom and Dad were always bragging about the two of you. Me? There was never anything to brag about. Average grades. Always picked last for games on the playground. Usually the last one called on in class if I actually knew something and got up the nerve to raise my hand."

"Aww, honey . . ." I put my arm around her shoulders. Closer to her, I could see tears in the corners of her eyes.

"But Nonna—she gave me something of my own. She taught me how to cook. By the time I was ten, I knew all her recipes by heart. She taught me everything I know about food and flavor and how to combine textures to perfection. The weekends I spent at her house were the best times of my childhood. When she died, I thought my life was over."

"Sweetie, I had no idea . . ." Ceil sat on Roe's other side. "Why didn't you say something?"

"Like what? What does a kid say when they're in pain and no one seems to notice?" She dug into her pocket and pulled out a tissue and blew her nose, then wiped her face with the tail of her shirt. "Anyway, she was my guiding star, my whole life." She blew her nose again. "Do either of you remember the night Nonna died?"

Ceil and I both nodded.

"The nurse had called and told Dad he should come over to the house, but she didn't tell him how bad things were. It was late when Mom and Dad returned home, and they both had red eyes from crying."

Roe nodded. "Dad came into my room and put something on my dresser. He was trying to be quiet. I woke up, but I didn't say anything. After he was gone and had closed the door behind him, I got out of bed and went to see what he'd left there. It was Nonna's recipe box. All her recipes, written in her hand, some of them in Italian, some in Italian and English. I knew without being told that she was gone." She fell silent for a moment, then added—as if we didn't already know—"That box and its handwritten notes are my treasures." Roe looked up at me. "Nonna knew me—saw me—in ways the rest of you didn't. I'm not blaming you. I was the pesky little sister and you two were so close, there wasn't any room for me."

"I'm so sorry," I said.

"Me too," Ceil told her. "I had no idea you felt that way."

"Neither did I." I swallowed back tears.

"It's okay. Really. But if you're wondering why I always saw myself through a lens that seemed a little dark, it's because I never felt I measured up, and when the one person who thought I was the best thing since sliced bread died, I felt like the lights went out and no one could see me. So yeah, everything in my life seemed to dim after that. What was there to be happy about? But coming here—I feel energized. I feel worthy of everything Nonna taught me. Everything she gave me. I feel like I've found my place, maybe even like she's here with me." Roe looked at me, then at Ceil. "I'm happy. For the first time since Nonna died, I feel like I'm in the right place."

"Come here, little sister." I went to hug her, but she pushed me away. At least she was laughing.

"Oh yeah. Sister hug." Ceil leaned in on Roe's other side. "Big one. All in."

"Stop! Go away!" Roe started to laugh. "Okay, fine. One hug. Then nachos."

"The nachos are gone," I told her as I pulled her closer. "But I know how to get more."

"In that case, you can both hug me." Roe was smiling, somewhat smugly, I thought, but it was okay.

Ceil and I both hugged her, and the three of us stayed in our group hug until the second round of nachos arrived. All in all, it had been a very good sisters' night, just like the ones we used to have back in Philly, but better. Roe was happy, and Ceil and I could see her very clearly.

Chapter Thirty

Breakfast the next morning was more subdued than usual. Roe begged off (wine headache), and Juliette was having breakfast in her suite with her friends, so it was Ceil and me for a while, then Ralphie showed up looking for leftovers.

"And how did the prince of the kingdom—er, duchy—spend his Saturday night?" I asked.

"My friend Henri stopped over and we watched a movie. He's Mila's brother, so he drove her over and stayed for a while." Ralphie ate a croissant or three before polishing off the last of the strawberries.

"What movie did you watch?" Ceil asked.

"A great American Christmas classic," Ralphie said. "*Die Hard.* Bruce Willis at his best."

Ceil snorted. "I'm sure that's not a Christmas movie."

"It takes place at Christmastime. It's a Christmas movie. Best. Ever."

"Jerk." Jules blew into the room. No Christmas spirit there.

"Good morning to you, too." I glanced behind her. "Where are your friends?"

"Remy's doing something with her grandmother, and Mila had to go to some family birthday thing," Juliette muttered.

"Her uncle's birthday party. Henri had to go, too," Ralphie said.

"Shut up. I hate you." Jules sat down in a huff.

"Whoa, what's going on?" It had been so long since the two of them had this sort of exchange, I'd thought she was kidding at first. But the look on her face told a different story.

"Okay, so me, Remy, and Mila were all set to watch our favorite movie, *Legally Blonde*, which stars Reese Witherspoon, only the best and coolest actress ever in the best movie in the entire history of movies and we know all the best lines and were psyched to watch it together? Then jerk-face and Henri came in and took off *our* movie and put on theirs." She was really getting into it. "I hate you."

"Hey, bros before ho—"

I jumped up and clapped my hand over his mouth. "Don't you even say it. Not one more word. Especially *that* word. I never want to hear that word come out of your mouth ever."

"Mom, it was just a joke." My son, who is almost six feet, two inches tall, tried to wiggle away from me, but I have an iron grip when I need one. I may be small, but I'm mighty.

"Really? And how was that funny? Explain to me the funny part, because it went over my head." I—as Mom and defender of my gender, and my daughter—was seeing red.

Juliette froze—she'd never seen me react like this before.

"Mom, everyone says—" Ralphie protested.

"You are not *everyone*. You are a *prince*. You're supposed to set an example." I loosened my grip but pushed him into the nearest chair. I had only begun to lecture. "You are not back in South Philly with your old friends, Ralphie. You're in a whole nother place now. You're an adult—well, almost. You have to decide who you are and who you want to be. You can be a smart-mouthed guy who thinks it's cool to hang out on a street corner for the rest of your life, or you can be something more. You can be the prince of the Grand Duchy of Saint Gilbert. But if you choose to be a prince, you'd better be worthy of it. You decide."

"Mom, I'm sorry." My son was ashen at this point. I guess maybe I'd gotten my point across. "I wasn't thinking about all that."

"Well, I hate to be the one to tell you, but from now on, you will have to be thinking about 'all that.' What you say and how you say it. There are a lot of little boys in this country who will learn from you either way. For better or for worse, they will look up to you and emulate you, their prince. Are you going to show them how to be a goof, a jerk, or a thoughtful young man?"

He paused. "Is this a trick question?"

I fought an urge to smack him. Not very royal on my part, but he knows better than to poke the bear. That would be me.

We stared at each other.

Finally, he said softly, "I get it, Mom."

"I hope so. Oh, I know everyone loves you right now. You leave the castle and people follow you and want to take their pictures with you. You visit a shop today and tomorrow there will be a photo in the newspaper along with an interview with the shopkeeper. 'What did he buy? What's he like?' The people of Saint Gilbert adore you. But they need to respect you as well. They need to see a solid example of a fine young man growing into adulthood, a young man worthy to represent their country." Okay, so I might have laid it on a little thick, but I was on a roll. Besides, desperate times, desperate measures. "You can do this through soccer, or by deciding on a career, or . . ."

"I thought my career was being a prince."

"A prince has to stand for something. He can't be a playboy. He can be a source of national pride or national embarrassment. He has to serve his country, earn his keep."

"So what are my choices?"

"Open your eyes. Look around, see what the country needs that you could help fulfill."

He pointed to his sister. "What's she fulfilling?"

"Juliette's videos already have gone viral. She's helping to build up what we hope will be a flourishing tourist industry. She's spreading the word to girls all over the world, and a lot of those young girls are showing their mamas those videos. They're going to want to come visit the country because Juliette is showcasing the highlights. They—and their mamas—could end up pumping some serious euros, not to mention American dollars, into the country's treasury."

Jules stuck her tongue out at her brother. He raised his middle finger in reply. Some things never changed.

I smacked his hand. "Knock it off, both of you."

I stared at Ralphie so he'd know I was still waiting for a response from him.

He finally caught on. "Can I choose soccer?"

"You can choose whatever you like, as long as it benefits the country in a positive way. Actually, soccer might be perfect. You could start up little soccer clubs in the villages and . . ." It really could be his niche.

"Organize tournaments." He nodded slowly. "Soccer for little guys. And girls, the girls can play, too."

"Raise money for a stadium," Ceil broke her silence and chimed in.

"I can do those things." Ralphie looked pensive. "I hope it's not going to be a problem that I can't remember to call it *football* here. It almost seems like a sacrilege."

"Understood," I said, because as a lifelong fan of the Philadelphia Eagles, this was tough for me, too. "You need to go to school, Ralphie. We haven't talked about school in a while, and you still have one more year of high school. You have to think about where you want to go."

"This could be my gap year. Then I could go to Switzerland for my twelfth year, or back to the States. Then I can go to college somewhere and get a degree in . . ." He paused and mulled it over.

"Maybe something like economics would be useful here in Saint Gilbert," I suggested.

"Economics sounds really hard, Mom. Maybe something easy. Like something to do with sports."

"Perfect." I knew if I knocked on that hard head of his long enough, something would get through.

"Oh, and by the way, Dad texted me. He wants me to come back to the States for a while." He tossed this out nonchalantly.

"Not a chance."

"That's what I told him," he said smugly and got up to leave the room.

"Whoa. Don't you have something to say?" I stopped him with a few pointed words.

"To who?" He looked surprised.

"To your sister, that's to *whom*," I said.

He looked at Juliette, who was once again glaring at him.

"I'm sorry, Jules. It won't happen again." He was trying to look contrite, but his sister wasn't buying it.

"Yeah, till the next time." She did know her brother well.

"Say it like you mean it, Ralphie," I told him. "And mean it this time."

"Jules, I am sorry."

"You ruined my first sleepover with my friends, Ralphie. They think I have the world's worst brother." She didn't say it, but the implied *and I do* was loud and clear.

"I'm *sorry*. You think of something I can do to make up for it, and I'll do it," he told her.

A slow smile spread across her lips. "Anything?"

"Okay," he agreed, but I could tell he wished he'd left that part out of his apology.

"So if I had my friends back again, you'll let us watch whatever movie we want?"

"Yeah."

"And you won't bother us except to make us popcorn and bring us snacks?"

He paused, then nodded. "Okay. I'll be your snack man for the night."

"Promise?" Juliette sat up. "Pinkie promise?"

"That's for little kids," he protested.

"Pinkie promise, Ralphie," she insisted.

"All right. Pinkie promise." He held out the pinkie of his left hand.

Jules shook her head. "Uh-uh. *Right*-hand pinkie. Everyone knows the left pinkie is for liars."

"Geez," he muttered as he grasped her right pinkie with his. "Right-hand pinkie promise."

"I forgive you for being such a jerk." Juliette dropped his finger and immediately turned her attention from her brother to the breakfast tray Ceil and I had shared, the same one Ralphie had plundered. "You guys ate all the croissants *and* all the strawberries?"

Ralphie had one hand on the doorknob. He looked at me, smiled, then channeled his best Diana Rigg as Olenna Tyrell in *Game of Thrones*. "Tell Juliette. I want her to know it was me."

Juliette tried to roll up a napkin to throw at him, but it was heavy linen so she didn't get much mileage out of it. Ralphie laughed and started through the door.

"Get dressed for church and meet us downstairs," I called to my son, then turned to my daughter and sister. "And you both should get moving as well. I'll meet you all in exactly thirty minutes at the front door."

"Mom, we went last week," Jules said.

"What did you promise your grandmother before she died?" I asked.

Grumble grumble, groan groan, but they were ready and waiting when Ceil and I arrived downstairs.

I had discovered there is a chapel in the castle. It's lovely and peaceful, and Claudette told me if I wanted to have the priest come there, he'd be happy to do that. But I liked going to the services at that sweet church in the city where generations of my family had worshipped. It really did make me feel that I was part of something so much bigger than myself. The royal family had a section off to the left side of the altar that reminded me of the box seats at the old Spectrum arena in Philly.

I'd been in one once when I was eighteen and won a contest the local sports radio station ran: be the sixth caller to name three of the Philadelphia Flyers who helped the team earn the nickname the Broad Street Bullies in the 1970s (Saleski, Schultz, Dupont). I took my dad to the game as my guest and we sat in a private box and it was the best night I ever had with my father. I think my love for Philadelphia sports was born that night.

Anyway. We went into the church through a special door in the back and filed into our seats. There was a fancy French-looking uphol-stered chair and an individual kneeler for each of us. The priest, Father Francisco, always seemed happy to see us and always asked the members of the congregation to pray for us, which I greatly appreciated. After the services, we went as a family to say a prayer at the graves of our ancestors in the cemetery behind the church before we left, something else that made me feel good.

Chapter Thirty-One

When we arrived back at the castle, Max was waiting in the reception area. After exchanging some pleasantries, he asked if I had plans for the afternoon. When I said I'd planned on working for a while—those remaining thank-you notes weren't going to write themselves—he suggested I change into something more casual and meet him out in the back courtyard after lunch. He wouldn't give me a hint of why, but since I'd meet him anywhere, at any time, for any reason, it didn't really matter.

So after lunch with my family, I changed into a pair of linen pants, a long blue tunic, and my ever-comfy white Keds. Escorted as usual by my two stoic guards—Sergei and Yves—I arrived at the grassy courtyard around two in the afternoon. I always loved coming out those wide French doors and stepping outside because the flower gardens were spectacular, colorful, and fragrant, the beds artfully placed. Whoever had designed them should be given a medal. I added that to my list of things to think about.

I saw Max standing midway between the castle and the lake with another man I didn't recognize. When they heard me approach, they both turned.

"Your Grace, may I introduce you to Fergus Taggart, who recently joined the castle staff as royal falconer." Max was smiling.

"Nice to meet—wait. We have a falconer?" My eyes grew wide at the thought. I'd been intrigued by the birds and the stories I'd heard about the falcon being my family's spirit animal. All the paintings and carvings throughout the castle had reinforced the tales.

"You have one now, madam. It's my pleasure to meet you." Fergus did a head bow.

"Fergus has come from Scotland, where he was a master falconer. He's agreed to reestablish the birds here in Saint Gilbert." Max said.

"Come and meet Sasha." Fergus gestured toward the old stables.

"Who's Sasha?" I fell into step next to him.

"She's the falcon I've been training for you," he said. "Let's hope you get along."

"You trained a falcon just for me?" I stopped midstep.

"I did, madam," Fergus replied in his rich brogue.

I had my own falcon! I could barely contain my excitement. I couldn't wait to see her and watch her fly.

I spent much of the afternoon getting to know Sasha and learning how to handle her. Watching her hunt on her own, seeing her soar off above the field and over the castle, I'd pray she'd come back to me and land on my leather glove–covered left hand and arm. She always did. It was exhilarating, watching that majestic bird catch the updraft and take to the sky, then seeming to float overhead before going into a lightning-quick dive. She was magnificent, and it was a thrill to watch. It was the single most fun I'd had since I arrived in Saint Gilbert, and I told Fergus so as he was returning Sasha to her cage.

"I can't thank you enough," I said. "This is the most wonderful gift. You've no idea how much I enjoyed these past few hours."

"You honor me, Your Grace, but thank your captain." Fergus nodded at Max. "He sought me out and lured me to Saint Gilbert with tales of how the monarchy and the royal falcons were linked. It's been my pleasure to train her. I hope you'll be back soon. The more you work with her, the more she will relate to you."

"I'll be back tomorrow," I promised.

"Sasha will be waiting." Fergus coaxed the bird onto a perch and replaced her hood.

"Thank you again." I looped my arm through Max's and we started back toward the castle. The terrain was slightly uneven, so I had a good excuse. "So you did this?"

"You'd expressed an interest," he reminded me. "I thought if we were going to bring back the falcons, we needed to find the best man for the task. I believe we did."

I wanted to put my arms around him and plant one big loving kiss right on his lips, but of course, I couldn't do that. Instead, I said, "Thank you. It was so thoughtful of you to find him and bring him here. I can't believe you kept this a secret. Sasha's the best gift ever."

"Well, we know that every grand duchess has had her own falcon. It seemed only right that you should have one, too."

"I'm going to come out here every chance I get and work with her. I'm going to become a real falconer."

"I have no doubt that you will. I think you can do anything you set your mind to."

We walked the rest of the way to the castle, the sun just starting to drop below the tree line. It was going to be a gorgeous sunset here in Beauchesne. As we drew closer and the ground flattened, I dropped my arm lest anyone see us and start rumors. It made me sad to know I had to be aware of such things, but it was for both our sakes. We reached the courtyard, and as we approached the back doors, two guards stepped out. They saluted Max, and he nodded in return.

"Which way, Annaliese?" Max asked once we were inside.

"My office," I said.

He escorted me to the door flanked by two guards, but before leaving, he went inside the suite with me. After looking around and deciding that no one had breached the security here, he turned to leave.

"Thank you again, Max."

"It was my pleasure."

"Same time tomorrow?" I asked.

"If your schedule permits."

I nodded. "We'll make it permit."

I turned on the light in my little office, and Max turned to go.

"Max, do you have a woman in your life?" I heard myself ask.

He smiled. "Several, Your Grace."

Of course he did. I should have assumed that. Why did I even ask? He was handsome and kind, he had a great sense of humor, he was honest, and damn it, if things were different, if I weren't the duchess and just Annaliese Gilberti and I was still living in South Philly, I'd have sent the kids to Ceil's house for the weekend and invited Max for dinner and whatever might happen after that. An image of the two of us flashed before my eyes. We were seated at the dining table at my little row house, enjoying a fabulous meal I'd cooked from scratch (so you know this is obviously a fantasy), sipping a nice wine and laughing at something he'd said. I'd put the flowers he'd brought me in my mother's favorite blue vase, and . . .

"Annaliese?" Max's voice broke through the vision. "Is there anything else I can do for you this afternoon?"

"No, thank you." I sat at my desk and pretended to go through some papers that I'd left the day before. "And thanks again for luring Fergus here."

Max smiled and left the room. I heard him speaking with the guards at the door for several minutes, then the hall fell as silent as the office. I tried to conjure up the dinner scene again, but the moment had passed and I couldn't seem to get it back. I picked up my pen and started in on another batch of thank-you notes.

I wish I hadn't asked about his love life. Competing with one surely gorgeous woman was one thing. (Would a man like him be romantically interested in anything less?) Competing with "several" was impossible.

Chapter Thirty-Two

It was late on Tuesday—so late I was thinking about dinner—when I heard someone in the outer office. Before I could get up from my desk to check it out, there was a soft rap on the door.

"Come in." Most likely it was Max or one of my kids, or my sisters. I was surprised to see our chancellor step into the room.

"I apologize for coming without an appointment, but I saw the light from your office and . . ."

"My door is always open to you, Chancellor. Please, sit." I tried to sound gracious, like I always told my kids to be. "What brings you to my office today? I don't recall a visit from you in the past."

"In the past, there'd been no cause, but something's happened that I feel you must be advised of." He paused as he tried to catch his breath. "We should probably call Captain Belleme as well. He needs to be alerted to this situation."

I picked up my phone and sent Max a text. My office please. I have company.

"The captain will be along shortly. In the meantime, tell me what has you concerned."

"I hardly know where to begin." He shifted nervously in the chair. "I am hearing rumors, most disturbing rumors questioning . . . I hesitate to say this, Your Grace, but questioning your legitimacy."

"My legitimacy?" I frowned. As far as I knew, my parents were married for several years before I was born.

"Your legitimacy to have inherited the crown," he explained, his eyes down. "The latest 'question' being circulated is, who is the true heir?"

It took that a moment to sink in.

"What are you talking about? My grandmother . . ."

"Oh, madam, please, do not misunderstand. I am not the one asking the question. I know exactly who you are, who your mother was, who your grandmother was. I was part of the committee who searched for the rightful heir to the throne. We were very diligent. There was no one else."

"Then why would someone . . . ?" I really felt confused.

"I do not know, other than to wonder if perhaps there is someone else who feels she—or he—had a claim as well. No such person—man, woman, or child—was revealed by our efforts, I assure you. No one stepped forward even after we sent out a call for anyone who thought they might have a case, even though we'd known about you since the day you were born."

I forced a smile. "There was a time when I wondered if perhaps you felt you had a claim to the throne."

Vincens's smile was more sincere than mine. "There was no real threat from me or my family. We know that the crown was to be passed within the family of the duchess. The duke's side of your family had no standing."

"Do you have any idea who might be behind this?"

"I have been pondering this for several days. Could it be a hoax, someone who simply likes to stir up controversy? I do not have a clue." Vincens held out his hands, palms up.

"Nor do I," Max said as he strode purposefully into the office.

"The chancellor was just telling me that he has heard the latest rumor. 'Who is Annaliese Gilberti?' is now being followed with, 'Who is the true heir?'"

Max pulled a nearby chair closer to the desk. "We've located the leader of the January protests, Joseph Andretti. We spoke earlier today. He swears his group is not behind any efforts to delegitimize you. He's taking the position that since the majority of his fellow countrymen had voted in favor of the monarchy, their votes must be respected and that any protests he might attempt to mount would be a waste of time. After the coronation, his group disbanded."

"A wise move on their part," Vincens said.

"But he did tell me this: a few weeks ago, there was a message left on his phone." Max was frowning, which told me he was more concerned than he was letting on. "The person calling did not identify himself, but he said plans were underway to reveal Annaliese Gilberti as a fraud, and if he were a true patriot, he'd join in the effort to return the rightful heir to the throne."

"Did Andretti tell you who the caller believed was the true heir?" I asked.

"He did not. He told Andretti to call him the Royal Watchdog. Andretti dismissed it as a hoax and pretty much forgot about it until I contacted him."

"Your Grace, I assure you, the captain and I were both generational members of the council who followed your grandmother—later your mother, then you—so that when the time came, no time would be wasted in bringing our duchess home to Saint Gilbert." I had to admit that Vincens, while annoying in other ways, apparently was sincere in this. This situation has shown me a different side of him.

"Generational?" I asked.

"The sacred duty, the responsibility, to protect the duchy fell first to our grandfathers, then our fathers, then to us," Max explained.

"I see." I knew the part Max's grandfather played in getting my grandmother out of the country when the Germans were at the door, but I had not been aware that Vincens had also inherited a 'sacred duty' to protect the monarchy. Who knew?

2

"So what do we do? How do we find this guy?" The thought of someone running around the country besmirching my name and accusing me of being anything other than legitimate made me see red. I wanted to find this guy and set him straight myself.

"We will of course be searching for him, but with no clues as to his identity, we can only hope he will come to us," Max said.

I felt myself frowning again. "Why would he do that?"

"Perhaps eventually he will realize he needs some help from the inside if his case is to be taken seriously." Max and Vincens stared at each other.

"Perhaps we should give him a nudge in the right direction," Vincens said, still looking at Max. There seemed to be some sort of unspoken agreement, sort of like a Vulcan mind meld going on.

Vincens reached for the pad of legal paper on my desk. "May I?"

"Of course."

He began to write, and while he did, Max and I tried not to stare too hard at each other. I was thinking that we had to get to the bottom of this nonsense as soon as possible, sooner if it turned out not to be nonsense. I had no intentions of going back to Philly, my tail between my legs, for the entire world to see. My lineage was well known to everyone. But if in fact there is someone out there with a stronger claim than mine, the council had better figure out how this person was missed while the vetting process was going on.

What if I really was illegitimately sitting on the throne?

But no, it wasn't possible. I knew the story by heart. *Everyone* knew the story and knew it to be true. There was no question that my grandmother was exactly who she and everyone else said she was. And if she was really who she claimed to be, then it followed that I was as well.

So who was this person stirring up doubt, and why now? Why not before I was coronated, like, during the week I visited here? Or when my family and I moved here? Why wasn't something said then?

Vincens put down his pen. "This statement can be sent to the TV stations, the newspapers, and all the social media platforms."

He cleared his throat.

"This statement is being issued directly by a spokesman from the Duke's Council: While we unanimously stand behind Her Royal Highness, Grand Duchess Annaliese Jacqueline Terese Gilberti, we request whoever may believe there is another potential heir to the throne to step forward now in order that we might evaluate their claim." He looked up from the paper. "If there is no objection from you, Your Highness, I'm going to call an emergency session of the council for tomorrow morning. I agree—the earlier we identify this person the sooner we can shut down the innuendos. It is not in the best interest of the country to have such baseless allegations made. We need to have them shown as being without merit, the sooner the better." He looked from me to Max, then back again. "But only if you agree, madam."

Before I could respond, Max said, "I'm not so sure I want to give this person a sense of legitimacy without knowing who he is or what he wants."

I shook my head. "I agree with the chancellor. I think this needs to go out there as soon as possible. I'd prefer to flush him out rather than sit around waiting for him to show his hand."

Max remained unconvinced. "Right now, he is a gnat. Give him legitimacy, and he becomes a wasp."

"Excuse me, but I spent a good many summers at the Jersey Shore. I know how to swat a gnat, and I know how to slap down a wasp. If someone is spreading untrue rumors, let him look me in the eye and say it to my face."

"Let's see how the other members of the council feel about this plan," Max suggested. I could tell by the set of his jaw what he was hoping the other council members would say.

I turned to Vincens. "Go ahead and contact the others. Tell them we'll meet at nine tomorrow morning."

"As you wish, madam."

"Anything else?" I looked at Max, and he shook his head. "Then I guess I'll see you both tomorrow morning."

Max and Vincens left me alone in my office. I wanted to just take a deep breath and continue on with what I'd been doing before Vincens knocked on my door. But the truth was, I was uneasy, not knowing where this anonymous person was going to take this campaign of his. Were his stupid little innuendos a prelude to something else? Did he have others behind him who were ready to, I don't know, mount a coup? I tried telling myself that I was in good hands, that Max would never, ever let things get that far out of hand, but I still felt the need to put a brown paper bag over my mouth and breathe into it to stop me from hyperventilating.

For the first time in my life, I knew what it was like to think like Roe.

Chapter Thirty-Three

I could barely wait to get to the council meeting. Since the rumors had started circulating, had one of the members suddenly remembered someone who could conceivably have a better claim to the throne than me? For all their vetting, stranger things had happened, right? Or maybe one of the dukes had heard something connecting someone to the rumors. I went into the meeting hoping we could get a handle on what was behind the rumors and soon. I had no time for something like this. There was serious work to do—roads to fix, soap to make and a spa to open, tourists to attract—and this was an unneeded distraction. At least, I hoped that was all it was.

Just as I was about to step into the council room, I noticed Ceil about ten feet away totally engaged in a quiet conversation with a man who looked vaguely familiar but I couldn't place. He was a few inches taller than Ceil and very good-looking in a professorial sort of way, with his tweed jacket and glasses. He had dark curly hair and a pleasant smile, and he appeared to be as absorbed by what she was saying as she was by him. Like, people were walking around them and neither seemed to notice. Hmmm. So un-Ceil-like. We'd skipped breakfast this morning because we both needed to get ready for this early meeting, so I hadn't seen her yet today, but I was going to get the scoop on this guy.

"Ceil," I called to her. "The meeting . . . ?"

She nodded, and I expected her to follow me into the conference room. Instead, she followed him in. Did he not know this was a closed meeting?

Before I could point this out, Ceil caught my arm, turned me partway around, and said, "Annie, have you met Carlo DellaVecchio? He's new on the council as well."

"Your Grace, we met briefly at your coronation but didn't have an opportunity to speak more than a greeting," he said.

"Oh. Yes. Carlo. The chancellor's son." Of course. That's why he looked familiar.

Vincens had introduced me to several members of his family that day, but honestly, I didn't remember many of them. I met hundreds of people. I couldn't say I was pleased that the man who was giving my sister a happy glow was a DellaVecchio—I mean, his brother was a lecher as far as I was concerned, and his father had been the occasional pain in my butt since the day I arrived. I know it wasn't fair to judge someone on the basis of their relatives—would I want my kids to be judged by the character of their father?

Gosh, that's a tough one. No.

Then again, last night Vincens had come directly to me with his concerns about the whole rumor thing. That, and his "sacred duty" to the crown speech, had come as a big surprise, but he'd seemed sincere. So I should keep an open mind about Carlo, right? And Max liked him and had been the one to nominate him for the council in the first place, so we'll see.

"Carlo." Max came up behind us and gave Carlo a friendly slap on the back. "Glad to see you accepted the opportunity to join the council."

"As am I." At this, he looked directly at Ceil, who blushed.

Blushed. Ceil the unflappable actually blushed.

"Carlo is researching the origin of the goats," Ceil said.

He laughed good-naturedly. "My first official duty as minister of agriculture: find out where the goats came from. It's not as simple as it sounds, but I've been told there are some men in one of the villages who might know. I'll be meeting with them this afternoon."

I have to admit, that did impress me. "Thank you for acting quickly, Carlo. It may sound funny, but the goats are a big part of our plan."

"Princess Cecilia has been explaining the overall strategy to me, and I think it's going to be the key to turning around our economy," he said as we began to move into the room. "Who would have guessed, all these years, that it would be our soap that saved us?"

Other members of the council came in and we took our seats, the two new members seated together at the end of the table. The chancellor called the meeting to order and outlined the reason for the emergency session.

"I trust you all have heard the rumors," he said.

"Regarding the legitimacy of our duchess?" Emile Rossi shook his head. "What nonsense. Every man in this room will recall the efforts we made to ensure that the proper heir was named." He turned to address me. "I hope Your Highness has not been overly concerned. I would hate to think you've been upset by someone's idea of a prank."

"Is it a prank? Or is it something more? Perhaps someone who believes he is rightfully the heir, whether or not he is. I think we need to shake my family tree a little harder and see who falls out. For example, did my great-uncle Theodore have children? I know my mother's brother has a daughter, but . . ."

"But she is—not to malign your family, madam—wholly unsuitable," Andre DiGiacoma pointed out.

"She does have a prison record, as I recall," Jacques Gilberti said.

"I was told that was all a misunderstanding." I felt I should toss this in, in defense of the family. But since it had been her father relating the story in a Facebook post—maybe not so much a misunderstanding as wishful thinking.

"In any case, we know that none of your great-grandparents' children had issue other than your grandmother and her siblings. We know who our duchess is," Vincens said. "What we don't know is who is behind these rumors and what their endgame might be, but we have to find out. This insult to the crown cannot be permitted to continue. I have discussed this matter with Her Highness, and with her permission, I will read a statement I prepared last night." He looked across the table at me, and I nodded.

When he was finished reading, there was silence.

"You're asking someone to meet with you?" Andre sounded as skeptical as Max had the night before. "How do you know this person isn't unhinged? He may be dangerous."

"I will not be meeting alone with him," Vincens replied. "I assume Captain Belleme will provide ample protection?"

"Of course," Max said, "though I'm still concerned that we are giving this person an even larger platform than the one he's making for himself."

"If there's a better way to find out what's behind this, I'd like to hear it. Otherwise, I agree with the chancellor." I looked around the table. "I propose we vote. All in agreement with releasing the chancellor's statement, say aye."

Seven ayes.

"Since there are ten of us, and seven have voted to release the statement, there's no point in asking for the nays." I turned to Vincens. "I would like you to send your statement to every newspaper, television, radio, and social media outlet in the country. Let's see if anyone speaks up. Until then, I suggest we continue on with our business of running this country."

From there, I proceeded to bring the council up to date on the plans to renovate one of the unoccupied castles to use as a spa and the part it—and the soap—would play in the overall resurgence of the country. I turned to Ceil and asked her to tell the others what she'd found, what she'd planned to do, and what we hoped would be the outcome. Since none of this involved golf, polo, or race cars, most of them merely nodded their agreement to what was being proposed while they checked their phones.

"Excellent idea. The ladies will come to the spa, and their men can play golf," Dominic Altrusi commented, after which the other men on the council seemed to wake up.

"Or," I said pointedly, "the ladies can play golf while their significant others can go to the spa."

"Yes, yes, of course," someone said as they discussed their plans for the golf course with much more enthusiasm than they'd shown for the spa. But they did have a point. Spa plus golf equaled more tourists.

The council was dismissed, and a few minutes later, I was back in my office, seated at my desk, hoping that Vincens's statement would encourage someone to show their hand sooner rather than later. I hated the feeling that there was a large question mark hanging over my head, like one of those big cartoon balloons in the annual Macy's Thanksgiving Day Parade. Like everywhere I went, that question mark was going to be bobbing along, following me.

Around eleven in the morning, Claudette poked her head into my office.

"Madam, there is someone here to see you."

She barely got the words out when Marianne literally ran into the room. I couldn't remember the last time I was that happy to see someone. I grabbed her and hugged her and held on.

"I thought you weren't coming for another week."

"I got your house rented sooner than I expected, so I decided to surprise you. My cousin Kevin—You know, the cop? He used to date Claire Murphy?—was looking for a small house to rent. I called him, he came down to look at your place, loved it, agreed to a one-year rental on the spot." Marianne was still hugging me, and I realized we were jumping up and down like a couple of five-year-olds on the playground.

"So I handed him the key, packed my bags, changed my flights, and here I am."

"How'd your boss take it?"

"Not well. It means he actually has to do some work until he can replace me."

"No one can replace you, Mare." I released my grip on her after giving her another quick hug.

"True." One of the things I liked about her was the fact that she had always been aware of her own worth.

"The castle seems so much bigger without so many people milling around," she noted. "That great hall where you first come in? It was crowded when I was here for your coronation, but it looks absolutely cavernous now."

I nodded, wondering why I had never thought to refer to that area inside the front entry as "the great hall." I'd try to remember to do so from now on.

"So tell me everything that's been happening," we both said at the same time, and we laughed. We'd been doing that all our lives, almost as if we simultaneously had the same thought.

We had a lot to catch up on. I closed up my office and took the arm of my longtime bestie to take her on a tour of the castle's first floor. Then I wanted to show her to her suite of rooms (across the hall from mine) and settle in for some long overdue gossip.

"So bring me up to date," I said as we prepared to eat lunch in my private sitting room.

"Same old, really." Marianne was still googly-eyed from her tour of her own suite of rooms—smaller than mine, naturally, but still, spacious and beautifully appointed. "Oh my God, look at those strawberries!"

"I know, right? They grow them in the garden right here on the castle grounds," I said with no small amount of pride.

"You said the food here was fabulous, and everything they served over the week of your coronation was delicious. I'm going to love being here." Marianne was grinning from ear to ear. She always was the first person in line at the buffet. "So tell me what I'm going to be doing now that I'm here."

I explained that she'd be more or less interning with Claudette while she learned her way around the castle and who was who but that mostly she'd be my assistant. Answer my mail, remind me of where I had to be and when, handle my social media platforms, that sort of thing.

"You have social media?" she asked.

"Just general stuff. Like, 'Good morning, Saint Gilbert. It's a beautiful day in the duchy.' Like that. No personal stuff. Just to, you know, make people feel like I'm in touch."

"I can do that." Marianne was a great schmoozer, so I knew she'd do a good job there. "Love Juliette's videos, by the way. The girl's a natural. She's going to grow up to be a TV anchor. The next, you know, what's her name. Gilda Radner used to be her on *Saturday Night Live*."

"Barbara Walters." I nodded. I could see my daughter doing important interviews and things like that. Once she outgrew the giggle, of course.

That's how the day went. Catching up with my friend and feeling happy to connect with her in person. We had dinner with my family, and everyone was happy to see her. Afterward, Ceil and Roe filled her in on the plans for the spa and promised to take her to see the castle. We talked about "the rumor," and she predictably expressed her indignation and placed an Irish curse on the perpetrator. When we finally called it a night and everyone retired to their own rooms and I crawled into my bed, all the apprehension I'd felt earlier had slipped away, and I knew that whoever was out there trying to steal my thunder was not going to succeed. I felt like we'd called out the cavalry, and it had shown up wearing yoga pants, an oversize sweater, slightly teased hair, stiletto heels, and plenty of attitude.

Chapter Thirty-Four

I was still in a good mood the next morning, still relaxed, still happy. I shared breakfast with my sisters, my best friend, my daughter, and my son. My heart was full, believe me, to have all the people I loved there with me.

Ceil was once again describing her plans for the castle spa I could tell had become her pet project.

"I'd love to see it," Marianne told her. "When can I see it?"

"Is there anything going on today I should know about?" Ceil asked me.

"Not a thing," I replied.

"Then today's a good day," Ceil said. "The weather is perfect for a ride out into the countryside." She turned to me. "Unless you have something pressing, you should come, too."

"You haven't seen it yet?" Marianne asked, and I shook my head.

"Only in pictures that Ceil took," I said.

"Then you have to come with us."

Marianne was right. I should go. I should see this place where our country's fortune was going to be made. So far I'd left it all in Ceil's hands, and while I knew when it came to renovating houses and decorating them she needs no help from me or anyone other than a good contractor, I should be more than a casual observer.

"All right. We'll all go," I announced.

"Count me out," Ralphie said. "I'm playing soccer with Henri and some guys he knows. I'll see you all later." And with that, he was gone.

"Annie, wait till you see the grounds. The vineyards and the gardens." Roe stood, eager to get going. "Well, they don't look like much right now, but when Roberto gets finished with them, they're going to be fabulous. Our spa ladies will sit on that beautiful patio and look out over colorful flower beds and beyond to the grapevines." Roe sighed.

"Oh, that sounds glorious." Marianne was already on her way to the door. "I'll be back in a jiff."

"I think it's the lure of maybe finding the fountain of youth that's going to sell it, but yeah, the beautiful surroundings will be the icing. Losing the marionette lines will be the cake." I stood.

"Count me out, Mom," Jules said. "We're filming again. Today I want to talk about Serafina."

On her way out of the room, she paused for a nanosec to kiss my cheek, then she was gone.

"Hurricane Juliette." Ceil laughed. "Don't get in her way."

"I wouldn't think of it. Now you two go, change into something casual enough for the country but nice enough in case there's someone around taking pictures."

∼

The drive from castle to castle was just beautiful. We passed field after field, some where goats and sheep grazed, some with cows, some with crops now reaching the end of their growing season, and some fields of wildflowers. We drove through villages of no more than a dozen houses that appeared to have been built centuries ago (which they probably were). There were vineyards where the grapes had been picked, and others where the vines were still laden with fruit. It was a perfect day to sightsee, clear blue skies and bright sun.

"I can see why you love Saint Gilbert so much," Marianne said after we'd driven through a picturesque village. "It's beautiful. We haven't passed by one house I wouldn't love to live in."

Before I could respond, Max pointed out that we were approaching our destination. "If you look off to the right, you can see the castle."

Marianne leaned forward. "Oh my God, I see it! It looks like a fairy-tale castle. Not as much as yours—I mean, your castle is straight out of a fantasy—but it sorta looks a little like yours only smaller and there are no turrets."

"It's perfect." Ceil was clearly in love with the place. "It's just the right size for what we want to do. Wait till you see inside, Annie. You're going to want to start the promo for the spa like, tomorrow, if not sooner."

"I can help you with that. I'm very good at writing promo," Marianne told her. "I did all the print promo for the insurance company Annie and I worked for. Of course, my boss took credit for it—he always said he just took my ideas but had to heavily edit them. Edit, my butt. He never changed a word. I know what I wrote."

"I'd forgotten all that."

"I didn't. Which is why it gave me immense satisfaction to give him notice I was leaving immediately. I spent the rest of the afternoon cleaning out my desk and saying goodbye to my friends, and there wasn't anything he could say that would change my mind. He threatened to tell any future employer that I was totally unreliable and had a bad attitude."

"Please. I've known about your attitude since we were in kindergarten. It's one of your finest qualities."

I could see Max's smirk in the rearview mirror, and I smiled when we made eye contact. I loved those quiet, secret moments when we seemed to be on the same wavelength. I just wished we could do something more than smile.

The castle came into full view as we rounded a curve. It sat on a rise overlooking the vineyards Roe had talked about and was as white as Castle Blanc.

"It looks so elegant," I said.

"Wait till you see the inside," Ceil said. "It's absolutely lovely."

As we drew closer, it became apparent the exterior could use a little work. Nothing major, just some touch-up here and there, and it needed some landscaping. Weeds were growing between the boxwood shrubs, and flowers popped up in random places. But those minor flaws did not detract from the simplistic beauty of the structure. Where it could have been embellished, it was restrained and sophisticated. I could imagine pulling up in front, two weeks of spa treatments already booked, and seeing this lovely building. I would definitely be impressed, no matter where I came from.

Max drove slowly to ease between two of those ubiquitous black cars. I guess our Bond team had arrived before us and were, assumedly, checking the interior for someone who wants to send me back to Philly.

"How many rooms, Ceil?" I asked.

"I think there are forty-five, thereabouts." Ceil was gathering up her bag, preparing to hop out of the car the second it stopped.

"Forty-five rooms?" Marianne's jaw dropped. "Definitely not in Kansas anymore."

Max stopped the car and, yup—off went Ceil as if she were racing someone unseen to be first inside. The rest of us got out and stood quietly admiring the castle and the setting.

"Roberto has been pruning the vines," Roe said. "He thinks we'll have grapes next year because the plants are well established. They just needed some cleaning up. Clip off the suckers, trim back the vines, that sort of thing. And then we can start making wine here, special for the spa." Roe closed her eyes and from the smile on her face, she was picturing the labels just as she'd once described to me.

"My little sister, the winemaker." I grabbed her arm and turned her in the direction of the front door. "Walk. We'll do the outside later."

She walked, and Marianne, Max, and I followed. Ceil was already somewhere inside. It was a warm day, but the castle was cool inside. The large windows let in lots of natural light, giving the marble tile in the entrance hall a glow. The ceilings were high and the chandeliers dripping with crystals.

"In here," Ceil called to us, and we followed the sound of her voice.

"This is what I'm assuming was used as a reception room. I'm thinking it should serve the same purpose now. You know, you arrive, you're welcomed at the door. There will be a huge arrangement of flowers on a table. Someone takes your bags up to your room, and you're led in here to have a glass of wine, maybe some cheese and some fruit. You sit and chat for a bit with the hostess." Ceil was drawing such a clear picture, I could almost get a whiff of that wine. "And then you're taken to your elegant room—your home away from home for the next two weeks—where a welcome basket is waiting for you."

"Oh, I can help with those," Marianne told Ceil. "I always did the gift baskets for our big clients at holiday times. Big baskets filled with goodies. Oh, you could do such fun souvenirs. You have that mermaid, right?" Marianne had been fascinated when I told her about Serafina after my first trip to Saint Gilbert. "You could do cute things with her as a logo."

"I'll definitely get back to you when we get closer to opening day," Ceil told her, but I couldn't tell if she was humoring Mare or if she really was intrigued at the thought of putting Serafina on souvenirs. With Ceil, you couldn't always tell.

"And check this out." Ceil lifted the covering from a settee, then stood back to show off its delicate white legs and rose-and-white-striped fabric. I ran a hand over the seat, and it sure felt like silk to me.

"Wow. It's beautiful." I went from one covered piece of furniture to another, peeking underneath the sheets, and I couldn't help but marvel at the treasures. "Ceil, any idea how long this stuff has been here? It's all in perfect condition. I can't believe someone didn't just come in and help themselves."

Marianne looked around the room. "Yeah, like, no graffiti or anything rude written on the walls. Back in Philly, a place like this would be trashed the minute someone left."

"I guess it would have fared the same in any city," Roe said.

I looked at Max, who was leaning against the doorway looking amused—one of my favorite looks for him. "Any thoughts on that?" I asked.

Max shook his head. "None, Your Grace."

I shot him a look and mouthed *Annaliese*. He nodded, but I knew in front of a group he was going to keep to formalities. We heard the sound of footsteps on the stairs, and he went to investigate.

"So how long do you think?" Mare asked. I peeked into the hall to see who'd come downstairs and saw a small band of Max's guards in quiet conference with him. He motioned to the room we were in, and four of the guards moved to stand in the doorway. Max followed several of the others up the steps.

". . . so who knows?" Ceil was saying when I tuned back in. "I asked Claudette what she knew about Gabrielle. She told me that Gabrielle and her family moved to Switzerland to sit out the war, and they took everything with them. Sometime in the late 1990s or the early 2000s, things were brought back by Gabrielle's grandson. Great-grandson? He died in 2017. Never married. No children."

I nodded as if I'd been listening all along when in fact, I was trying to figure out what had sent Max up the steps so quickly.

"Now, come into the dining room," Ceil was saying. "It's extraordinary." She continued talking as she led us on through the house. "Look at that chandelier! I've never seen one that big or that beautiful. The scrollwork around the top piece was all hand-painted. And check out this table! I feel like all these lovely things have been waiting for me to find them and bring life back into this place."

And so it went, room to room, Ceil calling our attention to this piece or that, all the time marveling at the artwork and the furniture, the rugs, and the many little things that had been sitting idle for years. Ceil clearly had hit the decorator's lottery. She showed us where she thought the spa should be located, where the aestheticians would do their thing, lathering up the faces and necks of the women—and of course the occasional man—who would come here seeking a new lease on life. Then we went upstairs and she showed off the bedroom suites where our future spa-goers would stay. Some had balconies; all had private baths and large closets and gorgeous views. The spa at Saint Gilbert was going to be like nothing else in the world. The very thought of such success made my head spin. This was going to happen.

"Ceil, we're going to need a timetable from the contractors. And a professional photographer. And some really effective ad copy. Mare"—I turned to her—"work with Ceil on that, and we'll see if what you come up with is . . . well, *good enough* won't be good enough. Not to be critical, but we have a lot at stake here. The copy has to have zing."

Marianne rolled her eyes. "Oh, please. Zing is my middle name."

"Then now's the time to bring it." I watched her and Ceil wink at each other, a good sign they'd work together to make our initial promotion a success. I had no doubt after the first wave or two of spa-goers, we wouldn't need as much promo. Word of mouth and unretouched photographs were going to sell this place.

I stood in the center of the second-floor landing—almost as large as the foyer below—and wondered where Max had disappeared. Except for the four of us chattering away, the rest of the house was silent.

"What's upstairs?" I asked.

"The ballroom and a few drawing rooms, a small private dining room. It's gorgeous, but I have no idea what we'd use it for. Then on the fourth floor, there are more bedrooms, smaller than these, though.

They probably used those originally for their live-in help. I'm sure they had a large staff of maids and cooks and whoever else a castle required to function. I'm not sure we would use those rooms. I wouldn't want anyone to feel as if they are second-class citizens."

"Good point." I looked up at the staircase.

"The fourth floor also has several large storage rooms. A trunk room with some of the old trunks still in there. They might be fun for Juliette and her friends to go through. Maybe there are some old dresses and hats. Remember how much we loved playing dress-up when we were little?"

"I do. I'll definitely tell Jules to check it out. That could be one of their videos." I was picturing the girls dressing up in old fashions. I was also thinking about going up and checking out those trunks myself when Roe grabbed my arm.

"Can I please show you the kitchen now?" She was almost pleading.

"I can't wait to see it, Roe." Actually, I could—I was more intrigued by the thought of finding fun things in the trunk room—but I knew the kitchen was all Roe's, and she was excited about the things she planned to do there.

We all went back down the wide staircase and through a hallway into a large open space in the back of the house.

"This is it." Roe's eyes were shining. "Okay, picture a huge stove right here, a second one right next to it. Then an enormous refrigerator over there, a double sink under the windows, and two extra-large dishwashers right alongside the sink." She spread her arms expansively and grinned as she described her vision. "I know we won't need double everything when we first start up, but down the road, we will. A mile of counter space for prep work. There's a butler's pantry behind that door." She walked across the room to show it off. "Come look at all the shelves. I can store a lot of stuff in here. Isn't it all just perfect?"

We all dutifully looked and oohed and ahhed for her sake.

"It is perfect," I agreed. If she was happy—and it was clear she was—I was happy. Plus her happiness would spill over into the food she made for our patrons, and that did make me happy.

"Oh, Roberto's here." Roe had glanced out the window, then she lit up like it was Christmas morning. "Looks like he's working on something in the orchard."

Roe sped off in the direction of the orchard, and we didn't see her again for a good half hour.

We were halfway through our tour of the grounds when Roe joined us. She had a goofy smile and didn't even chide us for starting off without her.

"Roberto's pruning the apple and cherry trees today. Tomorrow, he'll work on the fig trees. When I think of what I could do with a big crop of figs . . ."

"I think you're imagining what you could do with Roberto," Ceil said.

"Funny. I was thinking the same thing," I chimed in.

Roe nodded without hesitation. "Oh yeah. That too."

"The grounds here are gorgeous," Marianne noted. "That back patio would make a perfect little café-like spot." She looked over the vast lawn leading to a reflection pool. "There's no end to what you could do with a property like this."

"I think right now we have more ideas than we know what to do with," I said. "We should write them all down and then go through them and see what makes the most sense to begin with."

"Speaking of much to do," Ceil began slowly. "Remember how we talked about using one of the castles or chateaus—not sure which is the proper term—"

"I think chateau might be French for little castle," Roe said.

"Whatever we want to call them. Uncle Theodore's place would be perfect for a wedding venue, like we talked about. It has such a grand staircase, and it also has a ballroom. I think maybe twenty bedrooms and baths—I meant to count but I forgot. And the grounds are so pretty. There's actually a small lake behind the castle. You can't see it from the back of the building because there are so many trees in the way. The place is empty—we'd need to furnish that one—but it could be a real moneymaker. We could also use it as a hotel."

"We could sell a package—a week before the wedding at the spa for the mother of the bride and/or groom, then the wedding at the castle," I mused.

"Don't forget the older brides," Marianne noted. "I'll bet there are a lot of older women getting married who'd love to wash a few years off."

"Or we could offer a discount for the older bride and groom together," Roe said. "We could call it the Senior Special."

We all chuckled, but Mare and Roe were both onto something that we should explore at some point. Just not today. Today we were all relaxed, and for a while it was just like old times when Marianne would come over to our house and the four of us would just sit and talk about *stuff*. But soon enough, Max appeared and announced it was time to leave.

Mare and Roe both fell asleep on the way home, but Ceil and I were wide awake with our thoughts, she thinking about her castle renovation, me wondering where Max and some of the other guards had disappeared for over an hour. When we returned to the castle, he excused himself, then took off as soon as we got out of the car, leaving us in the care of the four guards who'd been with us at the castle, and me wondering where he'd gone in such a hurry.

Chapter Thirty-Five

By breakfast the next morning, I thought I knew what had put the bee in Max's bonnet. A new full-page announcement in yesterday's local paper—and apparently in all the papers in the country as well as on the social media accounts of someone who called himself the Royal Watchdog—asked, *Why does a foreigner sit on our throne?* I would have missed it completely if I hadn't left the paper on the table next to the love seat in my sitting room. I hadn't had time to look through it in the morning, so I'd left it to read when I got back from our outing but forgot about it until this morning.

Why does a foreigner sit on our throne?

Well, I suppose that was food for thought, but what exactly did he—Andretti had confirmed a male voice had left the message on his phone—want? Was he expecting me to quietly leave Saint Gilbert?

Don't hold your breath.

I tried not to think about it too much. I had a meeting with Jacques Gilberti and his son, Alaine, the engineer, who'd flown in earlier in the week to evaluate our existing roads and to see where new roads might be most efficiently built. I wanted to give them my undistracted attention because the roads were a big deal. That took most of the day, since we talked at length, then had lunch, then had taken a drive to see where Alaine had suggested repairs and where he thought new roads would most logically be cut in. At the end of the day, I was optimistic, because there was little we could really do to lift up this country if we couldn't get around in it. I told Alaine I'd like him to address the council directly, which he agreed to do if we could schedule that within the next week.

After dinner and a short visit with my family, we all agreed to turn in a bit early. The last few days had been busy, and we were all tired. Then I turned on the TV in my sitting room and bam! The city's major television station was covering the "who is Annie and why is she on our throne" story. At first, both the anchors appeared to be treating it as a joke. But toward the end of their banter, one said to the other, "I do recall the Duke's Council's announcement that the heir to the throne had been located in Philadelphia in the United States and that a contingent had been sent to discuss with her the possibility of returning to Saint Gilbert to take over where her great-grandmother had left off. As I recall, everyone was pretty happy about it."

"Right," newsperson number two agreed. "A spokesman described in detail how, through the years, members of the council had been in touch with the exiled former duchess and how they'd searched every inch of the Gilberti family tree and were one hundred percent positive that Annaliese Gilberti was in fact the rightful heir. The *only* rightful heir. So what's the point in starting these rumors when we all know the truth? Who do you think is behind it?"

The first anchor shook his head. "I have no idea. I think it's silliness, frankly, and a waste of our time to even talk about it. But there's one rumor I hope proves true: I heard there are plans to repair the roads between Beauchesne and the ski slopes."

"I hope it's more than a rumor. The slopes have been off limits since I was a child because the roads are a mess and the lifts are unsafe and . . ."

I turned off the TV and sat on the love seat, staring at the wall. I could probably have overlooked *Who is Annaliese Gilberti?* if everyone else had let it drop. I mean, it could have been some promo for a hastily written book, right? Even "who is the true heir?" didn't get under my skin the way this latest did. This felt different. It felt mean and personal, and its intent seemed to be to get people to talk about that very thing: Why was I, born in the USA, ruling their country? Everyone knew the story and seemed to be fine with it—except this one person. So the real question was, who is this person?

I know Max and his "eyes and ears" were on high alert, and I believe even Vincens was making an honest effort to find out who and why. But the more I thought about it, the crazier it was going to make me. The best thing I could do for myself right now would be to go to sleep.

Just as I was about to change into a nightgown—I'd purposely tossed my old nightshirts because if something happened in the middle of the night and I had to leave my room, how embarrassing it would be for me to appear in the hall wearing a long, faded *Nutcracker* T-shirt— my phone rang. Max. Calling no doubt to see if I was up for some fun in the moonlight.

A girl can dream, can't she?

So I answered the phone, and before I could speak, Max said, "I think we should talk."

"Now?"

"Yes."

"Did something happen? Did our anonymous friend respond to the chancellor's invitation?"

"Not to my knowledge. But I do need to speak with you."

I looked down at my bare feet and thought about finding my flats or my slippers, then figured the hell with it.

"You're going to have to come up here," I said. "I'm too tired to make myself presentable."

He hesitated for a moment.

"If you're worried that someone will start a rumor about you coming into my room at night, you're just going to have to live with it."

"I'll be there in a few minutes."

"I'll have coffee waiting." I went into the bathroom and checked my appearance in the full-length mirror. There was no time to do anything more than put on a minimal amount of makeup—mascara and maybe a little blush.

"Thank you. That would be appreciated."

We hung up and I called the kitchen. After apologizing for the late call, I told the person who answered the phone what I would like brought up. I knew from experience that when I requested something, it showed up in the snap of my fingers. Tonight was no different. While I was speedy with a mascara wand and a blush brush, the kitchen was just as quick. A tray with coffee and the ham biscuits, pastries, and fruit I'd asked for arrived at almost the same time as I turned off the bathroom light. Max was at my door minutes after the tray arrived. The timing all around was perfect.

"Please sit," I told him. "You look exhausted."

He nodded and sat on the settee in the bedroom. "It's been a long day."

I poured coffee for both of us and handed him a cup.

"You've no idea how welcome this is." He took a few sips.

"Did you have time to eat today?"

He shook his head, no.

"I suspected as much." I uncovered the plate of sandwiches and told him to help himself.

"We need to talk first," he protested.

"I want to make sure you don't pass out from hunger or fatigue in the middle of the telling." I pointed to the plate of biscuits, and he put two on a small plate.

While he ate, I talked, and he responded.

"Max, where do you live? You don't live here in the castle, do you?" It occurred to me to ask since he seemed to be just minutes away at all times.

"I have a home, a small chateau, outside the city," he said.

"Does Claudette live with you?"

"She has a town house here in Beauchesne, but when I have things to do at night, she will stay with Remy either at my place or at hers. Sometimes my daughter prefers to be in the city, closer to her friends."

I admit to being really curious about the things he did at night, but I didn't have the nerve to ask. Someone once told me to never ask a question if I wasn't sure I'd like the answer. Words to live by.

"Has Remy shown you the video she and Juliette made?"

He finished chewing a bite. "It's surprisingly good. I didn't know what to expect when she told me what they were doing. But I must say, I'm impressed with what I've seen."

"It's the perfect promotion piece for Saint Gilbert right now, an excellent introduction to the country. They're gaining thousands of watchers every day."

He finished both biscuits and took a few more sips of coffee before returning the cup to the saucer. "Thank you, Annaliese. That was very thoughtful of you."

"You're welcome. Now, what's so important it couldn't wait until the morning?" I asked. Not that I objected to having him there.

Max leaned forward a bit toward the table, his forearms resting on his thighs. On the opposite side of the table, I did the same. Another foot and we'd have been forehead to forehead. I wished.

"Calls have been made to the castle regarding the identity of the person who's planted the rumors. This self-proclaimed Royal Watchdog."

"You have a name?" My heart sped up. Oh, how I wanted to have my turn interrogating this guy.

"Not yet. But several of the callers have described the same person. A man a few inches less than six feet tall, slender build, dark hair, slightly receding hairline, between the ages of forty and fifty. He's been in some of the local pubs over the past week talking to whomever will listen."

"Talking about . . . ?"

"You. All the callers say he seems obsessed with you and your family. He thinks the council was hasty in accepting you, talks about how there is someone more deserving to be in your place, that sort of thing."

"Do you have a list of the callers? Can you bring them in so we can talk to them?" I remembered my old claim adjuster days, how sometimes stories changed when you sat down and looked a witness in the eye. Sometimes a casual conversation could help bring to light things they'd forgotten.

"We have their names and numbers recorded on the castle line. We will spend tomorrow tracking them down. In the meantime, I have guards in plain clothes in all the pubs this man has been known to frequent."

"I want to be in on any conversations you have with anyone he's talked to," I told him.

"Of course."

"He's saying someone else is more deserving but he's not saying who?" Curious, I thought. Why not just put it out there?

"Not yet, but I suspect that's coming."

"So we won't know until he tells us, or until he's found." I'd been hoping for more definitive news, but okay, this was something we didn't have this morning. "So, about yesterday. At Gabrielle's castle. Where'd you disappear to?" I think he believed I hadn't noticed.

"Hmmm. I do not recall disappearing."

"Yes you do. You took off up the steps to the upper floors like a rocket. What was up there?" I narrowed my eyes, hoping he understood that meant I knew he was withholding something and I wasn't going to let him get away with it.

He sighed. "In checking the castle before you and your family arrived, the guards found that someone has been sleeping in one of the third-floor bedrooms. Now, it could be a vagrant, it could be young people who think they've found a place to be alone, a safe lovers' rendezvous, perhaps. Or it could be something else. We're not sure. But there was a glass in one of the bathrooms that we took to have tested for . . ."

"DNA." Of course Max would jump on that. "Which would only be useful if that person's DNA was on record somewhere where he could be identified, or if it matched someone else. If you're looking to match someone in the Gilberti line, of course, you're going to start with me. That's the thinking, right? This person is related to me?" I started pacing, forgetting my bare feet. "Isn't that most logical? Who would even think of questioning my right other than someone who felt they were more entitled? The underlying message from this guy seems to be that the council picked the wrong person, even though you all were certain there was no one else. I know you must be wondering if you looked hard enough."

"I don't know where else—how else—we could have searched. We went through every branch of your family, generation after generation. We were—we still are—positive we got it right." Max was adamant, certain they had not made an error.

"And yet someone is convinced you got it wrong."

"So it would seem."

"So you test that glass for DNA and you compare it to mine—I'm available for swabbing anytime—and see if we're related. It won't tell us who he is, but at least we'll have a better idea what we're dealing with." I thought for a moment. "It can't be a coincidence that someone's staying in Gabrielle's castle at the same time all these rumors have started. Are we certain that none of her descendants are still alive?"

"We saw the death certificates of all three of her children. The last of her line died in 2017. It's well documented."

"Could someone have fallen through the cracks? Maybe she had another child after she and her family moved to Switzerland."

"I can't believe no one would have known. Surely a record would have been made. But it wouldn't have made any difference. Gabrielle's mother was never in line for the throne, nor was she. Therefore, none of her descendants would be. Your great-grandmother was always destined to become the grand duchess. The crown rightfully passed to your grandmother even though she never had a chance to wear it after her mother's hasty abdication."

"Maybe someone doesn't know that Gabrielle was never in the queue."

"If someone believed they were the legitimate heir, why would they have waited this long to make their case? And why not bring the matter directly to the Duke's Council if you believe you have a case? Why all this nonsense?" Max rubbed the back of his neck.

"I don't know. Maybe he believes if he gets people to thinking about me not being the real duchess, they'll be more amenable to accepting someone else. Then where does he think he could go from there? Stir up a revolution, then reveal himself as the real deal so he can step into my place?"

"We'll have to find him before he can make any of that happen. But we will find him." Max stood. "It's late. I should go and let you get some sleep. Thank you for seeing me at this hour. I wanted you to hear directly from me what was transpiring."

"Thank you, Max. Anytime." And I meant that. *Any* time.

There were voices in the hall outside my door, and I startled.

"It's just the changing of the guard," Max explained. "It's midnight. But . . ."

"But . . . ?"

"It's a bit awkward with the two of them out there and me in here."

"You can wait it out, if you want. Stay as long as you want." I was trying not to be too blatant.

He smiled, and I thought, *Yes!*

Then he said, "I should have thought of it sooner. Your sitting room is through that door?" He pointed.

"Yes . . . ?" Was he thinking about bunking in on the love seat? Nowhere near big enough for a man as tall as he is.

"Come with me." He grabbed my hand, and my hopes started to rise as he led me into the sitting room.

Then he dropped my hand and began to feel his way along the molding next to the fireplace.

What the hell?

"Max, what are you doing?" I turned on a lamp.

"There should be a . . . ah yes, here it is." He looked over his shoulder at me, and I thought I saw a gleam of mischief there, right at the same time a panel slid away and disappeared behind the fireplace.

"A secret passage?" I momentarily forgot my disappointment. "There's a secret passage in my room? Oh, I wonder who built it. Who used it?" I raised my eyebrows.

"The passages, like the secret rooms, were built in when the castle was first designed. Now, for what purpose?" He shrugged. "Maybe it was an escape route in case the castle was attacked."

"Maybe it was intended to keep secrets," I offered.

"Maybe. But tonight, it will serve to deflect any rumors that might start if someone saw me leaving your room at midnight." He stepped halfway into the opening. "I'll see you tomorrow."

"Max, are we in danger from this guy?"

He shook his head. "He will never get near you, Annaliese. Every man and woman in the castle guard would lay down their lives for you."

"Would you?"

He responded without hesitation. "Without question."

Without thinking, I stepped forward and raised my hand to touch the side of his face, and oh my God, it was just like a scene from a movie, only better, because it was real. We stared into each other's eyes, and I went up on my tippy-toes to kiss him, but he beat me to it. He kissed me. Max Belleme kissed me. And oh, mama, what a kiss it was! It was hot and sweet at the same time, and may I say, I know more than a few men who could take lessons from the captain. (Let's be real—I've been divorced for a long time and during those years, this duchess has kissed her share of toads.) Honest to God, I thought my heart was going to burst right out of my chest, it was beating so fast. Max wrapped those arms around me—like iron bands, he is one strong guy—and I just about melted into a puddle. As kisses go, this was an A-plus-plus-plus. When we finally broke apart—neither my idea nor my move—we just looked at each other.

I said, "If you are thinking about apologizing, so help me God, I will have you locked in the dungeon and chained to the wall."

He gently touched the side of my face, then bam! He disappeared into the dark passage.

I stood alone in the sitting room for a long time, just savoring the moment. I'd wanted to kiss that man since . . . well, practically the first time I met him. Was it worth the wait? Oh yeah.

My only regret was that it had to end.

Chapter Thirty-Six

I was still feeling a little swoony the next morning. I'd been awake half the night thinking about it, and I woke up, not exactly singing, but I could have. For a short time, I forgot about the mystery man—the Royal Watchdog—and his rumors and just wanted to sit with my legs curled under me, a cup of the divine castle coffee in my hand, and relive that moment when I kissed Max and he kissed me back. Or had he kissed me and I kissed him back? In any case, he hadn't pushed me away or looked as if he wished I hadn't done it. Frankly, he looked pretty pleased with himself. However, family members were gathering for breakfast and there was work to do.

I dressed quickly and joined the others, who were already chowing down on soft-boiled eggs, croissants, and pastries filled with cream cheese and blackberries. I followed the banter without chiming in for several minutes before Marianne tapped me on the knee.

"So what's with you this morning? You're awfully quiet," she noted.

"Tough to get a word in, the way you guys go on," I said.

"And in the past, that had stopped you . . . when?" Ceil asked.

"I guess I just have a lot on my mind." I couldn't bring myself to announce *I kissed a duke and I liked it.*

"Well, you do, what with everything you're trying to do—that list of yours is as long as Mrs. Rinaldi's grocery lists. Remember her?" Ceil, who sat next to me on the settee, nudged me, and we both laughed.

"Who's Mrs. Rinaldi?" Marianne asked.

"She lived across the street from us when we were growing up. She used to give Ceil and me a dollar each to go to the market for her. She'd give us a list with everything she wanted and enough money to pay for it all, down to the penny."

Ceil bit off the last bit of the blackberry pastry. "This is so good. Honestly, the pastry chef here could work anywhere in the world. She is that good."

"Yeah, but don't tell her. I'd hate for her to leave us for some fancy restaurant somewhere." Marianne sighed. "Keep feeding me like this, and I'll never go back to Philly."

"That's sort of the idea," I said. "Since I've made up mine that I'm never leaving. I can't remember when I've ever been happier. I really have grown to love this country."

"I have to admit, I'm pretty happy myself," Ceil said. "When would I ever get a chance to do over a freaking castle? I'm not going anywhere."

"Chef for life here." Roe pointed to herself. "I'm not leaving, either."

"I am," Juliette announced. When the adults in the room all turned to stare at her, she added, "Well, not right now. Mom, do you think we could get a tutor for me this year? I wanted to go to school in Switzerland with my friends, but you have to speak French fluently to get in, and I don't speak a word other than, like, you know, *croissant* and *merci* and *bonjour*."

"Well, they're three words less you'll have to learn." I stood and stretched. "We'll look into a tutor. Right now, it's time to get moving. I have a meeting at nine with Andre DiGiacoma about money. What are the rest of you doing today?"

"I'm working in the greenhouse with Roberto," Roe said, a silly grin on her face. "I told him I was going to want microgreens for salads for the castle and for the spa kitchen, so he told me I should learn to grow them myself. I'm excited."

"As anyone would be," Ceil deadpanned.

"You'll thank me when your salads are bursting with nutritious sprouts."

Ceil nodded. "I'll be sure to do that."

"And what does the day hold for Cecilia?" I asked.

"Looking at fabric with Gisele. I don't know anyone else in the city who has a direct line to fabric manufacturers, so I thought I'd go over our spa needs with her. You know, upholstery and drapes and such. Oh, and I thought I'd talk to the wool lady."

"The wool lady?" *We have a wool lady?*

"The woman who owns the yarn shop. She's the one the sheep farmers bring their wool to, and she cleans it and does whatever it is you do with raw wool to turn it into yarn. She has blankets knitted from that yarn that Gisele tells me are heavenly. I thought we'd look into having her make some throws for the spa."

"Great idea. Maybe use the colors from the flag. You know, that pretty blue and the white."

"That's the idea," Ceil said.

"I'm making a video with Remy," Juliette announced.

"Where?" I asked.

"Not sure. We have a few ideas."

I thought about the nameless guy chatting up strangers in the pubs. Regardless of how many guards Max might have, I still felt uneasy.

"Stick close to home today, okay?" I thought about the Royal Watchdog and wondered if he was watching anyone besides me. "But if you feel it necessary to leave the castle grounds, take your guards. Maybe an extra one or two."

She blew me a kiss and was gone that fast.

"Don't go anywhere without your guards, Jules." Too late. She was already gone. But I needn't worry. The guards would never let her leave the castle alone. Just like they never let Ralphie take off on his morning run or for his afternoon pickup soccer games without at least two guards. "That goes for everyone else, too. If you have to leave the castle, you have extra guards."

I'd been skeptical when Max first told me he was expanding the castle guard, but now I was grateful for the protection.

"I need to go, too. I'm supposed to get together with Claudette in her office." Marianne drained her coffee cup, then stood. "Today she's going to take me through every room in the castle."

I gave her a thumbs-up. "Wear comfy shoes. This place has miles of hallways."

She stopped on her way to the door to hold up a sneakered foot. "Already figured that out."

A few minutes later, Ceil and Roe left as well. I dressed for my meeting—a black (natch) dress with short sleeves and a modest neckline that was just right for a modest strand of pearls. I looked at myself in the mirror and thought I looked pretty good for going on forty-five. I pushed my hair back behind my ears, popped some pearl earrings in my lobes, grabbed my bag, and out I went.

I walked down the steps flanked by two guards. They escorted me to the suite of first-floor offices and took up their places outside the door. I went inside to the waiting room and through to Claudette's office, which was empty. Once in my office, I turned on the light and lifted my laptop out of a desk drawer. I had just started scrolling through emails when I heard first Claudette, then Marianne, talking in the front office. Moments later Andre arrived and was shown in to me.

"Right on time," I said as I closed the laptop.

"It wouldn't do to keep our duchess waiting," he said as he sat in a side chair, then opened his own laptop and held it on his lap until I pointed to the end of the desk, indicating he should set it there. "We've got so much good news this morning, I don't know where to start."

"Really? I could use some good news right about now."

"I hope Your Grace hasn't been disturbed by the . . . the . . ."

"Rumors about me not being the rightful duchess?" I finished his sentence since he seemed reluctant to do so. "I admit I've been a bit distracted, but that has nothing to do with what you and I have to discuss, so we'll put it aside for now and we'll talk about something much more pleasant. Money."

"Specifically, money the Swiss overseer has agreed to send us to fund the roads once the estimates and the engineer's report has been received," he said. "Now, I understand that Alaine Gilberti is at the moment writing his report and will enclose it with the estimate he's going to be getting from the paving company he contacted. That company is in France, but the owner is to meet with Alaine and his father on Wednesday. Alaine has given us a ballpark figure, and that is the amount the Swiss will send us without waiting for the official estimate. They have been warned it will be a large amount. Alaine will impress upon the contractor the urgency of not only having the full, itemized estimate prepared as soon as humanly possible but scheduling the work as well. We need those roads before we can accomplish the other goals we have set."

"Exactly what I've been saying." We spent the next half hour discussing Ceil's plans for the spa and the castle renovations, then the possibility of having Louis Bondersan, the contactor she was working with, look at several smaller chateaus that had been proposed as future hotels.

"Your Grace, if I may say so, you coming to Saint Gilbert—bringing your enthusiasm and your ideas and foresight—has breathed new life into this country. Everyone will benefit from the projects you have proposed. We have been honored by your acceptance of your heritage."

"Thank you, Andre. I appreciate that more than you know." I meant that. I don't think of myself as a needy person, but right now, words like the ones he'd just spoken made me feel more confident that we would put out this fire the Royal Watchdog had started.

We discussed the efforts he was making to modernize our banking system and the search for someone who was experienced with the technical aspects of setting up the new system, and the possibility of a rail system. While the country was small, a railroad that went north to south from Switzerland to Italy with stops in between would complete the picture. I promised to support his proposal to the council whenever he felt ready to bring it up. By the time our meeting ended and I'd seen him out, I was positive we were going to accomplish everything I'd set out to do. We were going to turn this country around in less time than anyone would have given us credit for. With the right people and the funding, we could do anything.

So far the day had gone well. Combined with what I hoped was a turned corner in my relationship with Max, I was pretty much walking on clouds. I celebrated by spending an hour with Sasha in the meadow, where we both enjoyed the sunshine and the gentle breezes. I was afraid the security detail, which now numbered six, might spook her, but most of the guards made an effort to blend in with the scenery, so I shouldn't have worried. Plus, Sasha, being the sassy little thing she was, seemed to be barely aware of them at all, as if they were beneath her notice. Watching my hawk grow bolder in her hunting and her flights gave me joy. The fact that she always returned to my arm when I signaled her made me feel even more connected to my Gilberti ancestors and appreciate the heritage we shared.

I returned to the castle with a happy heart—and my security detail, which had somehow grown to eight. When had that happened? Something must be afoot. I rang for Max as soon as I got into my office.

"What's up?" I asked as I sorted through a pile of phone messages Marianne had left for me in three piles: Return Call, Call Sometime, Ignore/Trash. I put them all in the Call Sometime stack.

"The Royal Watchdog is back in the news. Literally, in the news." He sounded exasperated with the whole thing. "He sent a video to all the news outlets explaining why you are not the rightful heir and chastising the Duke's Council for having done such a shoddy job of researching the lineage."

"He sent a video? So you know what he looks like and you can . . ."

"Would that it could be that easy. He blacked himself out. All you can see is the dark outline of a man seated in a chair. He made no effort to disguise his voice, however."

"Wait—he said your research was 'shoddy'?"

"He also said we were lazy, unprofessional, and unworthy to participate in the functioning of the government. That as we had predetermined our selection, we therefore made no effort to look beyond who we perceived as the obvious choice, and therefore the entire Duke's Council has to be removed and replaced with only the lawful heir." He paused. "There may have been more, but you get the picture."

"Sounds as if the Royal Watchdog is an autocrat at heart."

"Autocrat or dictator. There's a fine line between the two, but in any case, it appears he wants to be solely in charge."

"Saint Gilbertians would never allow such a thing," I said. "Would they?"

"No. There's a reason the Duke's Council has survived for hundreds of years. The council keeps a check on the monarch, and the monarch keeps a check on the council. It's worked since the sixteen hundreds. It isn't going to change now."

"And yet you're annoyed anyway." I could hear it in his voice.

"Of course I'm annoyed. The people of this country have been without their duchess for *eighty-two years*, Annaliese. We finally have you here, finally have plans in place to lift this country up and restore it to its place on the world stage, and now we have to deal with this? We have no time for such distractions."

"I agree," I said calmly. "So you do your thing and find him as quickly as possible, and let's hear his case."

"I would rather we, in America I think they say, feed him to the fishes."

I laughed out loud. "Now who's sounding like an autocrat?"

"Apologies. You're right, of course. We just need to find him and shut this down."

"I guess he didn't bother to explain who he thinks is the legitimate heir."

"That would make this all too easy. I'm beginning to think he's some deluded individual whose family history repeats some myth about them being a direct descendant of the first duke and duchess."

"Right. Like the way every other person with Scottish blood says they're a direct descendant of Mary, Queen of Scots."

Now he did laugh. "Yes, like that."

"Maybe we should have Vincens issue another invitation to this person to meet with him."

"That's an excellent idea. He should respond in video form as well so everyone can see him. The chancellor can do *sincere* very well. And by him doing that, it shows we have nothing to hide."

"So go do your thing, big guy." I paused, wanting to say more, something like, *So, can I look forward to another midnight visit?* "Call the chancellor."

"I'll be in touch." And like that—gone, and I'd missed my chance to issue a loaded invitation.

I called Marianne and asked her to go to my suite and bring both my sisters with her. I went upstairs accompanied by my now constant companions, who I left at the door. Ceil, Mare, and Roe were already waiting in the front room.

"You saw it," Ceil said glumly. "I was hoping you hadn't seen it yet. You were in such a good mood this morning."

"No, I haven't seen it, though judging from your faces, the three of you have." I sat on the love seat and toed off my shoes. "Max told me."

"What are you going to do?"

"Max is trying to find him, and Vincens is going to make a video inviting him to meet with him or the council or whomever this guy wants to meet with. Me if he wants. We just need to shut him down."

"He sounds a bit unhinged," Marianne said.

"Max thinks so, too. He thinks he's deluded. Which means he may or may not be dangerous." I leaned back. "Which means we all are going to take this as a serious threat, so no one goes anywhere without guards." I thought about the additional detail I'd had today. "Extra guards for everyone, got it?"

They all did. I would remind the kids at dinner, and again at breakfast the next morning.

And I did.

"Ralph, when you run this morning . . . ," I began.

He nodded. "Right. Extra guards." He bit a croissant in half and chewed what he'd bitten off. "I saw the news. Some crazy guy sent a video to the TV stations. He thinks we should be sent home." He swallowed what was in his mouth, then grinned. "But we are home, and we're not going anywhere."

"Spoken like a true Gilberti," Ceil told him, and he beamed.

"That was . . . very . . . *princely* of you," I said.

"I thought so." He grabbed the last chocolate croissant and a couple of berries and took off.

"Where's your sister?" I called after him.

"Don't know. Haven't seen her today." The door closed behind him.

Juliette strolled in, yawning, a few minutes later.

"Late night?"

"I'm learning how to edit the videos so I can do it myself after Mila goes back to school." She helped herself to breakfast, in between bites telling us what they'd filmed yesterday and how she was certain everyone who saw it would be *dying* to come to Saint Gilbert.

And that was pretty much the way it went for the rest of the week. The Royal Watchdog's video was played over and over on every news broadcast, the speculation and controversy taking on a life of its own. There were debates on talk shows where those with opposing views faced off.

"If the Duke's Council had made a mistake, shouldn't we know?" versus "The search played out before our eyes. Everyone knows the rightful heir has been crowned, and from all I've heard, she's doing a remarkable job."

By the end of the week, the story began to lose some of its steam. While still in the news, the televised segments became shorter and shorter, and the calls into the castle were fewer and more vague. We kept one eye on the Royal Watchdog but gradually turned our focus to other things.

But there were more ups and downs still to come. The clouds didn't begin to darken until we all met in the family dining room for dinner at six the following Monday evening.

After everyone had arrived and taken their seats, I realized someone was missing.

"Where is Juliette?"

Chapter Thirty-Seven

"Where's Juliette?" I repeated.

Everyone looked at each other but no one responded.

Finally, Ceil said, "Maybe she's still in her room doing something with her latest video and she's lost track of time. I'll run up and check."

"No, I'll go." If she was up there with her nose in her phone, I would chastise her for being late to the table. If she wasn't there, I'd . . .

I didn't know what I'd do. She knew the rules. Six o'clock sharp in the dining room. The cooks went to great lengths to make our amazing meals, and they deserved the courtesy of us being there on time to enjoy them as they were brought from the kitchen, not ten or fifteen minutes later. Not even five. Anything less was disrespectful to the people who served us so well.

I left the dining room and started down the hall so quickly my guards had to hustle to keep up. I climbed the stairs like a demon and practically ran to her room, pausing only to ask the guards if they'd seen her.

"No, my lady."

I opened the door to her suite and called her. Three times. Four. But the room was empty and silent. I looked around for her bag, her phone, anything to show she was around somewhere, but her bag and her phone were gone. I went back into the hall and told the guard to let me know immediately if she arrived. I cannot explain the sense of dread that began to wash over me.

I went into my own room and sat on the settee and called Max.

My hands were shaking so hard I could barely tap out his number.

"I can't find Juliette," I said when he answered.

"What?"

"I said I can't find Juliette. She hasn't shown up for dinner and she's not in her room."

"Maybe she's just running late, or . . ."

"No. Something's happened to her. I can feel it."

"Where are you?" I could hear him starting to move.

"In my room."

"Go back to the dining room. Maybe she's there now."

"Will you meet me there?"

"I'm already on my way."

The second I walked into the dining room, Marianne asked, "Annie, what the hell is going on? You're shaking."

"I don't know where Juliette is. She should be here and she isn't and she isn't upstairs."

"Maybe she's with Remy," Ralphie offered.

Max came into the room. "I just checked with my mother. Remy hasn't come home yet, either."

"I'm sure there's a good explanation." Ceil, ever wise and rational, remained calm while I was starting to disintegrate. "Why are you getting so upset because she's late to dinner?"

I couldn't put words to the feeling I had. It was as if I knew—*I just knew*—something had happened to her and it wasn't good. I felt fear—a deep, heavy, clawed-into-my-gut fear. It was the fear a parent knows when they can't find their child.

Like the time I lost Juliette in the Springfield Mall when she was four. A friend at work was doing a charity fashion show and asked Jules to be one of the kid models. We went into the store where the clothes were being tried on, and I turned my back for, honest to God, no more than twenty seconds, and when I turned back she was gone. We looked all around the store, even the dressing rooms, thinking she'd followed a friend, but she wasn't there. I went out into the mall and called her, but she wasn't in front of the store, either. I had never in my life felt so helpless. I dashed down the mall frantically calling her name, and finally, I saw her way ahead of me, by the fountain, leaning over the edge staring into the water. When I reached her, she nonchalantly pointed to the bottom of the pool and said, "Mommy, someone lost their pennies."

I had damn near collapsed. The depth of my fear had exhausted me. Yes, that time I had found her. This time, I knew it was different than a four-year-old taking off to see what she could see.

"Juliette said they were going to shoot a video today." My spinning brain recalled that much.

Ralphie stood up, his face white. "I was going to go with them because . . . because I think Mila is cute and I wanted to get to know her. But then something came up and Jules said Mila wasn't going, so I didn't go."

"Did she say where they were going?"

"I guess. I wasn't really paying much attention." He looked away for a second, a guilty look crossing his face. "Mom, I'm sorry. I should have."

Max was on the phone. He'd turned his back and had taken a few steps away and lowered his voice. I was practically bent in half trying to eavesdrop.

"Mom," Ralphie said, but I shushed him. "Mom."

Finally he waved a hand in front of my face. "Mom! I just remembered. I think she said something about the woods."

I grabbed his arm. "What woods?"

"The woods across the lake."

"Where the assassinations took place?"

"Maybe. I don't remember."

I waved to Max, and he finished his call quickly. I had Ralphie repeat what he'd told me.

"Where are the guards who'd have gone with them?" Ceil asked.

"We're going to find that out." Max's jaw was solidly set. "I'll have a detail dispatched to the woods immediately. I'll meet them there. If the girls are there, we'll find them."

"I'm going with you." Ralphie went to the door.

"You are not," I told him.

He shook his head. "If I'd listened to her, I'd know what her plans were. I'd know where they are."

"Honey, you're not responsible for . . ." I couldn't even say what.

"She's my little sister. I have to go." He looked at Max and said, "After you, Captain."

Max waited for me to approve or not. As much as I hated the thought of both my kids out there in the night, I saw how distraught my son was at the thought of something possibly having happened to his sister. I nodded to Max, and we held each other's gaze before he turned and left the room, Ralphie at his heels.

Despite my fear, I felt as if I were watching my son grow up in front of my eyes.

Ceil got up and guided me to my chair. "Come sit." She handed me a glass of water.

"I can't sit," I protested.

"Just for a minute." She practically pushed me into the chair.

"Why would she choose the place where our ancestors were murdered?" I asked, the very idea macabre as far as I was concerned.

"Maybe as part of her tour of Saint Gilbert, her retelling of the history of the country," Roe suggested. "She did say she was going to talk about the war and what had happened here, remember?"

I nodded. She'd touched on that in her first video.

"How would they have gotten across the lake?" I asked.

"The guards would have had to row them," Marianne pointed out. "The girls wouldn't have done that on their own. Rowing is tough when you don't know what you're doing."

"I'm sure there's a very simple, innocent reason why she's not here." Ceil maintained her position as the voice of reason.

"Yeah, look at you being negative. That's what you always accuse me of doing," Roe pointed out.

"I don't know how to explain it." I felt fat tears begin to roll down my face. "I have this feeling . . . like I know even though I don't know."

"Well, that explains it." I know Roe was trying to be funny, but I was not in the mood.

"Stop. Annie's really worried." Ceil sat in the chair next to me and took my hands and just waited for me to speak.

"I know it sounds crazy, but I can feel it in every part of me that something is terribly wrong. I can't explain how I know. I just *know*."

"Mom used to get like that sometimes," Ceil said quietly. "Like the time Dad . . ."

She paused, so I finished the sentence for her.

"The time Dad didn't come home because he'd had a heart attack."

"Oh, Annie, I didn't mean . . . this isn't like that. I just meant that Mom got feelings about things."

I leaned back in my chair. There had been times over the years when I'd "just known" things—sometimes things that were good, sometimes not so good. Granted, I hadn't seen this whole duchess thing coming, but I had known before Mom did that she had cancer. And I'd known that Ralph Senior had been cheating on me, but then again, he hadn't been real subtle, so maybe that shouldn't count. There were other times, not a whole lot but enough to make me wonder. Then again, there was never a pattern to it, so I couldn't claim to be psychic.

"Wherever Juliette is, right now, she's scared," I told them.

"Naw. She and Remy are probably filming the whole thing to add to their video," Roe chimed in. "She's fourteen, Annie. She's going to make the most of any opportunity for a little drama."

"Under other circumstances, that would be a reasonable suggestion," I told her.

"What other circumstances?" Marianne moved to the chair on my other side.

"If my gut wasn't telling me otherwise." Now the tears were really flowing, and both Ceil and Marianne put an arm over my back.

"Let's just not get too far ahead of ourselves," Ceil said. "Let's wait until we hear from Max, okay? Maybe the girls were there, and he'll be bringing them back before you know it."

"He would have called." I tried to focus on my daughter, tried to get a feel for where she might be. If I were truly psychic, I'd pick up something, right? Except nothing came to me but feelings of dread and fear. I had to admit to myself that the fear I was experiencing could be mine and not Juliette's.

Claudette called to see if we'd heard anything and offered to come to the castle to wait with us, but I told her to stay where she was in case Remy came home. The dinner the kitchen staff had prepared for us sat untouched on the table, and we dismissed the servers. We all just sat where we were, mostly not talking, just sitting inside our own heads.

~

By the time another hour had passed, I wasn't the only one who was worried. Ceil had gotten up and started to pace around the room, making a show of looking at something on the sideboard, or studying a painting, but it was all to cover up her growing anxiety. Roe and Marianne opened a bottle of wine and kept topping off their glasses. Finally, my phone rang, loud and harsh in the quiet room, and we all jumped. I answered before it could ring a second time and held my breath.

"Max, did you find them?"

"We found Remy alone on the opposite side of the lake. She said Juliette was tired of being followed by guards every time she poked her head out of the castle, so they decided to sneak out this morning through one of the back doors. They ran around the lake and rented a boat. But since neither of them knew what to do with the oars, they didn't get very far."

I could picture them, each with an oar they couldn't control, at first laughing as the boat went around in circles. After a while, their arms and backs aching, it wouldn't have been quite as funny.

"There was a man near the boats, watching them," Max said, "and after a few minutes, he was telling them how to row, but they just couldn't get the rhythm. When he offered to row them across, they were delighted. They said he was very nice and promised to come back for them later."

I covered my face with my hands.

"He did come back, but in a smaller boat. He said he could only take one girl at a time, so of course, he took the princess first."

"And never came back for Remy." I said what he did not.

"She had no cell phone reception there, so all she could do was wait for someone to realize she hadn't come home."

"Poor Remy. I can't even begin to imagine what must have been going through her mind."

"She knew I'd find her eventually, but she was very worried about the princess. She said she knew after waiting ten or fifteen minutes that something bad had happened." I heard the dread in his voice as clearly as I heard it in my own. "We have men searching the woods and the city. She gave us a very good description of the man. It matches the description of the rumormonger from the pubs. I have men searching the city for anyone who might have seen him at the lake today."

"Max . . ." I couldn't seem to voice another word.

"Just stay there and I'll get back to you." His voice was soft, but the underlying ice was unmistakable. "We will find her, Annaliese. Trust me."

"Okay." No, I didn't think everything was okay, but what else could I say? The call ended, and I put the phone on the table.

I looked around at the others in the room and told them, "They're still looking."

"I'm sure Max will have the guards and the city police force scour every inch of the entire city," Marianne said.

Ceil poured two glasses of wine and handed one to me.

"No, thanks," I said. "If I start drinking, I'll pass out."

"That could be a blessing. At least you won't be giving yourself agita while we wait." She took a long sip of hers and nudged my glass closer. "You know, I've always said the answer is rarely in wine, but tonight, I make an exception."

"You have a point." I picked up the glass and took a drink. The wine was delicious, so I took another.

"We're going to have to open another bottle." Roe got up and went to the kitchen to see what she could find. Moments later she came back to the dining room, a bottle in each hand. "If we're going to drink, we might as well drink the good stuff."

She opened one of the bottles. "Who's ready?"

Marianne held up her glass and Roe filled it, then filled her own. I waved her away. "You know, you don't have to sit here with me. You can go to bed, or go watch TV, or whatever."

"I'm not going anywhere," Ceil announced.

"Me either." Marianne raised her glass in a toast. "Tonight we are one."

I didn't bother to ask how much wine she'd consumed, having watched her and Roe for the past hour, but it was all right. We were each trying to get through the wait in our own way. Ceil paced. Roe and Marianne drank. I cried and prayed that my daughter was found unharmed and soon before I lost it completely.

I put my head back against the chair and closed my eyes. I had a headache, and my eyes hurt from crying. In my mind's eye, I was seeing Jules as a tiny girl, standing on the edge of the pool at the Y where I'd taken her for swimming lessons. You know how there are people who like to dive right in and others who have to ease their way? Jules was an *easer*. She'd sit at the edge of the pool and put in first one foot, then the other. She grew to love water and love swimming, but she never did learn to dive in without testing the water first.

For a second, I could swear I smelled water.

I sat bolt upright and grabbed my phone, speed-dialing Max.

"I think she must still be near the lake somewhere," I told him when he answered. "Did you check all around the entire lake?"

"Yes. We found nothing." He hesitated. "Why do you think . . . ?"

"I smelled water," I said.

"You smelled water?" I could hear confusion in his voice. "Water doesn't really have much of a smell, Annaliese."

"She's near water," I insisted. "Check the area around the lake again. Please, Max."

"Of course. I'll have some guards go back immediately."

"It's him, isn't it. The Royal Watchdog, whoever that is." I knew it without him telling me.

"It would appear so. We're tracing every possible lead. We have people in the pubs right now, and we have others knocking on the doors of the callers who'd alerted the castle about the man they'd seen. So far, no one has a name or any information that would help us find him. The only thing we know right now is that he hasn't been seen in any of his usual haunts. But we've got men and women in all those places in case he shows up."

"Keep in touch," I said before I clicked off.

I walked down to the gallery, barely seeing the portraits I passed. Through the tall arched windows, I could see faint spots of light in the woods beyond the lake. Members of the castle guard, no doubt, still searching. I stood there a long time and watched as the lights moved around the lake, shining into the coves and along the beaches at the edge of the water. None stopped. The lights continued to move, growing fainter as they moved farther away from where they'd started. I hadn't realized how big that lake was.

I thought about my mom and how much I missed her. How I wished she were here. She'd know what to do.

"Mom," I whispered, "we could use a little help. Maybe ask Gran where we should look. Maybe she has some insight we don't have since she was born here. I'm sorry you never got to come here, Mom. You'd have loved it."

I went back to the dining room where Ceil was pacing again and Roe and Marianne were just about lights-out and the second bottle of wine was empty.

"Nothing yet?" Ceil's eyes were red. She'd been crying, too.

I shook my head. "They're going to look all around the perimeter of the lake again. You know, there are lots of coves there, and a few beaches. Maybe . . ." I shrugged. I didn't know *maybe* what.

But still—there'd been that scent of water . . .

I don't know why I didn't think of it before.

I called Max back. "Gabrielle's castle. There's a pond there, behind the trees, remember? There's an overgrown woods, then the pond."

"Annaliese, we're already there. Not at the pond, but at the castle. There's no one here."

"Check the pond," I insisted.

"On my way."

That's one thing I loved about that man. He got me. He didn't argue with me, he just . . .

Uh-oh. I said *love*. I can't even think about what that might mean right now.

I went upstairs and changed into a pair of jeans and a sweater, then searched the closet for my old Keds. So unroyal, I know, but right now I was a mama, not a duchess, and I was off in search of my babe. I grabbed my bag, left the room, and looked at the two guards standing outside the door.

"Which one of you knows where the car keys are kept?"

It turned out that Yves had his own car, and over his protests and after telling Ceil and the others to stay there in case Jules came back to the castle, I had him drive the three of us—Sergei being the other guard—to Gabrielle's castle. Yves knew exactly where I wanted to go, and twenty minutes later, I was jumping out of the car and running up the steps of the castle.

Max saw me coming and stood in the front door like the goalie on a World Cup team.

"Annaliese, what are you doing here?"

"I couldn't just sit around and wait any longer," I told him. I was out of shape and slightly winded from running from the car. I wanted to put my arms around him and have him hold on to me, but I knew that wasn't going to happen.

He did take my hands, though, and simply held them for a moment or two.

"We just finished searching the pond," he said. "There's no trace of her."

I pointed to the outbuildings off to one side of the castle. "And you looked in all those?"

"Yes, of course. The stables, the barns . . . everywhere. If she's here, she's very well hidden."

I felt totally deflated. I sat on the top step and pulled Max down with me and draped his arm around my shoulders, and I didn't care who saw us. I put my head on his shoulder and cried.

After I was cried out, I said, "What do we do now?"

"Now, we are going to assume the person who kidnapped her wants something, and we're going to have to wait to see who that someone is, and what it is that they want."

"And then?"

"Then we will know what we are dealing with, and how to get your daughter back."

Chapter Thirty-Eight

I got back to the castle around two in the morning and went straight up to my room. I took my phone into the bathroom while I showered—my skin felt old and tired. There was plenty of battery left on the phone, but I put it on the charger anyway, just in case. I curled up atop the blankets on my bed and prayed that Juliette, wherever she was, knew I'd walk over hot coals for her, that I would move heaven and earth for her, if only I knew where to look. I went to the little chapel in the castle and knelt down and prayed she was okay and that she knew Max and I were searching for her. Well, Max was. Mostly I was crying and wishing I was in fact psychic, but I was lost. Dazed and confused, as the song went. The more hours that passed, the more helpless I felt. Not hopeless, though. I knew in my heart Max would turn this country upside down to find her.

At the same time, I was scared out of my mind that something terrible would happen to her before she was found.

Juliette's birthday was in a few weeks. I remembered when she was born, thinking that inside my child—inside every child—was a mystery. Who they were and who they'd become. What kind of person would they be, what would hurt them and what would bring them joy, who they would love. Like every mother, I wanted my daughter to have a wonderful, happy life, and I couldn't stand the thought of anything changing what her life should be. Then I thought of the forces that had prevented my grandmother from having the life she should have had, and I felt sick all over again.

I went back to my room and lay across the bed, tissue box close at hand. I must have fallen asleep at some point because the next thing I was aware of was Ceil shaking me. Claudette came into the room, and Ralphie was right behind her. Ceil pulled me from the bed and handed me a phone.

"He's been calling the castle for the past ten minutes, but he'll only speak with you."

"Who . . . ?"

"The Royal Watchdog, that's who."

I grabbed the phone with both hands. "Hello?"

"Who is this?" the voice demanded.

"Annaliese Gilberti. Who is this?"

"You will call me back at this number on the See-Me-Now app on your phone. I assume you have that function?"

"Of course. Give me a second to . . ."

"Thirty seconds, Ms. Gilberti." He hung up.

"Call Max," I told Ceil as I jumped off the bed. With shaking hands, I opened the app on my phone and called the number. The jerk let it ring almost ten times before he answered, no doubt trying to make me more anxious than I already felt.

But I had my first look at him, this man who was terrorizing my family. He was seated, so it was hard to tell how tall he was, but his shoulders were slender and his hairline receding. His eyes were small and his face round and his complexion ruddy—exactly as the callers had reported.

"Ah, there you are, Annaliese. I may call you Annaliese?"

I nodded. "And what do I call you?"

"You may call me cousin."

"I was told I had no cousins." I thought of Beth the embezzler, but I was pretty sure this had nothing to do with her.

"You were misled."

"You know my name. What's yours?"

"Alberto Mathias Gilberti," he said proudly. "But you may call me 'Your Highness' since I am the rightful heir to the throne you have stolen from me."

"And you have stolen something from me, haven't you?"

"Indeed I have." He stepped out of the frame and swept the camera to his left. Juliette sat motionless on a small sofa. Oddly enough, she didn't look as frightened as I thought she would.

"Jules—"

He reappeared. "No, no, there will be none of that. We have yet to come to a deal."

I wanted to scream, *Yes! Anything!* But I tried to remain outwardly calm. Something told me the more fear I showed him, the longer he would drag this out.

"What is it you want?" I asked, as if we were talking about something inconsequential instead of my heart.

"A trade." He smiled with obvious satisfaction, drawing out the moment, not offering details. He would make me ask, so I did.

"What are we trading, cousin?" Of course I knew what we were to trade. And of course he knew I'd agree to it.

Ah, he liked that. He smiled, but his eyes narrowed, and I knew without question this man was not rational.

Swell.

"Thank you for acknowledging the relationship. I appreciate that. But I have to say, after hearing the Duke's Council tout your intelligence, I'm surprised that you have not figured out the nature of our relationship."

"You said we were cousins, and I know you've been staying in Gabrielle's castle, so I'm assuming you're descended from her."

"Gabrielle was a cousin to *both* our great-grandparents. She did play a small role, however, in the story. Think, Annaliese. Who else was there?"

I had to think. My great-grandmother had three daughters: Jacqueline, who died with her, Gran, and her sister Amelia.

"I was told Amelia had no children," I said thoughtfully.

"Not Amelia!" he snapped.

"I'm sorry, I don't know who else . . ." I paused. "Gran had a brother, Theodore . . ."

"Bingo." He rolled his eyes. "It took you long enough."

"I was told Theodore never married, that he died with his parents and his sister." I really was confused.

"But not before fathering a child with the mistress he kept at his castle, one your sisters can't wait to get their hands on."

"Why . . ." I had so many questions I didn't even know where to begin.

"Why didn't the duke's 'thorough and meticulous' search find me? Because they were looking only on one side of the sheets, shall we say. That one of their grand dukes may have produced a child out of wedlock never occurred to them."

"Why did you wait so long? Where have you been? Why didn't you speak up if you thought you were . . ."

"So many questions."

He sighed a fake sigh. Like he was humoring me. It pissed me off, to tell you the truth. Add that to the anger I already felt. There would be a reckoning.

But there was nothing I could do but act like I was interested and that I cared about his story. Trust me, I did not, other than some small degree of curiosity. All I really cared about was getting Juliette home safely.

"I've been right here, in Saint Gilbert all my life. While you were in America, I was here, going to our schools and working in our vineyards. And then there was a vote to restore the monarchy, and the next thing we knew, here was this woman from a foreign country stepping into the spotlight."

"I did not ask for that."

"It doesn't matter. The Duke's Council anointed you. I didn't know then what I know now."

"Which is?"

"My grandfather, who died a month ago, talked of all sorts of things in his last days. After watching your coronation on TV, he told me that the new duchess was my cousin. He said his father had told him that his father—my great-grandfather—was Grand Duke Theodore, who died before he could marry my great-grandmother in the church. He said there may have been some written proof of this, but he didn't know where, that if I had any interest now that the monarchy was brought back to Saint Gilbert, I should find whatever proof there might be."

I nodded. "And did you?"

"It took me a while, but what I found was that when Gabrielle's things were brought back from Switzerland, all the books were placed in the library in her castle—including her diary. I found that diary. It took me weeks, but I found what I needed."

"You were staying in Gabrielle's castle?"

"While I looked through her things hoping to find her diary. But once I read it, I knew. I knew my grandfather was right. Gabrielle wrote about how the woman Theodore had intended to marry had a child before they could be wed, and that tragically, he was murdered before the wedding could take place. That she—Gabrielle—had taken the woman and the child to Switzerland with her." He sat up a little straighter. "I am the descendant of that child—and rightful heir."

"I was told the oldest daughter was always the rightful heir."

"You were told wrong." Unexpectedly, he stood and shouted. "My great-grandfather was the *first*born child of the grand duchess. His son should have been crowned, not your grandmother."

"Of course," I said soothingly, even knowing how wrong he was. "Why didn't you simply go to the council and show them Gabrielle's diary? Why bother to spread rumors? Why didn't you just speak up?"

"I had to lay the groundwork, don't you see? So the people would start to question who you were so they'd be receptive to me. You'd already been crowned. The Duke's Council had announced that you were the duchess, and everyone believed them and accepted you. The council members never would have admitted they'd made a mistake." He shook his head stubbornly. "Annaliese, you have to stand up in front of everyone and say that I am the rightful one. Don't you see? You have to be the one to proclaim it. The council will have to agree. And then they will have to resign as well for their incompetency. How could I rule with those fools on the council? Who could I trust to advise me? No, no. They have to go as well."

So much crazy talk, and he was becoming agitated. I didn't like what that might mean for my daughter.

"What is it you want from me, Cousin Alberto?"

"I want you to go to the Duke's Council and relinquish all claim to the crown," he said fiercely. "Then I want you to publicly announce that I am the true heir and that you are abdicating in my favor. The Duke's Council will have to admit their error, and you and your son and your sisters will leave the country."

"And my daughter?"

"She will be released once you have left Saint Gilbert. When you are back in America."

I shook my head adamantly. No way was I leaving the country without Juliette. "She goes with me."

"This isn't negotiable. You must do it my way or you will not see her again." He smiled again. God, I hated that smile.

Now I really was panicking. I tried to think of some other way to appease him that would not require me leaving my girl behind where any number of things could happen to her. But I had to think fast.

Then I remembered who I was, and I asked myself the question of the day: Who was the best settlement negotiator in the entire history of the Philadelphia Fire, Casualty, and Liability Insurance Company?

I was. Damn right I was.

"I will submit my resignation to the Duke's Council, and I will publicly announce that an error had been made and that you are the true heir. But I will not leave without my daughter. You can meet me at the airport in Switzerland, and she will get on the plane with me. You can watch it take off. When we are gone, you may do whatever you want. I do not care."

He frowned. "That was not my plan."

"Plans can change. Besides, Alberto, think of the good publicity for you. The entire country will know that you were so kind to come to see us off. They will applaud the way you handled what could have been an awkward and uncomfortable situation. Everyone will see that you are gracious and worthy to be the grand duke."

He nodded his head as if considering some weighty problem. Finally, he said, "That could work. Yes. They will all see me for the kind and caring man I am, seeing my dear cousins off to return to their lives in Pennsylvania." Then he chuckled, and I decided if I ever got close enough to do him bodily harm in some way, I would do it.

"I will call the Duke's Council for an emergency meeting immediately." I couldn't make this happen soon enough.

"You will have to do this publicly. Not behind closed doors."

"The Duke's Council is always closed to outsiders, so if you expect them to welcome you and accept you, you will have to respect their rules. We will video my address to the council and their admission of error. The video of me abdicating in your favor will be shown immediately on every television station in the country. Then I and my family will leave the castle and we will drive straight to the airport. You will meet us there with Juliette. The video of the council accepting my resignation and apologizing to you and naming you the new grand duke will be telecast once we are on the plane. You get what you want, I get what I want. However, if you arrive at the airport without my daughter, all bets are off."

Cousin Alberto—ugh—stared into the camera. I could see he was calculating how much to give in, and whether he could trust me. I had to push him a bit.

"Please, Your Grace." Gag. "I don't care about being the duchess. I just want my daughter."

He was still thinking.

"I would not want to wear a crown I'm not entitled to," I added softly and with as much sincerity as I could muster. "And no throne means as much to me as my children."

I could lay it on really thick when I needed to.

He nodded slowly.

"Go ahead and call the council. When I see the video of you stepping down and then getting into the car that will take you out of the country, I will leave the city with your daughter. If I arrive at the airport and I sense something is amiss, I will turn around and come back to Saint Gilbert, and you will never see your daughter again. No castle guards. No police. Understood?"

"Of course."

"I will watch for your video to be televised, Annaliese. Do not disappoint me."

"You can trust me, cousin." I gave him my most sincere smile, then piled it as high as I possibly could. "I would not want to keep what is rightfully yours."

I disconnected the call and realized that Max had come into the room. "Get dressed as if you're going on a long trip," I told my sisters and my son. "Bring some suitcases with you."

"There's not enough time to pack everything," Roe protested.

"I didn't say *pack* the suitcases, I just said *bring* them." I tossed my phone on the bed. "Now get moving, and get out. I need to talk to Max."

"Annie, I can't believe you're going along with this guy. How do you know he's who he says he is?" Roe asked. "I mean, you didn't even ask him for proof. Why didn't you even ask him to show you something, a birth certificate or . . ."

"Because I don't care who he is, Rosalie. It doesn't *matter* who he is. He could be the reincarnation of Freddie Mercury and I wouldn't care. All that matters is that he believes he's the true grand duke and he's been robbed of his throne, and I'm the only person who can give it to him. And the only thing I really care about is getting Juliette back safely. So if I have to play his game to make that happen, that's what I'll do."

Ceil crossed her arms over her chest and grinned.

"You're going to double-cross the little bastard, aren't you?"

That Ceil. She knew me so well.

Chapter Thirty-Nine

"Her Highness has called this special meeting of the council to discuss a matter of the greatest import and urgency," the chancellor led off once all the members of the council had taken their seats.

While I was preparing my speech, Max had filled Vincens in on what had transpired and what we were planning to do. He was incensed at Alberto's audacity—aghast that he'd been so bold as to kidnap the royal princess!—but understood what was at stake and agreed to taking his part and sticking to the agenda.

Had Vincens alerted the others in so short a time? I guess we would find out.

I cleared my throat, then nodded to Yves, who'd been enlisted to video my announcement. I'd worn a plain black dress and no jewelry. I rose from my seat and stood unadorned except for the crown, which I'd had taken from its safe and which now sat upon my head. My statement was brief and to the point, and in accordance with what I had promised Alberto.

"It has come to my attention that one more deserving than I to sit upon the throne of Saint Gilbert has stepped forward. In order that the rightful heir may be crowned, I am immediately relinquishing any and all claims I might have and hereby abdicate the throne in favor of my cousin, Alberto Mathias Gilberti, a true descendant of Grand Duke Theodore Philippe Emile. I wish to thank the members of the council for their faith in me, and for allowing me the opportunity to serve the people of Saint Gilbert."

And with that, I removed the crown from my head and placed it on the table, then left the room amid the many gasps and assorted exclamations: "What did she say?" (no doubt that was Pierre Belloque, who I'd noticed was a bit hard of hearing) and "No, no!" and "What nonsense is this?" and "Grand duke? What grand duke? What is she talking about?"

Yves knew exactly what to do with the video, and I trusted him to carry out his instructions. I couldn't afford a single snag when my daughter's safety—and possibly her life—was at stake. Clearly Alberto was deranged, but no one knew just how dangerous he might be. Kidnapping is one thing. What his next step might be—well, I had no desire to test him. I would uphold my part of the bargain—to a point, of course—and hoped he would deliver Jules to the airport.

I went to the front door and ran to the waiting car, which already held my sisters, my son, and Marianne, with Sergei at the wheel. Max and some others were already on their way and knew what to do when they arrived at the small private airport just over the border with Switzerland. I swear every minute of that ride felt like an hour, and I was more convinced than ever we really needed those roads repaired. But soon enough, we were there, and as arranged, Sergei drove onto the tarmac and parked next to the waiting plane. Everyone boarded except me. I remained in the car and tried to will myself not to sweat. I kept watching the time. Alberto should have been there by now. What was keeping him?

Just as I started to panic, I noticed an older-model Peugeot slowly crossing the tarmac. Thanks to Max, all flights had been halted, and his men had been moved into positions as pilots and mechanics working on the other planes, where they could spot Alberto's car when he arrived. One of the castle guards—er, airport employees—would offer to escort Alberto to the runway, an offer my "cousin" would undoubtedly accept. We would know immediately if Juliette was in the car.

Alberto drove up next to the plane and stopped the car. He got out first and walked toward me. The guard remained with the car, standing next to the rear passenger door like a sentinel, which made me think Jules was in the back seat.

"Where's my daughter?" I called to him.

"Patience. She's here. I just needed to see you face-to-face."

"You see me. Now release my daughter."

"And here I was trying to be friendly."

"I don't want your friendship. I want my daughter and I want to get out of here."

"Fair enough, then." He walked back to his car, and the guard opened the back door. Juliette hopped out and ran to me. She nearly knocked me over, but I was okay with that. She was safe and back where she belonged.

I looked into my daughter's beautiful face and said, "I'm sorry. Sweetie, I'm so sorry."

Jules, who having been rescued was now as cool and calm as could be, pulled back and looked up at me. "I bet you were more worried than I was."

"I don't know if more than you, but I was worried sick."

"I knew you'd think of something. You always do."

Ah, if only she would always have such faith in me. But I knew the "best" of her teen years were still ahead of us, so I didn't waste time patting myself on the back.

"Did he hurt you at all?"

Jules shot Alberto a dirty look. "He just fed me crap food, and I was cold all night last night. But I'm okay."

Alberto looked amused at this, but I could see he was eager to get to the castle, where he probably imagined he'd be welcomed with open arms.

"I'll see you leave before I go," he told me. "Get onto the plane. Now."

Before I could take two steps, Max crept behind Alberto and grabbed him by the back of his neck. He forced him to his knees—with one hand, mind you—and the would-be ruler of Saint Gilbert was yelling and cursing as his hands were secured behind him. In the blink of an eye, the castle guards who'd been "working" on the other planes had hauled him to his feet.

"You promised!" Alberto sputtered as he watched my family rush from the plane to welcome Juliette back into the fold.

I shrugged. "I did what I said I would do. Well, all but, you know, actually leaving."

"You won't get away with this. Everyone now knows I'm the rightful one. The Duke's Council released a statement accepting your abdication. The whole country knows by now that by your own admission, you are not the rightful heir." He was fighting the restraints, trying to get away from the two guards Max had handed him over to. "You lied to me! Everyone will know you're a liar!"

"Did you really think I'd go quietly? And seriously, did you think for one minute I'd feel any remorse at having lied to a man who would *kidnap my daughter*?" I lowered my voice. "You do not come between a bear and her cub, Alberto. It never ends well."

He was led away, still yelling and cursing, but I can't say I didn't enjoy the moment.

I turned to Max. "Where are they taking him?"

"Where would you like him to go, madam?"

I smiled. "I would like him taken to the castle dungeon. Chain him to the wall."

"I believe the orders were to take him to the police station in Beauchesne, but perhaps I can catch up with them."

"I'd like that. Thank you."

He leaned closer. "You played it brilliantly. Some of the members of the council are still in shock."

"Vincens hasn't told them yet?"

"He's waiting for me to confirm that all is well. Then he will issue a statement and explain everything. I suppose you should think about addressing the country yourself."

I nodded. He was right. I should do that. And first thing in the morning, I would. Right now I wanted to be with my daughter and just be grateful that I can be.

"We will talk tomorrow."

"We will. Thank you, Max." It was all I could do not to kiss him, right there in front of everyone.

I waved to my family, who'd gathered at the bottom of the plane's steps.

"Let's go home," I called to them.

"And hallelujah!" Ceil raised her arm in triumph. "Home is still the castle."

~

When we returned to the castle, I expected it to be dark because it was very late. I figured everyone had gone to bed. But as soon as we neared the city, we could see the castle ablaze with light. As we drove up the long lane leading to the front entrance, the doors opened and what looked like the entire staff spilled out onto the courtyard. When we got out of the car, they applauded.

I would like to say I pulled up those royal panties of mine and acted like a grown woman, but I cried. I couldn't hold it back. These wonderful people who served us and assisted us every day had waited for us through this ordeal—the story apparently had spread through the castle—and they cheered us on our return. There were no words to tell how that outpouring of loyalty and love made me feel: that despite what we'd just gone through, being the grand duchess of the Duchy of Saint Gilbert was probably the best job in the world.

I still had a thousand questions for my daughter, but I thought I should wait till the morning. You know, give her some space from the ordeal. But as Roe had reminded me earlier, Juliette was fourteen and therefore thrived on drama.

"Mom, I know you always tell us not to talk to strangers, but this guy was standing there on the shore while we were trying to figure out how to row that boat. If we got it to move at all, it just went around in circles! We were laughing, and he was laughing with us. He seemed so nice. When he saw we weren't going to make it across the lake, he offered to row the boat for us. He even said he'd come back in an hour or two to bring us back. We never thought he was someone bad or that he'd do something to us. I mean, I'm the *princess* and Remy is the daughter of a *duke*—the captain of the castle guard!—and everyone in the country knows us."

"How did he get you to go with him?" We were seated on my bed drinking milkshakes the kitchen had sent up because they knew she loved them. Okay, I loved them, too, so they sent one for me as well.

"He was so smart." She sat cross-legged atop the puffy comforter. "He came back for us in a smaller boat. Like a two-person rowboat? He said it was the only one left to rent so he'd have to take us one at a time but he should take me first, because I was the princess. So okay, I get in the boat, and he's rowing, and we're talking and he seemed really nice. He said he'd grown up in Saint Gilbert and how did I like living here and that sort of thing. When we got to the other side of the lake, I said I should maybe call someone to come and get me because it was getting late and if I wasn't at dinner by six, my mom was going to read me the riot act. That's what Gramma always said when she was really mad. Anyway, he said he'd drive me, to get into his car. Well, I did, and then I remembered that Remy was still over in the woods. He got into the car and I said, 'But my friend is still over there.' And he said he'd call someone to come for her. But he drove really fast past the castle and started to drive out of the city and my car door wouldn't open, and

I knew something bad was happening and I started to yell at him. He told me if I made a fuss, he wouldn't tell anyone where Remy was and she'd be stuck over there all night in the dark. So I stopped yelling." She paused. "He didn't send anyone to get her, did he?"

"No, honey. He didn't. Captain Belleme found her and took her home. She's fine."

"That's good." Juliette finished the last of her milkshake, and I took the glass from her hand. She yawned and lay down next to me. The adrenaline from all the excitement was beginning to wear off, and she was starting to fade.

I grabbed a warm throw from the bottom of the bed and covered her. I thought she was falling asleep, but she kept talking. Definitely her mother's daughter.

"I kept thinking about her all night and hoping she wasn't alone in the woods in the dark."

"She wasn't alone for long," I assured her.

"Good."

"I'm sorry you were alone."

"I wasn't alone. Gramma was with me. After she came, I wasn't even scared anymore. I knew she'd never let anything happen to me."

"Jules, who are you talking about?"

She yawned. "Gramma."

"You don't mean my mother?"

"Yeah. I couldn't see her—you know, because of the blindfold?— but I could smell her perfume. You know, the one she used to wear all the time?"

I did know. Dior's Poison.

"Did she speak to you?"

Jules shook her head. "No. But she didn't have to. I knew she was there, and I knew I was going to be all right. I knew you'd figure out how to make him let me come home."

I was stunned. My mother—I couldn't even put my thoughts together.

Juliette smiled a sleepy smile. "I know it sounds weird, Mom, but I know she was there."

Then she closed her eyes again and nodded off, leaving me with a lot to think about.

Like had my mother really shown up in Saint Gilbert to keep her granddaughter company and keep her from harm, or had that been Juliette's imagination, maybe wishful thinking? Mom and Jules had been very close, so I guess stranger things have happened. And after all, I had called on my mother last night to watch over Jules, so who knows?

Chapter Forty

The next morning I awoke still on top of the comforter, my daughter still wrapped in the blanket I'd put over her the night before. I was overwhelmed with a feeling of gratitude so strong that I could barely contain it. The sun was shining through the open windows, and I could hear a hawk calling from out near the woods. I got up slowly so as not to disturb Jules and peered out the window. Fergus was working a new falcon, and I wondered who this one was intended for. I watched for a few minutes as the falconer taught the bird how to come when it was called. Then from the corner of my eye, I saw my son walking from the back of the castle to the field, where he stopped and spoke to Fergus. Ralphie took a large black glove from the pocket of his jacket and slipped it on his left arm. I guess he'd decided to go full-on Gilberti and do something besides play soccer. The thought of it cheered me.

Breakfast was a quiet affair, at least for a few minutes. Jules got up to join me, then Ceil tapped tentatively on my door. Roe and Marianne followed not too long after. Soon we were all sitting there drinking coffee and eating scones and fruit. Did our menu ever vary? Other than the occasional egg, no, though it could have. We've never been big breakfast people in our family, so the fare provided by the castle was just right. We could have had eggs and sausage and toast and that sort of thing every morning, but it just wasn't our style. Maybe not the healthiest breakfast in some people's minds, but it made us feel like we started every day with a party.

"So how's my favorite niece feeling this morning?" Ceil asked Jules.

"I'm your only niece, and I'm good." Jules nodded as if she hadn't spent the previous day and night in the company of a deranged kidnapper. "I'm fine." She spread a scone with strawberry jam and took a big bite, sending some jam down the front of the shirt she'd slept in the night before. I handed her a napkin but didn't bother to say a word. For a while I feared we'd lost her, so today she was getting a pass on just about everything.

"Jules, you know you're going to have to talk to the police and Captain Belleme about what happened, right?"

"Good. I want to talk to them. I want to tell them what a whack job that guy—Alberto—is."

"Perhaps a different term might be more appropriate," I suggested.

"Mom, he is definitely deluded."

"Then maybe use that word instead of *whack job*."

Juliette shrugged. "They mean pretty much the same thing, but okay. I mean, he kept talking about what a fraud you were, which ticked me off a lot. Maybe that's why Gramma came to be with me. She probably didn't like hearing him talk about you like that."

Ceil and Roe exchanged long looks.

"Tell me about Gramma coming to see you," Ceil said.

Juliette did. Roe and Ceil accepted it without question, so I silently apologized to my mother for my skepticism and thanked her for taking care of Jules.

"Where did he take you?" Ceil asked.

"I don't know where I was, but it was someplace near water. I could hear things splashing during the night, like, you know, the way frogs plop into a pond? Like that."

"Do you remember anything else?" I asked.

"Yeah, I slept on the floor because the place we were in had no furniture. It got cold overnight."

"Theodore's castle," Ceil said. "There's a little pond in a garden right off the terrace, and there's no furniture in the place. Which is why Alberto was sleeping at Gabrielle's."

"He talked about her. Gabrielle. He had her diary, and he let me read a few pages when I said I didn't believe he was related to us."

My ears perked up. "You saw Gabrielle's diary?"

"Yup. See, Gabrielle was this guy Theodore's cousin, and they were like the same age and best friends. When she heard the country was going to be invaded, she packed all her stuff and was going to take her family to Switzerland. Before they left, Theodore asked her to take his girlfriend, so Gabrielle did, and she had a baby boy while they were there. Alberto said he was descended from her baby. The girlfriend had a baby, not Gabrielle. But Theodore never got to see the baby or marry his girlfriend because the Germans came here and killed him and his parents and his sister." She turned to me. "That's the story we were going to tell out in the woods by the marker where those murders took place, not the part about the girlfriend and the baby, but that might make a good story to add on. It's sad, isn't it? I guess that's why Alberto is so messed up."

"Did the diary say what the girlfriend's name was?"

"Uh-huh." She raised her arms to pull her hair back into a ponytail. "It was Isabella. Isabella DellaVecchio."

~

Later in the day, news reporters from the local TV stations and newspapers had been summoned to the castle, and I reiterated everything that had happened since the day before. Afterward I answered questions for what seemed to be hours, but I didn't mind. The people in Saint

Gilbert had the right to know what had happened. Everything was fine until someone asked, "So, are you okay with this cousin of yours now?"

I just about snapped. "How okay would you be with someone who'd kidnapped your daughter?"

That was the end of the Q and A for the day.

Max walked me back to my office.

"Come in and have coffee with me?" I asked.

"I would like that, yes." As we passed through Claudette's office, I paused to ask Madeleine to have a tray sent in. One of the duties she was learning was how to anticipate my needs. She brought in coffee, then discreetly closed the door behind her.

"So how is the princess this morning?" he asked.

"She's fine. Now that she's safe and home, she and the girls are planning a video about the entire experience."

Max laughed. "So that's what Remy was talking about this morning on her phone. They don't understand how quickly that might have turned ugly."

"Wait, I thought you said there was no real danger."

"Did I say that? In any case, she's fine, Remy's fine. You're fine." He took one of my hands. "You are fine, aren't you?"

"I am now, but I was terrified, Max."

"Of course you were, and I'm so sorry. I feel responsible. I was part of the council that was so sure, so certain, there wasn't anyone else who could even challenge you. The situation with Alberto was exactly what we'd wanted to avoid. We'd spent months filling out every line's family tree. We never saw him coming."

"It's not your fault, not the council's fault. If anything, I owe you thanks for helping me set up the trap. For bringing out the full force of the castle guard to make sure he did not get away with his scheme." I was very much aware of the light pressure of his fingers as they moved back and forth across my hand. "And without you, Max, I never would have known the castle had hidden passages."

He smiled. "You might like to explore those passages sometime, Annaliese. You might be surprised where they could lead."

"Why, Captain Belleme. Is that an invitation to explore those hidden places with you?"

"It is if it suits Your Grace." Ahh, that half smile. Gets me every time. But first, there was something that needed to be cleared up. "You should know, I don't like to share. I asked you once if you had a woman in your life, and you said several. So tell me, how many women are in your life these days?"

"The same, my lady."

"Well, that's a mood killer."

Max laughed. "There's my daughter, my sisters, my mother. And of course, there's my duchess." He raised my hand to his lips and kissed the palm. "There hasn't been anyone else since the first time I saw you in that market in Philadelphia."

I might have sighed out loud.

"So those hidden places you mentioned—would tonight be too soon?"

I'd like to say that we spent several hours winding our way through the castle's innards, led by a flashlight, where we'd have been wiping away cobwebs and probably scaring the mice. But it didn't happen that way.

Around ten thirty I shooed everyone out of my room and took a quick shower. I'd just finished drying my hair and I'd slipped into my robe—the silk one that had belonged to my great-grandmother. Believe me, few things made you feel sexier than heirloom silk, just saying.

Anyway, I'd just gone back into my bedroom when I heard the swoosh of the panel sliding open in the drawing room. I had a choice right then—I could ask Max to wait there until I could get dressed, or I could step right into the drawing room in that sexy, silky robe.

Reader, I seduced him.

Okay, not exactly, but the opening was there, and I couldn't resist it.

Let me just say that Max took one look at me and smiled. I smiled back.

"So is this how the royals dress for exploring?" he asked.

"Yes." I held my hand out to him and tugged him closer. I wanted him to kiss me the way he'd kissed me the other night, but I didn't want it to feel like an order from the duchess.

I needn't have worried. Max didn't wait for instructions.

You should know I'm not one to kiss and tell, so let's just say that it had been a very, *very* long, lonely drought for this duchess, but by the time the sun came up, the dry spell was over.

And that's all I'm going to say about that.

Chapter Forty-One

Three Months Later

The spa actually opened ahead of time.

Ceil is probably the most savvy person on the planet. She showed up at the worksite every single day so the contractors and their subs all knew she was present. But she did more than just make them feel as if she were the watchdog. She asked questions so they all got to know her. After a while she wasn't just the princess to them—she was the boss. Some days she brought them coffee and pastries from the castle, so they'd have a little break and she'd eat with them. On days when it was warm or the job was particularly dusty, she brought water in a cooler.

Later, after the kitchen was finished, Ceil got Roe into the act. Rosalie would spend the morning in the kitchen, then right around noon, she'd invite the guys to sample what she'd made.

"Hey," she'd tell them, "I just tried out a new recipe. Who wants to be my guinea pig?"

Of course, they all did.

As a result, absenteeism on the job was practically nonexistent, which meant the job was finished early. Another result? Every one of the subs asked to work on Ceil's next project. The guys loved her.

Marianne worked with Ceil on the promo, and I must say, my bestie hit that out of the park. For the letters to our targeted demographic, they chose a gorgeous heavy vellum paper. A golden crown sat at the top of the page, and the letter itself was handwritten in royal blue with a fountain pen, though not by me. My penmanship was abominable. Marianne's, on the other hand, was gorgeous. She even calligraphed the addresses. The result was splendid—understated elegance, which was exactly how Ceil envisioned the entire project.

I gave Mare the list of ladies who'd been intrigued by the "secret" and who'd wanted to be among the first to know when we were ready to share, along with a list of media personalities who'd interviewed me before I moved to Saint Gilbert. To accompany the letter—or the invitation, as we liked to call it—Mare had designed a color brochure with photographs of the countryside as well as Gabrielle's castle. "Come to the castle and allow us to treat you like royalty" was the slogan she and Ceil were trying out, and it must have hit home, because we sold out the first two weeks, then another, and then another.

By the time the first session had ended, we were sold out through the New Year. We had to hire a new IT tech to create a website for the spa separate from the one we had for the country. That site kept crashing once word about the spa began to spread. We hired more and more people to make soap, and more and more people to work at the spa. Ceil finally brought in a few aestheticians from France to train some young Saint Gilbertian women who wanted to work at the spa but who lacked all the full-service skills we were offering.

Gotta love those Saint Gilbert goats. The first of which, by the way, Carlo had determined had accompanied the first Gilberti duchess who'd inherited from her father the wedge of land that became this country. Unfortunately, Carlo'd been unable to trace them back further than that, though he did learn from an old farmer that the goats had never been bred to a different breed. So maybe the magical qualities in the soap were the result of something to do with these goats that had been purely bred for hundreds of years. Or maybe not. We still don't know.

At this point, as long as the goat milk soap continued to perform miracles, I guess we stopped caring where the goats came from.

Our wines were so popular and so well received we had to start taking orders for next year because we sold out of what we'd allotted for the spa, and I wasn't about to tap into the castle's allotment. I wasn't crazy. Besides, as word about the country's beauty began to spread, we found ourselves entertaining at the castle more and more frequently. That might have had something to do with the fact that I'd asked the chancellor to draw up a list of his recommendations for ambassadors to other countries. I'd pretty much given him free rein in the appointments, though I did have Max look them over before they were announced. He knew everyone much better than I did. So we soon had ambassadors from other countries wanting to come to Saint Gilbert, which I was starting to enjoy.

Jacques Gilberti's son, Alaine, quit his job in the States and moved with his family to Beauchesne to oversee the building of the roads. We're now getting bids for the proposed golf course, which really was a brilliant move. When Ceil finishes her next project, there will be a newly renovated chateau to serve as our first grand hotel.

If I said I wasn't excited about all this, I'd be lying through my teeth. This was my vision when I first came here, and I am so happy—grateful happy—I am here to see it through.

Juliette's ordeal didn't seem to have had any lingering adverse effect on her. I mean, to the extent that she was telling people about her abduction as if it were a badge of honor. I heard her tell Mila it meant she was still South Philly tough. I'm not sure what that meant in Saint Gilbert terms, but there it is.

But then one day about three weeks after it was over, she came into the library during my afternoon time-out. She sat on a chair facing me, so I knew she wanted to talk.

"Mom, would you really have given all this up for me?" she'd asked. "I mean, when Alberto said for you to tell everyone you were a bogus duchess and he was the real deal or you wouldn't see me again, how long did you think about it?"

"I didn't have to think about it at all, Jules." I'd closed the book I was reading.

"You really would do that? Give up being the duchess?"

"Of course. You're my girl. I could always go back to my life in Philly and find another job if I had to, but I couldn't make another you. You're irreplaceable."

"So are you, Mom."

Ah, my heart just melted. Warm fuzzies are so rare when you have a teenager.

"Thanks, sweetie."

"Wouldn't you miss living in this castle and having people cooking your food and doing stuff for you? Wouldn't you miss Claudette and Madeleine and everyone? I know you'd miss Max," she'd teased.

"I'd miss everyone and everything about this country. But I'd still trade it for you if I had to."

"Wow. I guess you must love me a lot."

"Wow," I'd said. "I guess I really do."

"Thanks, Mom." She'd kissed me on the cheek, and with that, she'd bounded out of the room. I could hear her laughing with the guard outside the door for a few moments, then all was quiet again.

My "me hour" was almost up. I closed my eyes and rested my head against the back of the chair, and I thought about how I really would have felt if things had gone differently with Alberto. What if he had been determined to be the rightful heir, or I had gotten on the plane with my family and flown home, leaving the Duke's Council to deal with him? Would I have regretted leaving Saint Gilbert? Damn right I would have. Don't misunderstand—I would always choose my children over anything else. Hands down, no contest. But I would miss my sunny private room on the second floor, not so totally private now that Max was a steady overnight visitor, but they were still mine—though I did enjoy the benefits of sharing. I'd miss the work I'd set out for myself, the people in this castle who do so much for me, the city of Beauchesne, the church where I was coronated, and the serene cemetery behind its gates where my ancestors lay. I'd miss the lake and I'd miss Serafina. And oh, I'd miss Sasha. I wondered if she'd miss me or if she'd be just as happy taking off from someone else's outstretched arm.

I've planned a trip to the States for the spring. It would be my first time back and would mark almost a year to the day when I first saw Max on Ninth Street. I thought he was a beautiful man then, but I had no idea of just how beautiful, through and through. I pinch myself every now and then. When I came here, love was the last thing I thought I'd find, but there it is. We haven't talked about the future too much, just enough that I know that we'll be together, and that's fine for now. People in the castle know we're a couple, and as far as I can see, everyone's happy for both of us. I know his mother is over the moon, and that makes me happy. She has been like a mother to me from day one in the castle.

I'm still totally focused on all the things I want to accomplish for the people of Saint Gilbert. They've accepted me and grown to love my family, and I couldn't ask for more from them than that.

Of course, the kids went back to see their father. They traveled (with guards) for the long Thanksgiving weekend. They both said the visit was fine, but they felt out of place. Ralph Senior and Lorraine were expecting another baby, and that was all they talked about. The one night the kids thought they'd have their dad to themselves, he took Lorraine out to dinner and left Ralphie and Jules to babysit their half brother and sister.

As Jules said, "Mom, it was a very uncool thing for them to do. Not that we don't like their kids, but it just wasn't cool. So when Dad complains that he never sees us, please remind him that we were there, and he wasn't."

Given the way I feel about my ex, you'd think I'd feel pretty smug about this, but I don't. I've never talked him down—though he's given me tons of material—and I've never tried to put the kids between us. It makes me sad that he isn't trying as hard as he should. Maybe he thinks they've chosen me over him, but if he were being logical, he'd be pleased that his kids were having such amazing experiences here and yet still want to go back to see him. I just wish he'd taken advantage of that time with them instead of using them as babysitters.

Anyway, Max is coming with us in the spring. I want him to see the Philly I know. I always said, if you want to know someone, know where they're from. The last time he was in Philly, it was all business. This time it will be for pleasure. The kids are looking forward to seeing their old friends—they hadn't made plans with anyone over Thanksgiving because they'd planned to spend the time with their dad. Ralphie has a prom date lined up with a girl he's known since kindergarten, and Juliette's friends planned a sleepover while she's there.

I'll be taking Max to see all the historic sites—the Liberty Bell, Independence Hall, McGillin's Old Ale House (the oldest continuously operated tavern in Philly, established in 1860), the old graveyards where the likes of Benjamin Franklin and other signers of the Declaration of Independence are buried. Maybe the one thing I'm most looking forward to is taking him and the kids to a Phillies game. I don't even care who they play.

Ceil and Roe opted out of the trip. Ceil said she's too busy with renovations and ordering furniture and yada yada yada. Yes, she's busy—busy with Carlo DellaVecchio, but no judgments here. (We still haven't told his father that Alberto's mother was a relative of his—not sure how we'll handle that going forward. That's the kind of news no one wants.) Roe's busy planting grapevines and learning how to graft heirloom apple trees with Roberto. He's a bit older than her—older than me, even—but they get along really well. He's an interesting guy, tall and broad and looks like he'd be able to play on the Eagles offensive line. Yeah, big like that. But he's quiet, doesn't talk much (which is okay, I guess, since Roe talks enough for both of them), and he seems to be a bit sweet on her, so we'll see where that goes, if anywhere. But he's teaching her all sorts of things about gardening and farming, and she's loving it, so that's a good thing.

Ralphie is still planning on that soccer stadium, but right now, he and his friends who've formed a team have to be content with a field to practice on. People who know (read: Max) say he's very good and could play on a national team if we had one. Max is looking into that, not just for Ralphie but for the other boys who love the sport (Max has to keep reminding me that over here, it's *football*). It would be a huge boost for the country if we had a team that could compete, so it's being taken seriously. We're even looking for a coach. Anything that raises the profile of Saint Gilbert is good for everyone, right? Oh, and Ralphie is taking French lessons along with his sister, who's being homeschooled (she calls it castle-schooled), and he's doing well with it, though I don't know if it's because he likes the language or because the tutor is a very pretty young mademoiselle.

There are signs that we're starting to develop a real tourist trade. I've walked into the city on several occasions—well guarded, of course—and I've seen people in the shops. I always stop and chat. Recently I've spoken with visitors from France, Italy, Germany, Belgium, the Netherlands, the UK, Switzerland, and—Michigan. Hopefully our reputation will grow beyond Europe and the States, but I'm proud of what we've accomplished in a very short time. A new gift shop in the city is selling souvenirs. T-shirts with Serafina on them, little metal statues of the mermaid. Refrigerator magnets with Castle Blanc, others with a scene of the lake. Hastily written guidebooks and bottles of wine. But no soap.

The other day I started looking through the books in the library hoping to find some information about all those stolen paintings I'd heard about. It's been bugging me since Max told me the story of how someone in the castle had been making forgeries—and bad ones at that—and selling the originals, none of which have ever shown up on the open market. At least, none that we know about. So I'm thinking that could be my personal project for the coming year. I'd love to find out who took them, who painted the forgeries, and who the originals were sold to. And then I'm going to get them back. Sounds like fun, doesn't it? Every girl needs a hobby.

Once upon a time, not so very long ago, I was a single mother with a mortgage and a job I was good at but one that didn't bring me joy. I was raising my kids mostly by myself, and I knew nothing about my mother's family. I went to sleep every night alone, and lonely.

Now, thanks to a twist of fate I never saw coming—so much for psychic abilities—my life is beyond anything I could ever have dreamed. I live in a castle with my family; I have a job that makes me happy every day (Jules's kidnapping aside). I'm surrounded by beautiful countryside in this place where my ancestors lived and loved and ruled. I've been able to fill in so many blanks about my family.

I know now who my grandmother really was, and who her mother had been—women of courage and determination, and so much more. I know and appreciate their stories, and I'm still learning. I understand the legacy that's been passed to me, and I'm hoping to pass that legacy to my daughter so that one day, she'll rule this country with the same wisdom as my great-grandmother, Grand Duchess Elizabet Maria Jacqueline.

I want to make sure my children and my grandchildren never forget the sacrifices that brave woman made for this country, and how, in sending away its wealth—and her daughter—she saved both and, in the end, helped restore Saint Gilbert. I want them to know my gran as I knew her, not as the dignified, quiet old lady who lived in the small castle-like house in a Philadelphia suburb but as a woman who did her best to keep alive what was important, even though death cut short her efforts.

But I remember, Gran, and I am proud to have been part of your journey. I hope you're proud to be part of mine.

Oh, there was one other surprise awaiting me in Saint Gilbert.

I found the love of my life, a man who loves me as much as I love him. Maybe not a prince, but a duke, and that's more than good enough for this duchess.

And I never go to sleep alone.

Friends, if that's not a fairy-tale ending, I'm not Her Royal Highness, Grand Duchess Annaliese Jacqueline Terese of the Duchy of Saint Gilbert.

ACKNOWLEDGMENTS

I started writing this book for my own amusement several years ago, never intending for it to be released into the wild. But then we went into lockdown / the pandemic, and some of us were starting to get a bit bored, so I played with it a little more. The more I played, the more the characters came to life. I mentioned this story-not-to-be-a-book to a writer friend who—also bored—wanted to read it. I emailed what I had to her, and she loved it. Loved it enough to want more. So I kept writing, and before I knew it, these characters had taken over and had given me an entire book, which my friend still loved. Long story short, I sent it to my agent, who also loved it. He sent it to my editor, who loved it. And now it's in your hands, and I'm hoping you love it, too!

One of the best things about being a writer is meeting and getting to know other writers. Some of them become your tribe and as such, your greatest cheerleaders, or when necessary, your biggest critics. Robyn Carr, I can't thank you enough for all your encouragement—I don't think I'd have gotten serious about finishing this book if you hadn't sworn to love it so much. Thanks for being such a good friend, and for egging me on when I needed a nudge or five. I didn't give up because you didn't give up.

Thanks also to my agent, Nick Mullendore, at Vertical Ink Agency, for insisting that we put this book out there before it was finished. It's the least of the things I thank you for.

Maureen Downey, thanks for being my right hand and doing all the things. Seriously. ALL the things. I don't know if I could function without you! You are the very best.

The Montlake team is phenomenal, and I'm so grateful to be working with them. Huge thanks to my editor, Maria Gomez, for loving this story. Anh Schluep, Jillian Kline, Karah Nichols, Alex Levenburg, Laura Stahl—thanks so much for all you do to take that first draft, wrestle it to the ground, and turn it into a book! Many thanks to the marketing team at Montlake and the art department for giving me the most beautiful covers. Angela James, my developmental editor, you did a yeoman's job and I thank you for your insights and suggestions. *The Head That Wears The Crown* is definitely better for having your hands in it!

Many thanks to Helen Egner for many years of friendship, and for her early read of this book, and for her encouragement, which never wavers, and that killer sense of humor. Jo Ellen Grossman, thanks for those Tuesday-morning chats, and for way-too-many-to-count years of friendship (we can count them—we just don't like publicly acknowledging how many years have gone by since we met in kindergarten!).

To my readers—the ones who started out with me on this journey when my first book was published in 1995, and those who have just discovered my books for the first time—thank you for spending some time with my characters. To my FB family and friends—you all know who you are—thanks for hanging out with me online and sharing this journey with me.

And to my family—my husband, Bill, who's been through the fire these past few years, our daughters Kate and Rebecca, and their merry offspring—Cole, Jack, Robb, Camryn, Charlotte, and Gethin. I love you and am grateful to my soul that you're part of my life, and of me.

ABOUT THE AUTHOR

Photo © 2016 Nicole Leigh

Mariah Stewart is the *New York Times, Publishers Weekly,* and *USA Today* bestselling author of several series, including Wyndham Beach, the Chesapeake Diaries, and the Hudson Sisters, as well as stand-alone novels, novellas, and short stories. A native of Hightstown, New Jersey, she lives with her husband and one sleepy rescued black-and-tan coonhound amid the rolling hills of Chester County, Pennsylvania, where she savors country life, tends her gardens, and works on her next novel. She's the proud mama of two fabulous daughters and six adorable (and, yes, fabulous) granddarlings. For more information, visit www.mariahstewart.com.